NO HIGHWAY

ABOUT THE AUTHOR

Nevil Shute was born in 1899 and educated at Shrewsbury School and Balliol College, Oxford. Having decided early on an aeronautical career, he went to work for the de Havilland Aircraft Company as an engineer, where he played a large part in the construction of the airship R100. His first novel, *Marazan* (1926), was written at this time. After the disaster to the R101, he turned his attention to aeroplane construction and founded his own firm, Airspeed Ltd, in 1931. In the war Nevil Shute served in the Navy, doing secret work for the Admiralty. He still found time to write, however, and during this time produced several novels including *Pied Piper, Pastoral* and *Most Secret*. These were followed in 1947 by *The Chequer Board* and, in 1948, *No Highway*, which became a great bestseller and an extremely popular film. In 1948 he went to Australia for two months, a trip that inspired his most popular novel, *A Town Like Alice*. He returned there for good with his family, and remained until his death in 1960. His later novels include *In the Wet, Requiem for a Wren, On the Beach,* and *Trustee from the Toolroom.*

NO HIGHWAY

NEVIL

SHUTE

General
— PAPERBACKS —
Toronto, Canada

Published in 1948 by
William Heinemann Ltd.

Published in 1963 by
Pan Books Ltd.

Published in 1987 by
General Publishing Paperbacks
34 Lesmill Road
Toronto, Canada
M3B 2T6

ISBN 0-7736-7154-4

The three stanzas by John Masefield from "The Wanderer"
are quoted by kind permission of Dr. John Masefield OM,
and the Society of Authors.

Cover Design: Falcom Design and Communications
Cover Illustration: Oni

Printed in Canada

. . . *Therefore, go forth, companion: when you find*
No highway more, no track, all being blind,
The way to go shall glimmer in the mind.

Though you have conquered Earth and charted Sea
And planned the courses of all Stars that be,
Adventure on, more wonders are in Thee.

Adventure on, for from the littlest clue
Has come whatever worth man ever knew;
The next to lighten all men may be you . . .

JOHN MASEFIELD

AUTHOR'S NOTE

THIS BOOK IS a work of fiction. None of the characters are drawn from real persons. The Reindeer aircraft in my story is not based on any particular commercial aircraft, nor do the troubles from which it suffered refer to any actual events.

In this story I have postulated an inefficient Inspector of Accidents, with a fictitious name and a fictitious character. Only one man can hold this post at a time, and I tender such apologies as may be necessary to the distinguished and efficient officer who holds it now. I would add this. The scrupulous and painstaking investigation of accidents is the key to all safety in the air, and demands the services of men of the very highest quality. If my story underlines this point, it will have served a useful purpose.

NEVIL SHUTE

1

WHEN I WAS put in charge of the Structural Department of the Royal Aircraft Establishment at Farnborough, I was thirty-four years old. That made a few small difficulties at first, because most of my research staff were a good deal older than I was, and most of them considered it a very odd appointment. Moreover, I wasn't a Farnborough man; I started in a stress office in the aircraft industry and came to Farnborough from Boscombe Down, where I had been technical assistant to the Director of Experimental Flying for three years. I had often been to Farnborough, of course, and I knew some of the staff of my new department slightly; I had always regarded them as rather a queer lot. On closer acquaintance with them, I did not change my views.

In spite of my appointment from outside I found them quite co-operative, but they were all getting on in years and beginning to think more about their pensions than about promotion. When I got settled in I found that each of them had his own little niche and his own bit of research. Mr Morrison, for example, was our expert on the three-dimensional concentrations of stress around riveted plate joints and he was toying with a fourth dimension, the effect of time. What he didn't know about polarised light wasn't worth knowing. He had been studying this subject for eight and a half years, and he had a whole room full of little plate and plastic models broken upon test. Every two years or so he produced a paper which was published as an R. and M., full of the most complicated mathematics proving to the aeroplane designer what he knew already from his own experience.

Mr Fox-Marvin was another of them. I discovered to my amazement when I had been in the department for a week that Fox-Marvin had been working since 1935 on the torsional instability of struts, with Miss Bucklin aiding and abetting him for much of the time. They were no laggards at the paper work, for in that time they had produced typescript totalling well over a million words, if words are a correct measure of reading matter that was mostly mathematical. At the end of all those years they had got the unstabilised, eccentrically loaded strut of varying section just about buttoned up, regardless of the fact that unstabilised struts are very rare today in any aircraft structure.

I knew that I had been appointed from outside the Royal Aircraft Establishment as a new broom to clean up this department, and I had to do a bit of sweeping. I hope I did it with sympathy and understanding, because the problem of the ageing civil servant engaged in research is not an easy one. There comes a time when the research worker, disappointed in promotion and secure in his old age if he avoids blotting his copybook, becomes detached from all reality. He tends to lose interest in the practical application of his work to the design of aeroplanes and turns more and more to the ethereal realms of mathematical theory; as bodily weakness gradually puts an end to physical adventure, he turns readily to the adventure of the mind, to the purest realms of thought where in the nature of things no unpleasant consequences can follow if he makes a mistake.

It is easy to blackguard these ageing men and to deride their unproductive work, easy and unprofitable and unwise. Short-term *ad hoc* experiments to solve a particular problem in the design of aircraft were the main work of my department, but I was very well aware that basic research also has a place in such a set-up, the firm groundwork of pure knowledge upon which all useful short-term work must be erected. In the great mass of typescript chaff turned out by the Fox-Marvins and the Morrisons within the RAE were hidden grains of truth. Callow young men entering the Establishment from the universities, avid for knowledge and enthusiastic in their early years, would read through all this guff and take it very seriously, and find and recognise the little grains of truth, and take them into their experience and use them as their tools for short-term work.

I had to steer a middle course, therefore, as every sensible new broom must do. Within the first year I had transferred two of the oldest of my scientific officers, and I had changed the line of three others. It was a busy year, because I got married soon after I went to Farnborough. Shirley was a local girl who had taught drawing and music in a little school in Farnham before the war; when the school evacuated she had become a tracer at the RAE. In the fourth year of the war she was sent to Boscombe Down to work in the drawing

8

office; she had her desk and drawing board just outside my little glass cubicle, so that every time I looked up from my calculations I saw her auburn head bent over her tracing, which didn't help the calculations. I stood it for a year, high-minded, thinking that one shouldn't make passes at the girls in the office. Then we started to behave very badly, and got engaged.

We got a flat in Farnham with some difficulty and got married into it soon after I took up my new job. It was a very small flat, with just one bedroom and a sitting-room and a bathroom, and a kitchen that we had our meals in. It was big enough for all we wanted, and we were very happy. There wasn't much for Shirley to do, since I was away all day, and we didn't plan to start a family for a year or so. So she went back to teaching music and drawing in the school that she had taught in before, and one of the girls she taught was Elspeth Honey.

She told me about Elspeth one evening when we were sitting after the nine-o'clock news. Shirley was sewing a slip or something, and I was working at the first paper that I had been asked to read before the Royal Aeronautical Society, which I called 'Performance Analysis of Aircraft Flying at High Mach Numbers'. It was something of a distinction that I had been asked to read this thing, and I was very busy working on it in the evenings.

Shirley told me about Elspeth as we sat there; she was teaching her to play the piano at that time. 'She's such a funny little thing,' she said thoughtfully. 'I can't make out if she's immensely clever or just plain bats.'

I looked up, laughing. 'I've been wondering that about her father ever since I took over the department.' Because Mr Theodore Honey was another one of the old gang of budding Einsteins that I had inherited. So far I had left him alone, feeling that the work that he was doing on fatigue in light alloy structures was probably useful. But I must admit that there were moments when I had my doubts, when I wondered if Mr Honey was not sliding quietly into an inoffensive form of technical mania.

Shirley bent over her sewing. 'She *looks* so odd,' she said presently, 'with her straight black hair and her white little face, and those ugly frocks she wears. She never seems to play with the other children. And she does say the queerest things sometimes.'

'What sort of things?' I asked. I was not quite happy in my mind about her father; subconsciously I was interested in anything to do with the Honey family.

Shirley looked up from her sewing, smiling. 'Pyramidology,' she said.

I stared at her. 'What's that?'

She mocked me. 'Call yourself a scientist, and you don't know pyramidology! Even Elspeth knows that.'

'Well, I don't. What is it?'

'It's all about the Great Pyramid, in Egypt. Prophecies and all that sort of thing.'

I grinned. 'That's not the sort of science that I learned at college. Is that what they teach at your school?'

She bent to her work again, and said quietly, 'No, it's just Elspeth. She came and asked me if she could do her practising in break on the school piano, and I asked her why she couldn't do it at home. She said there wasn't time now, because she was helping her Daddy with his pyramidology. I asked her what that was, and she told me all about it. It seems that there's a sort of directional bearing from two points in the Great Pyramid which is lined up on Iceland, just like a radar beam, and that's where Our Lord will come down to earth at the end of the world, and that's going to be quite soon. But Elspeth says her Daddy found a mistake in the calculations and he's working it all out again, and she's been helping him with the sums. She says it's all terribly exciting because her Daddy thinks it will turn out that the ray goes through Glastonbury, because Jesus Christ came to live in Glastonbury when He was a young man and so He'll probably want to go back there when He comes again. But Elspeth hopes that the ray will go through Farnborough because that's the most important place in the world and, besides, it's where her Daddy works.'

Shirley said all this without a smile, concentrated on her sewing. I stared at her incredulously. 'Does Mr Honey believe all this?'

She looked up at me. 'He must do, mustn't he. Or he wouldn't have told Elspeth. It's such a pity that she hasn't got a mother. It's rather unnatural for a kid of twelve to go on like that, don't you think?'

'What happened to her mother?' Anything about Honey

was of interest to me now.

'I think she died during the war. Elspeth and her father live in one of those little houses in Copse Road.'

I nodded, visualising the small villas. 'Who looks after them?'

'I don't think anybody does. I believe they've got a char-woman who comes in now and then. But Mr Honey does the cooking for them both. I know that, because Elspeth told me that she cooks the breakfast on Sundays, but next year she's going to be allowed to do it every day.'

'She's twelve, is she.'

'Just twelve – her birthday was last month. But she's small for her age. You wouldn't think to look at her that she was more than ten.'

I sat deep in thought. I was visualising my Mr Honey going home each evening to his little house to cook a high tea for his little girl, and then to spend an hour telling her about the tangled prophecies connected with the Great Pyramid, and then putting her to bed. Did he hear her say her prayers, and if so, were they all about the Pyramid? And after that, alone in his small villa, what did he do? Did he go out to the cinema? I did not think that he was one to spend the evening in a pub – or was he. Did he spend the evenings pondering the energy absorption factor of light alloy structures, or checking the position of the stars in the year 2141 BC, the datum year of the Great Pyramid. I wanted to know all I could about his background, because I had not then made up my mind if he was a useful research scientist or not. What Shirley had told me was not very reassuring.

'I was talking to Sykie about Elspeth,' she said quietly. 'Of course, Sykie doesn't really know much botany, only just enough to teach the children something elementary. Elspeth got her floored in class the other day by saying that a butter-cup was pentamerous, and Sykie didn't know if that was something rude or not. And so she made Elspeth tell them what she meant, and what she meant was that the buttercup has five of everything – five sepals in the calyx, five petals in the corolla, five carpels in the pistil, and so on. Sykie looked it up in the book afterwards, and she was quite right. But then she went on to say that the Bible was septamerous be-cause it had seven of everything, and that's why seven was a holy number. Sykie got out of that one by saying that it wasn't botany.'

'Did Mr Honey tell her that – about the Bible.'

'I suppose he must have done. She didn't learn it at the school.'

I went to the department next day resolved to give a good part of my time to checking up on Mr Honey and the progress of his research. I had not bothered him a great deal up till then, because it seemed to me that the work he was engaged on was of real importance to the modern aircraft, which was more than could be said for some of the other stuff that I had found going on in the place. Because the work was of importance to the aviation world it was imperative that it should be properly conducted, and although Mr Honey's religious beliefs were no concern of mine a man who is eccentric in one sphere of his interests may well be eccentric in another.

As I have said, Mr Honey was working on fatigue in aircraft structures. Fatigue may be described as a disease of metal. When metals are subjected to an alternating load, after a great many reversals the whole character of the metal may alter, and this change can happen very suddenly. An aluminium alloy which has stood up quite well to many thousands of hours in flight may suddenly become crystalline and break under quite small forces, with most unpleasant consequences to the aeroplane. That is the general story of the effect that we call fatigue in aircraft structures, and we don't know a great deal about it. Mr Honey's duty was to try and find out more.

I went down to his stamping ground to see what he was doing. The Farnborough buildings at that time were a mixture of the old and the new, and Mr Honey occupied a shabby little room of glass and beaverboard in the annexe to the old balloon shed. Here he sat all day and covered sheet after sheet of foolscap paper with the records of his research, or pored over the work of scientists in many languages; he could read both French and German fluently. Outside his office an area of the ground floor of the balloon shed had been allocated to his work, and here he had quite a major experiment in progress.

The Rutland Reindeer was the current Transatlantic airliner at that time, and still is, of course; the Mark I model, which went into production first, had radial engines, though

12

now they all have jets. Two years before I came upon the scene the strength tests of the tailplane had been carried out in my department, and for this two tailplanes had been provided by the Company for test to destruction. They were quite big units, fifty-five feet in span, as big as a twin-engined bomber's wing. It had only been necessary to break one of these expensive tailplanes for the strength tests for the airworthiness of the machine, and the other one remained upon our hands until eighteen months later Mr Honey put in a plea for it, and got it.

He had set it up in the balloon shed, horizontally as it would be in flight. He had designed a considerable structure of steel girders to support it at the centre section as it would be held in the aircraft, and this structure was pivoted in such a way that it could be vibrated, or jiggeted, by a whacking great electric motor driving a whole battery of cams to simulate the various harmonics that occur in flight. He had chosen a loading for the tailplane that would reproduce the normal cruising flight conditions, and he had started up the motor a couple of months before and sat back to wait for something to happen.

All that was going on as I was settling in to my new job and as my predecessor had authorised it I had to let it take its course, though I was not too happy about it. I had a feeling that a competent researcher could have got his data from a less expensive test, and apart from that the thing was a considerable nuisance for the noise it made. It may be possible to make mechanical vibrations without making noise, but it's not often done, and this thing could be heard all over the Establishment. And apparently it was going to go on for ever, because nobody but Mr Honey thought that tail would ever break by reason of what he was doing to it. It looked much too strong.

Honey got up as I went into his office. He was a smaller man than I am, with black hair turning grey; he was dressed in a very shabby suit that had been cheap to start with. He always looked a bit dirty and down at heels, and his appearance did not help him, because he was one of the ugliest men I have ever met. He had a sallow face with the features of a frog, and rather a tired and discontented frog at that. He wore steel-rimmed spectacles with very thick glasses, and he was as blind as a bat without them. Looking at him, my wife's description of his daughter came into my mind, the dark-haired, white-faced, ugly little girl. Of course, she would be like that.

I said, 'Morning, Mr Honey. I've just come down to have a look at your tailplane. Anything happening to it yet?'

He said, 'Oh no – everything is going on quite normally, so far. We can't expect much yet, you know.' He had a few strain gauges mounted on various parts of the structure and he was reading them every three hours and graphing the readings. He showed me the curves illustrating the daily deformations of the structure as the test went on; after a few initial disturbances, due to the rivets bedding down, the curves flattened out and went along as a straight line. It was behaving just exactly as one would expect a safe structure to behave.

We stood and looked at it, and walked around it in the noise. Then we went back into his office, where the noise level was lower, and talked about it for a bit. I cannot say I was impressed with what I saw and heard. But for the expense of the set-up, I should have been very much tempted to call off the entire experiment.

'What's your prognostication, Mr Honey?' I asked presently. 'How long do you think it will go on for?'

He smiled nervously, as the pure researchers always do when you try to pin them down to something definite. 'One has to make so many assumptions,' he said. 'The mass energy absorption factor, the factor that I call U_m in my papers – that varies somewhat with each type of structure, and one really has to do a preliminary experiment to establish that.'

That sounded like an old story to me, and I was not impressed. 'You mean, with a tailplane like this you've got to break one first under a fatigue test, just like this, to establish the factor?'

'Yes,' he said eagerly, 'that's right.'

'And then,' I said, rather naughtily, 'having found out the factor you can calculate back and find out when it broke.'

He glanced at me, uncertain if I were laughing at him or not. 'Of course, you can then apply that factor to other tails of similar design, vibrated on a different range of frequencies.'

I said doubtfully, 'Yes, I suppose so, when you've built up a good deal of experience.'

I spent most of the rest of the morning going through his papers with him and getting acquainted with his theory. I knew the broad outline of his ideas already, and because I knew them I had avoided going into them in more detail until I really had to. Because, like all my other Einsteins, Mr Honey in his research upon fatigue had gone all nuclear.

When the fundamental theories about atomic fission became generally known to scientists in 1945, they came as a godsend to all middle-aged researchers. Here was a completely new field of pure thought to explore, whether it had anything to do with their immediate job or not. Each of them very soon convinced himself that in an application and extension of nuclear theory lay the solution to all his problems, whether they were concerned with the effect of sunlight on paint or the formation of sludge in engine-lubricating oil. It seemed at times that every scientist in the Establishment had made himself into an expert upon nuclear matters, all but me, who had come from the material and earthly pursuit of testing aeroplanes in flight, and so had started late in the race. I didn't know much about the atom, and I was very sceptical if nuclear matters really affected my department at all.

However, Mr Honey was convinced they did, and he had built up an imposing structure of theory upon a nuclear basis. Quite simply, what he held was that when a structure like a tailplane is vibrated a tiny quantity of energy is absorbed into it, proportionate to the mass of the structure and the time that the treatment goes on for and a certain integral of strain. He had some evidence for this assertion, for he produced papers by Koestlinger of Basle University and by Schiltgrad of Upsala indicating that something of the sort does happen. Schiltgrad had made attempts to trace what happens to this lost energy, and had produced the negative result that it did not appear in any of the normal forms, as heat, electrical potential, or momentum. Mr Honey, sitting brooding over all this work, had convinced himself that this small energy flow produced a state of tension within the nucleus of aluminium of which the alloy is mainly composed, and that when this tension has built up to a certain degree one or more neutrons are released, resulting in an isotopic form of aluminium with crystalline affinities. This was the bare bones of his theory, and it was supported by about seventy pages of pure mathematics. It all seemed a bit like the Great Pyramid to me, and as difficult to criticise.

At the end of an hour or so with him I said, 'What value have you assigned to this quantity U_m for that tailplane out there?'

He said, 'Well – provisionally – just for getting a rough idea of how long the trial is likely to go on for, you see, I made a rough estimate —' He fumbled with his papers, shuffled them, dropped one on the floor and scrabbled after it, picked it up, looked at it upside down, turned it right way up, and said, 'Here it is. $2 \cdot 863 \times 10^{-7}$. That's in CGS units, of course.'

I took the sheet from him and studied it. It was untidy work, half in pencil and half in ink, written in a vile hand, rather dirty. 'Those are just the rough notes,' he said nervously. 'I shall write it all up properly later on.'

I nodded. One must not, must not ever, be influenced by *gaucheries* when dealing with these people. Untidiness may be a sign of slovenly thinking in an adult man, but it can also be a sign of an immensely quick intellect that gives no time for neat and patient writing. Mr Honey was obviously nervous of me, and he was showing at his worst.

'This figure, $2 \cdot 863$,' I said at last. 'That's a pretty exact figure, Mr Honey – four-figure accuracy. When that constant goes into your theory, the time to reach fatigue failure will be directly proportional to that, won't it?' I turned to one of the final sheets of mathematics that he had displayed before me.

'That's right,' he said. 'The time to nuclear separation is directly proportional to U_m.'

'Well, I don't call that a rough estimate,' I said. 'That's a pretty detailed estimate, surely? I mean, that figure says that in a given case something may be going to happen in two thousand eight hundred and sixty-three hours. I should have said a rough estimate was one that said something would happen between two and three thousand hours.' I glanced at him.

He shifted uneasily. 'Well, naturally, I went into it as carefully as I could.' He showed me what he had based his estimate upon. It was a pile about three feet high of the Proceedings of practically every engineering learned body in Europe and America. 'I couldn't find anything about light alloy

16

structures in fatigue prior to the year 1927,' he said dolefully. 'I don't know if there's anything else I ought to have got hold of.'

I laughed. 'I shouldn't think so, Mr Honey. If you've gone back to 1927 you've probably got everything there is.'

'I hope I have,' he said.

I turned over the sheafs of papers that were his analysis of previous trials and from which he had deduced the value of $2 \cdot 863 \times 10^{-7}$ for U_m, and I came to the conclusion that whatever bees he might have in his bonnet, he was at any rate a patient and an indefatigable worker, if rather an untidy one. At the end of ten minutes I said, 'Well, if this is what you call a rough estimate, Mr Honey, I'd like to see a detailed one.'

He flushed angrily, but did not speak. I had not meant to be offensive.

I turned over the papers before me. 'What does that mean to that tailplane out there?' I indicated the Reindeer tail upon the framework outside, booming and droning, filling the whole building with its noise. 'When do you expect something to happen?'

He said, 'There should be some evidence of nuclear separation in about 1,440 hours – taking that value for U_m.'

'That's till it breaks? It ought to break in 1,440 hours?'

He hesitated. 'I rather think that the material could be expected to suffer some change about that time,' he said, hedging. 'Under the normal loads imposed upon it – yes, I think that failure would probably occur.' He shifted uneasily and said, as if in self-defence, 'The isotope is probably crystalline.'

'I see.' I stood for a moment looking at the test through his window. 'How long has it been going on for now?'

'About two months,' he said. 'We started on the twenty-sixth of May. Up till this morning it had run four hundred and twenty-three hours. It only runs in the daytime – the Director wouldn't allow it to run on night shift. It's basic research, you see.'

I calculated in my head. 'So it's got another four or five months to go?'

He said, 'Well – yes, about that time. I was expecting to learn something from it before Christmas, anyway.'

I stood silent for a minute, deep in thought. 'Well, that's

all very interesting, Mr Honey,' I said at last. 'May I take what you've re-written so far and glance it over in my office? It all takes a bit of absorbing, you know.'

He sorted out a bunch of papers and gave them to me, and I tucked them under my arm, and walked back to my office in a brown study. Mr Honey was experimenting on a Reindeer tail, and what Mr Honey had lost sight of altogether was that Reindeer aircraft had come into service on the Atlantic route that summer. They were flying the Atlantic daily with full loads of passengers, from Heath Row to Gander, from Gander to New York or Montreal.

Although he didn't seem to realise it, Mr Honey had now said that the Reindeer tail was quite unsafe, that in his opinion it would break, suddenly and without warning, after 1,440 hours of flying.

It was the end of the morning. I left the papers in my office and walked up to the senior staff lunch-room. I found the Director there drinking a sherry; I waited for an opportunity when he was disengaged, and said, 'Have you got a quarter of an hour free this afternoon, sir?'

'I think so,' he replied. 'What is it, Scott?'

'It's about Mr Honey and his fatigue test,' I said. 'I'd like you to be aware of what's going on.'

'Can't help being aware of it,' he answered. 'You can hear the damn thing at the other end of the factory – it's worse than the wind tunnels. When is it coming to an end?'

'He says it's going on till Christmas,' I replied. 'I think it ought to be accelerated. But if I can come along this afternoon I'll tell you about it.'

'Quarter-past three?'

'I'll be there, sir.'

I turned away to go in to have lunch, but he detained me. 'Has Honey been all right recently?'

'All right? I think so, sir. I don't think he's had any time off.'

'I'm glad to hear that.' There was a momentary pause. 'You know,' he said, 'there has been a little trouble in the past. He seems to hold very firm ideas on certain semi-religious subjects.' I glanced at him in inquiry. 'About the lost ten tribes of Israel and their identity with Britain, and that sort of thing.'

'I hadn't heard that one,' I said, 'What I heard was something to do with the Great Pyramid.'

He laughed. 'Oh, that's another part of it – that comes in as well.' He spoke more seriously. 'No, just before you came there was a procession of these people in Woking, and it got broken up by a number of Jewish rowdies, and Honey was taken up and charged with creating a breach of the peace. He got bound over. I mention that because it's one of the matters that one has to bear in mind, that he has rather odd ideas on certain subjects.'

I nodded. 'Thank you for telling me, sir.'

'Poor old Honey,' he said thoughtfully. 'He's a man I'm very sorry for. But if you should decide at any time that a change would be desirable, I wouldn't oppose it.'

I went in to lunch aware that the Director didn't think a lot of Mr Honey. Anderson was there, who looks after radar equipment and development for civil air lines. I sat down next to him and said, 'I say, you can tell me. How many Reindeers are Central Air Transport Organisation operating now?'

He said, 'Five or six.'

'Do you know at all how many hours they've done?'

He shook his head. 'Not much, anyway. They only put them on the route last month, because they waited until four had been delivered. I shouldn't think any of the machines had done more than two or three hundred hours yet.'

I thought with relief that we had a bit of time. 'How do they like it?'

'Like the Reindeer? Oh, they're very pleased with it. It's a lovely job, you know – nice to fly in and nice to handle. I think it's going to be a great success.'

I went back to my office after lunch and sat turning over Mr Honey's papers, studying his Goodman diagrams, thinking out what I was going to say to the Director. Nuclear fission was quite outside my experience; I did not know enough about it even to read Mr Honey's work intelligently, let alone criticise it or determine for myself the truth of his prognosis. And turning over his pages, disconsolate, I saw one or two sentences that made me wonder if Mr Honey knew much more than I did, for all his pages of mathematics.

I went down to the Director that afternoon and told him all about it. 'On his estimates, he reckons that the Reindeer tail, the front spar, will fail by fatigue in 1,440 hours,' I said.

'I don't much like the sound of that. The Reindeers are in service now.'

'What is this estimate based on?' he asked.

I told him all about the nuclear fission theory and the separation of the neutron that produced an isotopic form of aluminium within the alloy. 'Quite frankly, sir,' I said, 'I don't understand all this myself. I'm not capable of criticising it. If he's correct it's very serious indeed, and all those aircraft should be grounded. But knowing something about Mr Honey – well, he may not be correct.'

He thought for a moment. 'The test will show. How long is that going on for?'

'It's only done four hundred and twenty-three hours,' I replied. 'He's not expecting it to break before next Christmas.' I paused, and then I said, 'I should think the aeroplanes are piling up hours quicker than the test. After all, they fly day and night, but the test only runs in our normal working hours.'

'What is the longest time that one of the aircraft has done?'

'I don't know, sir. One of them flew into a hill the other day, in Labrador or somewhere. I asked Anderson at lunch how many hours the rest of them had done. He said they'd only done two or three hundred hours each.'

'That gives us a little time,' he said. 'I didn't know they'd lost one of them.'

'It was in all the papers,' I told him. 'The Russian Ambassador to Ottawa was killed in it, Mr Oskonikoff or something. All the lot of them were killed.'

'Oh, that one – I remember. Was that a Reindeer?'

I nodded. 'That was the prototype Reindeer, the one we had here for the trials. But that's a clear case; it flew into the mountain. Hit just at the top of a precipice and fell about five hundred feet down into the forest, in flames. It always beats me how a pilot manages to get into that sort of position, with all the aids we give them.'

'It's the human factor,' he said. 'Still – I agree, you wouldn't expect mistakes of that sort in a decent air line.' He turned to the papers. 'I don't quite know what to say about all this, Scott. I'm like you – I can't criticise this nuclear stuff, myself. It's clearly a matter of urgency. I think we ought to put it up to ISARB, on a high priority.'

The Inter-Services Atomic Research Board were certainly

the proper people to advise us upon Mr Honey's stuff, provided they would do it quick. 'I'm very nervous about any delay,' I said. 'Could you send it personally, sir?' I hesitated. 'I'd really like to ground those Reindeers till we get the thing cleared up, but I suppose that isn't practical.'

He stared out of the window. 'That means, stop the entire operation of CATO's Atlantic service . . . I think we'll have to get some supporting evidence for Mr Honey's theories before we could do that. But I agree with you, Scott, this thing has to be taken seriously. I'll send it to Sir Phillip Dolbear tonight, with a personal note.'

I went back to my office satisfied with this; I knew Dolbear to be acute and hardworking, a good chairman for the Atomic Board. I sent for Mr Honey and told him what was in the wind. I reminded him that he was playing with a real Reindeer tail, and that when he said blithely that his experiment would culminate at 1,440 hours, he really meant that real aeroplanes would crash after that flying time.

He blinked at me through his heavy glasses. 'Of course, I know that,' he said. 'But till the research work is completed, everyone is guessing in the dark. You must realise that in all this kind of work one has to feel one's way. I may be very much in error, very much indeed. There's nothing definite about it yet.'

'Do you think it could fail sooner?' I asked.

'Oh, I shouldn't think so. In fact, I've been preparing myself for a real disappointment about Christmas time. It could quite well go on till April, or even longer.'

He lived and thought in quite a different world from me if he could contemplate waiting a year for data on a thing like this. He was pure scientist all through, and I suppose I'm not. I told him that Sir Phillip Dolbear would probably want to have a talk with him in a day or two, and he went away.

At the end of the week Mr Honey went to London at the request of Sir Phillip. I sent for him next day and asked him how he had got on.

He looked uneasy and unhappy. 'I don't think he was really very much interested in the subject,' he said.

'What makes you think that?' I asked quietly. It looked as if they had not agreed too well.

He was silent for a minute. 'He was just out to pick holes in it,' he said at last. 'You aren't going to get a very good report. He's the sort of man who wants everything docketed and proved, and each stage made secure and buttoned up before you go on to the next. Well, as I told you, there's a great deal still to be confirmed in the entire basic theory. It will take years to do that. These experiments we are doing now are meant to confirm all the points that I have made assumptions on, one by one. I told him that. But he insisted on regarding the test we're doing now as a test of the Reindeer tail. I told him it was nothing of the sort. It's a test to find our errors in the theory.'

'But Mr Honey,' I said, 'this test is, in fact, a fatigue test of the Reindeer tailplane. The Reindeer is out and flying, carrying passengers across the Atlantic, and what you say is that the tailplane will break up in 1,440 hours of flying. That's a very serious thing to say. It means that all those aircraft should be grounded.'

He said unhappily, 'I never said anything of the sort. I told you I was quite prepared for a disappointment. Theoretically, and if all the assumptions I have made should be exactly and precisely correct, a separation of the neutron should occur at 1,440 hours. The purpose of this test is to show where the assumptions are wrong and to correct the theory. You're trying to turn a piece of basic research into an *ad hoc* experiment. Well, you can't do that.'

He glared at me angrily through his thick glasses. He was very much upset.

'I see your point,' I said slowly. 'But that doesn't help us in deciding what to do about the Reindeers that are in service now.'

'I don't know anything about that,' he retorted. 'It certainly won't help them to keep badgering me like this. Sir Phillip Dolbear didn't believe a word I said, and he's quite right. Nothing is proved yet, nothing is confirmed. You're trying to make me run before I can walk, and the result is I just look a fool. Well, that's not very helpful.'

'I didn't mean to do that, Mr Honey,' I said. 'I'm just trying to find out what we ought to do about these aircraft that are in service now.'

'Well, I can't help you there,' he said. 'I've told you all I can, and I'm not going to be bullied into saying any more. You've got your troubles, and I've got mine.' He did not say that most of his troubles were of my making, but he meant it.

He went away, and I rang up Ferguson in the Department of Experiment and Research at the Ministry, who serves as our London office: 'Ferguson,' I said, 'this is Scott speaking. Look, we're getting a bit doubtful about the Reindeer tailplane; there's a suggestion that fatigue might crop up at a fairly early stage. It's got rather an exaggerated aspect ratio, you know. I believe I'm right in saying that CATO are operating five or six of them on the Atlantic route. Could you get on to the Corporation or the ARB – without alarming anyone unduly, because I think it may be a mare's nest – and find out how many hours flying these machines have done?'

He said at once, 'They can't have done much. They've only been operational for about a month. What number of hours represents the danger point?'

'Mr Honey's estimate is 1,440 hours. But as I say, I think it's a mare's nest.'

He laughed over the telephone. 'Oh, this is Honey, is it? In that case, I should think it might be. I'll find out from the Corporation, and let you know.' He rang back later in the morning. The longest time that any of the machines had done was 305 hours, up to the evening before.

Next day at about tea-time Shirley rang me up in the office. She said, 'Dennis, darling, I'm sorry to worry you. I've got Elspeth Honey here because she wanted to listen to the Pastoral Symphony on the wireless, and theirs is bust. I'm just going to give her tea. She wanted to let her father know where she is, because she won't be home when he gets there. I was wondering if you'd like to bring him back with you to pick up Elspeth.'

'Okay, dear,' I said. 'I'll do that.'

I rang up Mr Honey and told him, and suggested that he came back with me in my car instead of going by the bus, as he usually did. I was rather pleased to have the opportunity to do something for him, because the last time that we had spoken our relations had not been exactly cordial, and I didn't like to feel that he was nursing a grievance against me. I was aware, too, that there was a good deal of reason on his side. He met me at the car at half-past five, and we drove out on the road to Farnham.

'It's very kind of Mrs Scott to invite Elspeth like this,' he said diffidently. 'She mustn't let her make herself a nuisance.'

'Not a bit,' I said. 'She's probably company for Shirley –

for my wife. It gets a bit slow for her sometimes when I'm away all day.'

'That is the trouble, of course,' he replied. 'I mean, with Elspeth. It's all right in the term time, but in the holidays it's sometimes very difficult.'

'I should think it is,' I said, thinking of his womanless menage. 'What do you do with her in the holidays?'

He said, 'There's a clergyman who runs a holiday home for children down at Bournemouth, and she goes there sometimes, but it's rather expensive. And he's started to take mental defectives now – very backward children, you know – so it's not quite so suitable as it used to be. But really, Elspeth's so good at playing by herself that I don't know that she isn't just as happy at home.'

The thought of his little girl of twelve spending her holidays alone all day in the villa in Copse Road was not an attractive one. 'It's very difficult,' I said.

'It's a great deal easier in term time,' he remarked. 'Elspeth likes being at school, and she's very fond of Mrs Scott. She talks about her a great deal.'

I was not surprised to hear that Elspeth liked being at school if her holidays were spent alone in a deserted house. 'You've met my wife, have you, Honey?' I asked. 'Miss Mansfield, who used to be a tracer in the Aerodynamics? A girl with fair, sort of auburn hair?'

He did not think that he remembered her.

At the flat we found Shirley and Elspeth sitting over tea in the sitting-room listening to the wireless; we went in quietly, not to disturb them. I made a fresh pot of tea for Honey and myself, and we sat listening to the symphony with them till it was finished. It was the first time I had seen Elspeth Honey, and this pause gave me an opportunity to study her. As Shirley had said, she was an ugly child, but this ugliness seemed to me to be more associated with her unbecoming clothes and the way her hair was cut than with the child herself. She had rather sharp, pale features; she was thin; and she looked intelligent. She did not look to be a very happy child. She had fine, well-shaped hands, and when she moved she did not seem to be clumsy. If she had had a mother, I reflected, she might have been very different.

The symphony came to an end, and Shirley reached over and switched off the set. She turned to the child. 'Like it?'

she asked.

The little girl nodded vigorously with closed lips. 'Mm.'

My wife got up and began to gather up the plates and put them on the trolley. 'I thought you would. They're going to do one every week. Would you like to come again?'

Honey said nervously, 'You mustn't let her be a nuisance, Mrs Scott.'

'I won't,' said Shirley. 'I like listening to symphonies.'

Elspeth said, 'I'd like that ever so. May I do the washing up?'

Shirley said, 'Of course not. I was only going to pile these things together and take them out.'

'They've got to be washed up sometime, Mrs Scott. I can do it – honestly, I can.'

Her father said, 'Do let her help you, please. She's very good at washing up.'

'I can do it,' the child repeated. 'Daddy drops things, so I always do it at home.'

My wife said, 'All right, we'll do it together.'

They took the trolley out with them, and I sat talking with Honey as we smoked. I had only half my mind on our conversation and I forget what it was about to start with. I was furtively studying the man that I was talking to and trying to sum him up, the man who said the Reindeer tail would come to bits in 1,440 hours. The man who believed that, and who also believed in the Great Pyramid and in the descent of Our Lord to earth at Glastonbury or Farnborough in the very near future. The man who lived alone, and seemed quite unconscious that by doing so he was denying most of the simple joys of childhood to his little girl. The man who took umbrage in the office at small slights; the man who lived in an unreal, scientific dream. The man who walked in some queer semi-religious procession in Woking, and got had up by the police for some brawl that arose from it. The man who said the Reindeer tail would come to bits in 1,440 hours. The man whose judgment we had to accept or discard.

And presently he added something to the picture I was building up. He was looking at the backs of my books in the bookcase, reading the titles, as one always does in a strange house. I woke up suddenly from my abstraction to hear him say, 'I see you've got Rutherford's book there.' And he indicated *The Aryan Flow* stuck in among the novels.

When I was at college I was interested for a very short time in the movements of the races of peoples about the world, and this volume was a relic of that passing enthusiasm. I had not opened it for at least ten years, but it was there still. I said idly, 'I think it's very good.'

He got up and picked the book out of the shelf, and turned the pages. 'Sharon Turner covers much of the same ground,' he said. 'But it's Rutherford who identifies the ten tribes with the Scythians. And after all, that must have been the most difficult part, mustn't it?'

I was a little at a loss. 'I've really rather forgotten,' I said. 'It's a long time since I read it.'

'You ought to look it over again,' he said earnestly. 'It was the most wonderful migration in the world.' He stared at me through his thick glasses. 'The ten tribes, led away into captivity by Shalmaneser, King of Assyria – that's all in the Second Book of Esdras. The Persians called them Sakae – our word Saxon, of course, and Rutherford proves their identity with the Scythians. And then, from his end, Sharon Turner traces back the Anglo-Saxons all through Europe to the Scythians. It's fascinating.'

I was completely out of my depth. 'Absolutely,' I said.

He went on. 'It explains so much. The Druidic forms of worship, that were nothing but the old religion of Israel brought here in its entirety.' He paused and then said, 'That's what impressed Joseph of Arimathea so much when first he came to England on his tin business. That's why he brought his nephew here when He was a little boy, because he saw the Child was something quite unusual, and he wanted Him to come in contact with the priests of England. That's why Our Lord came back to Glastonbury as a young man and lived here for years before His ministry, because He had to live in the precepts of the old Israel which the Druid priests had kept here undebased. That's why Joseph came back to Glastonbury with Martha and Mary and Lazarus after the death of Christ, because they wanted to settle down and found His church in the place that He had loved so well.'

The Reindeer tail, he said, would come to bits in 1,440 hours. 'I'm not very well up in all this, I'm afraid,' I said.

He put the book back carefully upon the shelf. 'It's the most fascinating story in the world,' he said quietly. 'It explains so much. That's why Simon Zelotes, His apostle, came

26

here as soon as he could. That's why St Paul came here.' He drew himself up, a short, earnest, spectacled figure, not unimpressive. 'That's why the English are the greatest people in the world and always will be, because in the beginning we were blessed by the advice and the example and the teaching of the greatest people who have ever lived.'

Elspeth came running into the room, and saved me from the necessity of commenting on that. Her father took off his thick glasses and wiped them, and said, 'Finished the washing up?'

She nodded. 'Daddy, Mrs Scott washes up with a little mop so that you never have to put your hands into the water at all! Isn't that a good idea? May we have a little mop like that?'

He blinked at her without his glasses. 'Mop?'

She pulled him by the sleeve. 'Daddy, come and see. And they've got hot water all the time, made by the electricity!' She drew him away into our little kitchenette to see these wonders for himself.

They went away soon after that, absurdly grateful for the trivial hospitality that we had shown to them. We closed the front door behind them and went back to the sitting-room. 'I rather like your Mr Honey,' Shirley said. 'But he does look a mess.'

'That's just what he is – a mess.' I turned to her. 'Tell me, had he really never seen a mop for washing up? Or an electric water-heater?'

She laughed. 'Honestly, I don't think he had. I don't know what his own kitchen can be like!'

I lit a cigarette and flopped down in a chair. 'Tired?' she asked.

'A bit.' He said the Reindeer tail would come to bits in 1,440 hours, but he didn't know what an electric water-heater looked like. Could that possibly make sense? Did he know enough about real life to speak with confidence on anything? Was his opinion of any value whatsoever? Could one trust his judgment? I did not know, and I sat there turning it over and over in my mind.

Shirley said, 'Here you are.' I roused myself to what was going on, and the wonderful girl had been out to the kitchen and got a tumbler of whisky and soda, and she was offering it to me. I kissed the hand she gave it to me with, and said,

27

'Like to go to the pictures tonight?'

'I'll look and see what's on.' She picked up the paper, turned the pages, and said, 'I heard your Mr Honey holding forth very earnestly about something or other while we were washing up. What was it all about?'

I blew a long cloud of smoke. 'It was about the lost ten tribes of Israel, and the Druids, and about Jesus Christ coming to Glastonbury, and all sorts of stuff like that.' I looked up at her. 'I wish to God I could make up my mind if he's plain crackers or something different.'

'Is it important?' she asked.

'It is rather,' I told her. 'You see, he says the Reindeer tail will come to bits in 1,440 hours. And I'm supposed to be able to check up on his work. And I can't do it. I'm not good enough. . . .'

The next week was a torment of anxiety and uncertainty. I had to keep the matter to myself; I did not want to keep on badgering Mr Honey or to go wailing to the Director. Every day, I knew, the Reindeers were flying over the Atlantic piling up the hours faster than Mr Honey's test, each machine probably doing the best part of a hundred hours a week towards the point when Mr Honey said their tails would break. On the sixth day I couldn't stand it any longer, and suggested to the Director that perhaps he might give Sir Phillip a jerk up on the telephone.

On the ninth day the report came in. The Director rang through to tell me he had got it, and I went down to him. He handed it to me, and I sat down in his office to read it through.

Sir Phillip said that he had examined the work submitted to him in detail and had received certain explanations verbally from Mr Honey. He accepted, with considerable reserve, the work of Koestlinger indicating that an energy loss occurred when a material was subjected to repeated reversals of stress and that this lost energy could not be accounted for by any balance of the normal forms. It was a wild assumption on the part of Mr Honey, said Sir Phillip, that this lost energy became absorbed into the structure of the atom in the form of nuclear strain. He could only regard that as an interesting hypothesis which might perhaps be a fit subject for research at some date in the future. If ever it should be confirmed that something of the sort did happen, then he was very doubtful if the stress induced would, in fact, produce a separation of the neutron that Mr Honey postulated. He said, a little caustically, that in his experience it was not so easy to split the atom as amateurs were apt to think. If such a separation should take place, he saw no present indication that the resulting new material would be the crystallamerous isotope that Mr Honey had observed in substances broken under a fatigue test. That, he seemed to think, was little more than wishful thinking on Mr Honey's part.

In spite of all this, he recommended that the trials of the Reindeer tail should be continued, as the subject was obviously important. If it was desired that research upon the problems of fatigue should be undertaken by the ISARB, no doubt the representative of the Ministry would bring the matter up at the next meeting of the Board, when the priority to be allocated to the investigation could be determined.

I could have wept. Sir Phillip Dolbear had seated himself firmly on the fence and had offered us no help at all. And the Reindeers were still flying the Atlantic.

I said heavily, 'Well, this doesn't take us very much further, sir.'

The Director raised his eyes from the other work that he was reading. 'I thought that myself. I had hoped that we should get more out of him.'

We discussed it glumly for a few minutes. 'I should like to think it over for the rest of the day,' I said at last. 'At the moment I can't see anything for it but to go back to our old rule-of-thumb methods of guessing if the tail was dangerously flexible, and so on. May I think it over for today, and come in and see you tomorrow morning?'

'By all means, Scott,' he said. 'I'll be thinking it over in the meantime myself. It's certainly a difficult position, but fortunately we've got time for a little thought.'

I picked up the report and turned to go. 'In any case,' I said, 'I think we must face up to the possibility of having to ground all those Reindeers after seven hundred hours. I don't think we should let them go for more than half the estimated time to failure.'

'No,' he said slowly, 'I don't think that we should, although I wouldn't put too much weight on Mr Honey's estimate after this. If we said seven hundred hours, how long does that give us?'

'About three weeks from now,' I said. 'I'll find out definitely before tomorrow, sir.'

I went back to my room and dumped the report, and then went down and out of the building, and walked down to the aerodrome, to the flight office. Squadron-Leader Penworthy was there. I said, 'I say, Penworthy. You did the flying on the prototype Reindeer, didn't you?'

'Most of it,' he said.

I offered him a cigarette. 'What was the tailplane like?' I asked. I explained myself. 'I know it was quite safe, but was it very flexible? Did it have much movement of the tip in flight?'

He said, 'Well, yes – it did. It never gave us any trouble, but it's got a very high aspect ratio, you know, so you'd expect a certain amount of waggle. On the ground you can push the tip up and down about six inches with your hand.'

I nodded slowly. 'Did it have much movement in the air?'

He hesitated. 'I don't think it had any continuous movement – it wasn't dithering all the time, or anything like that. You could see it flexing in a bump, from the aft windows of the cabin.'

I turned this over in my mind. 'Was that in very bumpy weather? What time of year was it?'

He said, 'We had it flying in all sorts of weather. It was here altogether for about three months.'

'So long as that? How many hours did it do?'

'Oh,' he said, 'it did a lot. I did about two hundred hours on it myself. Before that there were the firm's trials, of course.'

A vague, black shadow was forming in my mind. 'What happened to it after it left here?'

'I flew it down to the CATO experimental flight,' he said.

I blew a long cloud of smoke, thoughtfully. 'Any idea how many hours it did there, before they put it into service?'

He shook his head. 'I'd only be guessing. But several hundred, I should think, because they did a whole lot of proving flights over the route before they put it into regular operation. They always do a lot of time on new machines before they go on service. They're pretty good, you know.'

I stared out over the aerodrome. 'That's the machine that flew into the hill in Labrador, isn't it?'

'That's right,' he said. 'Somewhere between Goose and

Montreal.'

I went back to the office with a terrible idea half formed in the back of my mind. I rang up Group-Captain Fisher of the Accidents Branch; I had had a good bit to do with him at Boscombe Down on various occasions that had not been great fun.

I said, 'You remember that Reindeer that flew into the hill in Labrador? Tell me, sir – could you let me know how many hours it had done before the crash?'

He said he'd look into the matter and let me know.

He came back on the telephone twenty minutes later. 'That figure that you asked about,' he remarked. 'The aircraft had done thirteen hundred and eighty-three hours, twenty minutes, up to the time of the take-off from Heath Row.'

I said quietly, 'Add about nine hours for the Atlantic crossing?'

'About that, I should think.'

'And say another hour from Goose on to the scene of the accident?'

'I should think so.'

'Making 1,393 hours in all?'

'That's about right.'

I put down the telephone, feeling rather sick. It was my job to stop that sort of thing from happening.

2

THAT AFTERNOON THE Director was in a conference; I was not able to get in to see him until six o'clock in the evening. He was tidying up his papers to go home, and I don't think he was very glad to see me at that time. 'Well, Scott, what is it?' he inquired.

'It's that Reindeer tail,' I said. 'Rather a disconcerting fact came to light this afternoon.'

'What's that?'

'You remember the prototype, the one that flew into the hill in Labrador or somewhere?' He nodded. 'Well, it had done 1,393 hours up to the moment of the crash.'

'Oh. ... Mr Honey's figure for tail failure was 1,440 hours, wasn't it?'

'That's right, sir.' I hesitated. 'The figures seem so close I thought you ought to know at once.'

'Quite right,' he said. 'But, Scott, in fact that machine *did* come to grief by flying into a hill, didn't it?'

I hesitated again. 'Well – that's what we're told, sir, and that's what everybody seems to have accepted. The story as I've heard it is that it hit the top of a mountain and fell down into a forest. Nobody saw it happen and everyone in it was killed. So there's no direct evidence about what happened to it.'

'Marks on the ground, to show where it hit first,' he said.

'Oh yes,' I said. 'I've no doubt that there was that sort of evidence. But if the tail came off at twenty thousand feet it would have to fall somewhere.'

'Is that what you think?'

I was silent for a moment. 'I don't know,' I said at last. 'I only know that this figure of 1,393 hours, the time that this machine did till it crashed – that figure's within three per cent of Mr Honey's estimate of the time to failure of the tail. I can't check that estimate and Sir Phillip Dolbear won't.' I paused in bitter thought, and then I said, 'And that three per cent is on the wrong side. It would be.'

'It certainly is a coincidence,' he said. 'Rather a disturbing one.' We stood in silence for a minute. 'Well,' he said, 'clearly the best thing is to establish what actually did happen to that aircraft. If it was a tailplane failure, then there must be some evidence of it in the wreckage. I should make a careful check of that upon the basis of Honey's theory. After all, a fatigue fracture is quite easily recognisable.'

I nodded. 'I was thinking on those lines, sir. I think the first thing is to get hold of the accident report and talk to the people who prepared it. If you agree I'd like to go to London in the morning and see Ferguson, and go with him to see Group-Captain Fisher in the Accidents Branch.'

'Will you take Honey with you?'

'Not unless you want me to particularly,' I replied. 'He isn't very good in conference, and I'd really rather that he stayed down here and got on with the job of verifying his theory. What I'd like to do would be to see him this evening and tell him that you've authorised the trial upon the Reindeer tail to go ahead by day and night from now on. I really think we ought to run a night shift on it, sir.'

'I think we should, Scott. Can you provide the staff?'

'I'll take young Simmons away from Mallory and put him to work with Honey,' I said. 'Simmons can watch the thing at night for the time being. He can have a camp bed in the office and an alarm clock. That'll do for a week or so; I'll have Dines to put on it when he comes back from leave.'

'All right, Scott. You can tell Honey that I'll see about the night shift in the morning.'

I was greatly relieved to have got that settled: at any rate we were now doing all we could upon the technical side. 'He'll have plenty to do tomorrow, sir, getting all that cracking. I'd rather he was down here doing that than coming up with me to London.'

It was nearly half-past six by the time I left the Director. I went back to my office and rang Honey's office, but there was no reply: he had probably gone home. I asked the exchange to give me his home number, and they said he hadn't got one. I packed up my work and went down to the balloon shed on my way out, to see if by any chance he was still there working late. But his office was locked and deserted. Outside, the great span of the tailplane stood upon its testing rig beneath the loading gantries, still and silent. It was not a happy thought that there were Reindeers in the air at that moment, putting up the hours towards the point when Mr Honey said their tails would break.

It was nearly half past seven by the time that I got home. Shirley had had dinner waiting for me for half an hour, and she was not too pleased about it. 'You might have rung me up,' she said.

I told her I was sorry. 'I've got to go out afterwards and dig up Honey,' I said. 'There's a bit of drama on.'

'What's the trouble?'

'It's that Reindeer tail,' I said.

'The one that Mr Honey says will come to bits in 1,440 hours?'

I nodded. 'Do you remember seeing in the paper that a Reindeer flew into a hill in Labrador a month or so ago? With the Russian Ambassador on board it?'

'I remember the Russians kicking up a stink,' she said. 'Was that a Reindeer?'

'That was the prototype Reindeer,' I replied. 'We heard this afternoon that it had done just on fourteen hundred hours when it came to grief.'

She had not worked at Boscombe Down all those years for nothing, and she knew quite a bit about aeroplanes. 'Oh, Dennis! Do you think it was the tail?'

'I just don't know,' I said unhappily. 'If it was, I suppose the bloody Russians will say we knew that it was going to happen, and we did it on purpose.'

She smiled. 'They couldn't say that, surely. Nobody suspected there was anything wrong with the tail when that one crashed.'

'Mr Honey did,' I said. There was no end to the trouble that might come out of this thing. But the first thing to do was to make darned sure that it could never happen again.

We had dinner, and washed up; then I went out and got into the car again, and drove round to Mr Honey's little house in Copse Road. It was about a quarter past eight when I got there; the door was locked. It was one of those suburban doors with a window in the top part; through this window I could see past the stairs down the narrow hall into the kitchen at the back. I pressed the bell; it rang, but there was no sign of life. Then as I waited there was a stir upstairs and footsteps coming down, and Honey appeared in the hall and opened the door for me.

He said, 'Oh, Dr Scott – I didn't expect to see you. Come in. I was just putting Elspeth to bed.'

I went into the hall with him. 'I'm sorry to disturb you, Honey,' I said. 'But something came up about the Reindeer tail this afternoon that I wanted to talk to you about. I've been with the Director this evening, and I've got to go to London in the morning. If you can spare a minute I'd like to have a talk about it now.'

He led the way into the front room, which would normally have been the parlour. It was furnished with a long table pushed against the wall, and with an enormous drawing-board in the bay window; on this was pinned a large-scale map of Europe and the Mediterranean Sea, but drawn to some curious projection with which I was not familiar. The other walls were lined with rather dirty, unpainted deal cupboards and bookshelves. Books and papers were everywhere, and overflowed in piles upon the floor. I noted some of the

34

titles of the books upon the table – *Numerics of the Bible, The Gate of Remembrance, Hysteresis in Non-Ferrous Materials, The Apocrypha in Modern Life,* and *A Critical Examination of the Pyramid.* The room was unswept and rather dirty, with cigarette ends stubbed out on the bare boards of the floor. There were two small upright wooden chairs; he pulled one forward for me.

'I'm afraid it's not very comfortable in here,' he said apologetically.

I smiled. 'It looks as if you do a bit of work, now and again.' I turned to the matter in hand. 'What I came about was this. You know that prototype Reindeer, the one that crashed in Labrador? The one that we all thought had flown into a hill?'

He said vaguely, 'I think I do remember something about it. It was in the papers, wasn't it?'

'That's right. It crashed and everyone was killed, so no one knows exactly what did happen to it. Well, I checked up on the hours that it had flown before the crash. It had done 1,393 hours.'

He stared at me. 'Had it? There'd be nothing to say that the crash wasn't due to tailplane failure?'

'That's just the point. I think the tail might possibly have failed. The crash wasn't seen by anyone, of course. It happened in the middle of Labrador.'

A slow smile spread over his face. 'Well, that's a real bit of luck,' he said.

I was staggered. 'Luck?'

He beamed at me. 'It's just what we wanted – it will shorten down our work enormously.' He explained himself. 'I mean, if this tail that we're testing now also fails at about 1,400 hours we shall have two trials, one confirming the other. We really shall feel that we're getting somewhere then.'

I said weakly, 'Well – that's one way of looking at it.'

From one of the rooms upstairs Elspeth called out, 'Daddy, Dad-dee!' She sounded impatient.

Honey turned to me, and said nervously, 'Would you mind excusing me for just a minute? I didn't pull her blind down.'

There was no point in playing the high executive, the little tin god; I had nothing else to do that evening. 'Not a bit,'

I said. 'Can I come up with you?'

'She'd be very thrilled if you came up to say good night to her,' he said. 'It would be kind of you.'

He took me up into a little bare bedroom at the back of the house; rather to my surprise it was all reasonably clean, though most unfeminine. Elspeth was lying on her back in bed, mathematically in the centre, with the sheet tucked smooth and unruffled across below her chin. Her eyes watched me as I paused in the doorway.

'Hullo,' I said. 'I've come to say good night.' And then I noticed that in bed with her, with its white-tasselled head beside her dark one on the pillow, was one of those little cotton mops that you use for washing up.

She saw me looking at it. 'Is that your dolly?' I asked, trying to be pleasant.

'No,' she said scornfully. 'That's a mop.'

Honey was busy at the window. I sat down for a moment on the end of her bed. 'Is it your best thing?' I asked. 'Is that why you've got it in bed with you?'

She nodded vigorously.

'I should use it for washing up,' I remarked. 'Then you won't have to put your hands in.'

She said, 'We've got another one for washing up. We went to Woolworth's and Daddy got two, and he said I could have this one to take to bed till we have to use it if the other one wears out. The other one's downstairs in the sink.'

Honey had finished at the window. He crossed to the bed, and bent down and kissed his daughter. 'Go to sleep now,' he said. 'Good night.'

I said, 'Good night, Elspeth. Sleep well.'

'Good night, Daddy. Good night, Dr Scott. Will you say good night to Mrs Scott for me?'

'I'll tell her. Good night from her.'

We went downstairs again to that dirty, littered room with the great drawing-board. 'It's all very well to think about the scientific value of that prototype crash,' I said, taking up from where we had left off. 'But thirty or forty people must have lost their lives in it, and if it was the tail we've got to make darned sure that doesn't happen again, Honey.'

'The important thing is to find out if the tailplane really was the cause of that accident,' he said. 'You see, it may affect the programme for this tail that we are testing now.

36

I've been thinking. A confirmatory experiment is valuable, of course, but it may not be making the best use of the material at our disposal. We might alter the frequency, for example. It's not easy to do that in the middle of a trial, but I'd like to think around it.'

'That's for the long-term programme,' I said patiently. 'What I'm bothered about is – ought we to ground all the Reindeers that are in service now?'

'I suppose that is important, too,' he said.

'It's the most important thing of all, Honey, because it's got to be decided now, or very soon, at any rate.'

He said thoughtfully, 'Of course, we don't really *know* any more than we did yesterday. We don't *know* that that tail failed in the air.'

'An examination of the wreckage will show that, though, won't it?'

'Oh, yes. If there's a fracture of the main spars of the tail, and if the structure of the metal at the fracture should be crystalline, that would be positive evidence of failure in fatigue.'

I stood for a moment deep in thought. Somebody would have to go and have another look at that tailplane; it really ought to be brought back to Farnborough for metallurgical examination. But it was a big unit to transport and it was urgent that the matter should be settled one way or the other. Where was the wreckage now? In Montreal? Or still in Labrador? I should have to find out that, and find out quick.

'I'm going up to London in the morning to see the Inspector of Accidents,' I said at last. 'That's why I came in tonight, Honey. I shan't be in the office tomorrow. But I saw the Director this evening and told him about this, and he agreed to running your trial night and day from now on.'

'Did he? That's very good news. I only wish he'd done it earlier, though. It's a pity that you have to have an accident to impress on people the urgency of basic research.'

I disregarded that one, and went on to tell him about young Simmons and to discuss with him the detailed arrangements that he would have to make next day in my absence. Mr Honey was quite wide awake and businesslike in any matter that concerned his trial, and having worked for so long in the RAE he knew all the ropes. At the end of ten minutes I was satisfied that everything would go ahead all right in my absence, and I turned to go.

'Well, I'm sorry to have disturbed you, Honey,' I said. 'I'll be away all day tomorrow, but I'll let you know what happens in London when I come in on Thursday.'

'It was good of you to come round,' he said. He came with me to the front door, and then he stopped me just as I was going out to the car. 'There's just one thing I wanted to ask you, if you could spare a minute . . .'

'Of course,' I said.

He hesitated. 'I wonder if you could tell me where you got that hot-water-heater? Are they very expensive things?'

'Why, no. They're very cheap. I don't know what they cost to buy outright, but you can hire them from the electricity company you know. We hire ours. I forget what it costs – something quite small. Two bob a quarter, or something like that.'

'Really – so little as that? They're very useful, aren't they? I mean, with one of those you've got hot water all the time.'

'That's right,' I said. 'We couldn't do without ours. You can get a big one for the bath, you know.'

'Can you!' He paused in thought. 'I think I must see about getting one for the kitchen, anyway. It's stupid to go on boiling kettles to wash up with.'

'It makes everything much easier,' I said. 'You know the electricity office in the High Street? Go in and tell them that you want to hire one. They'll fix you up all right.'

'I'll do that,' he said. 'Thank you for telling me. It does seem to be a thing worth having.'

I got into my car and drove home, and put it in the garage at the back of the flats, deep in thought. It seemed long odds to me that the tailplane of the prototype Reindeer would be still lying where it fell, in some Labrador forest. It was most urgent to get hold of it for technical examination; we must have a report on it within a week at the very latest, unless we were prepared to ground the Reindeers upon Mr Honey's word alone. One thing I was resolved upon, that no Reindeer should go on flying after seven hundred hours unless this thing had been cleared up. But to achieve that end, to stop the whole British Transatlantic air service before another accident happened, I should have to show some better evidence than I had got up to date that Reindeers were unsafe.

Shirley was waiting for me in the flat. 'Did Mr Honey

take it seriously?' she asked.

'And how!' I said, sinking down into my chair. 'He was as pleased as Punch about it. He thought it was a wonderful thing to have happened.' And I told her all about it.

She heard me to the end. 'He *is* a funny little man.' And then she said, 'Tell me, Dennis – do you really think, yourself, that Honey's right? Are the Reindeer tails dangerous?'

'There's not a shred of evidence that you can hang your hat on that there's anything wrong with them at all,' I said evenly. 'But – yes, I think he's probably right.'

'Why do you think that,' she asked quietly, 'if there isn't any evidence?'

'Fifteen years in the aircraft industry,' I said. 'One gets to know the smell of things like this.'

I reached for the cigarettes and gave her one, and lit one myself. We sat in silence for a time; I lay back in my chair and watched the blue clouds rising slowly to the ceiling, deep in thought. And presently she asked, 'What's Mr Honey going to do about it?'

I grinned at her. 'He's going to hire an electric hot-water-heater,' I said. 'He's already bought a mop.'

I went up to the Ministry in London first thing next morning and saw Ferguson; I told him the whole thing. He was inclined to regard it as a mare's nest, having had some experience of Mr Honey over the lunch-table while he had been at the RAE himself. 'I don't want to say anything against a member of your staff, Scott,' he remarked. 'But there may be things you wouldn't know about, that you really ought to know. Poor old Honey had a lot of trouble at the end of the war, you know – he lost his wife. That changed him a lot – he's never been the same man since. It was very distressing, that.'

He paused, and glanced at me. 'Did he ever tell you about his experiments with planchette?'

I was not now surprised at anything to do with Mr Honey. 'You mean, spiritualistic stuff?' I asked. 'I've heard a lot about him, but I hadn't heard that one.'

He hesitated. 'I dare say it's all over now. It was probably an effect of the distress he suffered at the time. But he used to do a lot with that.'

I was suddenly deeply sorry for the uncouth little man. 'Trying to get in touch with her, and all that sort of thing?'

He nodded.

I thought about it for a minute. 'I hadn't heard of that,' I said at last. 'I knew that he was religious, in an eccentric sort of way. But I don't think any of that really concerns us now. What I feel is this – that we can't let this thing slide, even if we both think that Honey's as mad as a hatter. He *has* made this forecast, for what it's worth, and the prototype did crash about that time. We've got to get to the bottom of it, now.'

'Oh yes, of course we have,' he replied. 'But in the meantime, I shan't lose much sleep myself.'

He rang through to Group-Captain Fisher in the Accidents Branch, and we went down to see him. After the preliminary greeting, I said:

'Look, sir – I've come up because we want to know a bit more about that accident to the prototype Reindeer.'

He nodded. 'You rang me up for the flying time. Just under 1,400 hours, if I remember right.'

'That's right, sir. We've been studying fatigue down at Farnborough, and a suggestion has been made that the tailplane might have failed on that machine.' I started in and told him the whole thing again, of course omitting the gossip about Mr Honey. I was getting to know my story off by heart by that time, from having told it to so many people.

As I talked, the frown deepened on his face. I came to the end, and he said, 'Do I understand, then, that there is a suggestion that my staff have been completely in error in their analysis of this accident?'

I hesitated. I did not want to get on the wrong side of the Group-Captain at the start. 'I wouldn't put it quite like that,' I said. 'We feel down at our place that this new evidence requires consideration alongside of all the evidence you have gathered up to date.'

He glowered at me. 'I don't know about new evidence,' he said. 'If I understood you correctly, you have an estimate from a research worker of what he hopes will happen in a trial which is in progress now. Is that right?'

I said, 'That's about it. We have been very much impressed with the way his estimate coincides with the flying time to crash of this first Reindeer.'

'Well, I'm not,' he said. 'There's no magic in the figure 1,400.' He rang a bell upon his desk. 'In this department, when we speak of evidence we mean evidence, sworn testimony that can be proved and that would stand up in a court of law. Not supposition and impressions.' A girl appeared, and stood in inquiry at the door. 'Get me the report upon the Reindeer accident, Miss Donaldson,' he said.

We sat in silence while the girl fetched the report; he did not seem to be in a very genial mood and I did not want to put my foot in it again, so I was saying as little as possible. She brought in a bulky folder bound up in the manner of a final report and handed it to him, and went away. He turned over the pages of it on his desk in silence for a time.

He said at last, 'Well, this is the report. The actual investigation was carried out by Ottawa, of course, with our representative assisting. I suggest you take it away and read it, as a first step. Then if you want any more information, we can have another talk.'

'That's very kind of you, sir,' I said. 'I'll read this through at once and get in touch with you again.'

I went back with Ferguson to his office. When we got there, 'What's eating the old boy?' I asked. 'I've always found him very helpful in the past.'

Ferguson said, 'Well, of course – this is a final report.' He took it in his hands thoughtfully, considering it. 'It's gone to the Minister, and there was a question in the House of Commons – the Minister based his reply on this. Because of the Russians, you know.' I nodded. 'Naturally, Fisher won't exactly jump for joy if you turn up and prove that it's all wrong.'

I said irritably, 'But damn it, man – we all make mistakes. I make them, so do you, and so does every living being in the world. One just has to admit them – Fisher's not a child. If this report is based on a misapprehension it'll have to be corrected – we can't hide things up. There's no future in that.'

'I know,' he said thoughtfully. 'The trouble is that Fisher's department has been making rather a lot of mistakes recently.' He paused. 'You heard about the Zulu crash at Whitney Sutton?'

'I heard the wings came off, or something. I didn't hear why.'

'That's right,' he said. 'It was diving at round about Mach unity, and the wings came off. The ailerons came off first and

41

then the wing broke up. Fisher's party got it all buttoned up as pilot's error of judgement. But then Cochrane from the Medical Research came in and proved pre-impact head wounds on the pilot's body. The windscreen broke up and crashed into the pilot's face – that's why it dived. It didn't do Fisher any good with the RAF types.'

I was interested. 'Is that established? Is that what really happened to it?'

He nodded. 'Keep it under your hat, old boy. No point in spreading things like that about.'

I settled down in Ferguson's armchair to read the report upon the accident to the prototype Reindeer.

It had flown from London Airport on the night of March 27th with a crew of nine and a passenger list of twenty-two persons, including the Russian Ambassador to Ottawa, thirty-one people in all. It had been diverted from Gander on account of fog and had landed at Goose at about 7 a.m. GMT on the morning of the 28th. It had refuelled there, and had taken off for Montreal at 9.17 in weather that was overcast and raining; the temperature was above freezing, unusual for the time of year. The crew had not reported any trouble at Goose. One wireless message of a routine character was received at 9.46 reporting that the aircraft was on course at 16,500 feet. That was the last that was heard of it.

It was three days before it was reported by one of the search aircraft, though the spot where it was finally located had been flown over several times. It was another two days before a party succeeded in getting to the wreckage. They flew up in a Norseman fitted with skis and landed in deep snow on a frozen lake called Small Pine Water; the landing was a hazardous one because of the alternate thaw and freeze: the skis mushed in beneath the icy crust. The party then had to force their way eleven miles over the snow-covered hills, thickly covered with a forest of spruce and alder. The night temperatures were as low as -45° Fahrenheit, making it a most difficult search: several of the party suffered from frostbite. In the deep snow and the forest growth they would never have found the crash at all but for the continuous guidance given by the aircraft working with them.

In the circumstances, it is hardly surprising that their investigation was, in some respects, perfunctory.

The spot where the Reindeer crashed was about 250 miles from Goose, about 50 miles west of the Moisie river and about 100 miles north of the sea coast in the Gulf of St Lawrence. It was just in Canada, in the Province of Quebec.

The bulk of the aircraft was found lying in deep snow among trees at the foot of a cliff, the estimated height of which was 340 feet. It had been on fire after the crash, and everything in it was totally destroyed. All the bodies were found within the flattened shell of the fuselage, indicating that nobody had survived the accident. The cliff face at that point ran approximately east and west along the aircraft's course, and the Reindeer had hit first at the top of this cliff, very near the edge. It had knocked down three trees, and here the starboard wing had been torn off; the wing was found at some distance from the rest of the machine, at the foot of the cliff. Two propeller blades and portions of the engine cowling were found on top of the cliff. The fuselage had then toppled over the cliff and had crashed down into the forest below, and burnt out.

From the damage to the trees it seemed that the original impact, the first touch, had been with the machine at a small angle of descent, probably not more than ten degrees below the horizontal. From that the investigators had deduced that the machine was under control up to the moment of impact, and from that that the pilot had been deliberately losing height through the overcast in order to check his position by a sight of the ground.

Ferguson, reading all this over my shoulder, said doubtfully, 'Well, that could be. But it sounds a bit odd to me. He was only an hour out from Goose. What should he want to check his position for?'

I shrugged my shoulders and turned to the photographs bound up with the report. The photographers were technicians, not sensation-mongers, and they had not gone out of their way to photograph the horrors; but it was not a pretty scene. The wreckage, of course, was hardly recognisable as an aircraft at all; in modern accidents it never is. It looked like the scrap heap of a tin factory. I turned the pages one by one, examining each photograph in turn minutely.

'I don't see the port tailplane anywhere,' I said at last.

'If it's missing, it'll be referred to somewhere in the text,' said Ferguson. 'Let me have a look.'

He turned the pages till we found what we were looking for. The passage read:

The party remained on the site of the accident for three days, during which time the 31 bodies were buried in individual graves. The whole of the units of the aircraft were not accounted for, due to the dense nature of the forest at this point. It was impossible to see further than three yards in any one direction because of the thickness of the undergrowth laden with snow, and no progress was possible except along paths cut for that purpose. The daytime thaw made all work wet and difficult and greatly hampered the search. The units of the aircraft unaccounted for were the starboard aileron, the outer starboard engine No. 6, the port tailplane and elevator, the port landing wheel assembly, No. 3 propeller (parted from the engine by a fracture of the crankshaft), and about five feet of the tip of the starboard wing.

I glanced at Ferguson. 'Port tailplane and elevator,' I said. 'There we are.'

He nodded. 'It's not evidence, of course,' he said. 'It keeps the fatigue theory in the field, in that if the tailplane had been there and intact it couldn't have come off in the air. But the mere fact that the port tailplane was missing, when so much else was missing, doesn't take us very far.'

'It's beginning to tot up,' I said. 'It's one more thing.'

I settled down to read the report through carefully; when I got to the end I turned back to the beginning and read it through again, making notes as I did so. It was clear from the circumstances of the accident that the wreckage could not possibly have been removed. It would still be lying where it fell three months before, with the new growth of the forest coming up around it and through it, gradually obliterating everything. There was my evidence, all right, there in the woods. In one of the photographs I could see the broken stump of the front spar of the port tailplane. It would not be necessary, perhaps, to search the woods for the tailplane itself. If that broken spar attached to the rear fuselage showed the typical form of fatigue crystallisation of the metal at the fracture, there would be all the evidence we needed. It would, of course, be better and would make the matter more complete if we could get the tailplane, too.

In the middle of the afternoon I went down to see the Group-Captain again, ready to be firm.

'I've read through this report,' I said. 'It's very interesting, sir – and, if I may say so, the most comprehensive report I've yet seen on an accident. It's very thorough.'

He smiled. 'Got all you want from it?'

'I think so,' I said. 'I should like to take it down to Farnborough to talk it over with the Director, if you could spare this copy for a few days?'

'That's all right,' he said.

I went on. 'Well, sir – about this suggestion that's been made about tailplane fatigue. You'll hear from us officially in the next day or two, if we want anything done. My present feeling – what I shall advise the Director – is that we should send an officer out there at once to make an examination of this broken tailplane spar.' His face darkened; I opened the report and showed him the photograph. 'This one. As the port tail was missing altogether we can't rule out this theory that has arisen. Of course, if it should be proved that fatigue is present in these aircraft at such an early stage, it's a matter of the greatest urgency to put it right.'

I stared down at the photograph before us; it was horrible. 'We don't want another one like this,' I said.

Fisher said stiffly, 'If you really think that necessary after the very careful investigation that has been already made, I suppose Ottawa can arrange it. If it comes at our request, of course, financial sanction will be necessary; these expeditions to out-of-the-way places like this are very costly, you know. It's in a dollar area, too, so the Secretariat will have to submit the matter to the Treasury. But if you people insist upon it, I suppose it can all be arranged.'

'I can only state my own view, sir,' I said. 'I think it's necessary and a matter of great urgency. That's what I shall tell the Director; I can't say, of course, what he'll decide. But I should like to see an officer on his way to Ottawa to-morrow, or the day after, at the latest.'

'It all seems rather ridiculous,' he grumbled. 'The matter was most carefully gone into.'

I did not want to argue it with him, and I had given him warning of what was coming, as was only fair. I said good-bye and left the office with Ferguson. He was rather amused; in the corridor outside the office he turned to me, and grinned.

45

'He's putting up a good fight,' he said. 'He knows all the tricks. He'll run round to the Secretariat tonight and tell them that your journey isn't really necessary.'

'He wouldn't do a thing like that,' I said. I was a little worried at the mere suggestion. 'He's a good old stick – I've known him for years. And this thing concerns the lives of people in the air. He wouldn't want to see another stinking crash like this.'

'Of course he wouldn't,' Ferguson replied. 'But you see – he thinks you're absolutely wrong and just kicking up a stink in his department irresponsibly. People believe what they want to believe.'

I got back to Farnborough too late to see the Director. I went home with the report under my arm, tired and depressed by what had been my reading for the day. I was due to read my paper on the 'Performance Analysis of Aircraft Flying at High Mach Numbers' on the following Thursday, the first paper that I had been asked to read before a learned society. When I got home I found that the advance printed copy of this thing had arrived, and that Shirley had been reading it all afternoon. She had taken it upstairs to show to Mrs Peters in the flat above; it was a great thing for us, because it was the first distinction we had managed to collect since we were married. Fingering it and turning over the pages, and discussing with Shirley the cuts that I would make when reading it, served as an anodyne; it took my mind off the Reindeer misery, so that I slept fairly well.

I went down to see the Director first thing next morning. I showed him the Reindeer accident report, and told him all about my interviews with Group-Captain Fisher. 'In spite of what he says, I think we ought to send somebody out there,' I remarked. 'I should like to see an officer from here sent out by air straight away, sir, to make a metallurgical report on that spar fracture.'

'I think you're right, Scott,' he said slowly. 'I believe that's the only thing to do. Who would you send?'

'I should send Honey.'

'You have sufficient confidence in Honey, Scott?'

I said, 'I have, sir. I'm beginning to get quite a respect for Mr Honey. I'm beginning to think he's right in this thing, and he's certainly the man in the Establishment who knows most about fatigue.'

'Yes, he is that.' He turned over the pages of the report, thoughtfully. 'This place where the accident is located – I understand it's eleven miles from a lake where you can land a seaplane? That's a journey of eleven miles through the Canadian woods?'

'I think so.'

'I'm not so sure that Honey is the right man for that sort of assignment, Scott. He isn't what I should describe as an outdoor type.' He paused. 'You wouldn't rather go yourself?'

I hesitated in my turn. I would have given my eyes to go off on a trip like that and it would have been a very welcome change from my office routine. But whoever went would have to go at once. 'I'd go like a shot, sir,' I said. 'But I've got this paper to read on Thursday of next week, the one on the performance of high Mach numbers. Of course, I could cancel it.'

He said, 'I had forgotten that.' He shook his head. 'You'll have to stay for that – after all, the Royal Aeronautical Society is an important body; you can't treat them like that. No, it will have to be Honey. You really think he will get on all right upon a trip like this?'

'I'm sure he will, sir,' I replied. 'Technically, he's certainly the best man we've got to send. And as regards the physical aspects of the journey, we can warn Ottawa that we're sending over somebody who isn't very fit. They'll make things easy for him, and push him through all right.'

We stood in silence for a minute; evidently he didn't like it much. 'I only wish he had a better presence,' the Director said at last. And then he straightened up. 'All right, Scott, I'll tell Ferguson what we've decided, and I'll get on to the Secretariat about the air passage. You'd like him to fly out at once?'

'Immediately, sir. I don't think we can afford to waste a day.'

I went up to my office and sent for Mr Honey. He came in blinking through his thick spectacles; his hair was untidy, his collar was dirty, and there was a smear of what I judged to be an egg upon the front of his waistcoat. He looked even more of a mess than usual. It was certainly a problem how to clean him up without hurting his feelings and making him bloody-minded, to make him look a little more presentable before I pushed him off to Ottawa.

I told him what had happened in London and I showed him the report of the accident. He did not seem to be very interested in the factual circumstances of the crash, but he seized on the photographs and looked for a long time at the stump of the tailplane front spar. 'It has all the appearance of a fatigue fracture,' he said at last. 'Look. There's no crumpling or elongation of the metal there. There's practically no distortion of the flange at all, right up to the point of fracture. That's not natural. That's a short fracture, that's what that is. The metal must have been terribly crystalline to break off short like that.'

I could see what he meant, though the detail was very tiny in the photograph. It was one more thing.

I told him that we had decided that an officer should fly to Ottawa at once, and that we were arranging for a seaplane or amphibian to take a party up to Small Pine Water immediately for a further technical examination of the wreckage. 'I want you to go and do that, Honey,' I said. 'I don't know anybody who could do it better.'

He stared at me. 'You mean – that I should go to Canada?'

'That's right,' I said. 'I want you to go at once, starting the day after tomorrow. It really is most urgent that we should get this matter settled up and find out if that tailplane failed in fatigue or not.'

'I don't know that there's all that rush about it,' he said. 'I agree – it's information that we must have ultimately, and the sooner we get it the better, I suppose. But we've still got to go on with the trial here, and I can't possibly get out even a preliminary report for limited circulation till November.'

'I know,' I said patiently. 'But that's the other aspect of it, Honey – the long-term research. What I'm concerned about now is – have we got to ground the Reindeers that are flying now?'

He said irritably, 'Oh, the *ad hoc* trial. Surely, anybody can do that, and leave me free to get on with the stuff that really matters.'

'This is the most important thing of all at the moment, Honey,' I said firmly. 'Look. You're an older man than I am, and probably a better scientist. Perhaps I'm better as an administrator than you would be – I don't know. In any case, here I am sitting in this office and it's part of my job to decide the priorities of work in this department. I think this trip to Canada is top priority of anything that's going on at Farnborough today and I want you to drop everything else and go and do it, because I can't think of anybody who could do it better. It's not an order, because we don't work that way. But I hope you'll accept my decision about priorities, because that's what I'm here for.'

He smiled, a shy, warm smile that I had never seen before. 'Of course,' he said. 'I wasn't trying to be difficult. I only hope I shan't have to spend too long away from here.'

I thought about that for a moment. 'I know it's important to get you back as soon as ever we can,' I said. 'I don't want to see the basic work held up. I'll see that you get an air passage home immediately the job is done. I should think you'd probably be away from here for ten days or a fortnight.'

His face fell. 'So long as that?'

'I don't believe you'd do it in much less. First, you've got to get from here to Ottawa. Then there's the flight back from Ottawa to north-east Quebec, and then to reach the site of the accident is a day's trek on foot. And then the whole thing in reverse again, to get back home.'

'It's an awful waste of time,' he grumbled.

'It's not,' I said. 'That's my sphere of decisions, Honey, and I tell you that it's not a waste of time.'

'It is from the point of view of the basic research.'

'So is eating your breakfast,' I remarked. 'But you've got to do that, too.'

I went through the various arrangements that would have to be made for carrying on his trials in his absence; he was quite business-like and alert where anything to do with basic trials was concerned, and in ten minutes we were through with that. 'Now about your trip,' I said. 'It's going to mean some days of living rough in the Canadian woods, I'm afraid. You'll be with the RCAF and they'll look after you, but I understand that there's a ten or fifteen mile walk from the lake you land on to the site of the crash, and the same back again. It'll probably be quite difficult going. Have you got an outfit of clothes that would do for that, Honey?'

'I've got some good strong boots. I haven't looked at them for years, but I think they're all right.' He paused, and then he said, 'We used to do a lot of hiking on Sundays, when my wife was alive. ....' He stared out of the window, and was silent for a moment; I did not care to interrupt him. 'We used to go in shorts ... I've got those somewhere, I think. Do you think shorts would be suitable?'

The thought of Mr Honey turning up in Ottawa in short hiking pants as a representative of the Royal Aircraft Establishment made me blench. 'I wouldn't take those,' I said. 'I don't believe they wear shorts in the woods, on account of the mosquitoes. I'll get a letter through to Ottawa asking them to kit you up for the trip, and we can charge it up as necessary expenses. I should take the boots with you, or ... no, they'll supply those too. But look, Honey, go in your best suit. You're going as the representative of this Establishment. Put on a bit of dog, you know. Don't let anybody sit on you in any technical matter; you're the expert, and you're the man that counts. We'll back you up from here in anything you feel you've got to insist on.'

He nodded. 'I'll remember that,' he said.

'Now, how about your personal affairs? Are you all right with those?'

He hesitated. 'Well, no, I'm not. I've got a man from the electricity company coming in one day next week to fit up that electric hot-water-heater. And then there's Elspeth – I shall have to see if I can get somebody to come and sleep in the house, I suppose. It's rather a long time for her to be alone.'

I was a bit staggered at the suggestion that he could leave Elspeth alone at all. 'What about her?' I asked. 'Have you got a relative who could come and stay with her?'

He shook his head. 'I don't think there's anybody like that.' He paused for a minute in thought, and then he said, 'Don't worry about that, Dr Scott – I'll think of something. I've left her for two days at a time, once or twice when I had to. Of course, she's older now, but I think this is much too long to do that. I think I can get Mrs Higgs – that's my charwoman – I think she'd come and sleep in while I'm away.'

The thought was distasteful to me, but it was at any rate a possible solution to his problem. If we had had a second bedroom at the flat I would have offered to put up his child myself, but we hadn't. Moreover, Honey's domestic affairs were really no concern of mine and there was a limit to the extent that I could allow them to influence me in the work of the Establishment. But I was sorry for Elspeth.

'I'll see that you get back as soon as ever we can manage it,' I said.

'That's very good of you – I really don't want to be away longer than is necessary, for a variety of reasons.' His eyes dropped to the accident report on the desk before us. 'Have you told the Rutland Company anything about this yet?'

I had forgotten all about the design staff who had produced the Reindeer, or if I had remembered them I had placed them in the background of my mind. 'I haven't told them anything about it yet,' I said slowly. 'I thought perhaps it was better to wait until the matter was rather more definite. Do you think we ought to get in touch with Prendergast now?'

'I don't want to,' he said quickly. 'I was wondering if you had.'

'No, I hadn't done anything about it.' The apprehension of a new series of difficulties swept over me. E. P. Prendergast was the Chief Designer of the Rutland Aircraft Company, and the author of the Reindeer. In person he was a big, dark man with bushy black eyebrows and the face of an ascetic monk. He was about six foot four in height and broad in proportion to his height; he was nearly sixty years old, but he was still a very powerful man. He was one of the oldest and most successful chief designers in the country, and the Reindeer was the last of a long line of lovely aircraft that had come out of his office. He was a very great artist at the business of designing aeroplanes, and like all great designers in the aircraft industry he was a perfect swine to deal with.

There is, of course, a good explanation in psychology for this universal characteristic of the greatest aeroplane designers. A beautiful aircraft is the expression of the genius of a great engineer who is also a great artist. It is impossible for that man to carry out the whole of the design himself; he works through a design office staffed by a hundred draughtsmen or more. A hundred minds, each with their own less competent ideas, are striving to modify the chief designer's original conception. If the design is to appear in the end as a great artistic unity, the chief designer must be a man of immensely powerful will, capable of imposing his idea and his way of doing things on each of his hundred draughtsmen, so that each one of them is too terrified to insert any of his own ideas. If the chief designer has not got this personality and strength of will, his original conception will be distorted in the design office and will appear as just another, not-so-good aeroplane. He will not then be ranked as a good chief designer.

All really first-class chief designers, for this reason, are both artists, engineers, and men of a powerful and an intolerant temper, quick to resist the least modification of their plans, energetic in fighting the least infringement upon what they regard as their own sphere of action. If they were not so, they could not produce good aeroplanes. For the Government official who detects an error in their work the path is not made easy, and of all men in the aircraft industry the most dangerous to cross was E. P. Prendergast. He was deeply religious in a narrow, Calvinistic way. He could be in turn a most courteous and charming host, a sympathetic and an understanding employer, and a hot-tempered fiend capable of making himself physically sick with his own passion, so that he would stalk out of a conference of bitter, angry words, and retire to the toilet and vomit, and go home to bed, and return to his office three days later, white and shaken with the violence of his illness. He was about the greatest engineer in England at that time and he produced the most lovely and successful aeroplanes. But he was not an easy man to deal with, E. P. Prendergast.

The Director sent for me again that evening. He had had Ferguson working all day on the matter; cables had been passing to and fro with Ottawa and the Treasury had been persuaded that it was necessary to spend the dollars. Priority had been allocated for the passage, and it looked as if Mr Honey would get off on Sunday.

After all that, I raised the matter of the Rutland Aircraft Company. I said, 'At what stage do you think we ought to get the firm in on this thing, sir?' I paused, and then I added, 'E. P. Prendergast . . .'

He glanced at me 'Yes . . . Prendergast.' He was silent for a minute, and I knew what he was thinking. If anybody dared to say the Reindeer tail was not above suspicion and could not produce good evidence for that assertion, E. P. Prendergast would go up in a sheet of flame. He would complain to the Minister, as he had done before, that he could not carry on his work in an atmosphere of petty backbiting and vilification by minor civil servants. He would offer, in the most dignified way, to give up his post and go to America if it would assist the Minister in his direction of the Industry. But if it was the desire of the Minister that he should continue to design British aircraft, then he must be protected from the expression of the petty jealousies of petty Government officials. As I have said, we had had some of this before.

The Director said, 'I doubt if Mr Prendergast would find Honey's theoretical work very convincing.'

'I'm damn sure he wouldn't,' I said. 'He'd chew him up and spit him out in no time.'

'I don't know that the time is quite ripe to inform the firm,' he said thoughtfully. 'After all, there's nothing they can do till it is proved that fatigue is actually taking place. We ought to have a cable from Honey in a few days which will indicate what really happened to that prototype machine. I think that would be the time when we should get the firm into the matter, when the question of some modification arises.'

'I think so, too,' I said. 'I think it's a bit early yet to worry them.'

I told Honey to make preparations for his passage on Sunday, and I put him into touch with Ferguson, who knew him well, over the matter of his passport and his money. Then I went home, and that evening over supper I told Shirley all about it. 'He's going to get the charwoman to come and sleep in the house with Elspeth,' I said.

'Oh, Dennis – the poor child! Is that the best he can do?'

'I asked him if he hadn't got a relation who could come in,' I said defensively. 'He said he hadn't got one.'

She was indignant. 'But do you mean to say she's going to be all alone for a fortnight, except for the charwoman? Dennis, you can't let him go away like that! He *must* make some better arrangement for her.'

'I can't help it if he goes away and leaves her like that,' I said irritably. 'I can't run his life for him. I'm his boss; I'm not a ruddy welfare worker.'

'I know.' She was silent for a minute, and then she said, 'Perhaps after he's gone we could go round there and see how she's getting on.'

'I think we ought to do that,' I agreed. 'It's a rotten way

to leave a child, but there doesn't seem to be much else that he can do. And he's the only man to go to Canada.'

3

IT WAS THE practice of the Central Air Transport Organisation at that time to fly the Atlantic by night. The aircraft took off from London Airport at about eleven o'clock, landed at Gander in Newfoundland to refuel before dawn, and continued on to arrive at Montreal or New York about the middle of the morning.

Mr Honey travelled up to the air terminal at Victoria after supper on Sunday night. He was tired and confused with the events of the day. He had had a good deal of trouble in persuading Mrs Higgs, his charwoman, to leave her husband and come to sleep in his house; in the end she had agreed to do it 'to oblige' and for ten shillings a night. He had had little sleep the night before because he had stayed up late making every possible arrangement he could think of for the comfort and security of his small daughter while he was away. Although by normal standards he looked after her very badly, he worked hard to do his best and he took his responsibility for her quite seriously. He had had much to do at the office, too, to secure the smooth progress of his trial by day and night during his absence. With all these responsibilities he started off upon his journey tired and a little worried lest he had forgotten something that he should have done.

At Victoria, however, the CATO travel organisation took him in its arms and wrapped him round as if with cotton-wool. While he was waiting in a deep armchair in the assembly hall a pretty stewardess brought him a cup of coffee with a couple of biscuits, and a choice of newspapers to read; he blinked and thanked her shyly. Presently his name was called out on a list, and he had to rise and walk a few steps to the motor-coach, where a rug was wrapped around to preserve him from the evening chill. He was driven to the airport and passed quickly through the emigration formalities; then he was ushered down a covered passage and into an aeroplane before he had even time to look at it. He probably would not have looked at it in any case, because he was not much interested in aeroplanes unless they had fatigue trouble.

In the warm, brightly lit cabin of the aircraft he was received by a tall, dark girl in the uniform of a stewardess, one of two that served the Reindeer passengers upon their flight. She showed him to his seat and took his coat and hat from him, and saw that he was comfortably settled down with magazines within his reach. Then she pulled out the safety belt from behind the seat and showed him how to clasp it round his body, talking to him brightly and cheerfully all the time. 'It's only just for taking off and landing that you have to do this,' she said. 'Just for the first five minutes. I'll come and tell you when you can undo it.' She adjusted the strap for him with quick, expert hands. 'There – is that quite comfortable?'

He said, 'Quite, thank you. You don't have to worry about me – I know something about all this. I work with aeroplanes.'

She smiled. 'Are you the gentleman from Farnborough, sir? There was an expert from Farnborough coming across with us tonight.'

He smiled up at her through his thick glasses, that shy, warm smile that had made me wonder once before. 'That's right,' he said.

'Oh well, then – you know everything.' She smiled down at him with a new interest, but habit was strong in her and she went on with her patter. 'Captain Samuelson says we've got a very good weather report. You'll see it will be quite fine half an hour after we get started.' She said that every time and she was always right, because they flew at a high altitude above the overcast.

She left him, and turned to attend to her other passengers. The aircraft was to cross with only about fifty per cent of its designed passenger load, so the stewardesses were putting one person only into each of the double seats; Mr Honey had room to spread his paper and his briefcase on the seat beside him. He sat in warm comfort staring round at the furnishings of the long cabin, exploring the reading-light switch and the control of his reclining chair. He was impressed with the comfort and security of everything, as he was meant to be. He had never been in such a comfortable and well-equipped aircraft cabin before, and for the first time he wondered idly what sort of aeroplane he was sitting in. He thought that he would ask the nice girl who had buttoned him into his safety belt, when she came to unbutton him.

He screwed round in his seat to look down the length of the wide cabin behind him, to the stewardesses' pantry and the toilets and the entrance door. The other passengers were mostly men, but there were three or four women. Mr Honey's eyes rested on a woman travelling alone; he paused, and stared at her in frank curiosity. She was seated two rows behind him, on the other side of the aisle. She was a very beautiful woman with deep auburn hair, carefully made up, wearing a most magnificent mink fur. In spite of all the trimmings her face remained keen and intelligent, giving added charm to her great beauty. Mr Honey knew her at first glance, and his heart rose in sudden emotion and he felt a tightening in his throat and tears welling up behind his eyes. She was Monica Teasdale.

When Honey had married one of the girl clerks in the Airworthiness Section back in 1934, he had married a girl as unsophisticated as he was. They were a very simple couple: they liked going for long hikes on Sundays with rucksacks on their backs; they liked amateur photography; and they did a bit of Morris dancing, too, with flying ribbons and little bells that jangled at the knee. They went a good deal to the movies, but they were discriminating picturegoers; if they didn't like the film they would walk out of it, preferring to lose their money than to sit through an unworthy show. They never walked out of anything with Monica Teasdale in it.

They loved Monica Teasdale with all the enthusiasm of very simple people; throughout their life together they did not miss one of her films. If they had been less inhibited they might have written to her to tell their admiration of her work: they talked of doing so a number of times, but when they came to frame the words upon paper once it seemed too stupid, and they never wrote. They did not do that, but they saw all of her pictures, and they remembered them and could discuss the details of the story with each other years afterwards. That went on from the day that they became engaged till Mary Honey was killed in the year 1944. That finished it abruptly; since that time Mr Honey had not been inside a picturehouse.

Monica Teasdale was for Mr Honey part of his lost life, a

part of the simple pleasures and enthusiasms he had shared with his young wife. She was inextricably associated in his mind with Mary Honey. As he stared at her across the aisle in the warm, bright cabin of the aircraft the tears welled up in his weak eyes behind the thick glasses of his spectacles; he had to turn away and blow his nose and take off his spectacles and polish them. The memory of his dead love was very vivid with him at that moment. He could see her sitting by the fire upon the rug one evening with a cup of cocoa in her hand, when they had just come in from seeing Monica Teasdale in *Temptation*. He could see her expression as she had looked up at him. 'Theo, darling – would you think it stupid if we went to see that one again? Before it comes off?'

He stared at the back of the seat in front of him, a worn, tired little man wiping his glasses.

Behind him the door closed; the chief steward passed by him on his way to the flight deck, a sheaf of papers in his hand and carrying a black briefcase. The forward door closed behind him and the engines started one by one, deep, re-assuring rumbles faintly heard as though from a great distance. Presently the cabin stirred beneath him. Mr Honey looked out of the window and saw the lights of the airport buildings pass him by as the aircraft moved down the ring road to the runway's end.

He never felt the machine leave the ground. At the runway's end she turned across the wind and cleared engines one by one; then before Mr Honey realised what was happening the runway lights were sliding past his window in acceleration and presently they fell away below. It was the first time he had ever travelled in an aeroplane with modern soundproofing and it took him by surprise, because he had expected to be warned for the take-off by a great burst of noise. But there was no such roar, and before he realised quite what was happening the airport was below and behind. Then there was nothing to be seen out of his window but a blackness that reflected his own face and everything in the brightly lit cabin.

He leaned back in his seat and relaxed, savouring the comfort. Presently the stewardess who was attending to the passengers at his end of the cabin came up the aisle, stopping by each passenger and saying a few words, helping to tuck away the safety belt, taking orders for meals upon a little pad. She came to Mr Honey presently, and said, 'I'm sure you'd like a little supper before settling down, sir. What can I get you?' She told him what he could have.

He ordered a cup of coffee and a plate of sandwiches; she noted it. And then he said, 'I say, is that Monica Teasdale sitting over there?'

The girl nodded. 'That's right. She came over about a fortnight ago. Quite a number of film actors and actresses travel with us – American as well as British. She always travels this way.'

He said in wonder, 'She looks just like she does in her pictures, doesn't she?'

'I know. But she looks old when you see her close up, in the early morning.' The stewardess laughed, and Mr Honey laughed with her. 'But she's ever so nice.'

'One more thing,' Mr Honey asked. 'What sort of aeroplane is this?'

The girl said, 'This is one of the latest, sir – what they call the Reindeer type. That isn't what we call them on the line, of course; this one is called "Redgauntlet". But it's the Reindeer type, made by the Rutland Aircraft Company. It's the very latest thing – we've only had them in service for a few weeks.' She broke off, smiling. 'I was forgetting sir. You must know all about them.'

He said, 'Oh, this is a Reindeer, is it?' He was not in the least perturbed, because he had complete confidence in the check that I was keeping on the flying time that all the Reindeers had done, but he looked about him with new interest. 'I must say it's very comfortable,' he said.

The stewardess said, 'I think it's lovely. I've only just come on to Reindeers; this is my first trip in one. I was working in Eagles up till last week. They're very nice, of course, but this is the most modern plane there is. You really must come down and see the galley later on, sir – it's a perfect dream. We've got everything we want, and a telephone to the flight deck. And plenty of room to work.'

She went away, and presently she came back with his coffee and sandwiches. Later she came and took away the tray, and asked him if he wanted to sleep. Although he had had a long and tiring day, Mr Honey was not ready for sleep; she adjusted the little reading-light for him and showed him the switch. 'We shall be turning off the main lights in a minute,' she said. 'If you feel sleepy, here's the switch for this one.'

He asked, 'What time do we land?'

'About seven o'clock of our time, at Gander. That's before dawn, on account of the change of time.'

The lights went down, and Mr Honey sat on, reading his magazine in a little pool of light. He looked round once or twice at Monica Teasdale but she had soon stopped reading and turned out her light, and now she lay resting or sleeping in her reclining chair, in the half darkness. Mr Honey never read a magazine in normal times, but these times were not normal; the novelty of his experiences had taken him out of his mental groove, and he found novelty in the little love stories and in the advertisements about unpleasant breath.

At about two o'clock in the morning the second pilot, a cheerful young man called Dobson, came down into the cabin and walked aft in the dim light, and went to the galley, where he stood drinking coffee and chatting to the stewardesses for ten minutes. Then he said:

'Which is the boffin?'

They laughed. 'What's a boffin?'

'The man from Farnborough. Everybody calls them boffins. Didn't you know?'

'No. Why are they called that?'

'I dunno. Because they behave like boffins, I suppose. Which of you is looking after him?'

'I am,' said Miss Corder. 'His name is Mr Honey.'

'The little half-pint size, with thick glasses?'

She nodded. 'Sitting on the starboard side, near the front.'

'I knew it. I knew that was the boffin when I saw him. You can't mistake them.'

'What about him?' asked Miss Corder. The joke was over, so far as she was concerned.

Dobson said, 'The captain sent me down to offer to show him the upper deck. Is he awake?'

She glanced down the aisle. 'I see his light's on still. Will you take him now, if he wants to go?'

He nodded. 'Get it over.'

'I'll ask him.' She walked down the aisle softly, with Dobson following behind her. 'Mr Honey,' she said. 'Captain Samuelson has asked if you would care to see the upper deck – the pilot's cockpit and the navigation and so on. Mr Dobson, here, could take you now, if you feel like it. Or would you rather go after Gander, on the run to Montreal?'

Mr Honey thought for a moment. He had no real interest in flying, though in the course of his work at the RAE he had picked up a fairly comprehensive knowledge of an aeroplane's controls. If it had been that alone, he would not have bothered to leave his seat, unless from a sense of duty or politeness. He was, however, genuinely interested in the navigation. His investigations in connection with the Pyramid had led him to a study of chart projections, and he was glad of the opportunity to examine the charts prepared especially for navigation over the Atlantic. It was unlikely that the charts used for the flight overland from Gander would show many novel features. 'That's very kind of the captain,' he said. 'I think I'd rather go now.'

The stewardess introduced him to the first officer, and with Dobson he went forward through the door and up the narrow duralumin stair that led to the flight deck. He found himself standing in a fairly spacious area, well lit, with windows showing the black night outside. An engineer was seated at a desk garnished with levers, before an instrument board a yard square that was completely filled with black-faced dials. A wireless operator was seated at the instruments, to one side of him the green trace of radar showed upon its screen. Behind him was the navigator's desk, and beyond that again the two pilots' seats with the flying controls, and the windscreen that showed nothing but the black night. A man of about fifty, Captain Samuelson, sat in the port seat, but his hands were not on the controls, which made tiny movements now and then upon their own. It was very peaceful up on the flight deck.

Mr Honey asked, 'What altitude are we flying at?'

Dobson said, 'About eighteen thousand feet.' He glanced at the sensitive altimeter above the navigating table. 'Eighteen thousand five hundred. Of course, we're pressurised. you know. The pressure in here corresponds to about seven thousand feet.'

The sense of solidity and security impressed Mr Honey very much; nothing, it seemed, could ever go wrong in a thing like this. 'This is a Reindeer, isn't it?' he asked.

'That's right.'

'How do you like it?'

plane. You must turn back to England at once.' He repeated earnestly, with a rising inflection in his voice, 'At once.'

The second pilot stared at him. 'Fatigue trouble? What's that? We can't go back to England, you know.'

'But you must.' His voice rose to a little nervous squeak. 'I tell you, this is very serious indeed. This aeroplane should not be flying at all. The tail is liable to fail at any moment – the front spar may fail. You've got a positive download on the tail in this condition. You'll go into a dive quite suddenly, and there'll be no control to get you out. I tell you, you must turn back at once. Turn back and land at the first aerodrome in Ireland.' The young man stared at him in growing tolerance and amusement. 'If you stop the inboard engines and reduce the revolutions on the middle ones right down to a minimum, there's just a chance that we may get back safely.'

'Take it easy,' Mr Dobson said. 'Whatever are you talking about? You must have heard of an airworthiness certificate, surely? This aircraft's all okay. I'll show you the daily inspection note, if you like.'

'This is something quite new,' said Mr Honey. 'No Reindeer is allowed to fly more than seven hundred hours until this question of the tail has been cleared up. And this one has flown double that, and that's right on the estimated time for failure. I assure you, something can happen any moment now. You really must turn back.'

'What's all this about a Reindeer not being allowed to do more than seven hundred hours?'

'It's true. They've all got to be grounded when they reach that time.'

Dobson stared at him; impatience and hostility were beginning to appear. 'First I've heard of it.' He beckoned to the engineer, who left his seat and came to them. 'Cousins, have you heard anything about Reindeers being grounded after seven hundred hours?'

'Not a thing,' the engineer said in wonder. 'I never heard of that. Who says so?'

'Chap from Farnborough,' Dobson said. He had forgotten Mr Honey's name.

'That's not right,' the engineer said scornfully. 'What do you think the Air Registration Board would have been doing?' He turned to Mr Honey. 'Who told you that?'

'It's true,' he said desperately. 'My chief, the head of my

department, Dr Scott – he was arranging all about it.' They stared at him in utter disbelief. 'Please – you must pay attention to this. Stop the inboard engines and turn back. If you stop the inboard engines it will break up the harmonic and modify the effective frequency, and the amplitude will be less, too.'

The engineer turned to Dobson and said, 'What on earth is he talking about?'

The second pilot said quietly, 'All right, Cousins – I'll handle this. I'll have a word with the captain.' The engineer went back to his seat, but kept a wary eye on Mr Honey. Eccentric passengers with odd ideas about the safety of the aircraft are never very welcome on the flight deck of an airliner on passage.

Mr Honey caught the last words. 'Please do that,' he said. 'I must have a talk with the captain. It's very serious indeed, really it is. We must turn back at once.'

Dobson crossed to where Captain Samuelson was sitting at the controls, and bent beside him. 'That passenger from Farnborough that you asked me to show round is up here now, sir. He's making a good deal of trouble.'

From the navigating desk Mr Honey could see them talking quietly together; he saw the captain turn in his seat to look at him. He stood at the desk waiting for them. His agitation was subsiding; already he was becoming aware that he had not got it in him to make these men believe that what he said was true. He had had so much of this in the past; he was accustomed to being right and being disbelieved on vital issues. It was what happened to him; other people could put across their convictions and win credence, but he had never been able to do that. Now it was happening again, probably for the last time. In the black night the aircraft moved on quietly across the sky above the cloud carpet, seen faintly in the starlight far below.

Captain Samuelson got out of his seat; the second pilot slipped into it, and sat at the controls. Samuelson crossed the floor to Honey, standing by the desk. He was a small, sandy-haired man of about fifty, rather fat; he had been sitting in the pilot's seat of airliners for over twenty years.

He introduced himself to Mr Honey, and said, 'I understand from Dobson that you're not quite happy about something, Mr Honey.'

He stood in silence while Honey poured out his tale, nodding every now and then. Honey was more collected now and told his story better, and in Samuelson he had an older and a more experienced man to talk to. The Senior Captain had heard of fatigue troubles once or twice, and he even knew something of the eccentricities of scientists. He knew something of the routine of the Ministry of Supply and a good deal about the routine of the Ministry of Civil Aviation. Presently he started asking questions, and they were informed and penetrating questions. He very soon uncovered the fact that officially there was nothing wrong whatever with the Reindeer aircraft, that there was no ban upon its operation after seven hundred hours, and that there was no real evidence that the tailplane was subject to fatigue trouble at all.

Mr Honey said miserably at last, 'I've got to tell you what I know. If you don't turn back to England now and do what I say about the engines, we'll all probably be killed.'

Samuelson stood deep in thought. Once or twice before in his career he had had over-excited passengers to deal with, who had required restraint during a flight; once he had had an attempted suicide, a woman who had been found struggling to open the main entrance door during the flight. He was not antagonistic, but he could not discount the likelihood that the excitement of the journey might have inflamed the fixed ideas of a man who, from his appearance, might well be a little bit unbalanced. He was, however, disposed to pay attention carefully to everything that Mr Honey said, and for a special reason that had not been spoken of between them. Captain Samuelson had known Captain Ward, the pilot of the Reindeer that had crashed in Labrador, very well indeed.

Samuelson and Bill Ward had both been short-service officers in the Royal Air Force in 1925; Samuelson had flown Bristol Fighters in Iraq and Ward had flown Sopwith Snipes in India. They had met as civil pilots in an air circus in 1927; they had met again as minor airline pilots in Canada in 1928. In 1932 they had come together once more, as pilots on the Hillman airline operating out of Romford in Essex; shortly after that both had joined Imperial Airways. From that time on they had met frequently, up till the time when Ward had received command of the first prototype Reindeer. Then

Ward had been killed.

The accident report, when it came out, was a great shock to Samuelson; he disbelieved it utterly. He had known Ward as a fellow pilot for more than twenty years. It was incredible to him that Ward should have done what the report said he did, that he should have descended through the overcast to zero altitude above the hills of Labrador to check up his position by a sight of the ground. There were things a Senior Captain of CATO just did not do, and that was one of them. Samuelson did not know what had happened to Bill Ward, but he did know one thing very certainly. The accident report was absolutely and completely wrong.

He had been flying for more than twenty-five years. Deep in his mind lay the feeling that there was something not right with the Reindeer; that this beautiful and efficient aircraft had a weakness that would presently show up. Some unknown Gremlin in it had leaped out upon Bill Ward suddenly, so suddenly that he had been unable to send word upon the radio, and it had killed him, and thirty other people with him. His instinct, bred of nearly twenty thousand hours in the air, told him that one day that thing would happen again.

He glanced at Mr Honey thoughtfully. He saw the weak eyes behind the thick glasses, the unimpressive figure, the shabby clothes, the nervous movements of the hands, the quivering wet lips. He thought, rather sadly, that he could not change his flight plan upon this man's word alone. Mr Honey looked a crank and what he said was unsubstantiated by any evidence at all. The captain decided, heavily, he must go on. If Honey turned out to be right, well, that was just too bad.

He said, 'Look, Mr Honey, I'm going to do this. I'm going to shut down the inboard engines as you say, and I can throttle down the middle ones to nineteen hundred revs. That drops our speed by fifty miles an hour and makes us nearly two hours late at Gander. I'll do that if you think it's the right thing to do. But I'm not going to turn back.'

'You're taking a great risk if you go on. You ought to turn back now – at once – and land in Ireland,' said Mr Honey.

'That's what you think,' the captain said quietly. 'But this decision rests with me, and we're going on.'

Mr Honey met his eyes, and that shy, warm smile spread

66

over his face, surprising to Samuelson as it had been to me. 'Well, let's wish ourselves luck,' he said.

At that moment, Samuelson very nearly became convinced. It was on the tip of his tongue to say they would turn back, but one could not chop and change. One had to take a line and stick to it. He turned to the flight engineer and gave him a few orders; then he crossed to the pilot's seat and spoke for a minute to Dobson. The second pilot got out of the seat and Samuelson slipped back into it, knocked out the automatic pilot and flew the aircraft manually while the inboard engines died and the note changed. Dobson crossed to Mr Honey at the navigating table.

'I'll take you back to the saloon,' he said. As they left the flight deck Samuelson motioned to the radio operator, demanding a signal pad.

In the saloon Dobson showed Honey to his seat with studied courtesy; then he went on down the cabin to the galley at the rear end. The tall dark stewardess was there, the one who was looking after Mr Honey.

He greeted her with a grin. 'Fun and games,' he said. 'The boffin's going mad.'

Miss Corder stared at him. 'What *do* you mean?'

'He's absolutely crackers. Says the tail's going to fall off.'

She asked quietly, 'Is it?'

'No, of course it's not. It's the altitude or something, even pressurised down like this. The captain wants him specially looked after – he's a bit excited. Got any bromide with your medicines?'

She turned to the medicine chest and pulled out a drawer, and examined two or three little flasks of tablets. 'I've got these.'

He took the flask from her and read the label. 'That looks all right,' he said. 'Give him two or three of these if he gets restless. But he's quiet enough now; I don't think he'll make any trouble. Give us a ring through if he does, and one or other of us'll come down.'

She nodded. 'What does he think is going to happen?'

He shrugged his shoulders. 'Says the tail's due to fall off after this number of hours. Says we ought to turn back and land in Ireland. It's all sheer nonsense – something he's made up. It really is a most fantastic place, that Farnborough. There's not a whisper of truth in it.'

'How do you know that?' she asked.

He laughed. 'Do you think the Inspection would have let this aircraft fly if there was any danger of that sort of thing? Be your age.'

She nodded slowly. 'That's right, of course. I suppose he's been overworking or something.'

'Overdrinking. Someone's given him an egg-cup full of ginger cordial.'

She said, 'He's a nice little man.' Above her head the telephone buzzer from the flight deck rang, she lifted her head microphone. 'Yes,' she said, 'he's here. I'll ask him to come up at once.'

She turned to Dobson. 'Captain wants you on the flight deck.'

'Okay. I like your idea of a nice little man. Ruddy little squirt, I call him, coming up with a tale like this and frightening us all into a fit.' He turned away, and moved forward up the aisle in the soft, dimmed lights of the quiet cabin, past the sleeping passengers stretched in their reclining seats. She watched him till he passed through the door at the forward end; then she moved up the aisle herself and stopped by Mr Honey. He was sitting upright in his seat, his hands playing nervously with the fringe of his overcoat upon his lap.

She said, 'Can I get you a hot drink, sir? We've got plenty of milk; would you like a cup of Ovaltine and a few biscuits?'

He said nervously, 'Oh no, thank you. I don't want anything.'

She said gently, 'Would you rather have some soup or a whisky and soda? It's better to have something when you can't sleep.'

He turned to her, roused from his obsession. Airline stewardesses are not chosen for their repellent qualities, and Miss Corder was a very charming girl. 'It's awfully kind of you,' he said. 'I'll be all right. It's – it's just a bit worrying, that's all.'

'Let me make you a hot milk drink,' she said. 'It's very good when you've got something on your mind. We've got Horlicks if you'd rather have that than Ovaltine.'

It was years since any woman had spoken in that way to Mr Honey; he was irresistibly reminded of his dead wife, and the tears welled up behind his eyes. It might have been

Mary speaking to him. 'All right,' he said thickly. 'I'd like Ovaltine.'

She went away to get it, and a minute or two later the door at the forward end opened, and Captain Samuelson came into the cabin. He moved down the aisle, nodding and smiling at Mr Honey as he passed. He went on past the galley, past the toilets, and opened a door in the rear wall and went through the aft luggage bay to the end of the pressurised cabin and the concave dome of the rear wall. There was a perspex window in the dome and a switch that turned on an electric light for the inspection of the tailplane and the elevator mechanism in the space behind. He stood peering through the perspex, looking for trouble.

Mr Honey saw him go through into the luggage bay towards the tail, and smiled, a little bitterly. He got out of his seat and followed him, passing Miss Corder as she tended a saucepan of hot milk over the electric stove. She turned and saw him go through into the luggage bay, following the captain; she said, 'Oh, damn!' and turned off the current of the hot plate, and went after him. It was one of her jobs to keep the passengers from wandering about the aircraft.

In the luggage bay Mr Honey came up behind Samuelson. 'It's no good looking at it,' he said a little bitterly. 'You won't find anything wrong.' Behind him the stewardess came up, but seeing that he was talking to the captain and that Samuelson was attending to what was being said, she did not intervene.

'If what you say is right, there might be some preliminary sign,' Samuelson said. 'But there's nothing to be seen at all. No paint cracking or anything. It's all perfectly all right. Have a look for yourself.'

'I don't need to,' Mr Honey said. 'The spar flanges are perfectly all right now, or we shouldn't be here. In half a minute it may be a very different story. When it happens, it happens as suddenly as that.' Captain Samuelson's brows wrinkled in a frown. 'If you cut a section of the front spar top flanges now and etched it for a microscopical examination, ten to one you'd find the structure of the metal absolutely normal. But all the same, it may be due for failure in ten minutes. There's nothing to be seen in the appearance of it that will tell you anything.'

Samuelson stood in silence for a moment, cursing his own

irresolution. This little insignificant man was getting terribly plausible. He had sent a radio signal to his Flight Control reporting briefly what Honey had said and stating his decision to go on; the signal had been acknowledged but not answered. He could hardly expect such guidance from his Flight Control in view of the difficulty of the technical points that were involved and the fact that it was then the middle of the night when all right-minded technicians would be in bed and sound asleep. The most that he could hope for would be guidance when they got to Gander, by which time it would be nine o'clock in the morning in England.

'I've shut down the inboard engines,' he said at last.

'That should help it,' Mr Honey said. 'But you ought to go back while there's time. Really you should.'

Samuelson smiled brightly and confidently, more for the benefit of the stewardess than for Mr Honey. 'Oh, I don't think so,' he remarked. 'I think we're quite all right.'

He ushered Mr Honey forward out of the luggage bay, and went forward up the aisle himself to the flight deck. Mr Honey stayed at the aft end of the cabin with Miss Corder, scrutinising the structure of the fuselage so far as could be seen by reason of the cabin furnishings; he opened the doors of the toilets and investigated the methods of staying the bulkheads, peering at everything through his thick glasses.

He was behaving very oddly, Miss Corder decided. She came to him, and said, 'I should go back to your seat, sir. I'll bring you the Ovaltine in a few minutes.'

'I'll go in just one moment,' he said meekly. 'Let me have a look at your stove first.' Thinking to humour him she showed him into the galley and began to explain the operation of the various switches and ovens to him, but she found he was not interested in that at all. He examined very carefully the methods of fixing the unit to the floor and the fuselage side; then he was through, and went back to his seat. She brought him a tray with his Ovaltine and biscuits a few minutes later, full of a queer, detached pity for him in his self-induced trouble. He seemed so very helpless.

She said quietly, 'I've brought you your Ovaltine, Mr Honey. Do you like these sweet biscuits? I've got some oatmeal ones if you'd rather have those.'

He said quickly, 'Oh, thank you so much. These will do splendidly.'

70

She smiled down at him. 'Would you like a little drop of rum in the Ovaltine to help you sleep?'

'Oh no, thank you. I never take spirits.'

'All right. Drink it while it's hot. I'll come back presently and take the tray.'

The Reindeer moved on steadily across the starlit sky, alone in space above the overcast seen dimly far below, shrouding the black, empty wastes of sea. In the quiet cabin Mr Honey sat sipping his Ovaltine, gradually relaxing with the warmth and comfort of the drink. His hands ceased to fiddle nervously, the tight, set muscles round about his mouth relaxed, and the feeling of a tight band round his forehead eased a little. He no longer sat tense waiting for the first movement of the aircraft that would herald the steep dive to their destruction; his ears were no longer strained to hear the first crack from the tail that would be the beginning of the sequence.

It now seemed to him that he could take things as they came. There were six hours more at least to go before they came to Gander; it seemed to him most probable that they would all be dead before that time was up. The thought did not now appal him as it had. Death came to everybody in its time; it had come to Mary earlier than they had dreamed it could. If now it came to him, well, that was just one of those things; he had a simple faith that somewhere, somehow after death he would catch up with Mary once again and they would be together.

He was saddened and distressed for Elspeth. But Elspeth was twelve years old; her character was formed for good or ill; it would not alter her so much if now he had to go. Materially he knew that she would be looked after by the Ministry; she would get as good an education as if he had lived. I am almost ashamed to record that for all the little homely pleasures that make the life of a child happy, he put his trust in Shirley and myself. I do not think he quite thought that we should adopt his daughter, but he did think very certainly that we should never let her suffer the lack of a home life; he thought that when he caught up with his Mary he could tell her that their daughter would be happy. I hope we should have lived up to his expectation of us. I don't know.

Miss Corder came to take away his tray. She bent to him,

and asked, 'Would you like another cup? I've got some more hot milk all ready, if you'd like it.'

He said, 'No, I've done excellently, thank you.' He blinked up at her through his thick glasses. 'It's been terribly kind of you to take all this trouble.'

She smiled at him, 'Oh no, sir. I'm so sorry you've got all this worry on your shoulders.'

This dark, kind girl would go too, when it happened. 'Are you married?' he inquired.

She stared at him in wonder; surely he wasn't one of those? She laughed. 'Me married?' she said. 'No.'

'That's a good thing,' he said quietly. 'Nor am I. There won't be a lot of trouble over us.'

The meaning of his words got through to her in a short pause. She hesitated for an instant, not knowing how to take it. She reached for a rug. 'Let me put your chair back for you and put this over you,' she said. 'Then you'll probably get a little sleep.'

She helped him to arrange his chair and tucked the rug around him; then she took the tray and went back to the galley. A quarter of an hour later she said to the other stewardess, 'I'm going up to the flight deck. Keep an eye on No. 11 for me, will you – Mr Honey. I think he's asleep.'

'That's the boffin? Is he liable to cut his throat, or anything?'

Miss Corder said, 'No, he's not. He's just a little, worried man, that's all. I'll be back in a few minutes. I just want to tell Dobson how he's going on.'

Mr Honey lay relaxed in his reclining chair. He did not want to sleep, so little time was left he had no use for that. His mind drifted to the accident as it would happen, objective and dispassionate. He began to calculate in his head, as he had calculated all his working life.

The download on the tail in this condition he knew to be about 6,000 lb. Assuming half of the tail failed only, leaving the rest of the plane intact, that meant a nose-down pitching moment of, say, 300,000 lb.-feet. He did not know the power of the one remaining elevator, but he guessed it might provide one half of that. The balance of the nose-down moment would be satisfied by an increase of speed by diving till the forces came in equilibrium. He figured for a time and came to the conclusion that a diving speed of 420 m.p.h., attainable at perhaps 7° of flight path to the horizontal, would be somewhere near it. With the maximum control that would be left to him, the pilot would not be able to do better for them than to dive at over four hundred miles an hour until he hit the sea.

He wondered what would happen when they hit. At that small angle they might well bounce up again and not plunge straight in, though there seemed to be a likelihood that the wings would be torn off. They might bounce once or twice, reducing speed each time. The impacts and decelerations would be very violent. After that the fuselage might float for a few moments before sinking; if anybody had survived the crash they might be able to get out into the sea, to float about in lifebelts till they died of cold. There was only one chance in a million that there would be a ship in the vicinity that could help, even if anyone got out.

He put all thought of safety from him; when it happened he would die. Now that he had become used to the idea he did not mind about that much; his mind was filled with memories of Mary. His life since Mary died had not been happy; he had no great ambition to hold on to it. Mary had gone before him; somehow, somewhere he would catch up with her again. Again they would go on hiking on long summer days over the Hog's Back, drink beer in little pubs together after the day's march, make love, go Morris dancing together with little bells and ribbons at the knee, buy a new enlarger and play with it together, go to the pictures and see all their favourites, David Niven, Monica Teasdale . . .

Monica Teasdale . . .

He thought ingenuously that it would be something to tell Mary when he met her, that he had seen Monica Teasdale in the flesh! she would be thrilled. His young wife was very real to him still. His mind dwelt on the actress, on her parts that they had seen together in the years gone by, on the pleasure she had given Mary. And suddenly it seemed to him to be important that the actress should be saved in the disaster that was coming to them all. He could not meet his Mary and tell her that he had neglected to do what was possible for Monica Teasdale, whom she had loved so well. All his knowledge must be used to save Miss Teasdale's life, or at any rate to give her a fighting chance of survival. He knew one place within the aircraft where a passenger could survive the impact with the water when it came. If then she drowned, well, that was just too bad, but with his knowledge he could get her through the crash.

He leaned up on one elbow and turned to look across the aisle to where the actress was reclining. She was not asleep, she was lying there awake, smoking a cigarette. There was an empty seat beside her.

He turned back his rug and got up, and moved down the aisle to her, and said, 'Please, Miss Teasdale, may I talk to you for a few moments?'

The shadow of a frown crossed her face; one travelled by air to get away from all that sort of thing. She had been at rest before this uncouth little man with the weak eyes had come to bother her. Then her professional charm took over and she withdrew herself within its mantle, and spoke the phrases she had used so often that they came mechanically. Half of her, at least, could go on resting while she said, 'Why certainly, I'd be pleased.' She spoke with a slight mid-Western accent.

He sat down beside her and plunged straight into his story. 'Miss Teasdale, my name is Honey. I'm a research worker at the RAE – the Royal Aircraft Establishment – that's the British experimental station for aeroplanes at Farnborough, you know. I've been doing some experiments recently on the tailplane of the Reindeer aircraft – that's this aircraft that we're travelling in now. I'm afraid we're all in rather a dangerous position.'

She said impassively, 'Is that so?' She noted his nervous movements, his excited urgency. It was a nuisance that she had attracted an unbalanced fan; in her career she had had that before, several times. She lay listening to him with one part of her mind only, waiting for an opportunity to be delivered from the nuisance of this wretched little man, making a soothing comment now and then.

Miss Corder, coming down into the cabin from the flight deck, was surprised and concerned to see that Mr Honey's seat was empty. She spotted him immediately talking to the actress and her lips tightened; she should have thought of that. Unbalanced people always make for actresses. As she approached them Miss Teasdale raised her eyebrows slightly in appeal; the stewardess stopped by the double seat and to her horror heard the actress say lazily:

'Mr Honey, can't I use the Ladies' Toilet? It seems more kind of suitable.'

He said earnestly, 'You see, the galley stove is up against the bulkhead of the other one, and that makes the bulkhead firm —' It was at that point that Miss Corder touched him on the arm, and said, 'Mr Honey, I'm sure Miss Teasdale wants to get some sleep. Will you come back to your own seat?'

He stared up at her, hurt and affronted. 'I've been trying ...' He glanced at the actress; she lay impassive and uninterested, her face a mask of indifference. 'I'm sorry,' he said with some dignity. 'I was only trying to help.'

'I'm sure you were,' Miss Teasdale said. 'Some other time, perhaps ...'

Without a word Mr Honey got up and went back to his seat, his face crimson. Miss Corder followed him, and tucked the rug around him once again. 'You shouldn't have done that,' she said quietly. 'You mustn't go alarming other passengers, Mr Honey. Will you promise me not to do that again? Promise to stay quiet in this seat?'

He said bitterly, 'If you say so. There's one place in this aircraft where a human body would be safe in the deceleration of a crash. I was trying to tell her what to do if things look bad. But if she doesn't want to know, I can't do more.'

The girl said, 'If I get you a small pill to help you get some sleep, will you take it?'

He said, 'No, I don't want that.'

'Will you promise not to talk to any of the other passengers?'

He knew that she was doing her duty; he knew that she was doing it with kindness and with tact. He warmed towards her in spite of the role of prisoner and warder that they were assuming. 'All right,' he said. 'I won't talk to anyone again.' He glanced up at her thoughtfully. 'What's your name?'

She smiled down at him. 'Corder,' she said. 'Marjorie Corder. What do you want to know that for?' It was her object to make him talk, to get his mind on something different from the accident he thought was going to happen.

He said quietly, 'You've been very nice to me, Miss Corder. I'd like to do something for you. Will you listen if I tell you what I was trying to tell Miss Teasdale?'

She said, 'Of course I will. But after that, will you try and get some sleep?'

He motioned to the empty chair beside him. 'Sit down there for a minute.'

She hesitated, and then sat down on the edge of the seat, turned towards him. 'What is it?' she asked.

He said evenly, 'I think this aircraft's going to crash in the next hour or so. You don't, nor does Captain Samuelson, nor anybody here. But I know more about it than the lot of you, and that is what I think. When that happens, there may be about three minutes from the time when you first know that something has gone wrong until the moment that we hit the sea.'

He paused. 'We shall most of us be killed,' he said quietly. 'We shall die with the deceleration of the crash. There's just one place to go to where a person could avoid that, and get out unhurt into the sea in a lifebelt. That doesn't give much chance for living, even then, but it's a better chance than all the rest of us will have. If I tell you where to go and what to do, will you do it?'

She said, 'Mr Honey, all this isn't going to happen, really it's not. But if it did, I've got my jobs to do.'

He said, 'If I tell you, will you listen?'

She nodded.

He said. 'You must go into the Gentleman's Toilet and sit down on the floor facing to the tail, with your back against the forward bulkhead and your head back in contact with the bulkhead, too. I was trying to tell this to Miss Teasdale, but she wouldn't listen. Get a pad of something – a towel or a blanket, and put it behind your head. The stove behind that bulkhead will hold it firm for the instant of the crash, and your body will be well supported. If you do that, you'll live through the impact. You must have your lifebelt on. When the machine comes to rest before it sinks, pull down the emergency hatch in the toilet roof, and get out at once. Don't stay to try and help the rest of us, or you'll be trapped and drown. Get out immediately the motion stops. There's just a chance you may be picked up when dawn comes.'

She stared at him. 'Is that what you were trying to tell Miss Teasdale?'

'That's right,' he said. 'She doesn't want to know. But will you remember what to do, if what I say is true?'

She said, 'I'll remember, Mr Honey. But I don't say I'll be able to do it.'

'Do your best,' he said quietly. 'If you get through this and we don't, get yourself married and bring up a family. I think you'd be good at that.'

She coloured a little, and laughed. 'Will you go to sleep now, if I leave you?'

'No,' said Mr Honey. 'But I'll lie down, if you say.'

'I do say,' she replied. She arranged the rug around him and saw that he was comfortable; then she turned away behind him down the aisle, her forehead furrowed deep with thought. For a madman, he was damnably convincing.

She stopped by the actress and said quietly, 'I'm so sorry you were troubled in that way, Miss Teasdale. It won't happen again.'

The woman turned her head, and said, 'Don't think of it. Is the little man nuts?'

'I'm afraid so,' said the stewardess. 'He seems to have some rather odd ideas. But he's quite quiet now.'

'I'll say he's got some odd ideas,' the actress said. 'He was trying to make me go into the Men's Room and sit down on the floor. If that's not an odd idea, I'd like to hear one.'

Miss Corder felt she could not leave the matter in that state. 'He's not as mad as all that,' she explained. 'He was trying to tell you what you ought to do if' – she hesitated – 'well, if anything should happen to make you feel that an accident was going to take place. It's probably true enough that in an accident the safest place would be sitting on the floor in there with your back against the bulkhead. He was trying to do his best for you.'

Miss Teasdale was more wide awake now. 'Well, that was nice of him,' she said. 'Who is the little guy anyway – apart from being nuts and apart from being a fan? Do you know anything about him?'

'Oh yes. He's a scientist from the Royal Aircraft Establishment, at Farnborough. He's an expert upon aeroplanes.'

'Well, what do you know? And he thinks that we're going to have a crash?'

Miss Corder said, 'Oh, nothing like that, Miss Teasdale. It's just that he's got into rather a nervous state. You mustn't pay any attention to him. I'm so sorry that he came and troubled you.'

The actress stared at her, and then sat up. 'He's not the only passenger that's in a nervous state right now,' she said.

77

4

MISS CORDER HAD a momentary, sickening feeling that the situation amongst her passengers was getting out of control. She made a valiant effort to restore it. 'There's no need to think of it again, Miss Teasdale,' she said brightly. 'Captain Samuelson himself has had a long talk with this passenger, and I'm afraid there is no doubt that he's a little bit unbalanced. It's probably the altitude or something. But he's quite quiet now.'

'More than I am,' said the actress. She was sitting up and smoothing out her clothes. 'If I'm going to meet my Maker, I won't go with my nylons down round my ankles. Say, where in heck did my shoes get to? Oh, thanks a lot.' She studied her face in the mirror of her powder compact. 'I was a darned fool not to travel in a US airplane,' she observed. 'But you haven't had so many accidents lately, and I thought I'd be safer. That's how one gets caught.'

Marjorie Corder said, 'I asure you, Miss Teasdale, there's nothing in what Mr Honey says. There's no chance of any accident. Can I get you a cup of coffee?'

The actress said a little sharply, 'Look, this scientist from Farnborough thinks this airplane's going to crack up pretty soon, and Captain Samuelson, he thinks it isn't going to crack up. And now you come along to give the casting vote, and put it with the captain's. Well, just you run along and get that cup of coffee, and bring it to me over there. You say his name is Honey? It would be. I'm going visiting with Mr Honey; bring my coffee there.'

The stewardess said anxiously, 'I wouldn't go and talk to him, Miss Teasdale – really. It'll only excite him again.'

'I can handle that, my girl,' the actress said. 'Just you go right down and get that coffee.'

Miss Corder hesitated, but there was nothing she could do against this strong-willed woman, twenty years older than herself. She went to get the coffee.

Miss Teasdale finished her appearance to her satisfaction and got up, and moved up the quiet aisle of the saloon to Mr Honey's seat. He was lying wide awake, in rather bitter reflection. He stirred as she approached, and looked up in surprise. It was about half-past three in the morning. The Reindeer was still flying steadily and quietly on course, above the overcast seen faintly down beneath them in the starlight.

Miss Teasdale said, 'Mr Honey, do you mind if I sit down here for a while?' He sat up, blinking at her through his glasses. 'I was half asleep when you were talking just now, and maybe I was just a little bit rude. I didn't mean to be, but you know how it is.'

He said, 'Oh, please – don't think of it. Do sit down.' He was a little flustered and confused. He had seen Monica Teasdale so often in the past upon the screen, had been stirred to deep emotion by her parts so many times, that he had difficulty now in knowing what to say to her in the flesh. When he had crossed the aisle to speak to her he had been carried away by the impulse to do something for the safety of this woman; he had something definite to tell her. Now he was flustered and nonplussed.

She said, 'That's real nice of you.' She sat down and turned to him. 'Say, when you started talking about going into the Men's Room, Mr Honey, I thought you were plain nuts. But then that stewardess came along and told me one or two things, and then it seemed to me that maybe I was nuts myself for having brushed you off. Would you mind starting off and say your piece again?'

He blinked at her through the thick glasses. This was not the ethereal girl that he had known upon the screen, the Madonna-like heroine of *Temptation*. This was someone very different, but someone who was out to make amends for a discourtesy, someone who was trying to be pleasant.

He said, 'I'm sorry – I'm afraid I ought not to have alarmed you, Miss Teasdale. I was just trying to help.'

She nodded slightly. She had had this so often, but more with adolescents than with grown-up men. Fans went to every kind of trouble to speak to her, but when she stopped and met them half-way they could only stammer platitudes, with nothing to say, so that she had to help them out of their embarrassment. She set herself to help out Mr Honey, and she said,

'The stewardess, she told me that you work at airplane research, Mr Honey? Is that the sort of work they do at Langley Field?'

79

He turned to her, pleased and surprised. 'Not quite,' he said. 'My work is on structures, more like what they do at Wright Field. We've got the whole of that work concentrated with the flying experimental side, at Farnborough. That's about forty miles south-west of London.'

She said, 'That must be interesting kind of work.' It was a part of her technique, this art of making men talk about themselves.

He said, 'Well, yes, it is. It's rather lengthy sometimes – you go on for a long time at a thing without seeing any results.' He smiled at her, that shy, revealing smile that he pulled out so unexpectedly from time to time.

'You must feel that it's something well worth doing, though,' she said.

'Well, yes – it is. There was the wing flutter on the Monsoon in the war.' He started in to tell her all about the research he had carried out into the wing flutter, and the effect of moving the mass of the guns and ammunition boxes six inches farther back upon the chord of the wing. From that she had little difficulty in steering him on to the Reindeer tail.

When Miss Corder came back with the coffee she found them deep in conversation, with Mr Honey talking freely to the actress. She was divided in her feelings over this; it was her duty to prevent the spread of alarm from one nervous passenger amongst the rest, but at the same time she had been troubled over Mr Honey. It was pleasant to see him animated and cheerful. She was grateful to the actress that she had done that for him. She went to get another cup of coffee for the little man.

Within a quarter of an hour Miss Teasdale knew a good deal more about the Reindeer tail than Captain Samuelson. She knew more of the background of the story; she knew something about Elspeth, and a little about Shirley, and a good deal about me, as Mr Honey's boss. She knew the way the matter had arisen, the urgency with which I regarded it, the sacrifice that Honey had made in leaving his small daughter to the uncertain mercies of a charwoman. Captain Samuelson knew the bald facts of the matter; he knew nothing of the background of those facts.

Miss Teasdale said, 'That's very, very interesting, Mr Honey. Tell me, have I got this right? You reckon that the stabiliser of this airplane that we're sitting in is kind of dying of old age?'

He blinked at her. 'Well, yes. Yes. I think that's a very good way to put it. It's not very old, as structures go, but – yes, it's dying of old age. In fact, it must be just about dead by now.'

'And when it dies it breaks? What happens – does it come right off the fuselage, so that we'd have no tail at all?'

'I think half would fail first. One side – yes, I think it would come off. I think it did in the first one, the one that fell in Labrador.'

She stared down the quiet aisle of the cabin. 'You never think, somehow, this sort of thing can ever happen to you,' she said.

'It may not happen,' Mr Honey said. 'I wasn't able to convince the captain or to make him land in Ireland. But he did agree to stop the inboard engines. That helps up, certainly.'

She thought for a minute. 'How much flying time did you say the one that fell in Labrador had done?'

'1,393 hours.'

'And this plane we're riding in – how long has that done up till now?'

'About 1,426 hours. I calculated that the tail would fail about 1,440, but it's not very easy to forecast as accurately as all that. The first one went at 1,393 hours; I'm afraid the only thing that one can say is that this one might go at any time. Dr Scott intended that no Reindeer should fly over 700 hours until this thing had been thrashed out. But this one's slipped through, somehow.'

She said, 'You told the captain all this, did you?'

He nodded. 'There's no real evidence yet that the captain could act on, I suppose. We don't *know* yet that the one in Labrador did crash for that reason. That's what I'm going out to Ottawa for now. But it looks as if I may not get to Ottawa. They may have to send out someone else.'

She said, 'Looks like Mossy Bauer'll have to look around for a new star for the new picture, too.'

He turned to her. 'You mustn't think of this as certain,' he said. 'We may quite well get safely to Gander. I – I just don't know. I only know that this machine is liable to accident at any moment now. But it might go on like this for another hundred hours, or even longer.'

She nodded. 'Say, would it help any if I were to have a talk with Captain Samuelson? I mean, there's all these other people to consider.' She indicated the sleeping passengers in the other seats.'

'I don't think it would do any good at all,' Mr Honey said. 'He thinks I'm just unduly nervous, and, really, there *is* no proper evidence at all yet that the tail is liable to failure. That's what I'm going to Ottawa to find out.' He outlined to her in detail what Samuelson had done. 'I really don't think it would be much good for you to talk to him. He's the captain and he's made his decision.' He hesitated. 'And anyway, we must be very near the point of no return by now.'

She said sharply, 'The point of no return?'

'That's the point when it is shorter to go on than to go back,' Mr Honey explained. 'Sort of half-way.'

She breathed. 'I thought you meant something different. So you think there's nothing we can do but sit here with our fingers crossed?'

'I don't see what else we can do,' he said. 'If we were going to turn back we should have done it long ago.'

His coffee came, brought on a small tray by the stewardess, who put it down upon his knees and left them. Mr Honey sipped it gratefully. If death was near at hand, there were worse ways to meet it than by sitting in the utmost comfort in a warm, delicately furnished cabin, sipping a cup of very good coffee, and talking to a very beautiful woman.

'Say,' she said, 'just to pass the time, then, you can tell me what you meant about the Men's Toilet.'

He coloured and said nervously, 'I wasn't trying to be rude. It's just that the safest place in the whole aircraft in a crash is sitting on the floor in there. And at the altitude we're flying, there'd be plenty of time for you to get back there and sit down.'

She stared at him. 'Say, why would that be any safer than staying right here where we are – with the safety belts on, of course?'

'Your body gets thrown forward, very violently. If the belt holds you, it could injure you so badly that you'd die in any case. But if you're facing backwards with your spine and your head pressed up against a firm support, you can stand a far greater deceleration without injury.' He went on to tell her all the details of what she ought to do, as he had told

Miss Corder.

She listened to him with attention. 'That's something to know about,' she said at last. 'Will I meet you in there when the time comes?'

He hesitated. 'I don't think so. I shall try and get to the flight cabin up forward when – when things start to happen. It's just possible that I could help the captain in some way.' He hesitated. 'I've been a long time in aircraft research,' he said. 'Something might happen after the tail fails that we could take advantage of, and that the captain might not recognise in time.'

She nodded without speaking. She had been travelling by air for twenty years and she knew a little about accidents. She knew that when a high-speed aircraft crashed those in the flight cabin were almost always killed, whereas those in the tail of the aircraft frequently escaped. She recognised that no one knew that better than Mr Honey who had sought out the safest place in the Reindeer and told her about it. She realised that this shabby, weak-eyed, insignificant little man who had been discredited by the crew was proposing to put aside the chance of safety and go to the point of maximum danger when the crisis came, following his calling to the end.

'Does anybody else know about this place in the Men's Room?' she asked. 'I mean, is there going to be a run on it? Because I'm kind of allergic to a crowd.'

He hesitated. 'I told the stewardess, Miss Corder,' he said. 'When – when I thought perhaps you didn't want to hear about it. But it's all right – the stove is quite wide enough. There'll be room for two if you crush up close together.'

The actress said, 'That's the girl who waited on us with the coffee?'

He nodded. 'She was so – so kind.'

There was a silence. Miss Teasdale sat staring up the cabin in front of her, thoughtful and silent. What she had heard bore the stamp of truth to her; in the quiet comfort of this aeroplane she realised that death might be very near. She could take that philosophically, so long as it was quick; with the Atlantic down beneath them it would be so. She would have liked to live, but she had no dependants; and as she sat there she knew that she had had the best of life. She had been born of middle-class parents in Terre Haute, Indiana; when she left school she had gone to work in an insurance office as a stenographer. Then, at the age of nineteen, she had won a beauty competition, becoming Miss Terre Haute; she had gained a screen test and her first job in Hollywood. She had been three times married, but never with success; twice she had created the divorce. The last time she had married Andy Summers, the band leader, and had divorced him after eighteen months; since then she had lived alone. She had never had a child. Twice she had visited her own state in glorious pageantry to start the Indianapolis Motor Race; these visits were to her the climax of a long career. She treasured the memory of them more dearly than her Oscars. She had a brother who ran a flourishing automobile agency in Louisville and a sister who had married an attorney and lived in Norfolk, Va.; she had not seen either of them for many years. When her star waned she planned to rent an apartment in Indianapolis, in her own state where people were proud of her, but she would spend her winters in Miami. There were indications at the box office that that time was not very far off now.

So, if it had to end, she would be missing little but old age and she could do without that, anyway.

Presently, she turned to Mr Honey. 'Why did you pick on me to give me the best seat in the house for this show?'

He said awkwardly, 'Well, you're a very well-known person, Miss Teasdale. You've given so much pleasure to so many people.'

All her life she had received compliments; they had become commonplace to her, just things that people said. With death very near, this one struck rather a new note and arrested her attention with its sincerity. She said quietly, 'You thought so much about my pictures? Do you go to the movies a great deal?' She had not taken him for an escapist.

He hesitated. 'Well – not now,' he said. 'I used to go a great deal when my wife was alive. But I've gone very little in the last five years. I'm afraid I haven't seen any of your recent films.'

'You haven't missed a lot,' she said. 'There was more adventure in the picture business in the 'thirties. Every picture that I made had something new about it then. Now – well, I don't know. Directors seem to have got cautious.'

'That's what we always said,' said Mr Honey eagerly. 'There was always something new about your pictures. I think we saw everything that you were in from the first day we got engaged right up to the end.'

She asked, 'When did your wife die, Mr Honey? Was it in the war?'

He nodded. 'It was at the time of the V.2s – the rockets, you remember. We had a flat in Surbiton.' He stared up the aisle. 'It was rather a long way from the factory, but there's a very good train service to Ash Vale. And there was always something going on in Surbiton: there was the Country Dancing Club and the Art Club and the Camera Club. We *did* have such fun . . .' He was silent for a minute, and then he said, 'I'd have been at home when it happened, only I was doing my turn firewatching at the factory. I didn't even hear about it till the morning. Elspeth was quite all right when they got her out – just a bit shocked, you know. But Mary – well, she died . . .'

She said impulsively, 'Oh, I'm sorry.' And then, to keep him talking and to ease the difficulty, she said, 'What did you do, Mr Honey? About Elspeth, I mean?'

'It was a terrible job,' he said simply. 'You see, all our furniture was gone, everything we had. We'd only just got the clothes that we were in – Elspeth was in her pyjamas. Of course, everyone was frightfully kind and we got fitted out all right, and lots of people offered to give Elspeth a home in the country right away from the bombing – places in Wales and Cornwall – all that sort of thing. But – well, there were only the two of us, and I thought that sending her away to be with strangers would do more harm than good.' The actress nodded thoughtfully. 'So I kept her with me and we managed to get digs in Farnham to start with; there wasn't much bombing there. And then we got a house, and bit by bit we got some furniture together. I think it was the best thing to do.'

'Who lives with you to keep house?' she asked.

'Nobody,' he said. 'We get along all right, Elspeth and I. Of course, now that she's growing up and can do things for herself it's getting a great deal easier.'

'How old was she when that happened?' Miss Teasdale asked.

'Eight,' he replied. 'It's bad luck to have a thing like that happen when you're only eight.'

She breathed, 'I'll say it is.'

They sat in thoughtful silence for a time. At last the actress asked, 'Was your wife a great movie fan, Mr Honey?'

He said, 'We both were, for good pictures like yours. We used to pick and choose. But Mary was terribly fond of your films.' He turned to her. 'That's really why I want you to do what I say and go and sit down in the Men's Toilet if anything happens. You will, won't you?'

There was a sudden watering behind her eyes. He certainly was the oddest little man. 'Surely,' she said gently. 'Of course I'll go.'

He stared past her through his thick glasses. 'I don't know if there's any truth in what they say in church about meeting people again,' he said. 'When the end of the world comes or when you die. Or if it all just finishes. It's an idea that kind of – helps, to think you'll meet people again. If it's true, I wouldn't want to go to Mary and tell her I hadn't done everything that could be done to help you. You see, you gave her so much pleasure.'

'I'll do just what you say,' the actress said humbly.

They sat in silence while the Reindeer moved across the night sky above the overcast, beneath the stars, in steady, effortless flight. From time to time this thing had happened to her before, that she had suddenly been brought face to face with the incredible power of the honky-tonk, of the synthetic, phoney film business. Story-teller, script writer, producer, director, cameraman, musician, cutter, actors and actresses, all came together for the purely commercial business of creating something that would sell; if they succeeded they created something that would sway the lives of men and women by the million, in all the countries of the world. That happened on the side. It was purely accidental to the business what they came together for, which was to make money.

She had few illusions about her profession; few film actresses have. In the endless, monotonous sequence of takes and retakes on the sets she had a faculty for carrying through the emotion of a scene from one shot to another taken ten days later, so that given the proper opportunities by her director she could turn quite an ordinary script into a masterpiece. That, with her beauty, had made star material of her, fit for publicity. She had few other talents; but for that knack she might still have been Miss Myra Tuppen, stenographer in the Century Insurance Office in Terre Haute. At first she had attributed her screen success to her young beauty, but soon she had discovered that in Hollywood beauties were two a penny, and it was years before she got an inkling what it was that differentiated her from all the stand-ins and the walkers-on. When she discovered what it was, that she had a knack that other women had not, a tenuous knack not clearly understood even by herself, she had been terrified for years that she would lose it. That fear had left her now; she had put away a fortune in safe stocks and real estate, and now she did not greatly care if she stayed on in the commercialised entertainment business that had been her life, or not. Sometimes she felt that her life might even have been more fun if she had remained Miss Tuppen of Terre Haute instead of becoming Miss Teasdale of Beverly Hills.

When such thoughts came to her she put them away; they were the discontents of middle age, and she must not be middle-aged while she remained in business. They were nonsense anyway; life had given her everything, everything but children. That was one thing that she had had to miss; her income had been much associated with her beauty, so that she could not afford to run risks with her figure. But treasonable thoughts returned from time to time, and recently she had wondered now and then what would have happened to her if she had not gone into the movies, if she had stayed on in the office. She would have married and settled down and raised a family, no doubt. Whom would she have married? One of her brother's friends in the automobile business? She hardly thought so. One of the boys she had met in High School – Dwight Henderson? Dwight had been a nice boy; she had heard of him during the war. He was Vice-President of a corporation that made women's shoes, in New York City. Her mind turned to the Century Insurance Office, well remembered after all these years, all these experiences. It would have been funny if she had married little Eddie Stillson the lame ledger clerk. . . .

Of all the people in the office, she remembered Eddie Stillson best. His desk was next to hers; because he was a low-grade clerk the noise of her machine was supposed not to disturb his work. She had been seventeen when she went to the Century office from her school of commercial typing; she supposed now that Eddie must have been twenty-one or twenty-two, but at that time she had thought him older. He had a pasty face and he wore steel-rimmed spectacles; one leg was shorter than the other, so that he could not take much exercise, or dance. He wore a sort of iron extension fitted to his right boot. Thinking back now more than thirty years in time, she remembered Eddie Stillson as one of the kindest men that she had ever known.

It had begun on the first morning, her first morning in her first job. At the school the machines had all been modern Remingtons. In the office she had been given a worn-out Underwood. It was just different enough to spoil her work; each time she forgot and worked up speed her flying fingers would depress two keys together or print $\frac{1}{2}$ instead of a stop, so that each letter that she typed was spoiled and messy with erasions. By the middle of the morning she was near to tears of apprehension and frustration, when the office boy put down upon the table by her side a glass of milk and a stick of chocolate.

'I always stop 'n take a lil' drink of something, middle of the morning,' Eddie had said, drinking his milk. 'I see they've given you the lousiest old machine in the office. Nobody else wouldn't have it.' After that, things had gone better.

She had worked in that office for two and a half years. Her evenings gradually became a whirl of dances, movies, and walks with various young men, though she found it better to cut out the walks as time went on. In all that time she never went out with Eddie Stillson. He never asked her to the movies; if he had done so she would have regarded it as a disaster, and would have told her friends about it, laughing. All she ever talked to him about was carbon papers, and the weather, and how many bits they owed the office boy for milk. Yet when opportunity came to her with a minor contract in Hollywood and she went round the office saying goodbye in a whirl of excitement and congratulations, the only leave-taking that left the smallest pang was that with Eddie Stillson, though it only took two minutes. In later years she knew he would have married her if she had so much as lifted her finger. She had sometimes thought that she would have had a very happy life if she had.

This man Honey was just such another one as Eddie Stillson, shy, insignificant, brave, and kind. With her experience of married life behind her, she now knew that such men made good husbands, though girls seldom realised it. There was security in them. She wondered what kind of girl his wife had been.

In the rear of the cabin Marjorie Corder sat with the other stewardess, Miss Peggy Ryan, by the galley. She had told Peggy all about Mr Honey's apprehensions, and they had agreed facilely that they were bunk. Now she sat silent, recalling her crash drill. Although in conversation she was prepared to write off Mr Honey as a nervous crank, she was not in the least prepared to do so deep in her own mind. If things started to go wrong with the aircraft she had certain duties to perform; she sat quietly, conning her drill over. Safety belts had to be fastened; she must go up and down her end of the cabin, not hurrying, smiling reassuringly, but seeing that the passengers did fasten them, helping those who were agitated. The upholstery rip cords must be pulled, disclosing the escape hatches, but on no account must the hatches be opened till the differential pressure indicator showed zero. She must be ready to jettison the cabin doors by pulling the hinge-pins. She must be ready with her first-aid box. She must be ready at the telephone to the flight deck for taking any orders that might come by it, and all the time she must be cheerful and composed and charming. Only by the sheerest chance would she be free to fling herself down on the deck in the Men's Toilet when the crash was imminent; in any case it would be wrong for her, the stewardess, to take the only place of safety in the aircraft. She could hardly do that.

Her home was in Ealing, a suburb to the west of London; her father was a vegetable merchant in Covent Garden. She had gone to the London Hospital as a probationer early in the war, and then she had exchanged into the RAF Nursing Service; she had given up nursing eighteen months before for the more varied life of an airline stewardess. She had been engaged during the war to an Ealing boy who had died in a Lancaster over Dortmund a month before her marriage; that had happened five years before, but she had not ventured into love again. She was rather older than the general run of stewardesses and had already exceeded the average length of service.

She sat quiet, thinking of the threat of death held by the Reindeer tail. It would be queer if it happened to her as it had to Donald, though his tail had been removed from the machine by AA fire. She still had his photograph upon the mantelpiece of her bedroom; she still heard from his mother at Christmas and on her birthday. If it had to happen to her now, it was a pity; she would go without the experience of marriage, motherhood, and children; she would go incomplete. She thought of Mr Honey and the queer thing he had said an hour or so ago – 'If you get through this and we don't, get yourself married and bring up a family. I think you'd be good at that.' Funny.

Mr Honey, she thought, was a very clever little man. He could see farther through a brick wall than most; he had penetrated her secret. She would be good at that, she knew. She knew that she would be able to be patient with a crying baby, loving with a fractious child. She knew that, but that Mr Honey should have known it too was a very queer thing. Of course, he must be terribly clever to be a research scientist at a place like Farnborough, and with that there came to her the certainty that he was right about the Reindeer tail. A man who had the perspicacity to be right in one thing was very likely to be right in another, and he had been very right about her.

Captain Samuelson sat in the first pilot's seat staring at the instruments in front of him, at the silvery cloud floor ahead and below them, at the bright stars above. It was very quiet and peaceful on a fine night at that altitude; he had time for thought. Although he flew continually from continent to continent he was a very ordinary man; his interests were essentially suburban. Nothing that he had ever seen in all his travels pleased him so much as his small home in Wimbledon, chosen for its proximity to the bowls club, of which he was vice-captain. He had three children, a son of nineteen in the RAF and a boy and a girl who were still at school. He did not believe that anything was going to happen to the Reindeer tail before they got to Gander; he thought that Mr Honey was a nervous crank, exaggerating the importance of his own work. At the same time, Bill Ward stood in the background of his mind. Something had killed Bill Ward, and it was not coming down through cloud to check up his position and so flying into the hill.

Samuelson was an experienced and a competent man. He had put the matter to his Flying Control in a radio signal and he had received no answer; the responsibility for the decision was left to him. He had decided to go on to Gander, anyway.

When they got to Gander he would have to make another decision, whether to continue the flight normally to Dorval, the airport of Montreal, or whether to ground the aircraft and stay at Gander till he did receive instructions. The latter would be quite a serious step to take upon his own responsibility; it meant stranding passengers at Gander and delaying the mail. He could hardly stop at Gander without evidence that something really was the matter with the aircraft. Like every pilot in the world, he veered instinctively away from a policy of playing safe. If he grounded the machine at Gander and it turned out to be quite all right, people would say that he was windy, that he was getting old. . . .

Another point bulked largely in his mind. There were no facilities at Gander for a major modification to the Reindeer, but there were all the facilities required at Dorval. Unless the aircraft proved to be completely unsafe, it would have to be flown from Gander to Dorval, or else back across the Atlantic to England, before any work could be done on it; if then it had to fly from Gander he might just as well continue on his scheduled flight without delay. He thought that he would turn all his engineers on to make a thorough check of the tailplane while the aircraft was refuelled at Gander; if that was satisfactory, he would go on. He had no great confidence that instructions from his Flying Control would have reached him by the time he was ready to leave Gander. Work would only just be starting in England at that time in the morning, and to ground an aircraft on a technical suspicion such as this would need a good deal of conferring between the various technicians who were involved.

The shadow of Bill Ward stayed by his side, perturbing him. This man Honey had at any rate provided a lucid and a feasible explanation of what could have killed Bill Ward, of what could kill them all that very night, perhaps. He sighed a little, in perplexity. If only this man wasn't such an obvious nervous crank. . . .

They passed the point of no return, and as a routine matter the navigator reported to him. He nodded, and handed over the control to Dobson, and got out of his seat, and went down into the saloon, and walked the length of it into the luggage bay to have another look at the tailplane structure through the little perspex window. He stood gloomily scrutinising the structure in the light of the rear fuselage lamp, flashing the beam of his powerful torch upon each point in turn. It all seemed perfectly all right, but that infernal little man had said it would, right up to the moment when it broke. He wondered if he ought to station one of the crew to stand by that perspex window looking through it all the time, a permanent watch. But what good would that do, anyway, if Mr Honey should in fact be right? They would know at the controls as soon as something happened.

Presently he turned and went back into the main saloon. As he passed the toilets he raised his eyebrows; was everybody crackers in this ship? The film actress, Miss Monica Teasdale, was standing at the door of the Men's Toilet, holding the door open, looking in.

He smiled brightly and said, 'I'm afraid you've got that wrong, Miss Teasdale. The Ladies' is on this side.'

She said, with cool irony, 'Say, what do you know?' And then she said, 'I was just kind of looking where I'd got to go in case we had an accident, Captain.'

It was true; everybody *was* crackers in this ship, or was it he himself? 'There's not the slightest prospect of an accident, Miss Teasdale,' he said, laughing brightly. 'If ever there was anything of the sort, the stewardess would come and help you fasten your safety belt. That's what the seats and belts are designed for, to hold you safely and to prevent injury in bumpy weather, or anything like that.'

She said, 'You don't say!'

He flushed a little, irritated. 'I should go back to your seat,' he said. 'There's nothing to see in there.'

She laughed, and she was very beautiful in her laughter, so that he was mollified. 'I believe you think that I've been playing "Peeping Tom".'

In all his years of experience as an airline captain he had never had this one before. 'Of course not,' he said weakly.

'Be your age,' the actress said. 'Mr Honey told me that was the place to go to in an accident, down on the floor and facing back, with your spine pressed flat against the partition. I've been taking a look around.'

He stared at her. 'Honey said that? But why?' He opened the door and stood inside, looking at the partition.

'Something to do with the kitchen stove,' he said.

'The stove? Oh, I see what he means.' He hesitated; there was no denying that it was a very safe place, very safe indeed against deceleration. He came out into the passage, closing the door behind him. 'I'm sorry Mr Honey has been bothering you, Miss Teasdale,' he said. 'I think he must have been overworking at Farnborough, and perhaps our altitude affects him too, if he's not used to flying. There's not the slightest foundation for thinking that there's anything the matter with this aircraft, I can assure you. I'm very sorry that he's troubled you with his ideas. I suppose he must have seen your pictures at some time.'

'You don't believe in his ideas?' the actress asked.

The pilot laughed. 'Of course not, Miss Teasdale. There's not the slightest evidence that there's anything the matter.'

Her eyes dropped to the torch he carried in his hand. 'That's why you've been taking a darned good look at our stabiliser, then.'

He smiled. 'I should go back to your seat and try to get some sleep.'

'Are we going to be on time at Gander, Captain?'

'No,' he said. 'We shall be about an hour and forty minutes late.'

'Is that because you've shut down on the inboard engines?'

He cursed Mr Honey in his mind for a talkative busybody. 'Partly,' he said. 'I think Mr Honey is a little bit unbalanced, between you and me. But I have given that much weight to his ideas, because he really does come from Farnborough; I've shut down the inboard engines at his request, although it's going to make us very late.'

She nodded. 'I don't think he's unbalanced,' she said. 'I think he's as sane as you or I. I've met a few unbalanced people in my time – fans, you know – and believe me, they don't talk that way. If I were you, Captain, I'd put a good amount of weight on what he says.'

They stood for a moment, thoughtful. 'I've not neglected it,' he said at last. 'I've done everything that he suggested, except turning back to land in Ireland. In any case, now, it's shorter to go on than to go back.'

'Okay, then,' said the actress. 'I'll just keep my fingers crossed.'

'Miss Teasdale, has Mr Honey been talking to any of the other passengers?'

She shook her head. 'He came across and spilled it all to me, but then the stewardess got after him for spreading

93

alarm; she did everything but take him across her knee and spank him, so he won't do that again. I don't think anybody else knows a thing about all this.'

He nodded. 'I'd just as soon it didn't go any further. There's absolutely nothing in it.'

'Says you,' she said rudely. 'Still, I don't see that it's going to help any to get the other passengers worked up. You needn't worry. I'll stay with him till we land at Gander, so that he won't talk to anyone.'

'That's really very good of you, Miss Teasdale. It's very helpful.'

'Don't thank me. I guess I kind of like the little man, and I'd not sleep now, anyway.' She turned to him. 'If I do that for you, Captain, will you do something for me?'

He said, 'If it's anything that I can do. What do you want?'

'If our stabiliser starts flying on its own,' she said, 'and things start going wrong, Mr Honey says he's going up to the flight deck. He's been a long time in airplane research, and maybe he could help you. If he comes up, will you listen to him and not shout him down?'

He knew that if that happened he would have little time and little inclination to listen to anybody about anything, but he said, 'Of course I will, Miss Teasdale.'

She said, 'I'll feel easier in my mind that way.'

They moved forward up the aisle past the galley. He said, 'Will you have a cup of coffee, or anything?'

She shook her head. 'Guess I'll go back and sit with Mr Honey. This is the darnedest flying trip I ever made.' She left him and moved quietly up the aisle in the dim light.

She sat down beside Mr Honey and began talking to him about other matters than the imminence of their disaster. They had said all that was to be said about that; now it remained only to wait and see if it happened. She asked him how it had happened that the aircraft had escaped our vigilance at Farnborough and in the Ministry – how it had managed to accumulate so many hours of flying unknown to any of us.

He told her what he had heard on the flight deck, about its loan to Anglo-Brazil Air Services for a trial. 'It slipped past everyone by sheer stupidity,' he said quietly. 'The Power of Evil in the world. It'll be different in fifty years from now.'

94

She asked, 'What'll be different?'

'Evil,' he said. 'This sort of thing won't happen after 1994. I shan't live to see that time, and you won't, even if we get through tonight. But my daughter will, when she is an old lady.'

She asked, 'What's going to happen in 1994?'

'Adam and Eve were expelled from the Garden of Eden in the year 4007 BC,' he said. 'Sin, foolishness, and evil came into the world then and are to last six thousand years. That finishes in the year AD 1994 at the autumn equinox on the twenty-first of September. After that we get another chance again, I think.'

She stared at him. 'Where did you get all that from?'

'You can work it all out from the prophetic calculations in the Talmud,' he said. 'It's confirmed by the measurements to the base of the Dead End passage in the Pyramid. That's a totally difference source, of course. There's no doubt at all that something absolutely cataclysmic is going to happen in the autumn of 1994. It's probably the end of this world, as we know it. The Talmud rather indicates that the millennium starts then, but that's a bit vague.'

She was startled. 'Say,' she said, 'do you believe all this?'

He said, 'Believe – that's not a scientific way to look at it. You don't believe in an hypothesis until it's proved to be true, and then it's a known fact, and doesn't have to be believed in. You don't believe in this seat you're sitting in, because it's *there*; you don't have to show your trust in it. I don't believe the end of the world is coming to us in 1994. But it's a theory that has been put forward by a number of very competent investigators, and the only theory that I know which forecasts what is going to happen to us in the future. Until a better theory turns up, one has to base one's life on that, because it's the only one.'

She stared at him. 'That kind of makes sense, when you look at it that way,' she said. 'You say the world is coming to an end in 1994? It doesn't mean a lot to you and me.'

'No,' he said. 'We shall probably just miss it. It's bad luck, after six thousand years, to miss it by ten years or so. But we prepare the people who will see it, and that's something. That's why we've got to work so hard and well, we people in the world today. We lay foundation stones.'

She thought of her work, of the endless, mean, commercial

haggling on story points, of jealousies and irritations on the set, of the endless manoeuvrings for star parts. 'I guess I don't lay many foundation stones,' she said bitterly.

He turned to her astonished. 'The whole world looks to you,' he said. 'People are finer and better for seeing one of your films; you give them an example. Do you really think you don't do any good? You can't think that!'

The power of the honky-tonk! She could not explain to him; if he believed that her films were conceived with a high motive, let him go on in that faith. She said quietly, 'I guess there's different ways of looking at these things. You kind of see the smutty side of any job you're working at, and maybe you forget about the rest.'

'I know. You've got to get away from a job and stand back, sometimes, and see what you've been doing in perspective.'

She turned to him. 'This daughter of yours, Mr Honey. Your little girl, Elspeth, what do you think that she's going to see in September 1994? What's going to happen then?'

It was quiet in the long saloon; the aircraft moved on steadily beneath the stars. The lights were dimmed for sleeping; it was a quiet place, a place fit for meditation before the end. 'I don't know what's going to happen,' he said quietly. 'Nobody knows. You and I will live our lives out without knowing; we may know in half an hour. But I have thought about it! I have read about it; I have worked on it – a lot. If you like, I'll tell you what I think may happen in September 1994.'

'Tell me,' she said.

He was silent for a moment. 'I think the Principle of Goodness will appear and take away all sin and evil from the world,' he said. 'I don't know how it will come about, but I think this, that to everybody in the world, Buddhist or Mohammedan, Christian or Jew, there will come a revelation of the truth, at the same time. Every religion in the world is due for a clean-up; I think they'll get it then. And when that is done, the Truth will be seen to be universal, and we shall all believe in the same things.'

She nodded slowly. 'That could be.'

'I think the revelation will be graded to our understanding,' he said. 'I think it will occur in terms that we can recognise. I shan't see it, but I think my little girl, Elspeth, will see it in the form that Our Lord will come to Glastonbury, to the place of meditation that He lived in as a boy. I think that's what the indicator sockets in the ascending passage of the Pyramid show, if you make allowance for the subsidence of the structure, as you must. I've done a great deal of work on this. I think something terrific is going to happen at Glastonbury, then.'

She stared at him; could he be nuts after all? 'Say,' she said, 'where is this place Glastonbury?'

'It's a little town in Somerset,' he said. 'The legend is that Jesus Christ came there to live in meditation as a young man, before His Ministry. His great-uncle, Joseph of Arimathea, brought Him there; he used to trade in the tin business between Palestine and Cornwall. He brought Jesus there, because Glastonbury was the religious centre of the Druids, who practised the original pure form of the Hebrew religion. Jesus is supposed to have lived in Glastonbury in meditation for a long time as a young man. That's the story, and there's a good deal to support it. You can believe it or not, as you like. I think I do.'

She said in wonder, 'I never heard that one.'

He went on to tell her all about it, talking with the quiet enthusiasm of a man with a hobby that he has worked at for years. She sat listening to him, her mind in the past. Eddie Stillson had been just such another one, but his hobby was monkeys. He had read a lot about the Origin of Man and he used to talk about the Missing Link, and one day he had produced from beneath his ledgers a book that had a lot of photographs of people's skulls, thousands and thousands of years old, dug up all over the world. It had photographs of human skulls in it and monkeys' skulls too, and she had listened with a sort of horrified fascination while he expounded to her all the differences and similarities. Looking back over all those years, she felt that he had meant it as a compliment to her, that he had revealed his secret interests in that way. After three marriages and thirty years of adult life, she now felt that you never really knew a man until you knew his secret interests. Mr Honey was extraordinarily like Eddie Stillson, the same insignificant appearance, the same warm, indefinable charm. It had taken her much of her life to realise it, but she had made a terrible mistake in losing touch with Eddie. When you were young and the world lay before you, you did that sort of thing. You met a man that you could really get to care about, and you thought there would be plenty of other ones, in Hollywood or wherever life took you to. It was only when you began to grow old that you realised they weren't as plentiful as all that, that you would have done better to stick to Eddie Stillson.

In the flight deck Dobson, the first officer, took a star sight with his bubble sextant through the astrodome; the navigator took another one to check it, and they plotted the position lines upon the chart. They had about two and a half hours flight to go before landing at Gander. Their hands were dirty and soiled the chart as they drew in the position line, for they had had some trouble in the flight deck. One of the electrical circuits of the undercarriage-operating mechanism had become defective and was blowing fuses with monotonous regularity; they had worked for two hours with the engineers in an attempt to rectify the fault, only to discover that it lay in the safety circuit of the retracting undercarriage mechanism and could be reached only from the ground; it was not important, so they had isolated that circuit and put it out of action. Then navigational necessities had intervened before they could wash, and they had taken their star sights with dirty hands.

Dobson walked down the saloon to the toilets; he noted with surprise that Mr Honey had got off with the actress; she was sitting by him, smiling at him, listening to what he said. He washed his hands and came out, and went into the galley, and said to Miss Corder, 'I see the boffin's got off.'

She put her head out and looked up the aisle. 'She's been sitting and talking with him for some time. How far off are we?'

'About two and a half hours. Had any more trouble with him?'

She shook her head. 'Have you had any trouble with the tail?'

He laughed. 'It's still there, so far as I know. Be still there in ten years' time, if you ask me.'

'It's funny,' she said thoughtfully. 'He was so positive that we were going to have an accident. But nothing's happened yet.'

He grinned. 'Nothing's going to happen either,' he said. 'He's got a bee in his bonnet – all those Farnborough types are the same. They just don't know what it's all about. It really is the most fantastic place. We might get some decent aircraft if it wasn't for them.'

He moved off up the aisle towards the flight deck.

The Reindeer flew on towards the last of the night, in rising moonlight. An hour later the navigator crossed to Samuelson sitting in the captain's seat and spoke a word to him. The captain spoke to Cousins, the engineer, and knocked out the automatic pilot; the engineer drew back the throttle levers a little, watching the boost gauges. The note of the engines dropped, the nose tilted down a fraction, and the Reindeer started on a slow descent, losing height at about two hundred feet a minute. Gander lay ahead

At ten thousand feet they started up the inboard engines at reduced power and went into the cloud layer. A quarter of an hour later they were below it in diffused moonlight. They made their landfall at a rocky, barren point of land that lay between two islands, seen dimly beneath them in the hazy, silvery light. At three thousand feet they flew for a quarter of an hour above fiords and inlets of the rocky coast, all full of ice. Then straight ahead of them appeared the twinkling runway lights and the cluster of lights round the airport buildings of Gander.

In the saloon the stewardesses were busy waking the passengers who were still asleep and making them do up their safety belts for the landing. Miss Corder, bending over Mr Honey, said, 'Well, we've got here all right.'

'I know,' he said. 'We're very lucky.'

Miss Teasdale had gone back to her own place. Mr Honey sat looking out of his window as they circled the airport and went off over the spruce woods and the river to turn into the runway. They turned in to land and the note of the engines died; the nose dropped a little, and he saw the flaps come down. The ground came closer and closer till the tops of the fir trees were near to the machine. Then there was the surface of the runway close beneath them, they sped over it, and suddenly a rumble and a forward tilt of the fuselage told him they were down.

Samuelson slowed the machine to a walking pace, and turned the Reindeer on to the taxiing track, towards the hangars and the airport buildings. He yawned. Cousins, the engineer, came forward to his elbow and said, 'Watch the undercart switch, sir. The safety locks are out.' He nodded.

Dobson leaned across to him, grinning, and said, 'Well,

we've still got our tail.'

Samuelson nodded; he had not yet reached the point when he could joke about it. He still had to decide whether to go on normally to Montreal or to ground his aircraft at Gander, one of the most bleak and desolate airports in the world at which to strand a load of passengers, and one where there were few facilities for any serious repair. He sat gloomily considering this as they rolled up to the tarmac. He had heard nothing from his Flying Control in reply to his signal stating Mr Honey's bleat. Perhaps a signal would be waiting for him here to give him guidance and to take the onus of deciding what to do from him.

It was then shortly before dawn, about nine o'clock in the morning by British time. The stewardesses disembarked the passengers and took them to the restaurant for breakfast; the refuelling tank trucks drew up to the Reindeer and began pumping in their load. Captain Samuelson went to the Control and asked if there was any signal waiting for him; there was nothing. He tightened his lips; the responsibility for the decision lay on him.

He sent Dobson to find the local Air Registration Board Inspector. Very naturally, Mr Symes was in bed, and he was not too pleased at being woken up at that hour in the morning to make a difficult decision. He was a man of fifty-seven and Gander was his last appointment before retirement. He had never risen very high in his profession because he had never shown initiative; in his view an inspector should stick closely to the rules as they were framed for him. That quality made him valuable enough at a place like Gander, where he was far from the control of his head office; his superiors could rest content that Mr Symes would never put a foot wrong or deviate one hair's breadth from the typescripts sent to him from time to time.

Dobson stayed with him while he pulled on his trousers, putting him *au fait* with the position. 'This little squirt from Farnborough, he's clean off his rocker, I believe. I don't know what you'll make of him, but that's what we all think. Of course, if there *is* anything the matter with the tail, we'll have to stop here, but Cousins hasn't heard a thing about it, nor have any of us. Captain Samuelson wanted you to have a good look at the structure with us, and see if it's all right.'

Mr Symes grunted. 'You get some funny sort of people

coming from those places,' he said. 'You remember Skues in the Airworthiness at Farnborough, back in 1928 or so? No – before your time. He always used to take his Siamese cat with him, in the offices, or into conferences – everywhere he went he took this blessed cat. . . .'

They walked together from the dormitory block where Mr Symes stayed back to the Reindeer on the tarmac. Dawn was just showing in the darkness as a grey line to the east; there was a bitterly cold north-east wind and Mr Symes had had no breakfast. Samuelson met them on the tarmac with Cousins, the engineer. A tall, wheeled gantry gave them access to the tailplane twenty feet above the ground; they commenced a meticulous examination of everything externally visible, moving the gantry from time to time. The bitter wind whipped round them mercilessly; very soon they were so cold that even holding torches became difficult.

They could find nothing wrong at all externally. They came down and went into the rear fuselage, behind the pressure cabin; clambering about in there they could see the structure of the tailplane spars where they passed through the fuselage and intersected with the fin girders. They twisted their bodies in amongst this structure, flashing their electric torches upon channels, webs, and ribs, laying the straight edges of steel rules along duralumin angles to check for any distortion, peering carefully at scratches on the paint and anodising. At the end of an hour of the most thorough examination they had finished; they had found nothing whatsoever wrong with the machine.

It was too cold to hold a conference outside or in the hangar. They went up into the heated flight deck of the Reindeer, and sent for Mr Honey from the restaurant. While they were waiting for him, Dobson and Cousins made an examination of the defective safety circuit of the undercarriage-retracting mechanism, climbing up the undercarriage legs from the ground into the engine nacelles. Mr Honey, hurrying across the tarmac to the Reindeer, saw them go back into the fuselage ahead of him; when he reached the flight deck the engineer was making his report to Samuelson.

'Port switch is burnt out, sir,' he said. 'We haven't got a spare. I've got both circuits isolated now. If Mr Symes agrees' – he indicated the inspector – 'I'd suggest we go on like we are to Dorval. They've got spare switches in the stores at Dorval.'

The inspector said, 'That means no safety locks are operating on the undercarriage.'

'That's right,' the engineer replied. 'It just means being careful not to trip the operating lever while you're getting in or out of the seat. That's while she's on the ground, of course; it wouldn't matter in the air.' Mr Honey waited his turn patiently in the background, till they were ready to attend to him. The inspector and the engineer and Samuelson moved over to the control pedestal between the pilots' seats. 'This one,' the engineer said, fingering the undercarriage lever. 'It's just a matter of being careful not to put this up while the auxiliary engine's running, like it is now.' It was running to provide the heat to keep the aircraft warm. 'When the auxiliary's stopped, of course, nothing could happen if you put this up, because there wouldn't be any current.'

They talked it over for a minute or two. 'All right,' the inspector said at last to Samuelson. 'You can go on like that. But have somebody standing by it all the time you're taxiing, just to watch that nobody's coat catches in it or anything.'

Samuelson nodded. 'I'll see to that.' He turned to Mr Honey and introduced him to the inspector. 'Look, Mr Honey — we've made a very careful inspection of the tailplane, and there's nothing wrong with it at all. I don't know if you'd care to tell Mr Symes here what you told us on the way across?'

Mr Honey started wearily to tell his tale again. He had had no sleep and he was overtired, blinking more even than usual. He had not shaved and he had not been able to eat his breakfast, spoiled as it had been by his anxieties; he was feeling rather sick. He told his story badly, defeated before he started by the atmosphere of utter disbelief he sensed around him.

Mr Symes gave him some little attention because he came from Farnborough, but his mind was already made up. He was a man who had never taken any action except on physical facts; it was not his business to assess the eccentric theories of wandering scientists and take a chance on them. There were no written instructions in his files that he should take any special precautions in regard to the Reindeer tail. On the suggestion that there was something wrong with it, he had made a thorough inspection and had found everything correct. That put him in the clear, and he had no intention of imperilling his pension by a rash display of individuality at that stage of his career.

They talked for a quarter of an hour. At last Samuelson said, 'Well, if Mr Symes agrees, I think the best thing we can do now is to go on to Dorval. I'm prepared to shut down the inboard engines after climbing up to operating height, as I did coming over, if you think that will ease things, Mr Honey. At Dorval we can assess the matter properly.'

Mr Honey, nearly in tears of weariness and frustration, said, 'I assure you ... I assure you that's the wrong thing to do. It's absolutely—' his voice cracked, and went up into a little nervous squeak – 'it's absolutely courting disaster to go on. You *must* ground this aircraft. Really you must.'

Samuelson glanced at Symes, and their eyes met in common agreement; this was not a normal, reasonable man. This was an eccentric plugging away at a fixed idea, a man whose mental balance was abnormal. 'If you would rather stay here, Mr Honey,' the captain said, 'I can make arrangements for you to finish the journey in another aircraft, probably to-morrow. But I'm afraid I can't listen to any more of this.'

The inspector nodded in agreement. This Reindeer would be off before long, and he could get back to bed and have a couple of hours more before breakfast. Then, in the course of the morning, he would write out a report upon the incident and send it in to his headquarters. Two copies would be sufficient, and one for his own file.

Honey said desperately, 'Is that your final decision? You're really going on?'

Samuelson turned aft, partly to hide a final irresolution. 'That's right,' he said. 'We're going on.'

'I assure you ...' Mr Honey's voice died in despair; it was useless to go on trying to convince these men. He turned forward to the pilots' seats. And then, quite nonchalantly, he put his hand upon the undercarriage lever and pulled it to UP.

He did it so quietly that it did not register with anybody for an instant; Symes was the only man who actually saw him do it, and it took a second or two for the inspector to appreciate what was happening. Then he cried, 'Here – stop that!'

The note of the auxiliary motor changed as the load came

on the dynamo. Samuelson turned, saw what Honey was doing, said, 'For Christ's sake!' and made a dive for the lever.

Mr Honey flung his body up against the pedestal, covering the controls. He said, half weeping, 'If you won't ground this aircraft, I will.'

The motors of the retracting mechanism groaned, the solid floor beneath their feet sagged ominously. Cousins, with quick wit, leaped for the electrical control panel and threw out the main switch to cut the current from all circuits. He was a fraction of a second too late. The undercarriage of the Reindeer was just over the dead centre. She paused for a moment; for an instant Samuelson thought that Cousins had saved her, as he struggled to pull Honey from the pedestal. Then she sagged forward, and the undercarriage folded up with a sharp whistling noise from the hydraulics. A pipe burst and fluid sprayed the ground beneath her, and she sank down on her belly on the concrete apron, all the seventy-two tons of her. By the mercy of Providence nobody was standing underneath her at the time.

The noise of the crumpling panels and propellers, a tinny, metallic, crunching noise, brought the mechanics running to the wide doors of the hangars. Marjorie Corder, going from the Reindeer to the reception and booking hall, turned at the mouth of the passage and stared aghast to see her Reindeer lying wrecked upon the tarmac. Instinctively she began to run back towards it, horrified; she met Dobson running from the machine to the Control.

She cried, 'What happened?'

He paused for an instant. 'The boffin did it,' he said furiously. 'I told you that he'd put the kiss of death on it. Well, now he has!'

5

THAT MONDAY was a bad day.

It began normally enough. I went to the office as usual. When I had left on Saturday the arrangements had been all set up that Mr Honey was to leave for Ottawa on Sunday night by CATO, I had seen nothing of him over the week-end, and I had not expected to. I went down to the old balloon shed at about ten o'clock as soon as I had cleared my desk, however, to see that he had really got away and to see that young Simmons was getting on all right with the responsibilities of the trial on the Reindeer tail.

The trial was running; I had heard it above the noise of my car when I was driving into the factory; it filled the whole district with its booming roar. In the old balloon shed it was deafening as usual; Simmons was up upon the gantry taking readings of the strain gauges; he saw me and came down, and came up to me smiling, and proffered his foolscap pad showing the rough daily graph of the deflections. We could not talk in the noise; I ran my eye over the results, and they were absolutely normal. The trial was going smoothly.

I led him into the office and shut the door; in there we could talk. 'Everything all right?' I asked. 'Did Mr Honey get away all right?'

'Oh yes, I think so, sir. He was in most of Sunday; I was here with him. He left at about four o'clock to go home and have a meal and pick up his luggage. He was catching the eight-forty up to London from Ash Vale.'

'That's fine.' I stayed with him for ten minutes going through the work; he was a clever, competent young man who only needed guidance now and then. I soon found that I had nothing to worry about. When I couldn't think of anything more to ask him, I looked around the littered little office before leaving; there was a neat pile of stamped and addressed letters on his desk, ready for the post. I glanced idly at them. The top one was addressed to Miss Elspeth Honey, No. 4, Copse Road, Farnham. I lifted it, and the second bore the same address, and the third, and all of them.

Simmons said, 'Don't get them out of order, sir. I've got to post one each day, and they're all dated.'

'Dated?'

'The letters inside are dated with consecutive days, as if he was writing to her every day. I've got to post one each day.'

I stared at them in wonder. 'How many are there?'

'Twenty-one, sir. He said that he was reckoning to be away three weeks.'

'Are all the letters different?'

'I don't know – I think they must be.' He picked up one of them and fingered it. 'From the feel, they've each got two sheets of paper, too.'

I was staggered by the magnitude of the work, because Honey had only had about three days' notice of his journey, and these three days had been very busy ones for him. I said, 'Well, I'm damned!'

Simmons smiled and said, 'He must be a very devoted father.'

The telephone bell rang then. It was the exchange trying to locate me; Ferguson had been on the line from the Ministry, but while looking for me they had lost the connection. I said I would go back and take it from my office.

I got through to Ferguson ten minutes later. He said, 'Scott, rather an awkward thing has just come up. CATO have had a radio signal from the Reindeer that left last night for Gander, the one with Honey on board. It seems that that machine has done over fourteen hundred hours, and Honey has been making a good deal of trouble during the flight. The pilot asks what action he should take.'

I had an awful feeling of apprehension in my stomach, suddenly. I said, 'That's terrible. The aircraft must be grounded at once. How on earth did it get through? I thought you told me none of them had done more than three or four hundred hours.'

He said anxiously, 'I know, old man – I did tell you that. I got that from CATO. The trouble is, this aircraft wasn't operating with them at that time.' He went on to tell me about its loan for trial operations with ABAS.

I bit my lip. It was the position that I had been anxious to avoid at any cost. 'Has it landed yet at Gander?' I asked.

'I haven't heard that it has,' he said. 'I should think it must have, by this time. Wait a minute – no – oh hell, their time's all different of course. I don't know exactly when it took off.'

'Look, Ferguson,' I said. 'It's got to be stopped at Gander. It mustn't fly one minute longer. Can you get through now to CATO and ground it, ground it positively and for good at Gander?'

He hesitated. 'I'd have to see the Director for that.'

I said, 'I'll have to see my own Director. But we've got to jump at this decision now, just you and me. We can clue up

106

the official side later. Will you get through to CATO and tell them that?'

'It's a bit awkward,' he said slowly. 'I don't know that we're justified in taking a snap decision, quite ... I mean, it might be very awkward if it turned out later there was nothing wrong with it. I think it should go through the proper channels.'

I said bitterly, 'We won't look quite so good at the court of inquiry if that tail fails in the air while you and I are looking for our senior officers. If you won't ring up CATO, I will.'

He said doubtfully, ' I could get through to them and say that's what you recommend, explaining that it's not official yet.'

'Will you tell them that I insist on grounding that machine?' I said. 'That's what I'm telling you. And that's what I should tell a court of inquiry.'

'You're taking a great deal of responsibility upon yourself,' he said resentfully.

'I am.'

'Have you got any evidence at all upon this tailplane yet?'

'Nothing,' I said. 'Nothing to call evidence.'

'But you insist that I ring up CATO and have that aircraft grounded here and now, before consulting anyone?'

'I do.'

'All right,' he said. 'I'll get through to them now.'

I put down the telephone, sick and angry at the position that we had been forced into. I picked it up again and asked for the Director's office. The operator said, 'I've got an outside call for you, Dr Scott.'

'Hold it,' I said. 'Put me through to the Director's office now. I'll take that outside call immediately I've finished.'

The Director's girl told me he was up in London for a meeting of the Aeronautical Research Committee. I swore; I should have thought of that. I could not now shelve my responsibility. I asked for the waiting call, thinking it was CATO, but it was Shirley.

She said urgently, 'Dennis, please, can you come and help me? I'm speaking from the call-box at the end of Copse Road. It's Elspeth Honey. I found her lying in a heap at the foot of the stairs in their house; she's quite unconscious and she's awfully cold. Please, do come at once.'

I hesitated. I could not take in properly the substance of

what she was saying; my mind was full of the blazing row that I had landed myself in by grounding a CATO aircraft at a place like Gander, without any previous notice and without any real evidence that there was anything the matter with it at all. I knew that it was only a question of minutes now before the storm burst; Ferguson must be already speaking to Carnegie, the Technical Superintendent. I forced my mind back to what Shirley was saying. 'Is she ill?' I asked foolishly. 'Couldn't you ring up the doctor – Dr Martin? His number's in the book.'

She said desperately, 'I've rung up Dr Martin – he's out on his rounds – I can't get hold of him till lunch time. I can't remember the name of anyone else. I've got her lying down and covered up with rugs – she's on the floor. There's nowhere else to put her downstairs – there's no couch or anything. I couldn't carry her up those stairs by myself. The old woman next door is boiling kettles up for hot-water bottles, but Dennis – she's looking awful – she's so blue. I'm frightened that she might be going to pass out. Do please come, Dennis.'

I could not leave her in the lurch; moreover, this was Honey's daughter. If the child Elspeth was really dangerously ill it would react straight back upon the grounding of the Reindeer. I should have to send Honey a cable, and he would obviously want to come home on the first available plane. If he did that, it would mean that the first Reindeer crash in Labrador would remain an enigma; we should not secure the evidence that we required to justify grounding the one at Gander. All this was running through my mind while I was listening to Shirley, and coupled with it was the thought that I had counted on two quiet days for finally rehearsing the paper that I was to read before the Royal Aeronautical Society on Thursday night upon the 'Performance Analysis of Aircraft Flying at High Mach Numbers'.

It was a blazing mess – just one thing after another. I said, 'All right, darling, I'll be with you in ten minutes. Keep her warm. I'll come right away, in the car.'

I put down the receiver and rang the bell for Miss Learoyd. But before she came, the telephone bell rang again, and it was Carnegie.

He said, 'Is that Dr Scott? Look, Dr Scott, I've had the most extraordinary request from Ferguson. He says you want to ground one of our Reindeers and ground it at Gander. Is that right?'

I said, 'That's right. We're getting rather concerned about the possibility of fatigue trouble in the tailplane. We've got people working on it on the highest priority now, and we've sent a member of the staff to Canada to have another look at the prototype Reindeer structure that crashed in Labrador. We've come to the conclusion that until this matter is cleared up no Reindeer ought to fly more than 700 hours. It was rather a shock when I heard this morning that one of your machines had done 1,400.'

'Well, it's very disconcerting having this sprung upon us at a moment's notice,' he said. 'I can't think what the Ministry are up to. They haven't said a word to us about it and the ARB don't know a thing about it, either.'

'It's not the Ministry,' I said. 'It hasn't got as far as them yet, on an official level, that is to say. Ferguson knows all about it, of course. It's all come up very recently, very recently indeed.'

He asked, 'The firm – Rutlands – do they know anything about it?'

I said, 'Not yet.'

'The only people who know anything about it, then, are your department down at Farnborough?' He was becoming hostile.

'That's right,' I said. 'Everything starts down here. As a matter of fact, we thought we had plenty of time to get the whole thing sorted out before any question of grounding your existing machines arose. We were told that none of your Reindeers had done more than 400 hours. Then we sent one of our staff across last night by CATO, and he seems to have discovered in the air that the machine that he was flying in had done over 1,400, which just about coincides with our theoretical estimate of the time to failure of the tailplane in fatigue.'

He broke in, 'Who told you that? Who told you that none of our machines had done more than 400 hours?'

I hesitated. 'Ferguson,' I said at last. Obviously everything was going to come out now. 'We put the inquiry through him.'

'It didn't come to me,' he retorted. 'I must say I would rather like to know why that was. Who did Ferguson get his information from – the office boy? If you people would only have the courtesy to come to the right person when you want to know anything, you might get the right answer.'

It would not do to tell him at this stage that I had asked Ferguson to get the information without calling too much attention to the inquiry. I said, 'Look, Mr Carnegie, let's settle on the action now and we can have the inquest and the slanging match later. I understand the Reindeer that our Mr Honey is travelling in is at or near Gander at this moment. We say it must be grounded right away, wherever it is. You must take my word for it that the machine is in a dangerous condition.'

There was a long silence. I said at last, 'Are you there, Carnegie?'

'I was just thinking,' he replied. 'I know nothing whatever about this, because you haven't thought fit to take me into your confidence. But at the same time I am responsible for the technical state of the aircraft of this organisation. What you suggest that I should do is to tell the Traffic side that this Reindeer is no longer airworthy, when I myself know of no technical reason why it shouldn't go on flying. Is that what you want?'

Put in that way it sounded very awkward. 'Yes I suppose so,' I said. 'I'm sorry to put you in that position, but we're all in a difficulty together over this.'

He said evenly, 'I'm sorry, too. And what's more, I won't do it. If you want that aircraft grounded without giving us more technical reasons than we have had up to date, you'll have to do it on a higher level.'

'Look, Mr Carnegie,' I said. 'I'll give you all the technical reasons that you want as soon as we can get together, but we can't do that over the phone. I'll come to you, or you come to me, and we'll have a session on it, this evening, if you like. But we've got to stop that Reindeer flying now, this minute.'

He said, 'All right. Get your Director to ring up my Chairman – Sir David's in his office. If you're making it a question of confidence because of the time element, then that's the way to do it.'

I bit my lip. 'I can't do that,' I said. 'The Director's in London, at a meeting of the Aeronautical Research Committee.'

He was on that one like a knife. 'Does he know anything about this?'

'He knows of our suspicions about fatigue trouble,' I said. 'He doesn't know that one of the machines has done 1,400 hours.'

'Well, don't you think you'd better take him into your confidence first of all, even if you don't take us?'

I became angry. 'Look, Mr Carnegie,' I said. 'All that can be settled later. I'm telling you now that in the view of this Establishment that Reindeer is in a grossly unsafe condition and should not fly one moment longer. The time is now eleven-fifteen, when I have told you that. If there's an accident, that will be my evidence at the court of inquiry. Whether you ground it now is entirely up to you, but you'll get a letter grounding it in the post tomorrow. That's all I've got to say to you.'

He said evenly, 'Well, Dr Scott, I hear what you say. And I will think it over and discuss it with my Chairman. The only thing I have to say now is that it's most difficult for us to do our job and keep the airline running if you people are allowed to carry on like this.'

I put down the receiver, breathing rather quickly, and glanced at my watch. We had been talking for ten minutes, and I had told Shirley that I would be with her by that time. I rang for Miss Learoyd again, and when she came I was at the door with my hat on. 'Miss Learoyd,' I said, 'I've got to go out for an hour, but I'm expecting several rather urgent calls. Will you sit in here and take them, and tell everyone that I'll ring them – oh, say at two o'clock.' I left her, and hurried away down to my car.

I stepped on it on my way to Farnham, because I was anxious to get Shirley settled up and get back to my office and my row. I could not imagine what had happened to Elspeth Honey, and I had an unpleasant feeling that whatever had happened to her was partly my fault, for having sent her father off to the other side of the world at such short notice that he hadn't had time to make proper arrangements for her.

The door of the house was ajar; I parked the car and went in. I heard Shirley's voice upstairs, and went up. Elspeth was lying in her bed, which was tumbled and slept in; she was an unpleasant greyish colour with a huge bruise on her forehead close up to the hair; she seemed to be unconscious. Shirley was there with an elderly woman, Mrs Stevens from next door.

Shirley and I withdrew on to the landing. 'What happened?' I asked.

She said, 'I really don't know, but I think she must have fallen downstairs some time in the night. I was just a bit worried, Dennis, because she didn't turn up at school this morning, and you know I never thought much of this charwoman arrangement. So I came round here at break, but the front door was locked, of course, and I couldn't get in. Well then I looked through the window in the door, and, darling – there she was, lying in a heap at the foot of the stairs, in her pyjamas. I couldn't make her hear, or anything, so I went round to the back and broke the kitchen window and got in, and there she was.'

I said, 'I'm frightfully sorry. But wasn't the charwoman here last night?'

'I don't think she can have been. But I don't know. I don't even know who she is.'

'How is she now?'

She shrugged her shoulders. 'Very much the same. I think she's warmer than she was – she was terribly cold. Mrs Stevens helped me to carry her upstairs to bed, and we've got three hot-water bottles in bed with her. I do wish the doctor would come.'

I stood by the door looking in. The little dark-haired girl lay in bed with eyes half open but immobile, like a dead rabbit; she looked very like her father. My wife said softly, 'Poor little brat. It *is* a shame.'

There was nothing more that we could do, for the moment, till Dr Martin turned up. I stood there with them in silence. Back in my office the telephone, I knew, would be ringing almost continuously as various infuriated people tried to find me; the storm would be mounting as frustrations multiplied because I was not at the office. Too bad; they would have to multiply. I had to tackle each of my responsibilities in turn; one thing at a time.

The doctor came at last; I knew him slightly. We told him all we knew; then he went in to her with Shirley. He came out after ten minutes, and we went down to the sitting-room, so called, that was Honey's drawing office.

'Well,' he said, 'she's got concussion, of course. I can't find any fracture. You think she fell downstairs; the bruising supports that. She was alone in the house ... I think that's very wrong, if I may say so.' He stared at us severely. 'A child of that age is much too young to be left alone at night.'

'I quite agree with you,' I said. 'Unfortunately, her father is abroad and the arrangements that he made for her seem to have broken down.'

He nodded. 'Well, she needs care now. She'll probably wake up before long, and when she does there may be a good deal of vomiting. She must stay in bed for at least a week. I'll look in again this afternoon. Who is in charge of her?'

There was an awkward pause. 'I don't think anybody is,' said Shirley. 'There's only us.'

I explained. 'I'm the head of his department at the RAE.'

'Well, who is going to look after her?'

I said doubtfully, 'Couldn't she go into a hospital?'

'Not here,' the doctor said. 'I haven't got a bed. We might be able to get her into Guildford or Woking.'

Shirley said, 'Dennis, we can take her. I mean, we *are* mixed up in it, in a sort of way. And if it's only being sick and that sort of thing – well, I can cope with that. I think we ought to take her. I'd hate to think of her waking up in hospital amongst strangers.'

I said, 'Yes, old thing – but where? You couldn't keep her here?'

She turned to the doctor. 'Could we take her to our flat? Can she be moved?'

In the end we telephoned for the ambulance and put her on the stretcher unconscious as she was, and took her to the flat and put her in bed. We both skated over the implications of that, because Shirley and I only had one bed between us and we put Elspeth in that one, and there was no other bed in the flat. We shelved the problem of where we were going to sleep ourselves till bedtime got a little nearer, and that was the quiet evening on which I had planned to sit down and run over my lecture on the 'Performance Analysis of Aircraft Flying at High Mach Numbers'.

By the time all that was done and sorted out it was ten minutes past two; I had had no lunch and had to get into my car and dash back to the office to catch up with my blazing row.

Miss Learoyd had a whole list of people who had left their numbers asking or demanding that I should ring them. There were Ferguson and Seabright in the Ministry, and Carter in the Ministry of Civil Aviation, and Sir David Moon of CATO, and Drinkwater in the Air Registration Board and – my heart sank – Mr Prendergast of the Rutland Aircraft Company, the designer of the Reindeer.

I asked Miss Learoyd to see if she could locate the Director. She asked his secretary, who told her that after his committee meeting he had intended to come back by Kew Gardens, to look at the flowers.

I sighed, and put in a call first of all to Ferguson. But before it came through, the exchange asked me if I would take an incoming call. It was from Sir David Moon, the Chairman of CATO.

He said, 'Is that Dr Scott?'

'This is Scott speaking,' I replied.

'Is a Mr Honey a member of your department, Dr Scott?'

'Yes,' I said. 'He's not here at the moment. He's in Canada.'

'I am very well aware of that,' he said. 'I have been trying to make contact with your Director, but he seems to be away. Are you aware of what your Mr Honey has been doing, Dr Scott?'

'No – I haven't heard from him yet. There's hardly been time.' I wondered what on earth the trouble was.

'Then you don't know that he has been responsible for destroying one of our aircraft?'

I had a sudden sickening feeling in my stomach. 'Destroying one of your aircraft? Whatever do you mean, sir?'

'I understand that he deliberately raised the undercarriage while the machine was standing on the ground at Gander. I need hardly say that the damage is very extensive indeed.'

I was staggered. 'But – but how could he have done that? There must be some mistake, sir. Our people don't make errors of that sort.'

'I tell you, this wasn't an error,' he said forcibly. 'It was done deliberately and maliciously, according to the report we have received.'

'I'm afraid I just can't believe that,' I said. 'I know Mr Honey very well. He's not a fool. You say this happened at Gander?' I was beginning to recover from the shock and think.

'That is correct.'

'What sort of aircraft was it?' I inquired.

'A Reindeer.'

'The Reindeer that he had flown over in last night? The one that was on loan to ABAS and had flown 1,400 hours?'

'I don't know how many hours it had flown. Thanks to the antics of your officer, it will be a long time before it flies again.'

I said, 'If that's the machine, Sir David, this may possibly be true. Have you seen Mr Carnegie since I spoke to him this morning, insisting that that aircraft should be grounded?'

He said, 'Yes, I have. And I may tell you here and now, Dr Scott, that this organisation will not tolerate technical secrecy where our aircraft are concerned. If you suspect at any time that there are latent defects in the aircraft that we operate, it is your duty to come forward and tell us immediately. I understand from Mr Carnegie that you have been considering a defect in the tailplane of the Reindeer for some weeks behind closed doors, till suddenly you came forward this morning and demanded that a certain aircraft should be grounded and put out of service at ten minutes' notice, without disclosing any technical reason for your action. Now, is that correct or not?'

'Broadly speaking,' I said slowly, 'that is quite correct. It came as a complete surprise to us this morning to learn that a Reindeer had done 1,400 hours. When we got that news quick action became necessary, and we decided that it must be grounded right away. Tell me, this machine that had the undercarriage accident at Gander – was that the same machine?'

'It was the machine that flew across last night,' he said. 'The one that had your representative on board.'

'Then it *was* the same machine,' I replied. 'You say that Mr Honey was responsible for retracting the undercarriage while the aircraft was standing on the ground?'

'That is so. The signal that we have received states that in the most explicit terms.'

'I can only say I'm very sorry this has happened,' I said. 'Where is Mr Honey now?'

'I presume that he's at Gander.'

I thought quickly. This new row over the smashed Reindeer was likely to overshadow the one about grounding the Reindeer; there would be a thumping repair bill to be paid by somebody. If it was true that Honey, a Government servant, had pulled up the undercarriage deliberately, inevitably the Treasury would come in at some stage or another; there was no knowing where the thing would end. Honey would have to come back to this country to tell us his end of it and the investigation of the crash in Labrador would have to wait for a few days. There was probably no urgency about that now, in any case.

'I think we ought to get Mr Honey back at once and hear his account,' I said.

He snorted. 'By all means, Dr Scott, so long as you don't ask for a passage for him in one of our aircraft. Get him back by all means.'

Gander is a day's journey in the train from St John's and the train goes twice a week; a steamer leaves St John's for Liverpool about once a month and takes a week or so to make the crossing.

I said, 'I think we ought to get him back without any delay.'

'Dr Scott,' he said, 'I have to make myself very clear. The signal that we have received suggests that Mr Honey is mentally unbalanced. He has already gravely damaged one of our aircraft. We do not consider him a fit person to travel by air, and I very much doubt if any other line will take him in the face of our refusal. If you consider that he should be brought back to this country by air, then your proper course is to send an aircraft of RAF Transport Command for him. And I should recommend you to send suitable medical attendants with it, to look after him upon the journey.'

This was simply terrible. I said, 'I can't believe that it is quite so bad as that, Sir David.'

He replied, 'I think I should like to speak to your Director, Dr Scott. Would you kindly put me through?'

'I'm afraid he isn't in,' I said. I could not say that he had snatched an afternoon to go and see the flowers in Kew Gardens. 'He's been up in London at a meeting of the Aeronautical Research Committee. I'm expecting him in later this afternoon.'

'Oh. Can I reach him on the telephone?'

'I don't think you can. He's probably on his way back here now.'

'Very well. Would you kindly ask him to telephone me immediately he arrives. I shall wait for his call in this office until six o'clock.'

'I'll tell him that, Sir David,' I said. 'I'll get him to call you up immediately he comes in.'

I put down the receiver in a cold sweat, but within half a minute the bell was ringing again, and it was Ferguson to tell me that Honey had ruined a Reindeer at Gander by pulling up its undercart. I said, 'I know. I've just had Sir David Moon upon the telephone.'

He said, 'Whatever can he have been thinking of? Do you think he's mad?'

'I don't know if he's mad or not,' I said angrily. 'I know that Reindeer had done 1,400 hours and that I asked you this morning to have it grounded. Well, now we hear that Honey's grounded it, so his action seems to be exactly in accordance with my own.'

'I don't think this is a time for flippancy, old man,' he said. 'The consequences of this thing are going to be very serious indeed.'

'I quite agree with you,' I said forcibly. 'The implications here are very serious indeed. We are the research establishment concerned, and we have asked that a certain aircraft should be grounded, because we think it dangerous to fly. There's been some hours of argument, and now we hear that our representative who is with the aircraft has taken energetic action to prevent that aircraft flying any farther. If it turns out that Honey did that as the only way to stop that Reindeer taking off from Gander, I shall support him. The lives of people are at stake in this affair, a fact that you chaps up in London tend to forget sometimes.'

'There's no need to talk like that,' he replied. 'We're just as much concerned to keep the airlines safe as you are. What worries us is that up to the present you don't seem to have any real technical justification for the action that you are taking.'

'That depends on what you regard as technical justification,' I replied. 'We suspect that trouble may occur at about 1,400 hours, and to some extent the first Reindeer accident confirms that. Till the matter is cleared up, no Reindeer is to fly more than 700 hours. Now, that's my attitude and I'm sticking to it. My staff work under me, and that's their attitude.'

'Is the Director back yet?' he inquired.

'No,' I said. 'I think he's looking at the flowers in Kew Gardens, if you really want to know where he is. And if you want the full story, Elspeth Honey, Honey's twelve-year-old daughter, fell downstairs last night, and she's unconscious with concussion and shock in my bed, and God knows where I'm going to sleep tonight.'

'I say, old man, I'm sorry about that. Can I do anything to help?'

'Yes, you can,' I said. 'You can keep these ruddy blood-hounds off my track and give me time to get things sorted out. We'll have to have a meeting of some sort tomorrow, I suppose, but I would like to get Honey back in time for it and hear what really happened at Gander. That bloody old fool Moon has just told me that he won't bring Honey back by air in case he wrecks another aeroplane. Will you see if you can get that one sorted out, and get Honey back here pronto?'

He said doubtfully. 'I'll do what I can. But I'm afraid they're taking rather a firm line.'

He rang off, and then Carter in the Ministry of Civil Aviation rang through to tell me that Mr Honey had ruined a Reindeer by pulling up its undercarriage while it was standing on the ground.

I got rid of him after ten minutes, and in a momentary breathing space I rang up Shirley. She said, 'Oh, Dennis dear, I'm so glad you are there. Dr Martin's been again. Yes, she's sort of half awake now, but I don't think she knows where she is; she hasn't said anything. Dr Martin said to keep her absolutely quiet – complete rest. He's given me a list of things we've got to get, but I can't leave her to go out to the chemist. Could you possibly get them on the way home, if I give you the list now?'

I blinked. 'What time do the shops shut?'

'I'm not quite sure. Five o'clock, don't they?'

I could not possibly leave the office by that time. I said, 'All right, dear – let's have the list and I'll do something about it. But I shan't be home before seven at the earliest. There's the hell of a row going on here, and I'm in a perfect shambles.'

'Oh, I *am* sorry, Dennis. Well, we've got to get another hot-water bottle and a bedpan and some tablets of Veganin ...' She went on with the list and I wrote it all down on my blotter and rang off, and then I rang for Miss Learoyd, and said, 'Miss Learoyd, can you drive my car?' But then the telephone bell rang again, and she waited while I answered it.

It was Seabright from the Ministry ringing up to tell me that Honey had crashed a Reindeer at Gander by pulling up its undercart.

Ten minutes later I resumed my conversation with Miss Learoyd. She said, 'I'm afraid I can't drive, Dr Scott.'

I said, 'Oh well, then, never mind.' Test pilots never have anything to do but stand around on the tarmac and goop at the aeroplanes; I rang through to the flight office and got hold of Flight-Lieutenant Wintringham, and said, 'Wintringham, are you doing much for the next hour?' He said he wasn't, and I got him to come up to my office and gave him the list for the chemist and the key of my car, and got him to go out and get the stuff and take it round to Shirley. Then Drinkwater in the ARB came on the telephone to tell me that a member of my department had damaged an aeroplane of CATO at Gander by pulling up its undercarriage.

And then Miss Learoyd, bless her, came in with a cup of tea.

I asked her to find out if the Director had come to life yet, but she came back in a couple of minutes and said he had not returned; his girl would let us know immediately he came in. I sighed and pulled my IN basket towards me, full of the arrears of work, but a quarter of an hour later I was speaking on the telephone again, this time to E. P. Prendergast, designer of the Reindeer.

He said, 'Is that Dr Scott?'

'Speaking, Mr Prendergast,' I said. 'It's very nice to hear you again.'

'Dr Scott, Mr Carnegie of CATO rang me up before lunch and told me rather a curious story about trouble with the Reindeer tail. He said you want to ground all our machines. Is that correct?'

'Not quite,' I said. 'We're not quite happy that the crash of the first Reindeer was, in fact, due to the pilot's error of judgment. Obviously I can't tell you the whole story over the phone, but we suspect that trouble with fatigue may crop up in the tailplane, due to the particular harmonic modes induced in cruising flight. We thought it wise to ground one Reindeer that has flown rather a long time until the matter is investigated further. We are quite happy to allow the others to go on, for the time being.'

'This is the very first that I have heard of it,' he said, 'when Mr Carnegie rang through today and told me that a Reindeer had been grounded at a moment's notice, and asked if it was done with my approval. I told him that of course it wasn't.'

'I know,' I said. 'I feel we owe you some explanation for that.' I searched my mind hurriedly to think up some sort of explanation that I could give. 'The matter came up very suddenly, I am afraid, and in connection with a piece of basic research upon fatigue, for which we used the second Reindeer tail that you delivered for experimental purposes.'

'I see, Dr Scott. Don't you think it would have been more courteous, if you suspected trouble with the aircraft designed by this company, to have taken us into your confidence? It is just possible that we might have been able to assist you. After all, we did give the design a great deal of consideration in this office, and we are not wholly inexperienced in problems of fatigue.'

I could not tell the truth, that Prendergast had become so difficult in recent years that one was most reluctant to approach him upon anything. I said, 'The thing moved very quickly from the basic research stage to the stage of immediate urgency. As a matter of fact, we had no idea until last night that any Reindeer had done anything like 1,400 hours. Our information was that they had all done about 400, and at that the matter was not urgent.'

'I see. Of course, you have your own way of doing things. I must say, I should appreciate it if we could be told before long what you think is the matter with our product.'

'Of course, Mr Prendergast,' I replied. 'I want to have a meeting on the thing as soon as possible, at which everybody will be represented. I'm going to fix that up as soon as ever I can get Mr Honey back from Gander, possibly tomorrow. But apart from that rather formal meeting, if you could come down here one morning we should be only too pleased to go into the matter thoroughly with you. In fact, I think a private meeting of that sort might well precede the formal conference.'

'I think it might,' he said. 'I think it might have happened some considerable time ago.' He paused. 'I think perhaps that it would be as well if I come down immediately,' he said. 'Would ten-thirty tomorrow morning be convenient for you?'

I hesitated. 'I think that maybe just a trifle too soon for us,' I said. 'Mr Honey has been doing all the work on this research, and I should very much prefer that he were present at our meeting. At present he's at Gander in Newfoundland, and I am expecting him to cross by air tonight.' I did not think it wise to mention that CATO had flatly refused to bring him back, because I hoped that Ferguson would get around that one. 'If I could give you a ring tomorrow morning, perhaps, and fix the date then?'

'Do I understand that Mr Honey is the only man at Farnborough who is conversant with the trouble that the Reindeer tail is supposed to be having?' he asked.

'Not at all, Mr Prendergast,' I replied. 'I am conversant with it myself, although I have not been able to work on problems of fatigue over a period of years, as Mr Honey has. You'll naturally want the fullest information that's available in this department, and so I think perhaps that we should wait till he gets back.'

'Mr Honey has been doing all the work on this research, then?'

'That's correct.'

'Mr Theodore Honey? A small man, with glasses?'

'That's right.'

'And you expect to get him back by air by tomorrow morning, from Gander?'

I could see myself being driven into a corner. 'I expect so. The Ministry are arranging for a passage now.'

'Oh. Are you aware, Dr Scott, that CATO have refused to carry this man in their aircraft, on the grounds that the mental instability from which he suffers makes him a danger to the safety of the other passengers? Are you aware of that?'

I coloured hotly at his tone. 'I know that that has been said in the heat of the moment,' I replied. 'It's perfect nonsense. I have told Mr Ferguson that we take a most serious view of allegations of that sort, and that Honey must come home by air at once.'

'I might reply that I take a serious view of allegations against the structural safety of the Reindeer, Dr Scott. I understand that Mr Honey has already destroyed one Reindeer standing on the ground at Gander. In the circumstances the action of CATO appears to me to be not unreasonable.'

I checked an angry retort. 'I think we'll have to leave that matter to be settled later, Mr Prendergast,' I said. 'What we have to decide now is the date when we shall meet. May I give you a ring tomorrow morning, making a proposal? I shall be able to see my way a little bit more clearly then.'

'If you wish it so,' he said. 'But I must make it clear to you, Dr Scott, that until these allegations, as you call them, about Mr Honey's health have been cleared up I shall be most unwilling to accept the results of his work, or even to waste much time in studying them.' He paused. 'I have worked in this industry for nearly forty years, Dr Scott. I have watched the personnel engaged in research come and go. I know the members of your staff. Probably I have known all of them longer than you have, I may even know some of them better. Take Mr Honey, for example. Did he not write a paper, published in the *Journal of the Interplanetary Society* in 1932 or 1933, advocating the construction of a rocket projectile for an exploratory journey to the moon?'

I felt rather helpless. 'I haven't the least idea,' I said. 'If he did, what of it?'

'I merely call your attention to the lines on which his mind appears to run,' he replied. 'I believe he has been Chairman of the Surbiton branch of the Society for Psychic Research, and that much of his leisure time has been spent in the detection of ghosts. I understand that he has been in trouble with the police arising out of his activities with the British Israelites. He has more than once forecast the coming dissolution of the world to members of my staff, over the lunch table. We now have a – er, an allegation by the officials of CATO that Mr Honey is mentally unbalanced. I must say that I should like to see that allegation disposed of before I am required to waste much of my time in an examination of his work upon the Reindeer tailplane.'

I said, 'Very well, Mr Prendergast. The most that I can do is to let you know tomorrow morning when we shall be ready to meet you to discuss the Reindeer tail. If then you prefer not to attend the meeting that we offer, that, of course, is your affair entirely. As regards these allegations against Mr Honey, we shall of course investigate them fully, and if we find that they have substance in them we shall reconsider our position. If we find that they are irresponsible slanders, we shall maintain our attitude, which is that till this matter is cleared up to the complete satisfaction of all parties, no Reindeer aircraft should fly more than 700 hours.' I put a little vehemence into the last words.

'Will you please transfer this call to your Director?' he asked.

'I'm afraid I can't do that,' I said. 'He isn't here this afternoon.'

'That is a great pity, Dr Scott. I had hoped to avoid troubling the Minister. Would you ask the Director to telephone to me as soon as it may be convenient to him?'

'Certainly,' I said. 'I don't suppose that that will be until tomorrow morning, by which time I hope the matter will have become rather clearer.'

He rang off, and I sat staring at the piles of work in my IN basket. The attack was developing, and it was going to take the form that Mr Honey was mad, and all his work upon the Reindeer tail was worthless rubbish. Inevitably it would come out that we had put it up to the Inter-Services Atomic Research Board, and that Sir Phillip Dolbear had thought nothing of it, that was bound to happen at some stage of the affair. Moreover, we had nothing positive to put upon the credit side. I had a hunch that he was right, a hunch derived from a study of the accident report on the first Reindeer and from a study of the little man himself. But could my hunch stand up against the formidable array of evidence now massing up that Honey was irresponsible and that his work was therefore worthless? Would the truth emerge that the Reindeer tail was quite safe after all? And if so, what would my position be?

The only other thing that happened on that most unpleasant afternoon was that Ferguson came through again, to say that CATO were adamant that they would not carry Mr Honey back across the Atlantic in one of their aircraft. He said that they were taking a firm stand upon the question of safety. They had no facilities in the aircraft or upon their staff for the control of passengers who might become unbalanced in the air, and in view of this man's record they would have nothing more to do with him. 'They just won't carry him, and that's all about it,' Ferguson said. 'I don't see that we can force them, in the circumstances. And I don't see that we can ask a foreign or Dominion line to take him, either. We'd have to go back to the Treasury for that and that would mean explaining all the circumstances there.'

I bit my lip. 'We must get him back,' I said. 'Until we have him here, we can't have a really effective meeting on the technicalities of this fatigue story. And everybody's clamouring for a meeting now.'

He said, 'Well, the only other way would be to get him back by means of RAF Transport Command. And that's really going just a bit above my head, you know. I think that that would have to be put through by your Director, on a higher level.'

'All right,' I said. 'That's how we'll have to do it.'

The Director came into his office soon after five; Miss Learoyd got the news, and I went down at once to see him. He was in a calm and cheerful frame of mind, and greeted me warmly. 'Good afternoon, Scott,' he said. 'I came back by Kew and spent an hour in the Gardens. You really ought to go and see them now – the rose gardens are perfect, and they've got the most magnificent hedge of sweet-peas that I have ever seen in all my life. You really ought to go. It's very delightful there at most times of the year, of course, especially in spring, but really I think I prefer the formal effects that you get in a made garden in July. I think I do. However. You've got something for me?'

'I'm afraid I have,' I said. 'I've got a major row.'

He made me sit down, and I told him all about it. It took a quarter of an hour. 'Well, there it is,' I said at last. 'I think that the immediate thing is to get Honey back here at once, and for that I'm afraid we'll have to ask for the assistance of Transport Command.'

'I see,' he said thoughtfully. 'You wouldn't let him go on now and do his job in Labrador?'

I met his eye. 'Do you think that anything he did in Labrador would be accepted as a valuable contribution, sir – after this?'

He stared out of the window. 'It's a question of fact. ... But I think that I agree with you, it might be better to recall

Honey and send out somebody to Labrador whose findings would be readily accepted by our critics.' He turned to me. 'We depend entirely on the evidence from the Labrador crash, do we not? We have nothing else to show, except Honey's theoretical investigations, which Sir Phillip Dolbear won't accept?'

I shook my head. 'Nothing, unless you count this photograph.' I had the accident report with me; I opened it upon his table and we studied the one print that showed the port tailplane front spar fracture at the fuselage. The print was an enlargement from a Leica frame, carried up already to a size at which the detail was becoming fuzzy; it would obviously go no bigger without losing definition. At that, the bit that interested us was no more than one-eighth of an inch long, and the really vital part considerably less than that. We studied it together with a magnifying glass. 'It certainly looks like a fatigue fracture,' he said quietly. 'It might come up more clearly in the stereoscope.'

He turned to me. 'That's all the evidence we've got to go upon, until we get this portion back from Labrador?'

I nodded. 'That's right, sir. That, and what we think of Mr Honey as a reliable research worker.'

'And what do you think of that, now?'

There was a long pause. 'I think the same as I did,' I said heavily at last. 'I think that there's a very fair chance that he's right. The fact that one Reindeer last night flew up to 1,430 hours or so before he wrecked it means nothing, of course; it might have been due to fail in the next hour. We don't yet know the full story of why he raised the undercarriage. But if, as I suppose, he felt it was the only way to stop that aircraft flying any more, I think that he was right. In his shoes I should probably have done the same, if I had had the guts. That hasn't shaken my opinion of his work.'

'It was a very extreme step to take,' he said thoughtfully. 'It's obviously going to make a lot of trouble.'

'It makes a lot of trouble when airliners crash, and people lose their lives,' I said.

He walked to the window and looked out upon the aerodrome, deep in thought. 'I made a mistake in this thing, Scott,' he said at last. 'I should have sent somebody upon this job who had more personality. I ought to have sent you. Honey's an inside man. I can quite see that in the circumstances that obtained at Gander, when the aircraft was due to fly on, he would have had difficulty in enforcing his point of view. Probably, in view of what both you and he feel on the likelihood of this fatigue trouble, he did as well as he could be expected to. He probably did right. But it will make a lot of trouble for us; I can see that coming.'

'I'm very sorry about that, sir,' I replied.

He smiled. 'It's none of your making.'

'I feel it is,' I said. 'If I could have handled things a bit more cleverly, all this could have been avoided.'

He shrugged his shoulders. 'We'll get over it.'

'What about Honey?' I asked. 'I presume that he's at Gander now. Will you start up something with Transport Command to get him back?'

He glanced at the clock. 'Not tonight. I think I'd like to sleep upon it, Scott, and take some action in the morning. It won't hurt Honey to stay there for another twelve hours or so.' He smiled at me. 'You sleep on it, too. Take your wife out tonight and forget about all this.'

I moved with him towards the door. 'I can't do that,' I said. 'I've got another spot of Honey trouble on my plate at home.' And I told him all about little Elspeth Honey falling downstairs in the middle of the night.

'But wasn't anybody looking after her?' he asked.

'I don't know,' I said. 'That's one of the things that hasn't been cleared up.'

I went back to my office and started my day's work, and for a merciful two hours I had respite from the telephone, so that by seven o'clock I had got well down into my IN basket. I gave it up then, and went home. Shirley was in the bedroom; she heard me in the little hall and came out to meet me.

'She's much better,' she said in a quiet voice. 'She's awake now.' We went into the sitting-room. 'Flight-Lieutenant Wintringham brought along the stuff from the chemist, and I've given her some of the Veganin, because her headache was so bad. She's been sick, but the doctor said that would happen. I think she's getting on as well as can be expected.'

I grunted. 'Well, that's one thing going on well, anyway.' I glanced at her. 'Her father's in a stinking mess over at Gander.'

'Mr Honey is? Why, Dennis?'

'I'm not quite certain why,' I said. 'But what happened was this. He pulled up the undercart of a Reindeer while it was standing on the ground. Retracted it.'

She stared at me. 'You mean, so that it sat down on its tummy?'

I nodded wearily. 'That's right.'

She said, 'What a naughty little man!' And then she laughed, and freed from the strain of the day, I hesitated for a moment, and then laughed with her. 'Oh,' she said, 'I would like to have seen him doing it!'

'All very well,' I said at last. 'But you just wouldn't believe the trouble that it's made.'

'Is the damage very serious, Dennis?'

'I simply don't know, yet.' I thought for a moment; somebody had once told me that the contract price of each Reindeer was £453,000. 'I suppose the repair bill will be something like fifty thousand pounds,' I said ruefully.

'Oh, Dennis, how bad of him! However did he come to do it?'

I started to tell her, and she went and got me a drink, so that I finished telling her about it in a more cheerful frame of mind. And then we went into the bedroom to see Elspeth.

She was lying in our bed, drowsy with the drug, but she opened her eyes when we came in. 'Hullo, Elspeth,' I said. 'How are you getting on?'

She said, 'I put on Daddy's warm dressing-gown and I trod on it and fell down.' And then she said, 'Will you tell Daddy that I want him?'

'He's coming back at once,' I said. 'He doesn't know you're ill yet, but he's coming home tomorrow or the day after at the latest.'

The little girl said, 'Was there a burglar?'

'A burglar – in your house last night do you mean? I don't think so.' Beside me Shirley shook her head. 'There was nobody there this morning but you, and everything was quite all right.'

She said, 'I heard a burglar, so I put on Daddy's warm dressing-gown, but I trod on it and fell down.'

'Don't worry about burglars now,' I said. 'You just get well again before your daddy gets back. He won't want to find you in bed, will he?'

She shook her head slightly on the pillow. The little movement drew my attention to the mop, its white cotton head, now rather grubby, on the pillow near her own. Shirley had found it in her bed and brought it round, to comfort her in her loneliness amongst strangers.

'Are you quite warm now?' I asked.

She said, 'I've got three hot-water bottles, all rubber ones.'

'Fine. Do you want any supper?'

'No, thank you, Dr Scott. I was sick three times and Mrs Scott held my head. May I go back and sleep in our house tonight?'

'I don't think that's a very good idea,' I said. 'I think you'd better stay with us till you're quite well again.'

'I must go back to our house,' she said in agitation, 'because it's empty and there'll be a burglar because of Daddy's work. It's very valuable, and burglars come and break into empty houses and steal valuable things. Please, Dr Scott, may I go back and sleep in our house? I'm quite all right now.'

'Your daddy's work will be quite safe,' I told her. 'Burglars don't come to steal that sort of valuable thing, because they can't sell it. They come and steal silver spoons and things like that.'

'Would they steal electro-plate, Dr Scott? It's just like silver.'

'No,' I said, 'they never steal electro-plate.'

'But there *was* a burglar last night, Dr Scott, because I heard him. And I put on Daddy's warm dressing-gown and I trod on it, and I fell down.'

This was where I had come in. I told her that I'd have a talk with Shirley and decide who was going to sleep where that night, and I left her, and went and found Shirley in the kitchen. 'I simply must eat something,' I said. 'I haven't had any lunch.'

'Oh, Dennis! Look, supper will be ready in about ten minutes. Have a couple of biscuits, and go in and eat them with Elspeth.'

I took the biscuits, but before I got to Elspeth there was a little wail, and Elspeth was in trouble again. What's more, she hadn't got her basin handy. I called to Shirley, 'All right, you go on cooking; I can cope with this.' And I did, and I can testify that there's no better anodyne to worry than coping with a vomiting child.

Presently supper was ready; I went to it with a reduced

appetite, partly on account of the biscuits. While we were eating I told Shirley about the burglars. 'That poor kid's got burglars on the brain, Dennis. She's been talking about them ever since she woke up. She's terribly upset that somebody will come and steal Mr Honey's work on the Great Pyramid.'

'Is that what's on her mind?'

She nodded.

'But that's absurd,' I said weakly.

'I know it is. But that's what's on her mind. She's got a great sense of responsibility.' She turned to the dresser and picked up a dirty halfsheet of notepaper. 'I do think it's a blasted shame,' she said vehemently. 'I went round to get her night things while Wintringham was here, and this is what I found in the kitchen.'

It was an ill-written note. It read:

Dear Miss,
I find I wont be able to come tonight as my husband is took poorly.

Yours respectfully,
E. Higgs.

I gave it back to her. 'Just like that,' I said.

'Just like that,' she said angrily. 'I'm keeping it to show to Mr Honey.'

I thought for a minute. 'About these bloody burglars,' I said. 'I've got to sleep somewhere, anyway, and so have you. I could sleep round there tonight if that would help.'

'I think it would help, Dennis,' she said. 'As a matter of fact, I don't quite know where else you *are* to sleep tonight, unless you went to a hotel. I thought I'd sleep on the sofa here.'

'All right,' I said. 'I'll go around and sleep there.' At any rate, I thought, it would be quiet, and I could take the 'Performance Analysis of Aircraft Flying at High Mach Numbers' with me.

'I'm awfully sorry,' Shirley said. 'But I think it might be quite a good thing if you did sleep there. I kicked the glass out of the kitchen window this morning, to get in to her, so there really might be a burglar tonight. I mean, the house is wide open.'

I went round there after supper, in the dusk. I found a piece of three-ply and a hammer and some tacks, and tacked the plywood up to the frame of the broken window; then I carried my bag up to the front bedroom, Honey's room, and made the bed. I took the typescript of my thesis from the bag and went down to the sitting-room, meaning to settle down in the one armchair that the house possessed and concentrate upon it.

The house was still and quiet, but I could not concentrate. The Honey matter was so urgent that here, surrounded by all Honey's personal belongings, I could not bring my mind to bear upon the aircraft flying at high Mach numbers. That afternoon various people had stated bluntly their opinion that Mr Honey was mad. I had taken my stand on my opinion that his work was valuable; very soon the matter would be decided one way or the other. If I was right there would be a complete disruption of CATO's Atlantic service. If events should prove that Honey's work was worthless, my position would be very much in question; it would hardly be possible for me to continue in charge of the Department after having been proved wrong in such a major row as this was going to be.

Probably I should have to leave the RAE, leave Government service altogether, having put up such a black as that. I should have to start again in industry; possibly it would be better to make a complete break and emigrate and start again in aviation in Australia, or in Canada perhaps. If Honey's work was worthless, that would be my future : to leave the country, go down in salary and in prestige, and start again in a strange place. But then, was Honey's work worthless?

My eyes strayed to his books, untidily arranged upon three long shelves. The *Psychology of the Transfiguration* rubbed shoulders with *An Experiment With Time*, and next came *A Discussion of the Infinite*. Then there was *The Serial Calculus Applied to Numerical Analysis* and then, surprisingly, *Great Motion Pictures, Past and Present*. I picked this out in curiosity and opened it; upon the flyleaf there was written, 'Mary with all my love, from Theo, March 16th, 1939'. I put it back, a little thoughtfully. There had been a human side at one time, long ago.

There was more such evidence farther along the shelf. Between *The Pyramid in History* and *The Stability of a Harmonic Series* there stood a large gift volume, richly illustrated and interspersed with musical scores, called *Country*

Dancing. This was inscribed 'Theo dear, from Mary, September 2nd, 1936'. It was a well-used book that lay open at any page : clearly it had seen some service on a music stand. Beside that was another well-worn, paper-covered volume called *Rambles in Old World Sussex*. I thought of the short hiker's pants and the good strong boots; they would be upstairs somewhere, probably with a rucksack. It would be interesting, I thought, to look and see if the good strong boots had been used recently, if Honey still went hiking, if he took any exercise at the week-ends. It would all add up.

The thought got me out of my chair and set me wandering about the empty house. On the kitchen table somebody had put three or four letters. All were bills or receipts saving one, addressed to Miss Elspeth Honey in her father's handwriting, the first from the pile standing on his office desk. I put it on one side to take to her in the morning.

The little house was rather dirty and rather bare of furniture. Upstairs there were three bedrooms, but one, although it had a bed set up in it, was clearly never used and served more for a box-room. At the back of the house looking over the small gardens of the row was Elspeth's room, which I had seen : a small, bare, rather bleak little room. On the mantelpiece there was a photograph of a dark-haired young woman with a pleasant, rather appealing expression. I stared at it in thought for a minute; would that be the mother who had died? I came to the conclusion that almost certainly it was.

I went into Honey's room, the room I was to sleep in. There was no such photograph there, and that seemed odd to me until it struck me that he might have taken it away with him in his bag, to Canada. In a cupboard in his room I found the strong hiking boots. There was mud on them, but it was very old and dry and flaked to dust beneath the pressure of my fingers. They had not been worn for years.

There was a small writing table, or bureau, by the window. I had lost all scruples by that time about intruding into his privacy; too much lay at stake for that. Here, alone in his house, I had the opportunity of learning more of Honey than I should ever get again. I wanted to find written arguments by him, essays, theses, papers for learned societies, or anything of that sort. I wanted to see how his mind worked, whether the conclusions and the inferences that he drew from

131

given facts were reasonable on other matters than the Reindeer tail.

The bureau yielded nothing much to help me. He kept his cheque-book and his unpaid bills and his receipts there; I did not hesitate to look into his affairs. I found them in good order. There were two life insurance policies and his Will, which I did not read because I could guess very well what would be in it. His bills were paid up to date, but this was evidently not usual, because a study of the counterfoils in his cheque-book showed that he had had a field-day at them before leaving for Canada. He had a credit of about three hundred pounds in the bank. I found no evidence of anything but a modest and a frugal life.

In a drawer, at the back, there were a large number of letters, faded, all in the same girlish hand, tied up in bundles with red tape out of the office. I did not look at any of those.

I went downstairs again to his living-room, more like a drawing-office than a parlour, and there in a big cupboard was a row of files containing what I was in search of. These files were all labelled on the back – PYRAMID DEDUCTIONS, MIGRATION (ANIMALS), and MIGRATION (MEN). Then there was one called HEBRAIC FORMS IN DRUID RITUAL, and another, PSYCHIC PHENOMENA. I was interested to notice one called INTERPLANETARY (MASS ATTRACTION OF CELESTIAL BODIES), and another, INTERPLANETARY (VEHICLES). And there was one simply entitled OSMOSIS. In all there must have been about fifteen of them.

I pulled a few of them out of the cupboard and sat down at his table to study them.

An hour later I sat back, filling a pipe, very thoughtful. In the year 1932 he was already writing about the bi-fuel propulsion of rockets and had demonstrated clearly how a three-stage rocket projectile could be constructed which would have sufficient energy and range to escape from the gravitational field of the Earth, with an intent to reach the Moon. He had made weight estimates and he had gone in some detail into the technique of launching. He had not dealt with matters of control, so far as I could discover. His work here seemed to parallel very closely the early German investigations; indeed, in point of date, it seemed to me that he was some years in advance of German work. I could not say that there was evidence of madness in this work of his, but there was sad evidence that we had not made use of genius that lay under our hand, in the last war.

Osmosis was the same story, so far as I could understand the technicalities involved, which were quite outside my beat. It had arisen, queerly, from the design of a radio valve for use in centimetre wave reception; this had apparently been a little mental relaxation from his normal work. In the course of it the properties of the metal thorium had seemed to him unusual when in the presence of argon, and upon this he had built up a considerable research, apparently all carried out in this front sitting-room. It had not been completed, for some reason that I was unable to discover, perhaps because of prior publication by some other research worker. But the work was careful, reasonable, and probably correct.

In the other subjects I was quite out of my depth; I knew nothing about the Pyramid and the Hebraic forms left me cold, except that they were interesting as evidence of his wide interests. Everybody, however ignorant, is attracted by psychic phenomena, or ghosts, and though I was growing sleepy, I pulled that towards me, and opened it at random.

The first part of this set of papers consisted of a series of temperature recordings taken in a house that was troubled by a poltergeist. The evidence was that the house, a modern villa occupied by the manager of a motor garage and his wife, was the scene of various unexplainable occurrences. At a time when the family was at dinner and there was nobody else in the house, the barometer which normally hung in the hall had been thrown with a clatter into the kitchen sink, through a closed door. In similar circumstances a disused paraffin lamp, normally kept in the loft, was thrown downstairs; and kitchen plates were broken with a crash under the bed of the main upstairs bedroom. Unlike the majority of such cases, there was no adolescent in the house. In every instance observers had noticed an apparent fall of temperature at the time of the occurrence. Honey had installed three recording thermographs, probably borrowed from the RAE, at different points in the house, and a mass of these records occupied the first part of the file. I could not find that the research had yielded much result.

The rest of the file was filled with records of communications by planchette; in some cases these were transcripts of the questions and answers and in other cases the actual sheets

covered with scrawled automatic writing were preserved.
Most of them were concerned with a Roman aqueduct and
water distribution system in the neighbourhood of Guildford; Honey had apparently selected this as a test case because the details of its plan had been lost in the passage of the
centuries, and anything discovered by planchette could be
verified fairly easily by excavation. He had amassed a thick
bundle of communications from a spirit called Armiger, who
was apparently a Roman soldier, but much of the other side
of the investigation, the verifying excavations, was missing.

Next came a thin sheaf of papers filed in an envelope;
upon the cover was the one word MARY. I hesitated over this,
and finally passed on, leaving them unread.

Last came a draft for a thesis, perhaps a paper he had read
before the local Society for Psychic Research; it was entitled
AUTOMATIC WRITING. It was a carefully prepared description of the Guildford experiments, which showed considerable verification by digging of the facts stated by the
planchette. What interested me most, however, as in every
technical paper that one scans through quickly, was the paragraph headed 'Conclusions'. Here Honey said:

'It is beyond question that information can be obtained by
automatic writing which is not obtainable in any other way,
provided that the matter is approached in a spirit of serious
inquiry, and that the investigator is not put off by the somewhat bizarre donors of information on the other side. It is not
possible to obtain information upon any subject that one
chooses. It is difficult, if not impossible, to obtain information
benefiting the inquirer. The information which appears to
come most readily is that benefiting mankind as a whole, or
which will benefit a third party who is not aware of the
inquiry.'

I put the files back thoughtfully, and went to bed.

6

I WENT TO SEE the Director when I got in first thing next
morning. 'I had E. P. Prendergast upon the telephone last
night, at my house,' he said. 'He's very much upset.'

'I suppose he told you that Honey's off his head,' I replied. 'I had him yesterday afternoon.'

'Yes, he said that. Of course, Honey lays himself wide open to that sort of thing, and that makes it rather difficult for us. Prendergast has been digging up a lot of Honey's activities in regard to ghosts. I must say, that was news to me.'

'It was news to me, too, yesterday,' I said. 'I know a bit more about it now.' There was nothing to be gained by concealing things; I told the Director that by no design of mine I had been forced to spend the night in Honey's house, and that I had spent the evening going through his private papers. He smiled gently. 'Very wise, if somewhat unconventional,' he said. 'And what do you think of him now, Scott?'

It was sunny and fresh that morning. 'I think exactly as I did,' I said. 'I think that there's a very fair chance that he's right about the Reindeer tail. I think he has a very logical mind. The fact that his interests spread very wide doesn't mean that he's mad. It means that he's sane.'

'And so you feel inclined to maintain your attitude?'

'I do indeed,' I said. 'I don't think we should dream of letting any Reindeer fly more than 700 hours.'

He smiled again, 'Well, I don't mind a fight.' He glanced at me. 'I think we must get Transport Command to fetch Honey back for us,' he said. 'I'll see to that this morning. Then there arises the problem of who to send to Labrador in place of him. When are you reading your paper before the Royal Aeronautical Society, Scott?'

'On Thursday,' I said.

He nodded. 'I want to come to that. But afterwards I think you had better go to Labrador yourself and get this thing cleared up. If we have the formal meeting on Thursday morning at the Ministry and then you read your paper on Thursday night, you should be able to get the night plane to Ottawa after that?'

'If CATO will consent to carry me,' I said. 'I think Honey is as sane as you or I, so they'll probably look a bit old-fashioned at me.'

He laughed. 'I want you to go yourself. It's getting on to quite a high level, this thing is, and it's obviously going to make some difficulties.'

'Well, I'd be very glad to go,' I said. 'I'm beginning to feel a trip to Canada would do me good.'

I went out of his office; on my way back to my own place I had to cross the road outside the main administration block. A very large blue Daimler limousine was just drawing up to the door, driven by a chauffeur; everything about it shone in the sunlight, including the buttons on the man. I wondered sardonically which of the aircraft firms had thought fit to send their representative to us that way, until I saw that the only passenger in it was a woman. I passed on without thinking any more about it.

Five minutes later, in my office, Miss Learoyd came in and said, 'There's a lady downstairs wants to see you, Dr Scott. Miss Teasdale.'

I stared at her. 'Who the hell's Miss Teasdale?'

'I don't know. Shall I ring down and ask what her business is?'

I nodded. 'Yes, do that. I'm very busy today.' I was, but I was rather intrigued; in my job it was quite unusual to have a stranger as a visitor, and especially a woman.

Miss Learoyd came back in a minute, round-eyed. 'It's Monica Teasdale, Dr Scott. She says she's come to see you about Mr Honey.'

The name was vaguely familiar in some way, and anything about Honey now concerned me very much indeed. I wrinkled my brows. 'Who is Monica Teasdale?' I asked.

Miss Learoyd gazed at me reproachfully. 'Wouldn't she be the film actress?'

I stared at her. 'Well, I don't know ...' The thought offended me; I was too busy to be bothered by that sort of person. On the other hand, the Honey matter was now vitally important, and if a movie star had anything to say about him, I should see her. 'You'd better tell them to send her up,' I said at last.

Miss Learoyd, pop-eyed, showed her in a few minutes later; I got up from my desk and met Monica Teasdale in the flesh, whom I had seen upon the screen so many times. She was an older woman than I had thought; she still had the same beauty and appeal, still the same slight figure, the same unwrinkled face, but there was an indefinable sense of age about her; she was not the young girl that I knew upon the screen. Later, I learned to my surprise that she was over fifty.

She came forward with a dazzling smile, with hand outstretched. 'Dr Scott?' she said. 'Dr Scott, I heard so much about you from Mr Honey that I thought, maybe, since there's a mite of trouble going on, I'd come right down and see you and tell you all about it.'

I said, 'Well, Miss Teasdale – that's very good of you. Er – have you known Mr Honey long?' And then I said, 'Would you sit down?'

She said 'I only met him night before last, flying over to Gander in an airplane.'

I was amazed. 'But . . . did you go to Gander?'

'Sure I did,' she said. 'I was at Gander with him yesterday, up till around midnight when my plane took off for London.'

'Then you know about the accident to the Reindeer?'

'Surely,' she said. 'I actually saw it happen. I could have died laughing.'

It was satisfactory, perhaps, to hear that somebody had got some fun out of this business. I leaned over and offered her a cigarette, which she refused, and said, 'But how did you get back here, then?'

She said, 'I flew right back last night. Out there, your Mr Honey's got himself in quite a spot, Doctor. I guess you know he pulled the landing wheels up, so "Redgauntlet" couldn't take off from Gander.' I nodded. 'Well, after that there was some trouble, as you'd suppose, and folks were going around declaring that he's mentally deranged – that's what they're saying out there.' I nodded. 'Well, I don't think he's mentally deranged at all, but it's got so that no airline will carry him away from Gander, and as there *is* no other way to get away from Gander, it looks like he'll stay there for quite a while. And that worried him a lot, because he thought he ought to get back and report to you, and tell you what he did.'

'I see,' I said thoughtfully. 'How do you come in on this, Miss Teasdale?'

'I got to kind of like the little man,' she said frankly. 'Seems like he's getting a raw deal. I said that I'd come right back myself and tell you just what happened. At first I couldn't get a passage – they said all the planes were full up, but I got a call long distance to New York – four hours it took to come through, would you believe it! – and I spoke to Solly Goldmann and I said, "Solly, this is Monica, I've just *got* to get a seat on that Trans-World Airline plane this evening back to London. I've just *got* to, Solly. Don't you ask me why, I'll tell you when I see you on the lot, but just you go right round and see the President for me and say that Monica's set down at Gander by the British and she's just *got* to get back to London on that plane tonight." That's what I said. Well, then I stuck around with Mr Honey, and sure enough when that plane landed around nine o'clock they had a seat for me, and here I am.'

'Did anybody else come back with you from Gander?' I inquired. 'Any of the crew?'

She shook her head. 'They're all sitting around grieving about their airplane, and trying to think of ways of getting it up on its wheels again. They say it weighs seventy tons, and that's a mean load to handle at a place like Gander, seemingly, where all the tools they've got is one jack from the tool-box of a Ford. I expect they'll be there some time with it.'

I asked her, 'Would you tell me exactly what did happen, Miss Teasdale? I'd like to know it all, right from the start.'

'Surely,' she said. 'I only came into the story half-way through, but we were barely clear of Ireland, only an hour or so out, when Mr Honey first discovered that that airplane had flown twice the hours it should have done.' She settled down to tell me the whole tale. Honey had briefed her well; she had a little paper of notes in her handbag and she had a letter for me, half a dozen lines scrawled in his vile handwriting, telling me I could depend upon her story, and asking me to cable him instructions whether to go on by land or to come back. In half an hour I had the picture very clearly in my mind of what had happened.

'It's been most kind of you to come back here and tell us all this,' I said at last. 'It's really very helpful.'

She said, 'Well, it seemed kind of wrong to go on to the Coast and leave it so.' She glanced at me. 'I like your Mr Honey,' she said quietly. 'I think he's a nice person.'

'It's good of you to say so,' I replied. 'I'm afraid he's interrupted your journey, though.'

She shrugged her shoulders. 'Guess I'd rather be sitting in this office than lying dead some place, even if I am back in England when I meant to be over on the Coast today.'

'You think that there was danger in going on?' I asked curiously. 'Honey convinced you, did he?'

'I don't know anything about these things,' she said. 'Out

there at Gander they're all saying that he's nuts. Well, I don't think that – and I've met some crackpots in my time, believe me. I'm just as glad I didn't have to fly on in that airplane, after hearing what he said.' She paused, and then she said, 'I reckon Captain Samuelson, the pilot of the plane, he was kind of relieved, too, when it sat down on its belly, though he was as mad as hell.'

I nodded thoughtfully. 'Miss Teasdale,' I said, 'would you mind waiting here a minute, while I go and see my chief – the Director of this Establishment? I think he might like to meet you.'

'Sure,' she said. 'Go right ahead.'

I went down to the Director; fortunately he was free. 'About this Honey business, sir,' I said rather desperately. 'I've got a film star here who knows a lot about it. Miss Monica Teasdale.' I had a feeling that my blazing row was getting altogether out of control.

He looked at me, smiling. 'Do you want me to see her, Scott?'

'I think you ought to,' I said. 'She travelled over with Honey and knows all about what happened on the crossing and at Gander. She came back specially to tell us all about it, and so far as I can make out she's the only witness who has come back to this country.'

'Are you going to put this lady from Hollywood up against Sir David Moon and E. P. Prendergast?' he asked. But he was grinning, and I knew that he was pulling my leg.

'I think you ought to see her,' I said stubbornly. 'I don't suppose you'll ever get another chance of moving in such high society.'

'By all means bring her down,' he said. 'I've never met a film star in the flesh.'

She came into his office with a radiant smile and hand a little bit outstretched, a perfect gesture from a very lovely woman. 'Say,' she said, 'it's just terribly nice of you to see me, and I'll try not to waste any of your time. I just wanted to tell you what a marvellous front your Mr Honey put up out at Gander, and how grateful to him I feel as a passenger.'

She launched into the story, as she had with me, and talked for about ten minutes. At the end of that the Director thanked her, talked to her about a few casual matters, asked if she would like to see the less secret parts of the Establishment, and asked me to show her round. I took her out on to the tarmac where the aeroplanes were parked awaiting test, and walked her round a little, and introduced her to Flight-Lieutenant Wintringham, who was properly impressed. And while we were chatting in among the aircraft, he inquired, 'How's Elspeth this morning?'

'Better,' I said. 'She's got a headache and she was sick again during the night – Shirley was up with her a good bit. But she's going on all right.'

'Honey know anything about it yet?'

'No,' I said. 'He's got enough on his plate out at Gander without bothering him with that.' It was common knowledge by that time what had happened.

He laughed boyishly. 'I would like to have seen him do it.'

'Miss Teasdale did,' I said. 'She saw the whole thing happen.'

He turned to her. 'You did?' But she was already speaking to me.

'Who is this Elspeth, anyway?' she asked. 'Not Mr Honey's little girl?'

'That's right,' I replied. 'She fell downstairs the night he went away, the night that you flew over to Gander, Sunday night. She's been rather bad.'

She stared at me. 'How did that happen? Mr Honey told me that he'd got the hired woman to come and stay in the house.'

'She didn't turn up,' I explained. 'Elspeth was alone in the house. She thought she heard a burglar in the middle of the night and got up to see, and fell downstairs and knocked her head. She was unconscious for over twelve hours; my wife found her about eleven o'clock on Monday morning, lying in a heap at the foot of the stairs. But she's getting on all right now.'

She stared at me in horror. 'The poor child! Where is she now?'

'As a matter of fact, she's lying in my bed,' I said ruefully. 'My wife's looking after her. I slept round at Honey's house last night, and I suppose I'll do the same tonight.'

She said slowly, 'I'm just terribly sorry to hear this, Dr Scott. I know how anxious Mr Honey's going to be when he gets to hear of it – he just thinks the world of his little girl. Is there anything that I can do?'

140

I smiled. 'It's quite all right, thanks. We shan't tell him about it till he gets back here, I don't think. She's getting on quite well, and it would only upset him.'

She said, 'Your Mr Honey was mighty nice to me, Doctor. Isn't there any little thing that I can do at all?'

I thought for a minute, wondering how far this actress was sincere or putting on an act. It would thrill Shirley to meet her, in any case. 'What are you doing for the rest of today, Miss Teasdale?' I inquired.

'Nothing,' she said. 'I'm completely free.'

'There is just one thing you could do,' I said. 'My wife's tired out; she got practically no sleep last night, sitting up with Elspeth. If you could go and sit with Elspeth while Shirley takes a nap on the sofa, it really would be very kind indeed.'

She said, 'Why, certainly.' She was more Miss Myra Tuppen than Miss Monica Teasdale at that moment; far from the honky-tonk, the simple past was opening before her. 'I'd be real glad to do that. Tell me, where do I go? And will you call your wife and tell her that I'll come right over?'

We went back to the offices and I rang up Shirley and told her simply that a friend of Honey's, a Miss Teasdale, was coming over to sit with Elspeth while Shirley got some sleep. I didn't feel equal to explaining to my tired wife upon the telephone that I was sending her a movie queen. Then we went down and she got into her enormous car, and I told the chauffeur where to find my little flat, and Wintringham and I were left as they moved off.

'The old devil!' he said with a note of admiration in his voice. 'Fancy Honey collecting a Popsie like that!'

It did seem rather curious when you came to think of it.

I went up to my office, but Miss Learoyd said the Director wanted me, and I went down again. He said, 'What have you done with our distinguished visitor, Scott?'

'I've sent her off to sit with Elspeth Honey while my wife gets some sleep,' I said. 'She seemed to want to help, so I took her at her word.'

He raised his eyebrows, 'And she went?'

I grinned. 'She did. Just like an ordinary woman.'

'Really ...' He asked me about Elspeth, and I told him. And then he said, 'You know, the thing that interested me most in Miss Teasdale's story was the reaction of the pilot,

Samuelson. He didn't seem to be sorry that it was impossible to fly that aircraft any farther.'

'I know,' I said. 'I think that wants looking into. He couldn't have diagnosed anything wrong with the machine, though, from his own experience. I wonder if old Honey shook his confidence a bit?'

'Maybe,' he said. 'About Honey, Scott. I've been talking to the Air Ministry. There's an old Lincoln from the Navigation School due to fly from Winnipeg back here one day this week, and they're instructing it to land at Gander and pick Honey up. I've got a draft signal here from us to him that I'd like you to look at.'

We got that off, and I went back to my office to deal with my overflowing IN basket.

Shirley, wearily cooking up a cup of arrowroot for Elspeth to see if she could keep that down, heard a ring at the door and thought it was the butcher; she was so tired she had already forgotten all about Miss Teasdale. She went with her overall on and a wisp of hair hanging down across her eyes and an enamel tray in her hand to receive the joint, and there was a most lovely and most beautifully turned-out woman standing at the head of the dark staircase that led up to our flat. Her face was vaguely familiar and her voice soft and husky and slightly Middle West.

She said, 'Say, it's Mrs Scott, is it?'

Shirley said, 'Oh ... of course. My husband rang me up.' She fumbled with the tray in her hands. 'I'm so sorry – I thought it was someone else. Please, do come in.'

Miss Teasdale said, 'I was visiting with Dr Scott this morning, and he told me what a time you're having with Mr Honey's little girl, and he suggested I could come and sit with her a while so you could get some sleep. I'd be glad to do that, if it suits you, Mrs Scott. I'm free all day.'

Shirley said mechanically, 'Oh, you don't need to bother – really.' She hesitated. 'Would you come in?'

Miss Teasdale took hold firmly as they went into the sitting-room. 'My dear, you're looking real tired,' she said. 'I'm a kind of friend of Mr Honey. I'm quite free to stay here up till ten o'clock tonight, or all night if it suits. Just show me where things are and where the little girl is, and then you get off to bed and get some sleep.'

Shirley stared at her. 'Aren't ... don't I know you?'

'Sure you know me, if you ever go to pictures,' said the actress. 'But that doesn't mean I can't look after a sick child, same as anybody else.'

'Monica Teasdale?'

'That's right.'

'But – do you know Mr Honey?'

'Surely. Now you just—' She stopped and glanced out of the window at the Daimler. 'Just one thing first of all, my dear,' she said quietly. 'We don't want any trouble here with Press or fans or anything. I don't think anybody noticed when I came in. Do you mind – would you go down and tell the chauffeur he's to go right back because I'm staying here a while? Say I'll call them at the office later in the day.'

Shirley went down to the car in a state of tired bemusement; the chauffeur touched his cap to her, and the great car moved off. When she got back to the flat Miss Teasdale was not in the sitting-room; Shirley went down the passage to the bedroom and there she was, standing in the doorway, leaning reflectively against the jamb, looking in at Elspeth, who was sleeping in our double bed, with a basin at her side.

She turned at Shirley's step. 'She's just the image of her father,' she said quietly.

Shirley stopped by her; together they stood looking at the sleeping child. 'She is and she isn't,' she said. 'She's got his features, but she's awfully well proportioned. Look at her hands. I think she may be beautiful when she gets older.'

The actress said quietly, 'That could be.' And then she said, 'Did you know her mother?'

Shirley shook her head. 'I only met Mr Honey a few days ago.' She drew away from the door. 'Don't let's wake her.'

They moved back to the sitting-room. 'Say, is that the only bed you've got?' the actress asked.

Shirley nodded. 'It's only a small flat,' she said. 'We've not been married very long.'

'Kind of difficult for nursing a sick child, isn't it?'

'It's a bit hard on Dennis – my husband. He had to go and sleep in Mr Honey's house last night.'

'Where did you sleep then?'

Shirley laughed. 'I didn't sleep much, anyway. I lay down on the sofa for a bit.'

'Well, you lie right down on that sofa again and get some

143

sleep. I'll sit in the bedroom to· be near her if she wakes.' She was tired herself after two nights sitting up in an aircraft, but she did not want to sleep. She could rest sufficiently by sitting quiet by the sleeping child.

Shirley said, 'It's awfully kind of you – I would like to lie down a bit. Let me get some lunch first.' They went together to the kitchen; the actress watched, a little helplessly, while Shirley got out the cold meat and salad and put on a kettle. And then she said, 'Would you like for me to take her up to Claridge's? We've got a suite there permanently reserved where she could have a bedroom and a private nurse and everything . . .'

Shirley said quickly, 'Oh thank you, but that wouldn't do. She'd be worried to death – she wants to get back into her father's house. She's worrying that all their things will get stolen. It wouldn't do to move her up to London – honestly it wouldn't.'

'Okay,' said the older woman. 'It was just an idea.' She watched Shirley for a minute, and then said, 'What were you doing before you got yourself married?'.

'I was a tracer.'

'In a drafting office?'

Shirley nodded. 'That's where I met Dennis.'

There was a long pause. 'I was a stenographer,' the older woman said. 'But that was quite a while ago.' She stood in thought, her mind full of memories of Eddie Stillson, the lame ledger clerk.

Shirley stared at her. 'Really? I thought you were always in films.'

'You don't get born that way,' Miss Teasdale said. 'How old are you?'

Shirley said, 'Twenty-four.'

'Well, I've been in pictures all your life, and maybe a bit longer. But I was a stenographer one time, in an insurance office.'

Shirley said curiously, 'How did you come to meet Mr Honey, Miss Teasdale?'

'It was this way.' They sat down to lunch at the dining-table in the little kitchen; as she heard all about it Shirley studied her visitor. She had never before sat and talked with any American; she was overwhelmed by the sophisticated, carefully tended beauty of the actress and confused by the real kindliness of the woman that lay under the sophistication. Above all, she was tired, too tired to take much in.

Miss Teasdale said, 'Now, you go right into that sitting-room and lie down with a rug over you, and let me see you make yourself real comfortable and warm.'

Shirley said, 'I'll just wash these things up first.'

'Wash – oh, the dishes. No, you leave those where they are. I'll see to them.'

It was too incongruous; the woman was not dressed for housework, her nails too carefully manicured for washing dishes, her costume too good. Shirley said, 'No – really, it won't take me a minute.'

'You do what I say.' Shirley was too tired to argue any more; she took off her overall and gave it to the actress, showed her the rusty tin that contained soda. 'This double saucepan's got arrowroot in it,' she said. 'Keep it warm and give Elspeth a cup if she wakes up. The sugar's here. She'd better not have anything else, and if she's sick, just empty the bowl down the lavatory and wash it out, you know. Dr Martin may look in this afternoon. It's awfully kind of you.'

She went into the sitting-room and let down the end of the sofa; under the disciplinary eye of the older woman she lay down and pulled a rug over her. In ten minutes she was fast asleep.

Back in the kitchen, Monica Teasdale started gingerly upon the washing up. She had not done that in years because her negro house servants were genuinely fond of her, and had seldom let her down, but long ago Myra Tuppen had done it after every meal as a matter of course. The greasy feel of hot wet plates stirred memories in her. Old tunes came creeping back into her mind as she stood there at the sink, the dance tunes of her early youth, *Redwing*, *That Mysterious Rag*. ... She stood there with these old tunes running through her head, washing the dishes mechanically, a middle-aged woman who had crept back into the past, when everything was bright and promising and new ...

She finished washing the dishes without breaking anything, and found places for them in the cupboard where they seemed to fit. Then she took off her overall and did up her face in the small mirror of her flapjack. If she had married Eddie Stillson this would have been her life, the kitchen and children in Terre Haute or in some other city of the Middle

West. She had done better for herself than that, or had she? She had seen India and China and the Philippines in films upon location, but Eddie Stillson's wife could have learned as much as she about those countries by seeing the films. She had travelled once or twice in Europe for her holidays between the wars, but Eddie Stillson's wife could have learned as much by reading the *Geographic Magazine* – possibly more. She had, however, tangible experiences that Eddie Stillson could not have provided. Twice she had started the Indianapolis Motor Race, in her own State. She had adventured three times into marriage. She had met interesting people in all walks of life; she had entertained Ambassadors. Now as her career was drawing to its close a life of idleness alone in an apartment lay ahead of her. All her experience and all the money she had earned had not secured for her a home and quiet interests for her old age, had not brought her children and grandchildren. She could never have those now, even if she married again. She smiled, a little cynically; for the fourth time. If ever she ventured into matrimony again she would look for very different qualities in a man.

She moved quietly to the sitting-room door and looked in; Shirley was asleep upon the sofa. She glanced around our room, thoughtfully, noting the second-hand carpet, the ten-year-old radio, the bookcases I had made in the evenings out of the planks of packing-cases stained with permanganate of potash. There were many flowers in the room because Shirley was fond of them; one spray of roses stood in a tall glass bottle etched with the legend MANOR FARM DAIRY. With a little pang she recognised the room for what it was, something she had never really known, the beginning of a home. Somehow, it seemed easier for folks to make a place like that when there wasn't very much money. When you built a bookcase with your own hands instead of ordering it by telephone from the department store complete with books, it was a little tenuous link that bound you to the home.

She was forgetting her charge; she moved down the short corridor to the bedroom. Elspeth had turned over in bed; as the actress came to the door she moved and blinked sleepily, her hair over her eyes, only half awake. Miss Teasdale said, 'It's all right, honey. Mrs Scott's having a nice sleep and I said I'd stay around and look after you.'

Elspeth said, 'What's your name?'

'Teasdale – Monica Teasdale. You'd better call me Monica.'

The child asked directly, 'Then why did you call me Honey?'

The actress laughed. 'Why, that's what we call folks back in America, in Indiana where I was raised. I didn't mean it for your name.'

'My name's Elspeth,' said the child. 'I've been sick six times.'

'Well, don't you be sick again till Mrs Scott wakes up, or maybe I'd not know what to do about it.'

'Why don't you call her Shirley?'

'I don't know – I only just met her today. That's her name, is it?'

The child nodded. Then she said, 'May I get up and go along the passage?'

'Surely,' said Miss Teasdale quickly. 'Wait – you'd better put something on.' She looked around a little helplessly.

'It's hanging up behind the door,' the child said. Miss Teasdale looked and found a very small, worn dressing-gown; Elspeth slipped it on, and put her feet in bedroom slippers, and went off. The actress moved to the bed, and smoothed out the bedclothes and pulled out the hot-water bottles, which were cold, and then Elspeth was back again and climbing into bed.

The actress watched the little active figure in pyjamas getting into bed, watched with her hands full of hot-water bottles and with her heart full of regret. She said, 'How do you feel now?'

The child said, 'My head aches when I move about.'

'Sure, it will do after giving it a bump like that. Does it hurt when you stay still?'

'Not till I think of it. It hurts then.'

Miss Teasdale laughed. 'I'll get these bottles filled.'

'I don't want them, please. They're too hot.'

'Okay. Mrs Scott left arrowroot upon the stove for you. Think you could take a cup of that?'

'No, thank you.'

The actress said, 'Come on, honey, try a little bit. It'll do you good.'

Elspeth said, 'It can't do me any good if I sick it all up.'

'You won't.'

'I did last time.'

'You won't this time.'

She went into the kitchen and found a cup and saucer and a tin of biscuits, and came back to the bedroom with the arrowroot and crackers on a little tray. The child obediently ate the food and said, 'Do you live in America?'

'Most of the time,' the actress said.

'My daddy's in America – not really in America. He's in Canada. He went on Sunday.'

'I know it. I travelled over with him – that's how I met him. Then I had to come back again directly, and he asked me if I'd come and see how you were getting on.'

Elspeth accepted this without much interest. 'When's he coming home?'

'Quite soon now, I think. Maybe this week.'

'He's been away an awfully long time.'

'Only since Sunday, honey. This is Tuesday.'

'It seems an awfully long time,' the child said.

There was a jigsaw puzzle started upon my drawing-board. 'Say,' said the actress, 'that's an elegant picture. Going to be Southampton Docks, isn't it, with all the liners?' She fetched the board, and they began doing it together.

When I got home that night at about half-past six I found Shirley just waking up upon the sofa; she sat up sleepily as I came in and asked what time it was. We went together to the bedroom. Miss Teasdale got up as we came in. She had been reading to Elspeth; the bed was littered with books from our bookcase: *The Oxford Book of English Verse*, *Puck of Pook's Hill*, and *The Earthly Paradise*. Elspeth had not been sick again, and they had had a cup of tea together and some bread and butter. 'We finished the puzzle,' said the actress. 'We've been reading for a while.'

Elspeth said to Shirley, 'She does read well, Mrs Scott. She reads much better than Miss Lansdowne or anybody at school. You sort of actually see things happening when she's reading out loud.'

Miss Teasdale laughed, a little self-consciously, which was odd in so sophisticated a woman. 'I guess I've had some practice,' she said quietly.

'She says she'll teach me to read like that when I get bigger,' Elspeth said.

'Sure I will, honey.' She gathered up the books. 'You've

148

got a nice selection of good books,' she said. 'This author, William Morris — I've never met his work before. Elspeth wanted me to read her some of this.'

Shirley took over to give Elspeth a bath and make her ready for bed; I took Miss Teasdale into the sitting-room and mixed her a drink. 'It's been terribly kind of you to come and help us out like this,' I said, lighting her cigarette. 'Shirley slept five hours this afternoon.'

She nodded. 'I might say it's kind of you folks to look after Mr Honey's little girl,' she said. 'As I see it, you hadn't any call to do so.'

I laughed. 'Well, it was I who sent her father off.'

She nodded. 'Surely.' And then she said, 'I don't know if you'll believe me if I say it's been a real pleasure to me, sitting here this afternoon, playing and reading with Elspeth.'

She hesitated. 'Some women have a lot to do with children, and some don't,' she said. 'I'm one of the ones who don't.'

I nodded. It seemed difficult to pursue that subject with this exotic woman. 'We fixed up about Mr Honey coming back from Gander,' I said. 'An RAF Lincoln is going to pick him up one day this week and bring him over.'

She nodded. 'And what happens after that?'

I laughed. 'Then we're going to have the hell of a row.'

'Say, not over what he did at Gander, pulling up the wheels?'

'Oh, not with him,' I said. 'We're on his side — I think he did quite right. The trouble is we haven't any evidence to prove it.'

I told her briefly what the row was all about, and mentioned that I should be going out to Labrador myself. Then I asked her plans, and persuaded her to stay and have supper with us. 'It'll probably only be the same bit of cold meat you had for lunch,' I said. 'We might cook up a Welsh rarebit or something, afterwards.' She called her office in Wardour Street and ordered the car for nine o'clock to take her back to Claridge's. Summoning the company's car forty miles out into the country to pick her up at that time of night seemed the most natural thing in the world to her.

She was interested in Honey, and kept leading the conversation round to him. She wanted to know what place he held in the organisation of the RAE, what we thought about him in the office. I had some difficulty in answering that one.

'He's an inside man,' I said, using the words that the Director had used about him to me. 'He's deeply interested in research and he doesn't concern himself very much with user problems. Opinions vary about him; lots of people think he's crackers.'

'Do you?' she asked.

I laughed. 'No – I think he's very good, within his own sphere. But I shan't send him out upon a job again. From now on he stays in the laboratory, where he belongs.'

'I don't think that's fair,' she said. 'He wants to get around and meet more people.'

I smiled at her. 'He can do that at the week-ends. I don't want any more Reindeers broken up.' That seemed badly phrased, and I regretted it as soon as the words were out of my mouth. 'I mean, a man who was more interested in operations would have found some other means of stopping that thing flying on.'

'I don't know about that,' she objected. 'The little man was in a mighty tough spot. Nobody believed him.'

'That's what I mean,' I said. 'He's an inside man. If he'd been an athletic type six foot two in height and weighing fourteen stone, with a red face and a fist like a ham, they'd have believed him all right, and he wouldn't have had to crash the aeroplane.'

'Maybe,' she said thoughtfully.

'He hated going, anyway,' I said. 'I had to force him, and now I'm sorry that I did. I thought he was the best man to send. He's only really happy on his own research.'

Later on, while we were eating the cold meat and salad, she said, 'Have you got a lot of scientists like Mr Honey in your organisation, Doctor?'

'Hundreds,' I said. 'I'm one of them. We're all bats in our own way.'

She said, 'He knows an awful lot about a lot of things. I never mixed with scientists before. He was telling me about the end of the world coming, all from the Great Pyramid. Say, do you believe in that?'

'No,' I said, 'I don't. But then I didn't really believe him first of all when he said the Reindeer tail was going bad on us. Now I think I do.' I turned to her. 'There's no doubt that he's got a very penetrating mind,' I said. 'He's full of scientific curiosity. We'd have done better in the war if we'd paid some attention to his crazy notions.' I was thinking of the rockets.

'I think he's a great little man,' she said quietly. 'With a brain like that and at the same time so simple and so kind.'

Her car came for her at nine o'clock. She said to Shirley almost diffidently, 'Mrs Scott, do you think I might come down tomorrow and sit with Elspeth? I certainly would like to do that.'

Shirley said, 'Oh please, don't bother. It's been terribly nice of you to help us out today, but we'll be all right now. I think she'll sleep tonight.'

The actress said, 'It wouldn't be a trouble. I'd be glad to do it. I did enjoy being with her this afternoon.'

Shirley said doubtfully, 'Would you really like to? Haven't you got more important things to do?'

Miss Teasdale shook her head. 'I've got nothing fixed. I've got to be back on the West Coast in ten days from now, but up till then I'm free. I certainly would like to spend another day with her.'

Shirley laughed. 'I won't say no to that. She's got to stay in bed a week, and keeping her amused is going to be a job.'

'Okay,' said the actress. 'I'll be with you in the morning, around eleven o'clock.'

We stood and watched the car move off. Elspeth was still occupying our only bed, so it was necessary for me to go and sleep in Honey's house again, while Shirley slept on the sofa. 'I rather like the sofa,' she said. 'I'll be all right there if Elspeth doesn't keep on being sick all night again.'

We went back into the house to get my bag with my night things in it. Shirley walked round to the little villa in Copse Road with me; it was only ten minutes away and she felt that she could leave Elspeth for that time. 'I was round there this morning,' she said as we went. 'Isn't it simply foul?'

I hadn't noticed anything much wrong with it. 'It hasn't got much furniture in the sitting-room,' I said.

'I don't mean that. Didn't you see the kitchen floor? It's absolutely filthy; and the scullery's disgusting. It can't have been properly washed out for years.'

We reached the house, and she took me and showed me all the horrors. They didn't seem very bad to me, but then I am a man. Shirley said, 'We can't send Elspeth back here with the place like this – it isn't healthy.' She thought for a minute. 'I'll come round tomorrow and have a go at it.'

'You don't have to do that,' I said. 'It's not our house and we've not made it dirty.'

'We can't leave it like this,' she said firmly. 'If Miss Teasdale turns up, I'll come round here tomorrow.'

'What about the school?'

'I've only got one period tomorrow.'

'I shouldn't bank upon Miss Teasdale,' I said. 'You'll probably get a phone call saying she can't make it.'

Shirley said, 'I think she'll come. Do you know—' She stopped.

'What?'

'Oh – nothing. It was just a stupid idea.'

'What's that?'

She hesitated. 'It would be funny if there was something between her and Mr Honey, wouldn't it?'

I stared at her. 'There couldn't be ...'

'I suppose there couldn't. But one or two things she said made me kind of wonder.'

She went away, and I got in a couple of hours upon the 'Aircraft Flying at High Mach Numbers' before I got too sleepy.

Next morning, in the office, the Director sent for me. 'I have arranged a meeting for eleven o'clock tomorrow morning,' he said, 'at the Ministry. It's going to be quite a big meeting, with representatives of CATO and the Company, and MCA, as well as the M. of S. and ourselves. You'll bring up everything we're likely to require?'

'Very good, sir. You'll be coming up yourself?'

'Oh, I think so. I think we shall need all the weight that we can muster, Scott.'

'What about Honey, sir?' I asked. 'Will he be back?'

'I rather doubt it. I think we may have to get along without him. I only know that the Lincoln is picking him up at Gander one day this week.'

'Pity,' I said. 'It would have been better if we could have had him there.'

He nodded. 'Carnegie wanted to see Sir Phillip Dolbear's letter about Honey's work. I sent him a copy of that yesterday.'

I made a grimace. It was impossible to hide up evidence like that, but it wasn't going to make it any easier for us to persuade them that the Reindeer tail was dangerous.

'They're getting back the pilot of the Reindeer, Captain Samuelson, in time for the meeting, I understand. We should get an informed account from him upon exactly what took place.'

'I don't like that,' I said. 'We're going to get the Organisation's account of what happened, but not our own. If we're going to have the pilot of the aircraft, we should have Honey too.'

He shrugged his shoulders. 'We've got to work on the assumption we shall get a fair account. You wouldn't suggest bringing in Miss Monica Teasdale, I suppose?'

I grinned. 'I don't think she could add much to our meeting, except glamour.'

He said grimly. 'Well, we may need light relief before this thing blows over.' He paused. 'I forgot to say, the Treasury are sending somebody, to hold a watching brief for the expenditures involved.'

I left him, and went down to the old balloon shed to see how the Reindeer tail on test was getting on. It was now running day and night; the graphs showed nothing yet that we could cite as any evidence of trouble. I had hoped that something would have turned up in the readings that I could take with me to the meeting as an evidence of abnormality, as a warning. There was nothing of that sort at all.

'I don't think there will be, sir,' young Simmons said. 'Mr Honey was convinced that it would go on like this right up to the end.'

While I was down there, Miss Learoyd rang through. 'There's a lady waiting in the Reception to see you,' she said. 'A Miss Corder.'

I said, 'Do you know who she is?'

'She's got a letter to give you from Mr Honey, sir.'

I blinked; another woman from Honey. 'All right,' I said. 'Have her shown up and ask her to wait. I'll be up in a few minutes.'

When I got up to my office there was a tall, dark girl sitting on an upright chair against the wall, waiting for me. She was dressed quietly in a dark blue coat and skirt; she wore a very simple hat. She was quite young, very attractive, and with the most beautiful features and colouring.

'I'm sorry to have kept you waiting,' I said. 'It's Miss

Corser, is it?'

She had risen to her feet as I entered. 'Corder,' she said. 'I have a letter for you, sir, from Mr Honey.' She opened her bag and gave it to me. 'He said that it was very urgent, so I thought it would be better if I brought it down by hand.'

'Oh – thank you,' I said. 'When did he give you this?'

'Last night, sir,' she said, 'at about ten o'clock – just before I left Gander.' She explained, 'I was one of the stewardesses on the Reindeer that got damaged at Gander, the one that Mr Honey crossed in. Most of the crew are staying at Gander with the aircraft, but we stewards were recalled to London. I suppose they'll put me in another aircraft; there's no point in keeping us with the machine till it's repaired. So as I was to come back last night, Mr Honey asked me if I would bring this letter with me and let you have it immediately I landed. I thought I'd better bring it down at once.'

'You landed this morning?'

'Yes, sir.'

She stood silent, holding her bag in her hands before her while I opened and read the letter.

It was not a very long one. He said that I must know all the facts by that time from Miss Teasdale. He had been thinking it all over, and while he did not see what else he could have done, he realised that his action must have let down the reputation of the RAE. He said that for some time past he had felt that perhaps he was out of place in the department, and it might well be that this was the time when he should make a break and find some other employment. He did not want to embarrass me in any way, but he would like me to consider that letter as his resignation.

I said quietly, 'Oh, damn . . .' and read it through again, biting my lip. It was another complication in this business; if Honey resigned, how could I maintain my attitude of taking a firm line by showing confidence in his judgment? He would have to be persuaded to withdraw his resignation and fight this thing through with me, and now he was in Gander, inaccessible. I raised my eyes, and the dark stewardess was staring at me in distress.

I said, 'Well . . . thank you for bringing me this, Miss Corder. I'll have to think it over.' I paused, and then said, 'Do you know what's in it?'

'I think so – more or less.' She stared at me appealingly.

'It's his resignation, isn't it?'

I nodded. 'That's right. I didn't want him to resign.'

'You didn't want him to? He thought you'd all be so angry with him.'

I cursed the comedy of misunderstandings. 'I'm not angry with him,' I replied. 'I wish he hadn't had to stop it flying in that way, but if that was the only way to ground it, then I think he did quite right. I'm backing him up all I can. Probably lose my own job over this before we're through.'

'Oh,' she said, relieved. 'I wish he'd known that.'

I chucked the letter on to my desk. 'You'll have a cup of tea?' She protested, but I opened the door and told Miss Learoyd to see if she could raise two cups of tea, and coming back I made the stewardess sit down beside my desk. I offered her a cigarette, which she refused. 'Tell me,' I said, 'how is Honey, in himself? Is he worrying about this very much?'

'He is, rather,' she said. 'You see, he hasn't anything to do, and the crew said some horrid things to him after it happened. Not Captain Samuelson, but some of the others.' I sat watching her as she talked, wondering who did the picking of the stewardesses and where they found such very charming girls. 'I thought a little exercise might take his mind off it, sir, so I got him to take me for a long walk yesterday, and I think that helped. He's very fond of hiking.'

I smiled. 'You've been looking after him, have you?'

'He was the only passenger I had left,' she replied. 'All the others went on, the same day.'

I nodded. 'Tell me just what happened.'

7

WHEN THE REINDEER settled down upon the tarmac she went slowly; the men standing in the flight deck staggered and reached for something to hang on to, but they were not thrown down. They stood petrified for an instant after the fuselage reached the ground, listening aghast to the rending and crashing noise of crumpling propeller blades and duralumin panels as the weight came on to yielding parts of the structure; then there was silence, and they came to life again.

Samuelson was the first to speak. He said dully, 'Well, that's the bloody limit.' And then he turned to Symes, the inspector. 'Come outside, Mr Symes.'

He turned away without a word to Mr Honey, who got up from the control pedestal that he had been embracing, his face scarlet and with tears running down his cheeks. The inspector looked him up and down, snorted, and followed the captain down into the saloon and so to the ground, to view the damage from outside.

In the control deck Dobson turned to Honey. 'You bloody little squirt,' he said. 'Pleased with what you've done?'

Mr Honey made a helpless gesture with his hands, but said nothing. Behind them the note of the auxiliary motor dropped and died; the engineer had switched it off, in case of fire.

Dobson said again, 'Pleased with what you've done?'

Honey raised his head. 'It was the only thing to do. You wouldn't believe me. If you'd gone on everybody might have been killed.'

Cousins, the engineer, pressed forward passionately. He loved his aircraft. He had worked upon it for three months before it flew; since then he had lived in it for much of the time, and he had tended it lovingly; he existed for nothing else. 'Nonsense,' he said passionately. 'There was nothing wrong with that tail, and you know it. Who the hell are you, anyway? Just a bloody penpusher and slide-rule merchant. What the hell do you know about aircraft?'

Dobson said, 'That's right. Have you ever flown anything? Ever piloted anything yourself? Come on, speak up.'

'No,' said Honey helplessly, 'I've never been a pilot.'

'What the hell do you know about aeroplanes, then, if you've never had to do with them? You say you come from Farnborough. God, I've heard some tales about that place, but this beats everything.'

Cousins laughed bitterly. 'That's what they do there, come around and smash things up. He'll get an OBE for this, you see.' He turned to Honey passionately. 'Get out of here, you dirty little swine, before I sock you one.'

Honey turned and went down into the saloon without a word. From the ground Samuelson called up to Dobson to bring down a signal pad. The two pilots stood in front of the wrecked Reindeer drafting a quick signal to their Flight Control in London; then Dobson went hurriedly with it to the control tower, passing Miss Corder on the way.

Mr Honey stood around upon the tarmac for an hour, with nobody paying any attention to him. There was a bitter north-east wind and he grew colder and colder; presently he got back into the fuselage and sat down in his seat, miserable and chilled. Miss Corder, coming to the aircraft presently to clean up and remove the unused food, observed him sitting in the unlit cabin half-way down the aisle.

She went up to him, 'I should go into the lounge, sir,' she said. 'In the restaurant building. All the other passengers are there.'

He said dolefully, 'I don't think they'd be very pleased to see me.'

She said, 'Oh . . . But have you had any breakfast?'

He shook his head. 'I don't want any.'

'But you must have some breakfast!' She thought for a moment. 'I know,' she said. 'There's a little private office you can use. Come with me.'

He followed her obediently out of the aircraft and across the tarmac and into the main building by a side door. She took him to a little room marked on the door PASSPORTS AND IMMIGRATION. It was rather a bare room with a deal table, ink-stained, and a few hard chairs, but it was warm and it was private. She said, 'Stay here and make yourself comfortable, Mr Honey. I'll bring you some breakfast.'

She came back presently with a tray of eggs and bacon and coffee and toast and marmalade, and set it down before him on the table. 'There,' she said. 'Get that in you and you'll feel better.'

He said warmly, 'It's terribly kind of you to look after me like this, especially when I've made such a lot of trouble.'

She smiled at him. 'You've not made any trouble for me,' she said.

'What about the other passengers? What's going to happen to them?'

'We've had a signal that a Hermes is coming up to fetch them,' she said. 'It's arriving about two o'clock.' She hesitated, and then said, 'Will you be going on with them, sir?'

'I don't know. I should like to have a talk with Captain

Samuelson as soon as he can spare the time.'

She nodded. 'I'll tell him. Now, eat your breakfast. I'll be along for the tray presently.'

Mr Honey was hungry, and made quite a substantial meal. When it was over he lit a cigarette, feeling more at ease. Samuelson, coming in to see him, found him sitting in a chair beside the radiator.

'Morning, Mr Honey,' he said. 'You wanted to see me?'

Honey got up from his chair. 'I wanted to apologise for all the trouble that I've caused you,' he said simply. 'Not for the Reindeer – that had to be grounded anyway. But I'm sorry about the work I've had to put on you and for the inconvenience to all the other passengers.'

The pilot laughed shortly. 'Don't bother about me. If I wasn't doing this I'd be doing something else.'

Mr Honey asked, 'Is the aircraft very much damaged?'

'I don't know. Until we raise her up we can't make a proper inspection, and that won't be for some time. There's no equipment here to lift an aircraft of this size. We've got no air bags. They'll have to be shipped from England. The whole job may take months.'

The scientist said nothing.

The captain said, 'I've had to send a full report about it all to Headquarters, Mr Honey. The other passengers are going on to Montreal this afternoon, but I'm rather doubtful if CATO will carry you – after this. I think you may have to do down to St John's and go on by boat.'

Mr Honey blinked at him. 'Oh . . .'

'Well, look at it from their point of view. They don't have to carry you if they're afraid of you damaging their equipment.'

'I don't make a habit of doing this,' said Honey unhappily. 'I don't do it every time.'

'No. Well, it will all have to be sorted out in London. I expect we'll get some signals as the day goes on.'

'I don't know what the RAE will want me to do,' said Mr Honey, 'after this. They may cable me and tell me to come home and not go on to Labrador.'

'I see . . .' The pilot glanced at him. 'You were going out to reopen an inquiry on Bill Ward's crash?'

'Er – the Reindeer that fell in Labrador.'

'That's right. The one that is supposed to have flown into

158

the hill. Bill Ward's crash.'

'That's the machine. I was to inspect the spar fractures in the tailplane and bring samples back for metallurgical examination.'

'You think the tail came off that aircraft in the air, don't you?'

'It might have done,' said Mr Honey. 'It had flown nearly 1,400 hours, which comes in very close accord with the estimated time to failure.'

The pilot stared out of the window. 'Bill Ward never flew into a hill,' he said. 'He couldn't have done. I knew that part of the accident report was utter nonsense from the first.'

Mr Honey blinked at him. 'You think that something else happened? Something like a tailplane failure?'

The pilot said, 'I just don't know, and it's not for me to guess. But strictly between you and me, Mr Honey, I'm not sorry personally that you've taken a strong line, in spite of all the trouble that it's going to mean for both of us. If I'd been able to, I'd have taken that machine on to Montreal. But as things are, I can't say that I'm sorry. I don't aim to be the bravest pilot in the world. Just the oldest.'

He went away, and crossing the waiting-room he had to run the gauntlet of the passengers. He answered a number of questions about transport on to Montreal; then came the film actress, Miss Teasdale.

She said, 'Say, Captain, I don't see Mr Honey anywhere around. Is he here some place?'

He told her where she could find him, and presently she tapped at Mr Honey's door. He called out, 'Er – come in,' and she opened the door and stood there looking at him quizzically.

'Well,' she said, 'you certainly have got the strength of your convictions, haven't you?'

He smiled weakly. 'You've got to do what you can. Won't you come in and sit down? I'm afraid it's not very clean in here.'

She seated herself on a hard chair on the other side of the table, and lit a cigarette with a gold lighter. 'How do you think your people back at Farnborough will react now?' she asked.

Honey said, 'I don't know and I don't much care. You've

got to do the best you can,' he repeated a little desperately. 'You've got to do what you think is the right thing to do.'

She nodded. He was terribly like what Eddie Stillson had been, thirty years ago – always worrying about doing the right thing. She asked, 'This Dr Scott that you were speaking of. He's the boss, isn't he? How will he take it?'

Honey said, 'I think he'll be all right. He's quite a young man, much younger than I am. I think he'll see it was the only thing to do. But he's not the head of the Establishment by any means – and then there's the Ministry over the whole lot of us. I'm afraid there'll be a great deal of trouble.'

She laughed. 'I'll say there'll be some trouble. You should hear the second pilot talking, Mr Dobson. He takes it kind of personally.' She paused. 'What do you plan to do now, Mr Honey? Will you go on to Labrador?'

He shook his head. 'I can't make up my mind. But from what the captain said I can't go anywhere – by air, that is. He says the company won't take me.'

She nodded. There had been some very frank talk in the waiting-room about the passenger who had become mentally deranged by the excitement of the flight. 'It's just a lot of hooey,' she said. 'But if they won't carry you by air you can't make them, though your office might be able to.'

'I don't know what to do,' he said irresolutely. 'If I write a letter it would take about three days to get to Farnborough. I suppose I ought to try and send a cable somehow, and ask what I'm to do.'

'What do you want to do, yourself?' she asked. 'Go on to Ottawa or go back to Farnborough?'

He replied, 'Oh, I'd like to go back. I didn't want to come away at all. You see, there's nobody looking after Elspeth except Mrs Higgs, and she isn't very reliable. I'd much rather go back to Farnborough. After all, the basic work is more important than this sort of thing.'

They talked about his movements for some time. She learned that he had little interest in his mission to Canada; the travelling, the change of scene, did not excite him. He regarded it as so much time wasted from the progress of his real work, as a distraction which he had been forced by discipline to submit to. She found him restless and unhappy, uncertain whether he could exploit the damage to the Reindeer as an excuse to give up his mission in Canada and to return to the work he loved, and to his home.

'I don't know what to do,' he said. 'I can't make up my mind. And one can't put it all into a cable, either.'

They sat talking of his difficulties for some time. For many years the actress had been out of touch with the hard realities of life. She had not been short of money for thirty years and she would never be again. All her working life had been spent in the facile world of honky-tonk, of synthetic emotion and of phoney glamour. Now she was getting a glimpse into a new world, a world of hard, stark facts, a world in which things had to be exactly right or people would be killed. There was no place for glamour or emotion in a world that had to say if the Reindeer tail was going to break or not. She was beginning to perceive that little insignificant men like Mr Honey were the brains behind that world, just as lame Eddie Stillson had been the coming brain of the Century Insurance office. The perception brought out everything that was still good in her; nineteen-year-old Myra Tuppen came to life again, suppressing Monica Teasdale. As she sat talking to Mr Honey the desire to help him grew; she felt that she could play a small part in a bigger production than any she had starred in. And help she could; in travelling Monica Teasdale had unquestioned priority.

She said, 'Say, Mr Honey, how would it be if I went back to England and took a letter to your Dr Scott? It would get to him first thing tomorrow morning, that way. I'd be real pleased to go, if it would help any.'

He was staggered at the suggestion. Unused to travelling himself, it seemed extraordinary to him. 'You mean, you'd fly back to England? But you're going on to Montreal, aren't you?'

She shrugged her shoulders. 'I'm not dated up. I've got to be in Hollywood on the twenty-seventh, but that's eleven days from now. I was reckoning I'd stop off in Indianapolis for a few days before flying on home, but I'd just as soon stop over those few days at Claridge's in London. I kind of like London, for all it's such a dirty town.'

He blinked at her. 'But it would be so expensive for you to go back.'

She said simply, 'I wouldn't pay. All my travelling goes on to the expense account. Honestly, Mr Honey, I'd be real glad to do that if it would help.'

He was bewildered by this woman, whom with his dead wife he had adored upon the movies; bewildered by her hard competence, by her sophistication, by her carefully tended beauty and her luxurious clothes, by the incongruous kindliness and small-town warmth of her consideration. He had never met anyone in the least like her before, never had dealings with anybody from her world. He said uncertainly, 'Well, that would be very helpful, certainly, Miss Teasdale. But it seems an awful lot to ask you to do.'

She said, 'I'm interested in this thing, Mr Honey, and I'd like to see it through. And if I can help any by going back instead of stopping in the Middle West a week, I'd like to do it. After all, it is kind of important, this, and Indiana's no novelty to me.'

He said, 'But can you get a passage back today?'

Her lips tightened. 'I can try.'

She left him to think out a letter to me that she could take with her, and found Dobson, and smiled dazzlingly at him so that he took her meekly to the Control, where she was very charming and just terribly sorry to be such a nuisance, but could she get a call down to New York? She delighted the Control Officer for four hours with her conscious charm, and left his office in the end with her return passage to London arranged and little lines of strained fatigue around her lovely eyes. Time was, she thought a little bitterly, when she could do that sort of thing just naturally. With the last remnants of her energy she charmed Dobson into arranging a bedroom for her use, and went and pulled the shade down and lay down upon the bed to rest.

Marjorie Corder was busy all the morning cleaning up the galley and the passengers' quarters of the wrecked Reindeer and in arranging lunch for the stranded passengers. She found time to visit Mr Honey with a cup of coffee in the middle of the morning, and to bring him a selection of magazines. She arrived just after Samuelson had visited him again, to break the news to him that CATO had refused to carry him any farther in their aircraft. She found him worried and distressed; he told her all about it.

'I don't know what to do,' he said. 'I suppose I'll have to try and get away from here by train. But now they say there isn't a train till Thursday.'

'Drink your coffee while it's hot,' she suggested. 'It'll all

162

come out all right, you see.'

He sipped it obediently. 'What are you doing?' he inquired. 'Are you going on with the passengers to Montreal?'

She shook her head. 'We shall stay here till we get some orders. The aircrew always stay with their own machine. The Hermes that's coming up will have its own steward.' She smiled. 'So after all the rest have gone on, I shall only have you to look after.'

He said diffidently, 'I'm terribly sorry to make so much trouble.'

She stood looking down upon him kindly. 'Last night you told me where to go if anything happened,' she said, 'where it would be safe. I don't suppose I'd have gone, but it was nice of you to tell me. I'm glad to be able to do something in return. It's my job to see that you're made comfortable, of course, but I'd want to do that anyway, for what you tried to do for me.'

He said awkwardly, 'I didn't do anything.'

She said, 'You'd rather have your lunch in here, sir, wouldn't you? You don't want to mix with the other passengers?'

He said, 'Er – if it's not an awful lot of trouble.'

'Of course it's not,' she said. 'I'll bring it you about one o'clock. There's cold meat or hot Irish stew, and I saw some cold salmon in the larder, but there's not enough of that to go round so I think the staff are having it. Would you like a salmon mayonnaise?'

He said, 'I'd love that, if it's going.' And he gave her one of his shy, warming smiles.

She nodded. 'There's treacle tart afterwards or semolina pudding.'

'Treacle tart, please.'

She nodded. 'And coffee?'

'Please.'

'Bottle of beer?'

'Well – if there is one – yes, that would be very nice.'

She nodded. 'Have you got enough to smoke?'

'Well – I would like another packet of cigarettes. Player's, if they've got them.'

'I'll get you those at once.'

She brought his cigarettes and a box of matches, and a few minutes later she took an easy chair from the lounge and carried it along the passage and put it in the office for him. Mr Honey sat reading the *Cosmopolitan* and smoking his cigarettes in some comfort, warmed by the solicitude of the girl. He felt in better spirits now, ready to face whatever might be coming to him.

The Hermes from Quebec came in and landed before lunch; Mr Honey stood at his window and watched it taxi in. Miss Corder brought him his tray of lunch, with the salmon and the bottle of beer. 'All the other passengers are having their lunch now,' she said. 'They're going on in the Hermes as soon as it's refuelled. All except Miss Teasdale, who's decided that she wants to go back to England.'

He said, 'She's very kindly offered to take a note back to Dr Scott for me. It seems an awful imposition, but she offered to, and it really is a great help.'

The girl said, 'I should think she's very nice, when you get to know her.'

'I think she is,' said Honey. 'Of course, one thinks one knows her from seeing her films, but really, she's quite a different person altogether.' He laughed. 'It's a bit confusing.'

Miss Corder said, 'I think her films are lovely. I never miss one if I can help it.'

She went out, and Mr Honey ate his lunch, and presently stood at his window watching the Hermes load up with its passengers and taxi out towards the runway's end, watched it as it left the ground and slid off into the distance. He turned again to the *Cosmopolitan*; presently the stewardess came back to take his tray.

'You don't have to use this office any longer, sir, unless you want to,' she said. 'There's nobody here now except the crew and Miss Teasdale.'

He said, 'Well – I'll sit in the lounge. Where is Miss Teasdale?'

'I think she's lying down, sir. Shall I bring your coffee to the lounge?'

'Oh – yes, please do.'

He stayed in the lounge all afternoon. Three or four aircraft landed to refuel, and there was a stream of passengers from them in and out, stretching their legs and gossiping together over cups of coffee or short drinks. Mr Honey sat insignificant in a corner, unhappy. Now that the first excitement had passed, he was miserably anxious about his own

164

position; clearly there was going to be a most appalling row about the Reindeer, and he was quite unused to rows and hated them. Personal unpleasantness always upset his work; he could not think clearly if his mind was full of hard things that had been said about him, and he liked thinking clearly. Rows frightened him; he would go to considerable lengths to avoid them. For the first time in years the thought of resigning his position at the RAE entered his mind.

If things got too nasty, he could always do that. He could resign and not go there any more. True, it would be a terrible wrench to part from the work he loved; true, he would have to find another job. But he was not unknown in the intimate, unpublicised, middle world of science; he was on blinking and smiling terms with the heads of several other research departments. Perhaps a little niche would open out for him at the National Physical Laboratory or the Admiralty Research Laboratory. He knew people at both places, and he could be happy there, though not so happy as he now felt he had been while dealing with fatigue in light alloy structures.

By tea-time he was in a state of deep dejection. When Marjorie Corder brought him his tea, unasked, she noticed his preoccupation. 'Haven't you been out?' she asked. 'Have you been sitting here all the time?'

He nodded. 'I've had a lot to think about.'

'It's nice outside,' she said. 'There's a cold wind, but if you wrap up well it's rather lovely.'

He was not listening to her words; he only heard her sympathy. 'I wish they'd cable and say what I'm to do,' he muttered. 'I'm afraid I shall have to resign.'

'Resign your job?' she said. She looked down at him with deep compassion; he was such an unhappy little man and yet so terribly clever. 'You mustn't think of that. They'll understand, back at your office.'

'I think I'll have to,' he said miserably. 'I think it's the only thing to do.'

She said gently, 'Look, I got you some buttered toast, and there's anchovy paste here and jam. I got you strawberry jam, but would you rather have apricot? There's apricot if you'd rather have that.'

He roused, and smiled at her. 'No – I like strawberry, thank you.'

165

She poured out his tea for him. 'Is that how you like it? I brought you a piece of cherry cake and a piece of madeira, but there's more of either if you want it.'

'Oh, thank you very much, but I don't think I shall want any more. I don't think I shall get through all of this.'

'Well, let's see you try.'

She went away and had her own tea in the staff room, but in her turn she was preoccupied. She recognised in Mr Honey a man of moods, capable of deep depression; all geniuses, she had read, were men like that. She was not a very talented girl herself, nor very highly educated; she had had to go to work too early. She was firmly convinced that Mr Honey was a genius and that he was right about the Reindeer tail. She could not help him in the matter of the Reindeer directly, but she might be able to do something to ease the burdens on his mind. It shocked her that he should be talking of resigning from the RAE. She felt dimly that if that were to happen her country would have suffered an irreparable loss, because he was the cleverest man that she had ever met. He had seen through into her secret places at one glance, and had known that she would be good with children.

When she went to take his tray, she asked, 'Do you play chess, Mr Honey?'

He looked up in surprise. 'Chess? I haven't played for years. My – my wife and I used to play in the evenings, sometimes. It's a very good game.'

'I can play a little,' she said. 'I'm not very good. Would you like a game or would you rather read?'

He roused. 'No – I'd like a game of chess. Are you sure that you can spare the time, though?'

'I've only got two passengers left now,' she said, 'you and Miss Teasdale, and she's still lying down. I'll bring the things along.' She took his tray.

She played three games with him, and beat him once; she suspected that he had contrived to be mated by her, and she liked him for it. In the course of the two and a half hours she had learned a good deal about Elspeth. 'What do you do about her clothes, Mr Honey?' she had asked curiously. 'Who buys those for you?'

He said, 'Oh, whenever she needs anything I take her to a shop in Farnham. The woman that keeps it is really very helpful, and I buy what she says.'

She stared at him. 'But do you just take what's in the one shop?'

He replied, 'Well, yes, I do. I suppose one ought to go to other shops sometimes, but it's so much easier to do it that way.' He hesitated. 'I've sometimes thought that Elspeth isn't dressed quite like the other girls at school,' he admitted. 'I suppose I ought to learn a bit more about what schoolgirls wear. Do you think if I took in *Vogue*, or some paper like that, it would help?'

She was at a loss. 'I don't think that's quite the right sort of paper,' she said. 'I'll think of something and let you know, if you like.'

'I wish you would,' he said. 'She's getting so big now that I think I ought to do something.' He paused, and then he said, 'Mrs Higgs gives me a lot of advice, but I don't know that Elspeth isn't outgrowing that.'

'Who's Mrs Higgs?'

'She's the charwoman. She's got a lot of children of her own, and she's really been very helpful.'

'Oh. . . .'

Later on she asked him, 'What do you do at the weekends?'

He said, 'Well, we don't do very much. Cleaning the house up takes us a lot of time, of course, and then there's the garden to be done and cooking. It just seems to go.' He turned to her. 'There never seems to be time for anything. When – when Mary was there we always had time to do things on a Sunday – photography or hiking in the summer. But now there just doesn't seem to be time.'

She nodded. 'Are you fond of hiking?'

'We used to do a lot,' he said.

'Staying in Youth Hostels?' she inquired, her eyes gleaming.

'Sometimes. Have you done that?' He was interested.

She nodded. 'I had a lovely holiday in the Lake District once,' she said thoughtfully. 'Four of us, staying in Youth Hostels every night, for a fortnight. It *was* fun.' She turned to him. 'That was when I was engaged,' she said simply.

'Oh . . ' He glanced at her hand, but there was no ring. She saw his glance. 'That was a long time ago,' she said. 'He was in Bomber Command and got shot down over Dortmund. I thought the end of the world had come. But I suppose it hadn't.'

'My dear,' said Mr Honey, 'I'm so very sorry.'

She roused herself. 'Your move,' she said.

She went away after the third game to assist in serving dinner, and presently Miss Teasdale appeared, looking fresh and radiant and about eighteen years old. She said, 'Say, Mr Honey, I just heard my plane's coming in around nine o'clock, so we'll have time for dinner before I go.' She ordered an Old-fashioned for herself and persuaded him to join her; beer was his normal drink and he took the novelty gingerly, and under the influence he pulled out his wallet and showed her a photograph of Elspeth.

'My,' said the actress, 'doesn't she look cute?'

He agreed. 'I think she's more intelligent than children of her age usually are,' he said. 'She's only twelve, but she's got a very good grasp of crystallography.'

She stared at him. 'What's that?'

He smiled. 'Everything,' he said. 'All matter is built up of the associations that result in crystals, like miniature universes. It's an extraordinary thing that schools don't teach more about it.' He turned to her. 'Schools only teach results,' he said. 'All the basic knowledge that Elspeth has, she seems to have got from me.'

'I'd believe that,' she replied. 'Say, does she get around at all – parties with boy friends and that sort of thing?'

'Who – Elspeth? She's only just a child.' He was amazed. 'She's only twelve years old.'

Miss Teasdale laughed. 'From what you say about her crystal – crystall – what you said, she sounds to be about forty. Still, maybe English children don't get around so early as they do at home. Has she got a flapjack?'

'What's that?'

She stared at him. 'For powder.' She rummaged in her bag. 'Like this.'

He was at a loss. 'No,' he said weakly. 'Ought she to have one?'

She laughed. 'It's not obligatory. I guess she ought to have it when she wants it.'

'I really don't think she's old enough for that,' he said. 'I don't think any of the other children at her school have those.'

168

'Maybe not.' And then she said, 'Tell me about this Dr Scott that I'm to go and see. And how do I get to this place you work at, Farnborough?'

He told her, and wrote a short letter for her to give to me, and presently they dined together. Then her plane landed to refuel and the lounge was filled with passengers stretching their legs after the flight up from New York. In the bustle he said good-bye to her as her luggage was carried out. 'I'll tell him just the way you're fixed,' she said. 'Leave it to me. And I'll say that you'd appreciate it if you could get back to your work in England.'

'Do please tell him that,' he said earnestly. 'I really feel I'm much more use in the Establishment than on this sort of thing.'

The passengers departed and the plane taxied away for the take-off for England in the dusk. Mr Honey was left reading the *Saturday Evening Post* in the deserted lounge. At ten o'clock the stewardess came up softly behind him. 'I've got a bedroom ready for you, sir,' she said. 'Would you like me to show you which it is? It's just over the road.'

He said, 'Oh thank you,' and got up and went with her out into the night. It was cold and bright and brilliantly starry out on the road. To the north the sky was shot with spears of glimmering white light reaching up towards the zenith. They paused for a minute, looking at it. 'That's the aurora,' the girl said. 'They call it Northern Lights here. We often see it.'

He said, 'It's associated with the cosmic rays, I believe. It would be interesting to find out more about it.' And then he said, unusually for him, 'It's very beautiful.'

'It's wild,' the girl said, 'and uncanny. I don't like it much.' She took him into a two-storeyed wooden hutment, one of a row upon the other side of the road, and opened a door. He saw rather a bare bedroom, but his bag had been unpacked for him, and his hairbrush and shaving things laid out neatly on the dressing-table, and his pyjamas put to air upon the radiator so that they would be warm for him to get into, and the bed was turned down invitingly. 'I put a hot-water bottle in the bed,' she said. 'I hope you'll find everything all right, sir.'

He had not been treated like that for years. 'Oh, thank you,' he said. 'It all looks most comfortable. Did you do all this for me?'

She smiled. 'It's what I'm here for, sir.' She hesitated. 'I hope you don't mind – I've taken two pairs of your socks to darn. They've both got holes in the toe. I'll bring them with your tea in the morning.'

He said, 'Oh please, you don't have to bother. They won't show.'

The girl said, 'I've got nothing else to do, and you can't go around like that.' She hesitated, 'I did notice your pyjama coat has a great tear in the back,' she said. 'If you let me have that tomorrow I'll mend it for you. It must be terribly uncomfortable wearing it like that.'

He flushed. 'It's so old,' he said. 'I ought to get another suit, but there never seem to be any coupons.'

She asked curiously, 'Who mends your clothes when you're at home?'

'Oh, I do that myself,' he said. 'It's really very little trouble, and Elspeth's getting quite good at it, too. We get along splendidly, only the coupons are so short.'

Coupons, she knew, were always short for the bad managers. 'I'll take your jacket anyway tomorrow,' she said. 'The material's quite good – it'll patch all right.'

'I don't like putting you to so much trouble,' he said.

'I'd like to do it,' the girl said. 'I like mending things.'

She went away, and Mr Honey went to bed in greater comfort than he had experienced for many years. He stood for a few moments in his torn pyjamas before opening the window, looking at the Northern Lights, noting the form of the radiation. Then he got into bed; with his feet resting snugly on the hot-water bottle he was able to relax and think about the geographical distribution of the cosmic rays, a subject that was beginning to intrigue him. He lay in warm comfort doing mental calculations of the strength of the earth's magnetic field in various latitudes and computing its effect upon the distribution of the protons and the positrons as they approach the planet, till sleep came to him.

He was roused a eight o'clock in the morning by the stewardess, who brought him a cup of tea and a few slices of bread and butter on a tray. She pulled his curtains and let in the sunlight. 'It's going to be a lovely day, sir,' she said. 'What would you like for breakfast?'

He smiled at her. 'What can I have?'

'Orange or pineapple juice,' she said. 'Porridge or cereals. Eggs anyway you like. Bacon, cold ham, sausages. Buckwheat cakes and syrup with a sausage on the side – that's very good. Toast, hot rolls . . .'

He considered this. 'Could I have porridge and bacon and eggs?'

'Two eggs?'

'Well – yes, if I can.'

'Coffee or tea?'

'Er – coffee, I think.'

She nodded. 'What time would you like it? It's eight o'clock now.'

'Oh, I don't take long. Half-past eight?'

'Very good, sir.' She paused, and then she said, 'I want to go out for a walk this morning – it's such a lovely day. Would you like to do that?'

He considered this. 'Well – yes, I would. It seems rather stupid to be in Newfoundland and see nothing of the country, doesn't it? May I come with you?'

'Of course,' she said. 'The Gander River's only about two miles away and there's a road down to that, but there's nothing much to do there except bathe, and it's frightfully cold still. But going the other way, out past the restaurant, there's a path that takes you to a lake; it's awfully pretty there. That's where people go to fish. Do you do any fishing, sir?'

He shook his head. 'I'm afraid I don't.'

'The staff, the people stationed here, go fishing there on their days off,' she said. 'They catch salmon and trout and all sorts of things. But apart from that, it's terribly pretty. We could go there, if you like.'

He said eagerly, leaning up upon one elbow in his bed, 'Do let's. I haven't done that sort of thing for years.'

She hesitated. 'Would you like to take out lunch? I could cut some sandwiches.'

He said doubtfully, 'It'd be fun. . . . But do you think I ought to be away all day? I mean, there might be a cable for me from the office.'

She smiled. 'It could wait. We'd be back anyway by four, and if you're ordered to go on or to go back, you won't miss a plane because they all come through at night. I think a day out in the country would do you good.'

He said, 'I think it would.'

She nodded. 'I'll see about the sandwiches. Oh, and here are your socks – I did them last night.'

He took them gratefully. 'It's terribly kind of you to do all this for me.'

'Not a bit,' she said. 'Let me have your pyjama jacket when we get back and I'll do that for you.' She glanced at the tear. 'You can't go on wearing it like that.'

'I know,' he said ruefully. 'It got bigger in the night.'

When she was gone he sat in bed sipping his tea and fingering his socks, full of pleasure. He had not been looked after like that since Mary died; since then he had battled on alone, doing everything for himself and most things for his little girl. When Mary had been killed he had resigned himself to a life of celibacy; it had never entered his head, as practical politics, that he should go looking for another girl. He would not have known how to set about it. He had not married Mary; she had married him, to the surprise and consternation of her friends in the office, who thought she might have done a great deal better for herself than that. Mary had just happened in his life, a rare, sweet interlude that he had done very little to provoke; when she had gone he had slipped back quietly into his bachelor ways, more complicated now that there was Elspeth to look after.

He got up presently, and as he dressed looked ruefully at his pyjama jacket; not only was it very badly torn but it was indisputably dirty. He could not hand it over to her to be mended in that state; he washed it ineffectively in the basin in his room and hung it over the radiator to dry. As a consequence he was late for breakfast and it was nearly ten o'clock before he was ready to start off.

He met her in the lounge. 'I say,' he said diffidently, 'I hope I haven't kept you waiting.'

'Not long,' she said. She had a small blue stewardess's bag in her hand. 'I've got the sandwiches, and I brought a thermos of coffee too.' She hesitated. 'I didn't ask you what sort of sandwiches you like,' she said. 'I made some chicken ones and some sardine and some cheese. Is that all right?'

'Oh – of course,' he said. 'That's fine.' Food did not mean a great deal in his life; his meals were either canteen meals at the factory or scrappy messes that he cooked himself at home; moreover, his mind was usually too full of other matters for him to pay much attention to what he was eating.

'I like all those,' he said.

She was relieved. 'I had an awful feeling that perhaps you wouldn't like sardine . . .'

They set out walking down the path away from the hangars; as they went he asked her how she knew the way so well. He learned a little of her life. She made three Atlantic crossings, on the average, each week; most times she came to Gander for a short stop to refuel. Sometimes, on the rare occasions of easterly gales in the Atlantic, the flight had been delayed there for a day or longer; once before she had been stranded there for several days due to defective motors in the aircraft. 'But we shan't have to stop here for weather in the future, I don't think,' she said. 'The Reindeer carries so much petrol we can make the crossing even against the worst gales in the winter. That's what Captain Samuelson was saying.'

Mr Honey said, 'Well, that will save a lot of trouble. But we've got to get its tailplane right, first of all.'

She nodded. 'How long do you think that will take, sir?'

He smiled up at her. 'Please – don't you think you might stop calling me sir? I mean, you're doing so much for me that you don't have to.'

She laughed. 'All right. But how long do you think the Reindeers will be grounded for?'

'I don't know,' he said vaguely. 'These things usually seem to take three or four months to put right. But that's supposing that what I think is correct.' His face clouded, and he was in distress again. 'It's just an estimate,' he said. 'I didn't want people to take me up on it like this. I should have had more time, and now there's all this row . . .'

She said sympathetically, 'I know. But it had to be done this way, didn't it?'

He shook his head. 'We should have gone on working in the department in the proper way until we had some positive results to show.'

She smiled. 'I'm glad you didn't.'

'Why?'

She said gently, 'I should have been killed.'

He blinked up at her, taller than he was, slim and lovely against a background of Newfoundland fir trees and blue sky. It was Mary all over again, incredible that girls like that should come to death. He stared at her, confused by the clash of the theoretical and the practical in his work. 'Jean Davenport and Betty Sherwood were the stewardesses in Captain Ward's Reindeer,' she said. 'That one that fell in Labrador. If you'd gone on working in the proper way, I should have been killed too.'

He said a little more timidly, 'Did you know them?'

'Of course I did. I knew them very well.'

'Oh. Were they people like you?'

She glanced at him curiously. 'They were both fair. Betty was smaller than me. I suppose Jean was much the same.'

'But were they young, like you?'

'I suppose they were about twenty-five,' she said. 'It's not a job for people much older than that. Most of us are round about that age.'

They walked on for a time in silence through the woods. 'I suppose Dr Scott was right,' he said at last. 'But there ought to be more time for scientific work. One can't produce results all in a hurry, out of the hat, like this.'

She said, 'It must be terribly difficult.'

He glanced up at her, distressed. 'I don't know what to do. There must be a tremendous row going on in England because I damaged this Reindeer. You see, there isn't any proof yet. Sir Phillip Dolbear didn't believe a word I said.'

She was sorry for him; if it would help him to tell her all about it she wanted him to do so. 'Who is Sir Phillip Dolbear?' she asked.

She listened while he told her the whole story. 'You see,' he said at last, 'there isn't any proof at all – it just rests on my estimate. I was on my way to Labrador to find out if the fracture of the tailplane of the crashed one is crystalline – if it supports the theory of failure in fatigue. They never meant me to do anything like this. They'll all be very angry about it, I know. But it seemed the only thing to do.'

'It *was* the only thing to do,' she said gently. 'It was playing safe. Captain Samuelson isn't angry about it. And after all, he's been flying nearly thirty years and he does know about things.'

He shook his head. 'I told them they'd do better to send someone else. I always do this sort of thing all wrong.'

To distract his mind she said, 'Look, there's the lake. It's lovely, isn't it?'

It lay blue and shimmering before them under the summer sky, fringed with tall fir trees, its shores broken up into little rocky bays. Waterfowl were dotted about upon its surface; three or four deer, grazing on a rocky sward beside the water half a mile away, looked up as they stopped and vanished into the woods. 'There are all sorts of wild things here,' she said. 'There's a stream running out at the far end where there were beavers last year. And there are bears here, too.'

He stared at her. 'Are they dangerous?'

She laughed. 'The only time I saw one he ran like a rabbit. They say they're all right unless you feed them; then they come after more and you get clawed. But if you let them alone they're quite harmless.'

The path ran alongside the lake, made by the fishermen from the airfield; they passed a couple of rough dorys moored to the bank. They went on and came to the place where the deer had been and studied their tracks, and on until they came to the beaver stream. But the beavers were gone and only fragments of their dam remained.

They laid out their lunch by the stream, on a bare rock. 'It's so quiet here,' she said. 'You might be a thousand miles from anywhere.'

'Apart from the airport,' Mr Honey said, 'we probably are.'

She nodded. 'It's a mistake to leave the path, they say,' she remarked. 'You can quite easily get lost in the woods, and that's not so funny. All this country looks the same.'

'Do people ever get lost?' he asked in wonder.

'Oh yes. Two of the boys from the airport got lost last year. One of them died; it was eight days before they were found.'

He thought this over for a minute. 'You have a very adventurous life,' he said at last. 'What will you do? Can you go on as a stewardess indefinitely?'

She smiled. 'I suppose you could if you wanted to,' she said. 'I don't know that I should want to, though.'

'Don't you like it?'

She picked up a twig of fir, and absently scratched a little furrow in the earth. 'It's been quite fun,' she said. 'It's been fun meeting people and going to new places. I went into it after the war when I was restless, with Donald being killed, and everything. But now – well, I don't know. I sometimes feel I'd like to give it up.'

'You'd find it rather difficult to settle down,' he said. 'After this.'

She said, 'When you've seen all the new places you've got no more new places to see. And anyway, one new place is just like another new place. . . . I used to like meeting new people every trip – and I still do. But those things, meeting new people, seeing new places, they aren't everything. And while you go on in that sort of life you can't have any real friends or any real home. Because you're never there . . .'

'You don't get worried about the risks?' he asked.

She shook her head. 'There's so little danger in flying now. I know Jean and Betty bought it in the first Reindeer, but that sort of thing happens so seldom.' She flashed a smile at him. 'Thanks to people like you.' He was confused, and she went on, 'No – it's fun living this sort of life, but there's nothing *permanent* about it, if you understand. Sometime I'd like to be a bit more permanent. . . .'

'You'll be looking for another job?' he asked.

'I suppose so.'

He said, 'So shall I.'

She glanced at him. 'Are you going to leave Farnborough?'

He nodded. 'I've decided to resign.'

'Oh. . . .' There was a pause, and then she said, 'Do you think that's necessary? Surely they'll understand?'

He shook his head. 'They've got nothing tangible on this fatigue at all – just my own hypotheses, which nobody really believes in but myself. And there's certain to be a row about this Reindeer, because I'm a Government servant and so the Government will have to pay for its repair. And that means the Treasury and – oh, all sorts of things. I thought it all out last night. I want to write a letter to Dr Scott putting in my resignation, and get it to him as soon as I can.'

She was convinced in her own mind that he was doing the wrong thing, but she knew too little of the problems that confronted him to argue. She said, 'But what will you do? What sort of a job would you look for, Mr Honey?'

He said, 'I think they might take me on at the National Physical Laboratory – I know a lot of people there. And the work might be quite similar. . . . I should try that first of all. Or else I might try teaching.'

She was distressed for him. With her wider knowledge of

the world she knew one thing very certainly; that Mr Honey would not be much good at keeping order in a class of boys. He would be ragged unmercifully, grow bitter and morose. She said, 'I should think the other one would be better.'

'I think it might be more interesting,' he said thoughtfully. 'There's such a lot of new stuff coming up about the earth's magnetic field and its relation to cosmography. It's all getting rather exciting.'

'I'm sure it must be,' she said. 'Look, try one of these chicken ones – they're rather nice.'

He brought his mind back to the matter in hand. 'They're very nice,' he said. 'Things you make yourself always taste better than what you get in a canteen, don't they?'

She said, 'You take a lot of your meals in the canteen, do you?'

He said, 'Well, yes, we do. We get our own breakfast, but then I always have lunch at the factory, and Elspeth has hers at school. There's a very good British Restaurant in Farnham and we go there sometimes in the evening, but it shuts at six and that sometimes isn't very convenient. It's such a lot of work getting meals at home, you know, when you're both working all day.'

She nodded slowly. 'It isn't very good, having so many meals out, is it?'

He said. 'It makes it rather expensive. I think you're right in a way – I get a lot of indigestion that I didn't seem to get before. But one can always take magnesia for that.'

She laughed. 'That's expensive, too.'

They sat by the lake for a couple of hours, talking, finding out about each other. In the middle of the afternoon they recalled the cables and the signals that might be waiting for them in the airport office from the outside world, and got up reluctantly and walked slowly back up the path.

At the edge of the airport clearances they stopped for a moment. 'It was terribly kind of you to suggest coming out like this,' Mr Honey said. 'I haven't had a day like this for years.'

'Nor I,' she said. 'I'm getting rather tired of aeroplanes, I think, and racketing around the world. A quiet day like this is rather a relief.'

Mr Honey hesitated, uncertain how to put in words what he wanted very badly to say. 'Do you think we might do it again some time in England,' he asked timidly, 'one Sunday? There are some lovely walks along the Hog's Back . . .'

She smiled down at him, 'I'd love to do that, Mr Honey,' she said. 'I'll give you my address.'

They went back together to the airport, rather quiet. In the CATO office there was a signal ordering her to take passage on the night aircraft for London; there was a cable for Honey telling him to stay at Gander till an RAF aircraft arrived later in the week to bring him back to England.

He wrote a short letter to me giving in his resignation, and gave it to Marjorie Corder to deliver; at dusk he walked with her to the plane.

'It's been terribly kind of you to do all that you have for me,' he said. And then he added wistfully, 'We'll meet again in England, won't we?'

For some odd reason, tears welled up behind her eyes. 'Or course, Mr Honey,' she said quietly. 'Of course we will.'

8

I SAT FINGERING Mr Honey's letter of resignation while Miss Corder was telling me what had been going on at Gander; I was only listening to her with half my mind. With the other half I was wondering if I dared put his letter in the wastepaper basket and tell him not to be a bloody fool when I saw him, or whether I ought to show it to the Director. I sat fingering it uncertainly as she talked.

I looked down at it when she had finished, and read it through again. 'I see,' I said thoughtfully. And then I said, 'I wish he hadn't written this.'

She said, 'He was so positive that you would all be very angry with him.'

'So we are,' I said. I raised my eyes and grinned at her. 'He's been a silly fool. There *must* have been other ways of stopping that thing flying on without wrecking it. But if that was the best way he could manage, then he did quite right to wreck it. I should never have forgiven him if he'd let it fly on.'

She stared at me, puzzled, trying to absorb that one. 'I

don't think he's quite the person to deal with things of that sort,' she said.

I nodded. 'You're quite right. He's an inside man. The fault was mine for ever sending him.' I waggled the letter in my fingers. 'But that doesn't help me in deciding what to do about this.'

She was silent.

I glanced at her. 'Did he write this reluctantly, because he thought it was the thing to do in the circumstances? Or does he really want to leave and get another job?'

'He doesn't want to leave,' she said. 'He thought that things would be so unpleasant for him if he came back here — well, he'd rather go somewhere else. He talked of going to some place called the National Physical Laboratory to try and get a job on cosmic radiations or something.'

I nodded; it was a likely story. He was quite capable of taking cosmic radiations in his stride. 'Things won't be unpleasant for him here,' I said. 'That Reindeer had to be stopped flying, and he stopped it.' I fingered the letter in my hand. 'I should be very sorry to lose him,' I said thoughtfully. 'I've got a feeling that he's working on the right lines in this matter of fatigue, and that we'll find in a few months' time that his estimates are very near the truth.' I raised my head and looked at her, thinking of what I should have to say at our formal conference next day. 'He's a valuable man in this department. I don't want to take this letter seriously. I think it would be a loss to the Establishment, and even to the country, if he left his work upon fatigue just at this stage.'

She said, 'If he's as important as all that, I can't understand why you don't look after him a bit better.'

I stared at her. 'How do you mean?'

She said firmly, 'He gets a terrible lot of indigestion and he's always taking pills for it. He'll be getting a duodenal ulcer if you don't look out, and then he won't be able to work for you at all.'

The indigestion was news to me, and there didn't seem to be much that I could do about that, but it fitted in with his complexion, and one bit more was added to the picture of him in my mind. 'I can't help that,' I said. 'I wish his home life was a little easier for him, but that's just one of those things.'

She got up to go. 'I know, sir,' she said. 'It was stupid of

179

me to say that. I know you can't help him in that way.' She hesitated. 'I told him that I'd go and see his daughter, Elspeth, while I was down here,' she said. 'There's only a charwoman looking after her. He lives in Copse Road, Farnham. What's the best way for me to get there, sir? Is there a bus?'

I blinked; another lovely woman to see Elspeth Honey. 'She's not there now,' I said. 'As a matter of fact, you'll find her in my flat. She had a bit of an accident.' And I told her shortly what had happened.

Miss Corder was upset. 'The poor kid!' she said. 'I *am* glad Mr Honey doesn't know about this – he'd be terribly worried. I mean, on top of all the other trouble.' She asked a few more questions, and then said,

'It's awfully kind of Mrs Scott to have done so much, sir. I was wondering if I could help at all? I went into the office at the airport this morning, and they've given me a few days' leave. I'm a nurse, you know. I trained at the London Hospital.' She paused. 'If I can help, I really would like to. Mr Honey was so kind to me , and I'm quite free.'

I thought quickly. There was some substance in this offer; Miss Teasdale, charming and good-hearted as she was, was not a trained nurse. But here was a trained nurse who felt herself to be under some obligation to Honey, and who was free for some days and anxious to assist. In fairness to Shirley I could not pass this over.

'It's very nice of you to say that,' I replied. 'As a matter of fact, Miss Monica Teasdale came down and helped a bit yesterday, and I think she's coming again today. But she's just an amateur; I know my wife would be awfully glad of your help.'

I told her how to get to my flat and that I would ring up Shirley; then I showed her out, because I had a lot to do that day. At the door she turned to me.

'You won't let him resign, will you, Dr Scott?' She looked up at me appealingly; she was a very lovely girl. 'He's not the sort for changes and adventures. He'd be much happier going on quietly here.'

I nodded. 'I don't want to lose him,' I said. 'I'll do what I can.'

She went, and I read Honey's letter of resignation again. Then I asked Miss Learoyd to find out if the Director was free; he was, and I went down to see him, forgetting all about my call to Shirley.

I said, 'Good morning, sir. I've got a letter from Mr Honey here, resigning his position with us. With your permission I'm going to tear it up and forget I ever had it.'

He smiled, and stretched out his hand. 'Let me see.'

He read it carefully, and then said, 'Why, particularly, do you want to destroy it?'

'We've got this conference tomorrow, sir,' I said. 'I still think he's probably right about this Reindeer tail, and as a member of my staff I'm going to back him up. But if we accept this letter, then he's not a member of my staff any longer, and I don't know where we are. We'll all look pretty good fools and the right decisions probably won't be made.'

He said thoughtfully, 'You are quite sure about him still?'

I was silent for a moment, thinking. 'I don't want to be stupid about this,' I said at last. 'I don't want to back him automatically, just because he *is* a member of my staff. I've got a strong feeling that he's probably right about the Reindeer tail, but that's not evidence. I'm basing my opinions more on the quality of his other work, the stuff I found in his private files. He's a fine mathematician, he's very well informed on physical chemistry, and he's got a very clear analytical mind. Apart altogether from the Reindeer tail, I think it would be a great loss if he left us, sir.'

He handed me back the letter. 'All right, tear it up.' He paused, and then said, 'How did that get here?'

I grinned. 'The stewardess from the Reindeer flew over last night and brought it down to me by hand. Miss Corder. She's a very beautiful young woman.'

He smiled. 'Stewardesses usually are. What have you done with her?'

'Sent her off to see Elspeth. It's just a procession of girl friends from Honey – two in two days.' I turned to him. 'Old Honey with his face like a frog. What's he got that we haven't, sir?'

He laughed. 'I can't tell you that – but I'm not a bit surprised. Mrs Honey, who had got killed, you know, she was a very beautiful girl.' He paused, reflectively. 'She used to work in the Airworthiness Department, when we had that here. Really lovely, she was.'

I stood in thought for a moment; every little thing I could

find out about Honey was important to me at that time. I was staking my career on my opinion that his work was valuable, that he was a credible person. 'When Mrs Honey was alive,' I said slowly, 'was he just the same as he is now? Or was he any different?'

The Director did not understand. 'He was younger,' he replied.

'I know. But was he different in himself? Was he always as touchy and difficult in the office?'

'Oh, I see what you mean. Yes, he was very different. He was much tidier in his dress and he had a better colour. Now you mention it, I don't think he was so difficult in the office. He used to make little jokes. He probably got better food at home and more exercise.'

The heavy boots came into my mind, and the indigestion. 'I should think that's right,' I said thoughtfully.

'Mary Honey did a great deal for him,' said the Director. 'It was a tragedy when she got killed. She was such a lovely girl.'

All this drove the thought of telephoning Shirley clean out of my mind; when I got back to my office I pulled my IN basket towards me and started on it, my mind still running upon what I had learned of Honey's past life. In consequence, when Shirley opened the door of my flat, she opened it on a completely strange young woman, who said, 'Good morning, Mrs Scott. I'm Miss Corder – Marjorie Corder.'

Shirley stared at her blankly; she had Miss Teasdale in the bedroom sitting with Elspeth, and she herself was just about to go round for a day of cleaning in Honey's house.

The stewardess said, 'Didn't Dr Scott ring you?'

'No. Ought he to have done?'

She explained. 'I've just come from him. I brought a note to him from Mr Honey in Newfoundland – I flew across last night. I told Mr Honey I could come and see his little girl, and Dr Scott told me to come here.'

Shirley's brain reeled; another beautiful stranger had flown the Atlantic with a message from Mr Honey and was diving deep into his private life. She said weakly, 'Do you know Miss Monica Teasdale? She's here.'

'I thought she might be. I was with her at Gander – I'm the stewardess, you see. Dr Scott told me that she might be here.'

Shirley nodded. 'She came yesterday. She's in the bedroom reading to Elspeth, now. Do come in.' She took Miss Corder into the sitting-room and explained to her.

The stewardess, laughed, flushing a little. 'You won't want the two of us fussing around, Mrs Scott,' she said. 'I'd just like to look in and see Elspeth for a moment, and then I'll go away. Unless there's anything I can do to help you?'

Shirley said, 'Oh – no, not really. I was just going round to clean up Mr Honey's house a bit, but I've got nothing else to do.'

'What's the matter with it? Is it dirty?'

'Perfectly filthy. The kitchen floor simply makes you sick.'

The stewardess laughed. 'Well, I can do that, Mrs Scott. I'm used to scrubbing.'

If there is one job Shirley loathes, it is scrubbing a floor. 'Would you really like to come and help?' she asked. 'I was going to take some lunch round there and make a day of it.'

'I'd love to.'

They made their plans together; then Shirley took Marjorie down the corridor to our bedroom, where Monica Teasdale was reading *Just So Stories* to Elspeth Honey, lying in bed. She looked up in surprise at the stewardess.

'Good morning, Miss Teasdale,' Marjorie said. 'I came over last night and brought another note from Mr Honey to Dr Scott. He asked me to come on and see Elspeth when I was down here.'

Elspeth from her bed said, 'Is Daddy coming home soon?'

'My name's Marjorie,' the stewardess said. 'I saw your daddy last night. Yes, he's coming back soon. In two or three days, perhaps.'

'Why can't he come sooner?'

'He's got to wait for an aeroplane to bring him. It's a long way across the Atlantic.'

'Didn't an aeroplane bring you?'

'Yes, but he has to wait for a special one, in two or three days' time.'

'Couldn't he have come on the same one that you came on?'

She shook her head. 'He's got to wait for a particular one, that has to do with his work.'

That satisfied Elspeth. 'My Daddy works on things to do with aeroplanes,' she said. 'He works at Farnborough. He's terribly clever.'

' I know,' said the stewardess. 'I know that.'

Miss Teasdale asked, 'They've fixed that difficulty there was about his passage home?'

The stewardess said, 'He's coming on an RAF aircraft of the School of Navigation. It's coming across some time this week.'

Shirley said, 'I'm just taking Marjorie down with me to your house, Elspeth, so that we can do some cleaning before your father gets back. Is there anything you want from there? We could bring it when we come.'

She shook her head. 'May I sleep at home tonight, Mrs Scott?'

'I don't think tonight, dear. Better stay here till you feel quite well.'

The child said in distress, 'If nobody's there, there'll be a burglar.'

'Don't worry about that,' Shirley said. 'Dennis – Dr Scott – slept there last night, and I expect he'll be there again tonight. One or other of us will be there. We won't leave the house empty.'

Elspeth said, 'I do want to go back.'

'You shall, the very minute you're well.'

Miss Teasdale said, 'You'll just have to hurry up and get well, honey.'

Elspeth snuggled down in bed. 'I like the way you always call me honey.'

Shirley collected scrubbers and soap and Vim and a dustpan and brush, and put them in a basket with the lunch, and started out with Marjorie Corder to Copse Road. As they walked through the surburban streets, the stewardess said, 'She's very anxious to get back into her own house, isn't she?'

'I know,' said Shirley. 'It's a sort of fixed idea. She feels responsible for all her father's papers, and she's terribly afraid a burglar will get in and steal them. As if anybody would want to steal that sort of stuff! But that's what she thinks. That's how she came to fall downstairs – she thought she heard a burglar.'

They came to the little house in Copse Road and opened it, and went through it with curious disdain. The products of Honey's creative research in the many files in the front room meant nothing to them, except that they were papers to collect a lot of dust. There was little in the house that they approved of. 'My dear, that kitchen!' Shirley said. 'The whole place wants doing out from top to bottom, really.'

Marjorie nodded. 'I'll start off on the kitchen floor, and after that I think I'll wash the walls,' she said. 'It wouldn't be a bad room if it was cleaned up. It's got quite a nice outlook.'

Shirley said, 'If you make a start on that I'll slip round to the builder and tell him to come and put some glass in this window, where I kicked it out. After that, I think I'd better start off in the bedrooms and turn those out, and work down.' She paused. 'I'll get some Harpic for that ghastly lavatory . . .'

They worked together till the middle of the afternoon; then Shirley left to do her own housekeeping. Marjorie stayed on in the house, partly because she was not yet tired and partly because the glazier was working on the window. She roamed through the house for a little, smoking a cigarette, touching and feeling things, rather as I had done two nights before. She stared in wonder at the many files and books and drawing instruments, relating them to the man she had known at Gander. This was what the home of a genius looked like. A genius who had no woman to look after him.

There was one small rug on the bare boards of the front room, that mixture of drawing-office and study. She took this rug up and fetched a bucket of hot water from the kitchen, and got down on her knees again to scrub the floor. Better to make a job of the whole house, while she was at it. And this was where he did his work, and so the most important room of all.

There was a step on the path outside, and the front door opened. She raised her head and knelt back on her heels, thinking to see Shirley again. But it was Miss Teasdale, delicately gowned and perfectly made up, who stood in the doorway looking down at Marjorie as she knelt on the scrubbing mat.

'Say,' she said, 'Mrs Scott just told me all that you've been doing. She's back in the apartment now for a while, so I just stepped around to see.'

Marjorie flushed a little. 'I was just going to start scrubbing this floor.'

'So I see.' The actress stared around her curiously. 'Is this some kind of a laboratory?'

'It's his study, where he does his work.'

Standing in the door, Miss Teasdale glanced out into the kitchen and the stairs leading to the rooms above. 'Which is the sitting-room, then?'

'This is it. It's the only sitting-room there is.'

She stared around her, at the drawing-board, the deal cupboards and shelves loaded with books and files, the bare floor. 'The little girl,' she said at last. 'Where does she go?'

The stewardess said, 'They've got a couple of armchairs in the kitchen – basket ones. I think they sit in there a good deal.' She stared around her. 'It doesn't have to be like this,' she said. 'I'm sure it doesn't. He could be much more comfortable.'

The actress glanced at the pail of steaming water. 'I see you're doing all you can to make it so.'

'Me? All I'm doing is to get rid of some of the dirt. But he could have curtains in this room and a carpet on the floor and some decent lampshades, as a start.'

The actress smiled. 'Kind of wants a woman round about the place?'

Their eyes met. Marjorie said evenly, 'I think he does.'

'Okay,' said Miss Teasdale. 'Just so as we know.' She turned and wandered into the kitchen. It was scrubbed and clean and smelling of antiseptic soap. The window was open and the sun streaming in; on the wooden table there was a small vase of flowers. A little pang struck at her heart again, as many pangs had in the last two days. Kitchens had been like that back in her youth in Indiana, before they got to look hygienic, like a hospital. She called over her shoulder, 'You've done a swell job in here.'

Marjorie got up from her knees in the sitting-room and came and stood behind the actress. 'It's clean now, anyway,' she said. But it's all so old-fashioned. It must seem terrible to you.'

'Maybe.' The actress stood for a moment in thought. 'I kind of like a scrubbed table,' she said at last. 'I haven't seen one in years. But they were all that way when I was young, and it carries you back.'

'All right if you haven't got to scrub them yourself,' the stewardess said. 'But the metal ones are so much easier.'

Miss Teasdale glanced at her. 'Kind of interested in housework, aren't you?'

Unaccountably, beside this sophisticated woman Marjorie Corder felt like a child. 'Everybody's interested in that,' she said defensively. 'Besides, I was a nurse once, before I went to the Air Transport Organisation. I know a lot about scrubbing.'

'Going to stay with the airline? Or leave and marry the boy friend?' She glanced at the stewardess's hand. 'Or isn't there a boy friend?'

The girl shook her head. 'Not now.'

'No? I'd have thought there'd have been plenty.'

'I got inoculated,' Marjorie said. 'There was one once, but he was killed. He was a bomber pilot.'

'In the war?'

She nodded.

'That was quite a while ago,' the actress said. And then she said, 'I see.'

Miss Corder flushed, in spite of herself. 'I don't know what it is you see,' she said. 'I've got this other floor to do.' And she went back to the sitting-room, and went down on her knees beside the pail.

'Okay,' the older woman said. 'You don't have to get worked up about it. Guess I'll go along now and get Mrs Scott to telephone the office for my car.'

Marjorie raised her head. 'All right,' she said. 'Tell her I'll be round in about half an hour for my coat.'

Miss Teasdale walked back slowly to our little flat, deep in thought; it did not now seem very important to her whether she was recognised or not. One or two women and three men, glanced at her curiously in the street, but no one spoke. She reached the garden gate just as I drove up from the factory; I had left early that night, resolved to get in a couple of hours more upon my lecture that evening, somehow and in some place. I had to give it the following night; indeed, the next day, with our full-dress meeting upon Reindeer fatigue in the morning and my lecture in the evening and flying to Montreal that night, was likely to be quite a heavy one.

I took her into the flat and telephoned for her car; it would take an hour or so to come from London. I poured her out a glass of sherry.

'Tired?' I said. She looked rather limp.

'Just a bit.' She roused herself. 'I walked around to see where Mr Honey lives. Miss Corder, she's still there scrubbing the floor. Says she'll be another half an hour. She's got energy, that kid has.'

'Well,' I said, 'she's young.' I could have bitten my tongue out an instant later for having said that.

The actress nodded briefly. Presently she said, 'Say, Dr Scott – this research on airplanes you and Mr Honey do. Can that be done any place? I mean, suppose a man had money, enough money to set up a swell laboratory, say, at some place like Palm Beach, and maybe another one in Vermont for the summer months. Could the work be done that way?'

'Research on aeroplanes?' I asked. 'You mean, the sort of things that we do here in Farnborough?'

'That's right. Fatigue, is that it?'

I shook my head. 'I don't think you could do any effective work upon fatigue effects in airframes in a private laboratory,' I said. 'You'd have no access to the secret information, for one thing, so you'd never be up to date. But apart from that, the expense would be prohibitive to any private individual.'

'What's that about secret information?'

'All the work done on military aeroplanes is secret,' I said. 'If the wings start coming off our latest bomber in a dive, we don't tell the world about it. Not until we get it put right, anyway. But at Farnborough, all that experience is at our disposal when we're dealing with the Reindeer tail – in fact, we should ourselves be working on the secret troubles of the bomber at the same time. A private research worker would always be behind, for that reason alone.'

'He wouldn't cut any ice, working that way?'

'I don't see how he could. Research on aeroplanes is a big business, too. I don't know what this fatigue story on the Reindeer is going to cost before we're through with it. Apart altogether from the repair of the one at Gander, what's going on at Farnborough may cost thirty thousand pounds before we're through with the first stage of it.'

She opened her eyes. 'A hundred and twenty thousand

dollars. That's quite a lot of money. How long would that be spread over?'

'About a year,' I said. 'But I don't think it could be done at all upon a private basis. There's the buildings and the plant to be considered too, you see.'

She nodded. 'Like the stages.'

I did not understand her. 'No, I mean the actual buildings to house the experimental work.'

'That's right. Like the stages that we put up the sets in, ready to start shooting the scene.'

I thought of the great barnlike buildings I had read about. 'Yes – just like that,' I said. 'You'd need something just about as big as that, and a corresponding staff.'

She turned the conversation and asked me about my lecture that I was to give upon the 'Performance Analysis of Aircraft Flying at High Mach Numbers.' Elspeth had told her about it, it seemed, and had confused Miss Teasdale with her erudition. The child, it seemed, knew quite a lot about high Mach numbers and the difficulties that aeroplanes get into in those regions. The actress had no idea what a Mach number was, high or low, and was hazy about the meaning of the word analysis. But she was a very beautiful and charming woman; I did not find the explanations tedious.

Shirley came in while that was going on, and almost immediately Miss Corder followed her. I poured them both out a glass of sherry. Monica Teasdale said, 'Dr Scott's been telling me about his lecture tomorrow night, Mrs Scott. Elspeth told me first. She said it was a great distinction for a young man like Dr Scott to be asked to read a paper to the Royal Aeronautical Society.' She glanced at me mischievously. 'I'm just repeating what she said.'

'I can quite believe it,' I replied. 'That child's got the mind of a woman of forty.'

Shirley said artlessly, 'I do wish I could come up and hear it.'

I stared at her; it had never entered my head that she would not be coming to London. 'Aren't you coming?' I suppose there was disappointment in my voice, because we had worked at it a good deal together. And then, it struck me that she was talking with a purpose.

'I *can't*, Dennis,' she said. 'There's Elspeth.'

Miss Teasdale sat motionless, staring at the sherry in her

glass. The faint lines upon her face seemed suddenly deeper.

Marjorie Corder burst out, 'But Mrs Scott, of course you must go! I've got a few days' leave. I'd love to come down again tomorrow and sit with her, or stay the night if you like. She'll be perfectly all right with me. If anything should happen, I *am* a nurse, you know.'

The actress sat silent, motionless.

Shirley said, 'Would you – really?'

'Of course, Mrs Scott. I'd love to do that.' The girl was bright-eyed and eager.

Shirley said, 'It really is most awfully kind of you – I do want to go, terribly.' And then we all said what a good idea it was and Shirley said, 'And after the lecture we can go on and have dinner somewhere, and then I'll come to the Airways place at Victoria and see you off.'

I grinned. 'Fine,' I said. 'But you'll miss the last train home.'

'Then I'll stay in Town, and make a night of it,' she said. She turned to Marjorie Corder. 'Did you really mean that you'd spend the night here with Elspeth? It means sleeping on the sofa, I'm afraid.'

'Of course, Mrs Scott. I'd love to do that.'

Presently I suggested that we'd better go and tell Elspeth about it, and we all walked down to see her in the bedroom. 'Guess what's going to happen tomorrow,' I said.

The child's face lit up. 'Am I going back to our house?'

Marjorie sat down on the bed and took her hand. 'Not quite that,' she said gently. 'But Mrs Scott wants to go to London to hear Dr Scott give his lecture, so I said I'd come and spend the night here and look after you. Would you like that?'

The stewardess, as I have mentioned before, was a very charming young woman. She made a sweet picture, sitting talking to the sallow little girl. Elspeth said, rather shyly, 'Yes.' And then she said, 'Will Dr Scott be coming back after the lecture?'

'No,' said Marjorie. 'He's got to fly to Montreal and he's leaving that night from London, and Mrs Scott's going to see him off and stay the night in Town. So there'll be just you and me alone down here tomorrow night.'

Elspeth said in distress, 'But that means there'll be nobody at all in our house, and there'll be a burglar.'

We stared at each other in consternation. We had all heard about this burglar in the last few days, sufficiently to realise that it was the sort of phobia that a child has to be led out of, that it may not be very good to repress. In Elspeth's case she certainly would not sleep while that house remained empty, and she was a mild concussion case.

Shirley said, 'Oh dear. I never thought of that.'

There was a momentary silence.

Marjorie Corder said slowly, 'Mrs Scott, would you think this very awful? I don't believe Mr Honey would mind me sleeping in his house, in the circumstances. They won't want me at Air Transport before the week-end, and Mr Honey will probably be back himself by then. What I was thinking was, we might move Elspeth back into her own house and her own bed tomorrow morning. I'd be very glad to sleep there tomorrow night and look after her there, and the next night, too, if that would help. I'm sure Mr Honey will be back in a day or two.'

I said, 'It'll only be a couple of days at the most. There's a Lincoln from the Navigation School picking him up this week.'

Shirley said slowly, 'I don't think it would matter a bit. After all, he did ask you to come and see if Elspeth was getting on all right. I don't think he could possibly mind if you moved in for a night or two to look after her, as things are. But surely, it's a great tie for you?'

The girl said, 'I'd like to do that, honestly.'

I said that I thought it would be a darned good idea. Shirley had had quite enough of sleeping on the sofa, I thought, and if I was to go away to Labrador upon this trip, I did not want to leave her with a sick child on her hands. If this Miss Corder who was a trained nurse wanted to take over and move Elspeth back into her own place and look after her there, I was all for it, and the sooner the better.

Everyone was very pleased about the decision we had taken, except possibly Miss Teasdale, who said very little. We made all the arrangements; Marjorie was to come down first thing in the morning, Shirley was to drive me to the station in the car and then bring back the car and transfer Elspeth back into her own house.

Soon after that, the stewardess went off to catch the bus to the station for the train that was to take her up to London.

As soon as she was gone, Miss Teasdale said, 'I guess I'll have to say good-bye, now, to you folks. I don't see any reason to come down again tomorrow.' She was brightly cheerful.

Shirley said in disappointment, 'Oh, can't you stay and see Mr Honey when he gets back? You've done such a lot for him.'

She smiled. 'It's you folks have done everything – all I did was read a while with Elspeth. I certainly did enjoy doing that. But now she's going to be all fixed up, and as for me, I've no right to be over on this side at all. I'm due back on the Coast in five days' time.'

She was emphatic that she had to go, and she went through into the bedroom again to say good-bye to Elspeth. 'One day,' she said, 'when you're a little older, I want you to come over to the States and spend a holiday with me. We'll go on a ranch up in the mountains, riding and swimming all day. In the spring, when all the flowers are out. Would you like that?'

The child nodded. 'Mm.'

'Okay, honey,' said the actress brightly. 'We'll look forward to it.' She paused, and then she said, 'If I write you sometimes, would you like to write me back and say what you've been doing?'

Elspeth nodded again. 'I'll write four pages,' she said.

'Okay, honey,' said Miss Teasdale again, 'that's a deal. I must go now.' She stooped and kissed the little sallow face. 'Tell your daddy I'm sorry that I couldn't wait to see him. Tell him I'll look forward to seeing you both again next time I'm over on this side.'

'How long will that be?' the child asked.

'A couple of years, maybe. But we'll write in the meantime, won't we?'

Elspeth nodded vigorously.

Miss Teasdale turned to the door, and waved her hand brightly. 'Good-by-ee,' she said, with rising American inflection.

As we walked down the passage there was a ring at the door, and it was the chauffeur. We went into the sitting-room, where she gathered up her things. And then she said, 'It's been swell knowing you folks. Going around the way I do, one never gets to know the real English people, the way you live and work. But this two days has been just like it used to be at home, as if you were all Hoosiers. It certainly has been grand knowing you.'

I forget what we said in reply; it doesn't matter. We walked down with her to her car, and this time there was a little crowd of ten or fifteen people on the pavement, for the news had leaked out. Two little girls with autograph albums stopped her as she crossed the pavement and said, 'Miss Teasdale, would you sign my book?' She smiled brilliantly, professionally, at them, scrawled her name, and got into the car; we stood and watched it as it slid away, conscious of the eyes of the small crowd now focused upon us, friends of the great.

Shirley asked, 'Dennis, what's a Hoosier?'

'Blowed if I know,' I said.

We went in and had supper, and gave Elspeth hers, and made her bed for her, and put her down to sleep. Then we washed up the supper things, and then I had to pack a suitcase with everything that I would need for a fortnight or three weeks in Ottawa and Labrador. By half-past nine I was finished, and could take my overnight bag and the printed script of my paper and go round to Honey's house to do a final trial reading of the thing, and finally, to sleep.

Shirley came with me to the gate of the front garden of our little block of flats. 'Goodnight, Dennis,' she said softly. 'Don't stay up later than midnight, will you?'

It was reasonable that I should get a good night's sleep. 'All right,' I said.

She stood for a moment, looking down the road in the dusk, in the direction that Miss Teasdale's car had gone. 'That poor woman,' she said thoughtfully.

I asked her, 'Why do you say that?'

She kicked absently at a tuft of grass. 'I don't know. I think she's having rather a rough time.' She turned back to the house. 'Mind now, don't stay up too late.'

I went off down the road, and the 'Performance Analysis of Aircraft Flying at High Mach Numbers' put the matter from my mind.

9

I TRAVELLED UP to London next morning with the Director
for our meeting at the Ministry of Supply. It took place in
one of those long, bleak conference rooms you sometimes
find in economical Government offices, furnished only with
a long table and about twenty hard seats. It was a very hot
day, with the sun streaming in across the table. Our Chairman was Stanley Morgan, the Director of Research and
Development. Ferguson was seated by his side, and on his
other hand was a chap from the Secretariat that I did not
know, and next to him there was a lean, cadaverous beggar
from the Treasury whose name I never learned. Then there
was Carter from the Ministry of Civil Aviation with some
stooge or other. Next was Sir David Moon, the Chairman of
CATO, with Carnegie beside him, and next to them and in
their party was a little sandy-haired man, rather stout, who
turned out to be Samuelson, the Captain of the Reindeer that
Honey had had his fun with. There were two chaps from
the Air Registration Board, and Group-Captain Fisher of
the Accidents Branch, with somebody to help him. Next
came E. P. Prendergast, the designer of the Reindeer, looking like thunder, and with him was a chap in a black jacket
who turned out to be the legal adviser to the Company.
Finally, there was the Director and myself. I don't know
what he felt like. I know I felt like a bag fox about to be let
loose in front of a pack of hounds.

The Chairman opened the meeting by saying that as there
was no formal agenda he would lay down terms of reference
right away. The meeting had been called to discuss the airworthiness of the Reindeer aircraft with particular reference
to tailplane failure by fatigue. He hoped that as a result of
our discussions we would reach agreement upon whether any
steps were necessary to restrict the operation of the aircraft,
either now or in the future. He wished to emphasise that any
decisions taken must be taken upon sound technical grounds
alone. At the same time, he said, the matter was of grave
political importance. The Reindeer aircraft was now main-
taining more than half of the British Transatlantic passenger

service, and by the end of the year would be doing the lot. If those aircraft had to be taken out of service the consequences would be very serious indeed. He was sure that the technicians present, of whom he was one, appreciated these hard facts. With that, he would ask the Director of the RAE to give a short account of the investigations which had been proceeding on the Reindeer tail.

The Director said that the matter arose from certain basic researches into the question of fatigue, for which the second Reindeer tailplane submitted for structural tests, and unbroken in those tests, was used. This choice had been entirely fortuitous; the tailplane happened to be there, and so we used it. The research was directly in the hands of Mr Honey, working under Dr Scott; it was unfortunate, he said dryly, that circumstances prevented Mr Honey from being present at that meeting. Sir David Moon tightened his lips and looked annoyed, but said nothing.

The Director went on to outline what had happened up to the point where the Reindeer crash in Labrador came into the picture. Here he called on me to speak. 'I was very much impressed with the coincidence of flying times,' I said carefully. 'The Reindeer crashed in somewhat mysterious circumstances when it had flown for 1,393 hours. Mr Honey's estimate of the time to tailplane failure, under normal weak mixture cruising conditions, was 1,440 hours – that is, $3\frac{1}{2}$ per cent greater than the point at which an accident occurred. $3\frac{1}{2}$ per cent is nothing in investigations of that sort, of course. Clearly, it is very possible that the accident may be related to the estimate.'

Group-Captain Fisher said, 'If I may say a word, Mr Chairman, Dr Scott speaks of the Reindeer accident – the *first* Reindeer accident, perhaps I should say – as having taken place in somewhat mysterious circumstances. I cannot agree with that. The accident was very fully investigated and was fully explained. There is no mystery about that accident at all.'

Morgan said, 'Quite so, Group-Captain Fisher. I think we may come on to that a little later.'

Prendergast raised his head. 'I should like to say a word, Mr Chairman. I quite agree that the coincidence of flying times deserves attention, provided that one has confidence in the estimate produced by Dr Scott and Mr Honey. May we hear a little of the nature of this research and of the substance of this estimate?'

The Chairman said, 'I was about to ask the RAE if they would deal with that next.'

The Director said, 'A point of difficulty arises here at once, sir. This estimate was produced by Mr Honey as an incidental to a programme of pure research into fatigue problems. In the course of this research Mr Honey has made a completely new approach to the fatigue problem. It is a very great pity that he could not have been brought here to tell you about it himself. However, I will do my best to outline it to you.'

He paused, and then he said, 'Mr Honey's work is nuclear. He bases it on the small energy loss of materials under strain detected first by Koestlinger and further investigated by Schiltgrad at Upsala University. That work is public property. Mr Honey related these investigations to certain work of a more secret character recently carried out at the NPL which, with your permission, sir, I propose to gloss over.'

The Chairman nodded.

'Arising out of these investigations,' the Director went on, 'Mr Honey produced a completely novel theory of the fatigue effects in light alloy structures, which involved a considerable extension of the accepted nuclear theory. If confirmed by experimental tests, this theory would present for the first time a firm basis for designing structures to resist fatigue, instead of the somewhat hit and miss empirical design factors that we have used to date. Accordingly we put in hand a test upon the Reindeer tail left over from the airworthiness investigations, to confirm or to disprove the theory. That test has now run for about five hundred and ten hours, and on the present rate of progress, running twenty-three hours a day, we expect to reach Mr Honey's figure of 1,440 hours' running time about the end of August.'

There was some discussion of the trial programme then and the nature of the test. I produced some photographs of it from my attaché case and circulated them around the table. Prendergast seized them at once and began studying them intently.

The Director went on. 'At the RAE we do not pretend to expert knowledge upon every branch of natural science. There are bodies in this country charged with the investigation of nuclear matters; we are not one of them. When nuclear matters come our way we submit them to the appropriate authority, and in this case we submitted Mr Honey's thesis to the Inter-Services Atomic Research Board for guidance. In addition, Mr Honey visited Sir Phillip Dolbear to discuss the matter. The letter from the Board is there, sir.'

The Chairman picked it up. 'Well, yes. I think I'd better read it to the meeting.'

He did so.

At the conclusion he smiled wryly. 'Well, gentlemen,' he said. 'We all appreciate that the Inter-Services Atomic Research Board has a very full programme, but unfortunately this letter does not take us very much further. In its concluding paragraph it expresses the willingness of the Board to put fatigue problems upon their programme, indicating that they consider that an extension of the nuclear theory may yield useful results in assessing the effects of fatigue; at the same time they clearly don't think very much of Mr Honey's work in this field. They do not go so far as to say that his work is inaccurate or worthless. They refer to it' – he glanced at the letter – 'as a wild assumption, which needs much experimental verification.'

I said, 'Which is what we are trying to do.'

'Exactly, Dr Scott. Well, gentlemen, I must confess I don't see what further steps the RAE could have taken in the matter. The confirmatory trial is running night and day, and such assistance as could be obtained has been obtained, from the ISARB. I understand that in the circumstances the RAE have a recommendation to make.'

The Director glanced at me.

'I have an opinion,' I said. 'A recommendation, if you like, sir. I don't think any Reindeer should fly more than 700 hours until this thing has been cleared up.'

The Chairman nodded. 'Any comments upon that?'

Carnegie, the technical superintendent of CATO, said, 'Well, sir, I should like to ask one or two questions. First of all, why seven hundred hours? What is the magic in that number?'

I said, 'It's half the estimated time to failure.'

'No, it's not,' he said. 'Half the estimated time to failure is seven hundred and twenty hours.'

I swallowed. 'All right,' I said. 'Make it seven hundred

and twenty hours, if you like. But I don't think any aircraft carrying passengers should fly more than half the estimated time to failure.'

Sir David Moon said, 'I don't want anyone to think this is a trivial point. Twenty more hours flying, on an average of six aircraft only, means twelve more Atlantic flights, which would earn a revenue of over sixty thousand pounds. I am very grateful to Dr Scott for allowing us to make that money by his concession.'

I flushed at his tone. The battle was evidently on.

'I have another question,' said Carnegie. 'Who decided this ratio of one half? We are all agreed that safety comes first, up to a point. If safety precautions are unreasonable, of course, they can stop aviation altogether, and we can all go home.'

He paused. 'I should like to suggest that it is perfectly safe to permit these aircraft to fly up to two-thirds of Mr Honey's estimated time to failure – that is, to 960 hours. As operations are going, some of the aircraft will reach seven hundred hours before the test reaches 1,440 hours. As far as I can see, when the test has reached 1,440 hours the first aircraft will have flown about 910 hours, and after that the test should keep ahead of the aircraft if it runs twenty-three hours a day, because the aircraft seldom exceed ten hours a day, operating as at present. Two-thirds seems to me to present a fair margin of safety.'

Prendergast said, 'I would certainly agree with that.'

The Chairman turned to me. 'Dr Scott.'

'I don't agree,' I said. 'I should like to. But we know too little about fatigue problems and their onset. All estimates that I have ever seen upon fatigue in built-up structures – and there aren't very many to see – have been very much in error, and in the majority of cases failure has taken place before the estimate. I think a factor of two is necessary in a case like this – seven hundred and twenty hours. I shouldn't like to see the aircraft flying on to nine hundred and sixty hours.'

Carnegie said, 'I take it, Dr Scott, that that is just your personal opinion.'

'My personal opinion,' I agreed. 'That's what I think.'

Prendergast said, 'Dr Scott, am I not right in saying that another Reindeer, the one that there has been some trouble with at Gander, has flown 1,429 hours, without any trouble at all?'

'I think that's about right,' I said.

'Well, in view of that, do you still feel that so large a factor of safety as two is desirable?'

'For all we know that one may be on the point of failure,' I replied. 'If it is, then I think a factor of two is necessary. We know too little about fatigue problems to sail nearer the wind than that, where passenger services are concerned. If it were a military aircraft, I might take a different view.'

Sparkes, of the Air Registration Board, spoke up. 'Mr Chairman, with every respect, the allocation of factors of safety is our responsibility, and not that of the RAE.'

'Certainly,' I said. 'I'm just telling you what I think.'

There was a short pause.

Then Sir David Moon said, 'Mr Chairman, nobody here wishes to subject the travelling public to any undue risk. But this factor of safety seems to be a matter of opinion. Opinions should be based upon the consideration of all the factors involved, including both the technical factors *and* the operational ones. Now, here there is a political issue. If these aircraft are grounded at 720 hours, the British Transatlantic air service will virtually come to an end, probably for several months, with the most deplorable results to the prestige of this country. If they are allowed to go on flying up to 960 hours and therefore to two-thirds of the time currently run by the test at Farnborough, there is a very good prospect that it may not be necessary to interrupt the services at all.' He paused. 'I should like to ask Dr Scott if he has taken that into consideration.'

The Chairman glanced at me.

I stuck my chin out. 'No, I haven't,' I said. 'This is a technical matter. For safety, I think this thing should carry a factor of two. That is, the aircraft should be grounded at 720 hours, subject to the further investigation of the fatigue problem.'

Sir David Moon said, 'That's a very positive statement, Dr Scott.'

'It is,' I agreed.

Prendergast leaned forward. 'Dr Scott,' he said. 'Is it not the fact that we have no evidence that there is any fatigue trouble in the Reindeer tail at all? Let me put it another way.

Mr Honey has produced a theory of fatigue which is unsupported as yet by any experimental evidence. This theory states that the Reindeer tail is dangerous. That is all we have to go upon?'

'Not quite,' I said. I opened the accident report lying on the table before me. 'The tailplane of the first Reindeer crash is still lying in Labrador, and a metallurgical examination of that in the region of the fracture will show if that tail failed in fatigue or not. Here's a photograph of that crash, and I've drawn a pencil circle round the stump of the front spar. It's very tiny, I'm afraid, but it looks not unlike a fatigue fracture to me.'

There was a pause while the report was passed eagerly round the table. Group-Captain Fisher said irritably, 'Nobody can possibly tell anything from that – it's only about a sixteenth of an inch long. The accident was very carefully sifted and all the parts examined. There's no question about what happened.'

Prendergast said, 'Have any steps been taken to recover these parts for examination?'

The Director said, 'We sent out Mr Honey to investigate the matter on the spot. Unfortunately circumstances have prevented him from doing so. Instead, Dr Scott is flying to Ottawa this evening to recover the parts and to carry out any other investigations that may be necessary, in conjunction with the Accidents Investigation Branch.'

The Chairman said, 'Dr Scott is going out there personally? That seems a very good thing.'

Prendergast said, 'But at this moment, all the evidence we have upon this matter is this photograph and Mr Honey's theories?'

I nodded. 'That is correct.' I knew that it was coming now, and it did.

He said, 'Dr Scott, leaving aside the photograph, have you got confidence in Mr Honey's theory of fatigue?'

'I'm not sure that that is quite a fair question,' I said slowly. 'I'll tell you quite frankly that I don't understand it very well, and I doubt if anybody in this room would understand it any better. I have a bowing acquaintance with nuclear theory, as many of us have. I don't know enough about it to criticise the work of somebody who has made a deep study of nuclear matters, as Mr Honey certainly has.

I'm sorry, gentlemen, but that's the way it is.'

The Chairman said, 'I think that is a reasonable answer. Dr Scott's appointment does not call for experience in nuclear matters – indeed, no appointment at the RAE has called for that experience up to the present. The RAE very properly applied for advice to the ISARB, and it is unfortunate for us that no very definite advice has been forthcoming. However, there it is, and we must make the best of it.'

Prendergast said, 'Making the best of it, Mr Chairman, may I ask another question? Dr Scott, are you satisfied with Mr Honey's work in general? In technical matters have you got confidence in him as a credible person?'

It was very hot in the conference room. I was beginning to perspire.

The Chairman said, 'Well, that's rather an unusual question.'

Sir David Moon said, 'These are rather unusual circumstances, Mr Chairman. So far as I can make out there is grave danger that we may be called upon to suspend the entire operation of the British Transatlantic air service because Mr Honey has produced a theory of fatigue which the ISARB think nothing of, and which nobody else has checked. Some of my staff have had experience with Mr Honey recently, as you know, and we are not at all impressed. Indeed, so little impressed were we with his mental stability that we have felt compelled to refuse him any further passages in our aircraft.'

There was a tense pause. I said, 'I should like to answer Mr Prendergast's question, if I may, sir. I have complete confidence in Mr Honey. I think his work, in general, is very advanced and very competent. I think that in this matter he is very likely to be right.'

And I thought to myself as I said that, there goes your job.

Prendergast said slowly, 'I am astonished.'

The Chairman said, 'I think we should accept the opinion of Dr Scott, Mr Prendergast. Mr Honey is a member of his staff, and he is better known to Dr Scott than to anybody in this room.'

Sir David Moon said, 'With every respect, Mr Chairman, I should like to say a word about that. In CATO we also know a good deal about Mr Honey. We consider him to be a man with an obsession on this question of fatigue that impels him to the most extravagant acts. I do not think I need go into what happened at Gander; I imagine we are all aware that Mr Honey has wrecked one of our aircraft in deference to his theory.'

'No,' I said. 'In deference to me. I told Mr Honey before he left England that no Reindeer was to fly more than seven hundred hours.'

Carnegie exclaimed, 'You did?' He turned to the Chairman. 'Really, sir, I think that was a little bit high-handed. This meeting has been called to consider that very point.'

I said, 'In emergencies, somebody has to say something. At that time we had no idea that any Reindeer had flown more than four hundred hours. But Mr Honey knew my views, and he acted on them to the best of his ability. I don't think he was backing up his theory by preventing that Reindeer from flying on. He was doing his best to ensure the safety of the travelling public.'

Sir David Moon said, 'Nobody questions that Mr Honey was doing his best, Dr Scott. What we feel in CATO is that it was the best of an unbalanced man. I do not know if you quite realise the seriousness of his acts. I have no exact figures yet of the cost of repair of the Reindeer which is now lying at Gander, nor the loss to which my Organisation will be subjected due to that aircraft being out of service for a period of many weeks. It does not seem possible to me that the sum of those two figures will be less than eighty thousand pounds. I do not feel that my Organisation should be liable for that amount.'

The Chairman pursed his lips and wrote down the figure on his pad.

'We feel in CATO that that large financial loss has been forced upon us lightly and unreasonably by an employee of the State who, let us say, thinks differently from ordinary people.' Sir David glanced at the chap from the Treasury, who made a note upon his pad in turn. The legal representative of the Rutland Aircraft Company was already scribbling busily; clearly there was going to be a fine dog-fight over who was to pay for that aircraft. 'Having had this experience of Mr Honey and his obsessions we are quite unwilling to accept him as a passenger again in any of our aircraft. And, equally, we shall be most reluctant to accept any reduction of our services based upon the uncorroborated work of this man, in view of our experience with him.'

Prendergast said, 'As one who has known Mr Honey by repute for a great many years, may I say a word, sir?' The Chairman nodded.

The designer said, 'I have worked in this industry for thirty nine years. I came into it as a boy two months after Bleriot flew the English Channel, and I have been working in it ever since. At that time the RAE was still known as the Balloon Factory. I have seen that establishment grow from practically nothing to its present size, and all that time I have been in close and intimate touch with it. I have seen scientists come and go at the RAE; I know them, and I know their ways, and many of them have been most able and devoted men. But I can tell this meeting frankly I consider Mr Honey to be exceptional. Scientists, like other men, are subject to mental disturbances, perhaps more so in view of the continuous mental efforts that they are required to make. Some scientists grow senile at an early age, they develop kleptomania and steal small articles from little shops' – he was speaking very slowly – 'or they behave indecently in the Park, or they engage in treasonable activities, or they slip into religious mania.'

The Director flushed. All these were true incidents that had bedevilled him within the last three years.

'All my life I have watched these men in their careers,' Prendergast continued. 'I fancy that I know the initial symptoms of a scientific mental decline by this time, and I could make a tolerably good guess of what the future holds for Mr Honey.' The Chairman stirred restively, but Prendergast was Prendergast, senior in age and in experience to the lot of us. 'We have here a man,' he continued, 'who takes a deep interest in psychic phenomena – that is, gentlemen, in ghosts. Mr Honey believes in ghosts; he has been chairman of a body dealing with psychic research. Apart from that, Mr Honey will forecast the date of the coming dissolution of the world to anyone who cares to listen to him. based, I believe, on the structure of the Great Pyramid. If you take fright at that, and wish to escape from a planet which is doomed to destruction' – there was infinite sarcasm in his tone – 'Mr Honey is your man again, because he has been concerned with the Interplanetary Society and at one time produced designs for a rocket-propelled Space Ship, I think he called it, for a projected journey to the moon.'

There were smiles around the table. I spoke up in a cold fury. 'I don't know much about the ghosts or the end of the world,' I said. 'I have looked over his work on interplanetary rockets, which was carried out in his own time in the years 1935 and 1936. So far as I can see, modern developments in guided missiles are following exactly on the lines that he forecast.'

Prendergast glared at me. 'I wish I could believe that certain other forecasts made by Mr Honey would come equally true,' he said harshly. 'As it is, they appear to me to be a particularly offensive form of blasphemy. Are you aware that Mr Honey expects Our Lord to descend to Earth in this country in the year 1994? Are you aware of that, Dr Scott?'

I said angrily, 'Are you aware that He won't?'

The Chairman said, 'Gentlemen, I don't think any of this is really relevant to our consideration of what action we should take, if any, in regard to the Reindeer.'

Prendergast said, 'Our action depends upon our confidence in Mr Honey's work, sir. For my part, I have no confidence at all. The eccentricities that I have mentioned are plain indications of mental decline. Unless fresh evidence, as from the Reindeer crash in Labrador, should be produced, I don't think we should take any action at all, though I would agree to Mr Carnegie's proposal to limit the flying time to two-thirds of the time done by the test.'

The Chairman said, 'Well, Mr Prendergast, as I understand the matter no question of grounding any aircraft upon Mr Honey's estimate alone is likely to arise. It has already been decided to send a representative of the RAE, Dr Scott, to make a fresh investigation of the wreckage in Labrador, in conjunction with the Accidents Department. How long do you suppose that that will take?' He turned to the Director.

'It should not take longer than a fortnight,' the Director said. 'That is, assuming that there is no further obstruction in regard to the air transport of my staff.' He said that very quietly.

Sir David Moon said, 'Sir, any action that we may have taken has been for the protection of the travelling public. If we consider any passenger, *any* passenger, to be mentally unstable, we refuse to carry him. We do not wish to obstruct the RAE in any way.'

The Director said gently, 'I should like to say a word upon this question of mental instability, if I may. A wiser man than I once said that an unusual man is apt to look unusual, gentlemen. I will admit that Mr Honey sometimes presents an unusual, an untidy appearance in his manner and his clothes. I do not condone that, but I should be sorry to see the RAE staffed entirely by correct young men in neat, conventional, civil service clothes, with neat, conventional, civil service minds.' A smile ran around the table. 'In my department,' he went on, 'we seek for original thinkers, for the untiring brain that pursues its object by day and by night. If the untiring brain refuses to leave its quest to attend to such matters as the neat arrangement of collar and tie or to removing food stains from its waistcoat, I do not greatly complain.'

He paused. 'As regards Mr Honey's other interests, I would say this. You cannot limit a keen intellect or try to fetter its activity. At times, perhaps, I have no job on hand for a few weeks that will wholly occupy the energies of some member of my staff, but I cannot put the untiring brain into cold storage or prevent the thinker from thinking. If there is a hiatus in the flow of work my research workers will start researching on their own, into the problems of thought transference, or ghosts, or the Lost Tribes of Israel, or the Great Pyramid and the coming dissolution of the world. That, gentlemen, does not mean that they are going mad. It means that I have picked my men well, because the true research worker cannot rest from research.'

Prendergast said acidly, 'May I ask if other members of your staff destroy aircraft when they are not fully occupied?'

The Chairman said hastily, 'I think, Mr Prendergast, we can pass on.'

Prendergast interrupted hotly, 'With every respect, I think we should hear more about the circumstances in which Mr Honey wrecked the Gander aircraft. We have the captain of the aircraft here, Captain Samuelson. May we not hear what he has to say about Mr Honey, sir?'

'If you wish,' the Chairman said reluctantly. 'Captain Samuelson?'

The pilot hesitated. 'Well, sir, I don't know what to say. At the time I thought he was off his head, but having heard all this it seems there's something on the other side as well.

I think it's a matter for the doctors,' he concluded weakly.

'Exactly,' said the Chairman. 'Well now, gentlemen—'

Samuelson spoke again. 'Excuse me, sir,' he said. 'May I add just one more thing?'

'Certainly.'

'Well, I've heard a great deal this morning that I don't really understand,' the pilot said. 'I mean, I'm just the b.f. who knows how to fly the thing. But one thing I'm quite certain of, and that's that that first accident report is wrong.' He pointed to the folder lying on the table before me. 'That thing says that Bill Ward came down through the overcast to check his position, and flew into a hill at about fifteen hundred feet. I never heard such bloody nonsense in all my life. I've known Bill Ward for twenty years. He was as senior as I am in the Organisation. It's just bloody nonsense to suggest that he'd have done a thing like that.'

Group-Captain Fisher, red as a turkey cock, said, 'The whole weight of the evidence supports that explanation of the accident.'

The pilot said, 'I don't give a mugger about that, sir. It's plain bloody nonsense. Senior pilots in the Organisation just don't do that sort of thing. Whatever happened to that Reindeer, it wasn't that.'

Sir David Moon stared down the table at his pilot thoughtfully. 'I think that we should give that view a great deal of consideration,' he said.

The Chairman said, 'I think we should. Well, gentlemen, I think we have heard all that can be said upon the matter at this stage. The RAE will recover the relevant parts of the wreckage of the first machine and will report to me, if possible within a fortnight.' He glanced at the calendar. 'That is, by the 25th. We cannot settle anything this morning, or, indeed, until we have that report upon the first machine. In the meantime, I will see Sir Phillip Dolbear and see if any interim investigation is possible, on high priority. If any action then seems necessary, we must have another meeting.'

Prendergast said sullenly, 'Very good, sir. If any action on our part is required, no doubt somebody will consent to let us know, sometime.'

The chap from the Air Registration Board said, 'It looks as if a little preliminary investigation for the modifications that may be required would be justified.'

Prendergast said sourly, 'It's rather difficult to do that when there is no fault apparent in the present structure. Certainly, I can invent a weakness and get out a modification to put it right, if that is what you wish.'

On that the meeting broke up; the various members stood about in little groups. Sir David Moon went down to the end of the room and stood in close conversation with his pilot, Samuelson; in a lull in the conversation I heard the little sandy-haired man expostulating, 'I tell you, it's all a lot of bloody nonsense, sir.' Group-Captain Fisher was complaining to the Chairman, who was trying to brush him off; he did so just as I was leaving the room with the Director, and bustled over to us.

'You're crossing over to Ottawa tonight, then, Scott?' he said.

'Yes, sir,' I replied.

'Fine,' he said. 'Do your best to get this settled quickly, one way or the other. It's very disturbing to everybody when these things drag on in uncertainty.'

I left then, and went to the Royal Aero Club for lunch. The Director had to go back to the RAE, so I lunched alone in the snack-bar and sat for half an hour smoking in the lounge over a cup of coffee. I was very tired. The last few days had been a bit of a strain and the tensions in the meeting that morning had left me feeling slack and ill. Hanging over my head was the lecture in the evening; it should have been the great day of my life, but now it was just another hour of tension to be battled through. I sat trying to rest and read an illustrated magazine till it was time to go back to the Ministry to see about my journey to Canada.

I went to see Ferguson first of all. 'I thought old Prendergast was going to break a blood-vessel this morning,' he said cheerfully. 'Specially when you picked him up on Jesus Christ. I must say, we do have fun at our meetings. That chap from the Treasury said he'd never been at one quite like it.'

I went with him to the Secretariat and spent an hour in various departments getting my passport and my tickets and my money. We got back to his office at about a quarter to four, and his secretary was waiting for me with a message from the Director of Research and Development, our chairman this morning. 'Dr Scott, Mr Morgan wants to see you . . .'

When I got into his office, he said, 'Sit down, Scott. I want to have a talk with you about this morning's meeting. How well do you know Mr Honey?'

'Not very well,' I said. 'This matter of fatigue is the first job of his that I've investigated. He was working on it when I took over the department.'

'Is he a friend of yours? Do you know him personally?'

'No,' I said. 'He's been to my house a couple of times, and I've had his daughter staying with me for the last two days.' I told him about Elspeth.

'I take it that you're friendly with him, then?'

'Not specially,' I said. 'I think he has rather a hard time, living alone after the death of his wife and all that, sir. And I think he's an able little man. As regards his daughter, I hope we'd do that much for any of my staff who got into a jam.'

'You think he's able?'

'I do, sir.'

He drummed on the table for a moment, staring out of the window. 'Well, I hope you're right,' he said at last. He raised his head and looked at me kindly. 'There's going to be a row about this Reindeer, either way,' he said. 'If it proves that there is real trouble in the tailplane, that you and Honey are right, then there's going to be Parliamentary trouble over the suspension of the North Atlantic service. People will start saying that this country can't build aircraft so we'd better give up trying.'

'We can plough through that one, sir,' I said.

He nodded. 'Of course we can. But if it goes the other way, and it turns out to be a mare's nest – that there's nothing wrong with the tailplane at all, then there'll be trouble of a different sort. Then the Treasury will come in over the payment for the aircraft Honey wrecked at Gander. I rather wish you hadn't thrown your weight on his side quite so definitely this morning, Scott.'

'There'll be a row about that, will there, sir?'

'I'm rather afraid there will. I had the Treasury man with me for half an hour after lunch. He's very much concerned about the action that Honey saw fit to take.'

'Too bad,' I said wearily. 'But I can't help that. Honey

knew my views and what he did was certainly influenced by what he knew my attitude to be. You can't go through life sitting on the fence. You've got to make decisions, and sometimes you're pretty sure to make them wrong. If you're going to chuck Honey to the lions, sir, you'll have to chuck me too.'

He said doubtfully, 'Oh, I don't think it will come to that.' He stared out of the window for a minute; it was hot in his office and I was sweating a little. 'You must have thought about this for a long time,' he said. 'What makes you so positive that he is right?'

I could not relate the sum of tiny things that had built up my judgment, the strong hiking boots, the rocket thesis, the quality of his discourse upon automatic writing, his spartan mode of life, the beauty and intelligence of the women who had loved him. 'I don't know,' I said. 'I've just got a hunch that he's right.'

'From your experience?'

I knew he understood. 'That's right, sir,' I said eagerly. 'I just kind of smell trouble here. Honestly, I think there's something the matter with the Reindeer tail.'

'I believe I agree with you,' he said slowly. He smiled. 'Well, we'll keep our fingers crossed and hope you bring something definite back with you from Canada.' He stood up and held out his hand. 'Good luck. You've got everything you want for the journey – money and tickets and all that?'

'Everything,' I said. 'I'll come back with the evidence all right, sir' – I smiled – 'for or against.'

I went back to Ferguson's office. 'What did he want?' he asked casually.

'He wanted to break it to me that if the Reindeer hasn't got fatigue trouble I could start looking for another job,' I said. 'But he didn't get around to putting it in so many words.'

I left the office and walked slowly across the Green Park towards the club. I was tired and dispirited; everything was massing up on me as if for a disaster. I had backed Mr Honey in his fatigue theory because one has to take a positive line. I had thought it out and come to the conclusion that he was probably right, and I had plumped for that, but I could not overlook the other side of the question. What if he were wrong? He had never seen a washing-up mop or an electric hot-water-heater; he had walked in a provocative procession and had been taken by the police and charged with creating a breach of the peace. Lucky that Prendergast did not bring out that one at the meeting! Suppose, in fact, he was a stupid, trivial man; suppose, in fact, I found nothing wrong at all with the wreckage in Labrador? My name would then be mud; it would take a long time to live down the stink that this would make in official circles. Probably it would mean that there would be no more promotion for me at the RAE. In that case I would do better to get out of the country, go down to the bottom and start again, perhaps in Australia or New Zealand.

I sat for a long time on a bench in the park tired and trying to rest, wondering miserably if my life in my own country was coming to an end.

Presently I got up and went back to the club. Shirley was waiting for me there, and I ordered tea. 'We got Elspeth moved all right,' she said. 'She's back in her own room now, with Miss Corder looking after her. She's a nice girl that, Dennis.'

'She is,' I said. 'Where's she sleeping?'

She looked at me reproachfully. 'In the little spare room, of course. All in among the suitcases. You didn't think she'd sleep in Mr Honey's bed?'

'Not yet,' I said. She aimed a kick at my ankle under the table. 'Is Elspeth happy to be back in her own place?'

'Oh yes. Marjorie was going to wash the stairs and the hall this afternoon, and she can talk to Elspeth while she's doing that. After tea they were going to make toffee.'

'Where's she going to get the sugar from?'

'Mr Honey's got about thirty pounds of it in the larder. It's their jam sugar ration for about four years. He doesn't know how to make jam.'

'She'd better make him some.'

'She's going to do that tomorrow. There are strawberries in the shops now, and they're reasonably cheap.'

She turned to me. 'How did the meeting go, Dennis?'

'Not too well,' I said. 'There's going to be the hell of a row if these machines have got fatigue and a worse one if they haven't.'

'Oh, darling, I *am* sorry.'

Presently we left the club and walked across the park to

the lecture hall; my lecture was at half-past six, but I had to go through the slides with the lantern operator first. Then came a period of waiting and nervous, distracted talk with various people in the industry while the hall filled up, till there was an audience of six or seven hundred people. Finally I went through with the President on to the platform, with the Secretary behind me, and sat nervously trying to control my twiddling fingers while the President introduced me as the lecturer on the 'Performance Analysis of Aircraft Flying at High Mach Numbers'.

When I got on my feet, all my nervousness vanished after the first few words. I was very tired and stale, but I knew my subject, and the familiar graphs and diagrams followed each other on the screen without a hitch. I spoke for about fifty minutes; at the end I was a little hoarse, and was glad to sit down and take a drink of water, happy that the damn thing was over. There was applause, of course; there always is. It seemed a terribly long time before it stopped; the next fence was the discussion, and then it would be over. To my dismay I saw Prendergast get heavily to his feet in the second row. I waited with sick anticipation for what he was going to say.

He said, 'Mr President and gentlemen. I have worked in this industry for nearly forty years, and during that time I have attended most of the meetings of this Society. I have several points on which I wish to cross swords with the lecturer, but at the outset I wish to pay my tribute to his clarity. I have very seldom listened to a lecture that explained so difficult a subject in such simple language. I am left with the feeling that the most inexperienced student in this hall must have learned as much as I have this evening, and I have learned a great deal which will be of value to me.'

I sat blinking as I listened to this incredible man. He changed like a chamelion, but I sat back sick with relief that he was not going to go for me in public as he had that morning at the meeting. The fact that he then proceeded to tear to pieces my analysis of the critical area of the pressure plate based upon the harmonic surges that occur when passing through the compressibility zone did not worry me a bit; it was done constructively and in one instance at least suggested a line well worth further investigation. Morgan was there and I could see that he was pleased. Other speakers took their tone from Prendergast, and the discussion went on for another three-quarters of an hour. I replied to the various points as best I could, and then it was all over.

Shirley met me in the lobby. 'Dennis, it was marvellous,' she said. 'Everybody said it was awfully good. Was that Mr Prendergast who spoke first?'

'That's right,' I said.

'What a nice man he must be. I can't think why people say such horrid things about him.'

I could, but I did not want to spoil her pleasure in the good reception that my talk had had, and so I marched her off back to the club and there we had dinner with a bottle of red Algerian wine to celebrate our success, and to put me to sleep on the plane, and a glass of port to follow. Then it was time to get a taxi and take my suitcase to the Airways terminal. On the steps I kissed Shirley good-bye.

'Back in about a fortnight,' I said. 'Look after yourself.'

'You look after yourself,' she said a little tremulously. 'Don't go and get eaten by a moose in Labrador, or anything, Dennis.'

I said I wouldn't, and we parted, and I went into the hall and showed my passport and my tickets. And as I turned away, a woman in a great fur came up behind me with a swirl, and it was Monica Teasdale.

'Evening, Miss Teasdale,' I said. 'Are you crossing over tonight?'

She stretched out a hand in her most dazzling, professional gesture, that made me feel that everybody in the hall was taking note of us. 'Say, Dr Scott, isn't this nice? Are you going over too?' And then she said, 'Did you give your lecture? How did it go?'

'All right,' I said. 'They didn't throw any eggs.'

There were several sleek young men with shiny black hair and flashing eyes with her to see her off, and one portly old gentleman with a very hooked nose; I drifted away and left her to her other life. We travelled down in different seats of the bus; at the airport I did not speak to her. I was amused to note that we were to travel in a Reindeer; I decided to ask no questions about that one and to refuse any invitation from the captain that I should go to the flight deck. What the eye doesn't see, the heart doesn't grieve over.

We took off, and as we climbed up on our way to the Atlantic I relaxed for the first time that day. The Algerian wine was doing its work; as I leaned back in the reclining chair fatigue came soaking out of me in great waves. Three rows ahead of me I could see Miss Teasdale's auburn hair; as on Honey's trip, the aircraft was only half full. After half an hour or so, when I was beginning to doze, she got up and went aft down the cabin; on her return she stopped beside me.

'Say, Dr Scott,' she asked, 'is this a Reindeer, too?'

I sat up. 'I'm afraid it is,' I said. 'But I don't think you need be afraid of anything going wrong this time.'

She smiled, 'Will we be landing at Gander again?'

'I imagine so,' I said.

She laughed. 'You'll be interested to meet your Mr Honey there,' she said. 'Mind if I sit down a little while and visit with you?'

'Do – please.' I picked my papers off the seat, and she sat down beside me. 'I hope Honey will be on his way home by this time. The Lincoln that was to pick him up was due through Gander today.'

'He won't be at Gander when we land?'

'I hope not. I hope he'll be at home.'

She was silent. I glanced at her after a moment, and was surprised to see the hard lines of age and suffering on her face as she stared up the cabin. People had told me that she was over fifty, but I had never really believed it till then.

I said, 'Are you going back to the West Coast?'

She nodded. 'I'll go from Montreal to Chicago, and pick up with the airline there. I kind of like this way of travelling, unless there's business in New York.'

'When will you be over here again?' I asked. 'Do let us know so that Honey can bring Elspeth up to see you.' It's extraordinary how cruel one can be, quite unintentionally, when one is too tired to be careful any more.

She turned to me, and she was every day of fifty. 'I don't just know when that will be,' she said. 'Maybe not for some years. I guess a person ought to stay in her own place.'

I was more awake now to the situation. 'Don't think like that,' I said. 'We've loved having you, and it's been terribly kind of you to spend so much time with Elspeth. It's taken a lot off Shirley.'

She said quietly, 'It's been real nice getting out of Wardour Street and Claridge's a little while, and getting to know you folks in your homes. I never knew that British people lived so much like folks in the US. But I guess if you've been born American you're better off in your own country. Maybe you British think the same way.'

'I think that's true, after a certain age,' I said. 'If you're going to make your life in a new country you should go before you're twenty-five. After that you start to get associations, little grooves and anchors, that make it difficult to change.'

She nodded. 'I know it. Not only living places, either — that goes for what you do. Take pictures, now. You get set in pictures when you're young and maybe you think you can give up and get right out of it any time you say, like marrying and bringing up a family like any other woman. But then when you come down to hard brass tacks, you find you can't. So many little grooves and anchors, like you said.'

I said thoughtfully, 'You mean you've got to make the pattern of your life before you're twenty-five. I never thought of that, but I dare say it's true.'

'I'd say that's true,' she replied. 'By that age you either go for marrying and raising a family and making a home or you go for a job and forget about the other. If it happens later, maybe it works out, maybe it doesn't. But if you want to be sure, then you've just got to drop the job and do the other by the time you're twenty-five.' She was about to add something, but checked herself.

I was fully awake by that time. I smiled; the woman wanted to talk. 'Marjorie Corder,' I said.

She turned to me. 'You're clever,' she said. 'I guess that's why they made you boss of your department, all about fatigue and things like that. Well, there's a case for you. I'd say she's around twenty-four or twenty-five. And now she's switching over.'

I glanced at her. 'You think she wants to marry Mr Honey?'

'She's moved into his house already,' she said bitterly.

There was a long pause. 'I don't say that I blame her,' she went on at last. 'He's a grand little guy, and he deserves a young wife.' Her face was lined and old. 'I guess she knows she wouldn't find a man like that so easily again; she's been around, that girl has, and she's got to know about men. I guess she's in love with him all right.'

There was a long silence. My eyes drooped in fatigue; sleep was not far away. But presently the actress said, 'It's funny the way those little quiet men get you. I knew a man one time, oh, years and years ago, before ever I went into pictures. In the office, that was, back in Terre Haute. He was so kind, but he was lame and I was a young fool and thought I'd meet ones like him around every corner, and get married when I wanted to. Well, I did get married, but it wasn't like it might have been if I had married Eddie Stillson. I'd have had about four kids then and no money, and a lot of work and worry and been old and tired and worn out by this time.'

'Sorry?' I inquired.

'Sometimes,' she said. 'I never did my stuff. Seems I've always been a kind of passenger.'

There was another of those long, slow pauses. 'It's too late to do anything about it now,' she said. 'That kind of man, he's got a right to have a family when he marries. It wouldn't be good for him to marry somebody like me, not now. That kind of man, he's got a right to a young wife, who'll have some children for him, and not mind living in a little house like that and working, with just two weeks in a summer camp some place each year. I couldn't do that, now.

'You can't put back the clock,' she said. 'You may want to, terribly badly. But some things you just can't do, and that's one of them.'

I was desperately tired, and closed my eyes for a moment to think this over. When I opened them again the lights in the saloon were dimmed and Miss Teasdale, the World's Pin-Up Girl, had gone back to her own seat three rows ahead of me. I turned on my pillow and slept again, and when next I woke the stewardess was standing over me, telling me to fasten my belt. We were going into Gander.

We came round in a great sweep, low over the forests in the moonlight. The approach lights came in view, the flaps came down and the runway appeared immediately beneath our wheels; then we were down and rolling towards the hangars and the office buildings. We drove up near the Reindeer lying on its belly on the tarmac.

As soon as we were allowed to disembark I went to the reception hall and asked for Honey at the CATO desk. But he had left about tea-time the day before in a Lincoln for

Shawbury; he must have been already in the British Isles when I took off for Gander. Probably by that time he would already have arrived back in Farnborough. I went and had a wash and a shave and then crossed the road to the restaurant; as I went in I passed Miss Teasdale coming out, fresh and blooming like a rose.

I stopped. 'I was terribly rude last night,' I said. 'I went clean off to sleep while we were talking.'

She laughed, and passers-by stared at me with interest and with envy. She said, 'You must have been tired after a day like that. I felt real sorry for you.'

'I've just heard that Honey left for home yesterday,' I said. 'He'll be there by now.'

'You see he stays there,' she said. 'He's a great little guy, but not the sort to go wandering around the world alone.'

'Too true,' I said. The sight of the first Reindeer lying on its belly was still fresh in my mind. 'What's the breakfast like in here?'

She laughed. 'I had just a cup of coffee – I never take more in the morning. The people at the next table had buckwheat cakes and syrup, with a sausage on the side.'

I asked anxiously, 'Can I get porridge, do you think?'

She laughed. 'I wouldn't know about that. You're on our side of the Atlantic now.'

I did not speak to her again. I breakfasted in a hurry on cornflakes and bacon and eggs, and then went out with one of the CATO officials to the tarmac to inspect the first Reindeer. It was a sad sight, the propellers, flaps, and engine cowlings crushed and distorted, and the belly of the fuselage on which it rested badly crumpled. The air bags to raise it had not yet arrived and were not expected for another week; when they came they would be placed under the delicate wing structure and inflated; by bearing on so large an area they would gently lift the great thing without further damage. The ARB inspector, Symes, appeared while I was looking at it, and the official introduced me.

He grunted. 'We got rid of your Mr Honey yesterday,' he said. Evidently he did not think much of Honey.

I asked, 'Have you made any examination of the tail?'

'It's perfect,' he replied. 'There's not a sign of trouble of any sort. Of course, I know that this fatigue may not give very much warning, but I'd stake my reputation that that tail's as perfect as when it left the factory. About the only thing that is,' he said gloomily, looking at the aircraft. 'Just wanton destruction, I call it.'

'There are two views on that,' I said. 'It's just possible that he might turn out to be right.'

'I've been in this industry since 1917,' he said. 'I don't say that fatigue never does occur. What I say is, that you don't very often meet it.'

We climbed up into the fuselage and went aft through the luggage bay. They had taken out a panel from the pressure bulkhead and I was able to crawl in and get all round the spars with an electric torch. What the inspector had said was quite true; the structure seemed in perfect condition. I knew that that meant nothing in the case of fatigue trouble, but it was depressing all the same. The evidence was running all in favour of the diehards.

Mr Symes clearly did not believe in the least that there was anything the matter with the machine at all, apart from what Honey had done to it. I had to leave them, because the passengers were being marshalled out to the other Reindeer, the one that I had come from England in. I followed them and we took off for Montreal.

We landed there at about 10 o'clock in the morning, local time. Miss Teasdale was surrounded in the reception hall by a little crowd of friends and fans; I was met by a flight-lieutenant of the RCAF, who had a four-seat Beaver waiting to fly me down to Ottawa. The actress was busily engaged and I was reluctant to keep my officer waiting; moreover, I had nothing more to say to her. I left her to her other life, and went with him to the Beaver and took off for Ottawa.

We got there in about an hour and there was a car to meet me. We drove straight to the Bureau of Civil Aviation, and in half an hour I was sitting in conference with the Director, a Group-Captain Porter, and the Inspector of Accidents, Squadron-Leader Russell.

A small population in a big country seems to breed a clearer-headed sort of man than we get in England, although they may be less well informed. These men knew all about my business and they were very ready to accept the possibility of fatigue in the Reindeer tail. Indeed, they were very interesting in their opinions of the onset of fatigue at sub-zero temperatures. When operating a certain high-speed jet-propelled medium bomber at temperatures exceeding thirty degrees below zero they had had two cases of structural failure by fatigue, one of a vertical fin and one of an elevator. They were convinced that temperature came into it, a new idea to me. They suggested that the life of Mr Honey's Reindeer had been prolonged by the fact that it had operated mostly in the tropics.

All this was very stimulating, and they were not less helpful in the practical investigation of the crash in Labrador. They had a Norseman seaplane all laid on for the journey, and all the equipment and provisions for a week or ten days in the woods already loaded into it. The pilot was to be a civilian bush-pilot called Hennessey, a thick-set tough who knew that country intimately; Russell and an assistant of his called Stubbs were coming with us, making a party of four. The programme was that we should fly up and land on Small Pine Water, about eleven miles from the wreck; from there a trail made by previous visitors to the scene led over the hills and through the forests. It was, of course, quite impossible to put a landplane down in such country.

'They say the trail's pretty well defined,' Russell said. 'There was our party first of all, and then there was a funeral party went up there, and then the Russians sent a third party to bring away the body of their ambassador for burial in Russia. They had the hell of a job carrying a coffin down that trail.'

'Our people were all buried up there, were they?' I inquired.

'Oh yes. It wasn't practical to bring the rest of them away. There were over thirty, and all would have had to be carried eleven miles. No, we buried them all up there; a padre went up for the funeral service.'

They were all ready to start, and were only waiting for me. We lunched and then they took me to a sort of store and fitted me out with a bush shirt, breeches, and high laced boots that buckled close below the knee. 'The mosquitoes are liable to be mighty bad this time of year,' Hennessey said. They had hammocks for sleeping in, provided with a sort of roof of waterproof fabric with a mosquito net attached.

I transferred some small personal kit from my suitcase into a small kitbag; then I was ready and we drove down to the dock, where the Norseman was moored. It was only about three o'clock in the afternoon, and we were all ready to start. 'I guess we'll make Ivanhoe by sundown,' Hennessey said. 'Tank up there, 'n have plenty up at the lake.'

The others agreed with this programme. 'How far is this place Ivanhoe?' I inquired.

Russell said, 'About five hundred and fifty miles. It's on the north shore of the St Lawrence, about a hundred miles from the crash.'

I said good-bye to the Director and thanked him for all his help; then we got into the machine. Hennessey started the engine and someone on the pontoon swung the wing-tip round; we taxied out into the lake, running up the engine in short bursts as we went. Then we headed into wind and took off after a long run, about fifty seconds. The machine was very heavily loaded for its power.

We circled the city and steadied on our course back over the route I had flown that morning. The machine was equipped for hard commercial work in the Canadian north, mostly for carrying freight. The passenger seats were small and rather hard, designed to be quickly removable; they wasted no weight upon blinds, and the cabin on that sunny afternoon became very hot. I sat drowsing and sweating and tired, but unable to sleep as we droned back past Montreal towards Quebec, a slow, interminable journey. Finally as the sun was getting down to the horizon we came to Ivanhoe, a little town of white wooden houses on the shore of an inlet of the sea. Behind it stretched the fir woods, apparently pathless, impenetrable. Such roads as there were came to an end immediately outside the town. There were three churches, with white wooden steeples, a little dock with a few fishing vessels and another seaplane moored to it, a small air-strip suitable for very little aeroplanes. That was all there was of Ivanhoe.

We saw all this as we circled round for the landing; then Hennessey put her down on the water gently; he was a very good pilot, on that aircraft anyway. She touched with a quick slapping of the small waves on the bottom of the floats; the floats bit down into the water and she leaned forward and decelerated, and slowed, and floated on the water off the town, pitching a little. Hennessey turned her, and we taxied into the pontoon.

A sergeant in the gay red tunic of the Royal Canadian

Mounted Police was there to meet us; he knew Hennessey, and said, 'Guess you folks'll have to sleep in the store tonight. Hotel's full of summer visitors.'

In the fading light he took us to a sort of marine store, a wooden shed full of old ships' ropes and other gear. There were big hooks down each wall, especially put there, it seemed, for slinging hammocks; it was frequently used as a dormitory. We slung ours, Stubbs assisting me and showing me how to do it, and made the seaplane fast at the pontoon; then we walked into the little town and sat down at the counter of the only café and ordered dinners of steak and onions and fried potatoes, from a girl who spoke nothing but French. Over the ice-cream and coffee we talked a little.

The crash was about four months' old, but Hennessey had been up there within the last month as a guide to the party of Russians who had come from the Embassy to disinter the body of their Ambassador and carry him away. 'Great big jars of stuff they had with them,' he said, 'and a kind of zinc tank with a lid you could screw down on a rubber gasket. He didn't smell so bad after they got him all sealed down. Eight handles it had, for carrying, but gee, that was a mean load. I never want another one like that again. Eleven miles, and a rough trail at that.'

He stared at his cup. 'I'm not sure even now they got the right one. It was the right grave, but when we buried them they weren't too easy to identify, and it didn't seem to matter which got which cross; they were all there together. We tossed a dime for which cross to put on some of them. Still, it wouldn't make a row of beans, anyway.'

We went back to the store in the soft darkness; at the pontoon near by the Norseman loomed with a great shadowy wing over the water. We undressed partially and got into our hammocks, but for a long while I could not sleep. I was overtired, and lay restless, wondering what the Director was saying to Honey in my absence, wondering what the next day would bring for me, wondering if corrosion would have destroyed the evidence for which I sought. Then, unhappily, I wondered if temperature did enter into this fatigue problem. If so, it might well mean a year's investigation before we could say definitely if the Reindeer was, in fact, unsafe. In that case it would be quicker to take the aircraft out of service and modify them whether they were dangerous or not, but what a stinking row there would be about that!

I rolled insecure, sleepless, overtired, and unhappy for most of the night. The store was full of rats, who scurried all around incessantly.

Early in the morning we were up and breakfasting in the same café, served by the same French-speaking girl. Then we began the weary task of filling six forty-gallon drums of petrol into the tanks of the Norseman through a semi-rotary pump. Each barrel had to be rolled from the petrol store a hundred yards away down to the pontoon, and the empties rolled back again. It took us about two hours, and by that time the sun was high and hot and we were tired and sweating. At last it was finished, and we got into the machine and started up the engine, and took off.

Small Pine Water is about an hour's flight from Ivanhoe. We left the St Lawrence and flew approximately north-east, over a desolate country covered in fir woods and fallen timber like spillikins, on hills which grew gradually higher beneath us as we went on inland. Presently Russell asked me if I would like to see the scene of the accident from the air before we landed on the lake. I said I would, and Hennessey brought the Norseman down to above five hundred feet above the tree tops and began circling around. But there was very little to be seen from the air. I saw a cliff that the aircraft had evidently hit, but it was not very conspicuous or very high. I saw a few shells of dulled duralumin between the fronds of new vegetation, and there was a little clearing where a few trees had been felled; in this clearing there were planted two rows of neat white crosses. That was all that could be seen from the air, and we turned back and landed on the lake.

When we were down, we turned and taxied in to a beach. People had been here before us, for the trees had been felled and undergrowth cleared at the landing. There were oil stains on the ground and a few empty tins, and burnt ashes in a fire-place built of stones, and stuck up in the fork of a tree there was a bundle tied around with sacking. The floats of the Norseman grounded upon rotting and decayed vegetation on the bottom of the lake about a couple of yards from the shore. We stopped the engine and got out on to the float, and walked along, and splashed through the shallow water to the shore. We took mooring lines with us and made the seaplane

221

fast to screw pickets; immediately the flies were all around us in a cloud.

It was then about noon. We unloaded all the gear out of the Norseman on to the beach, and Stubbs set about cooking a meal. It was arranged that he should stay there at the beach to look after the aircraft while Hennessey and Russell and I walked the eleven miles up to the crash, carrying upon our backs the packs containing our hammocks, blankets, ammunition, and food for two days. In addition each of us carried an axe and Hennessey carried a rifle, Russell a shot-gun.

I am ashamed to say how much that walk distressed me. It was a very hot summer afternoon, for one thing. My pack weighed about fifty pounds and it was comfortable enough on a light duralumin frame carrier. But I was out of condition with years of office work, whereas both Russell and Hennessey were wiry and perfectly fit. They took an easy pace to avoid tiring me too much and several times they offered to carry my pack for me, but pride made me refuse. It took us nearly five hours to get there, blind and drenched with sweat and tormented by the flies.

The country that we passed through was appalling. It was a forest of spruce and alder; in some parts the trees were no more than three feet apart. It was full of the rotting trunks of fallen trees, and these trees and the decaying vegetation round them made a queer, stifling aroma that was more a gasp than a smell. For much of the way the ground was soft muskeg in which the feet sank up to six inches. It was impossible to see more than a few yards in any direction; at the same time the trees were fairly small, so that they gave little shelter from the sun. The trail wound in and out among the fallen trunks marked here and there by a fading blaze upon a standing tree, but it was difficult to discern except to the practised eye, and in no way resembled a path. In places it was swampy, and here if you put a foot down incautiously you would go in knee deep. And always the flies were an incessant torment.

When finally we came out into the clearing with the double row of wooden crosses I was practically foundered. I slid the pack from my back and sat down on it for a moment with my head swimming and the flies in a great cloud around me. I thanked God in my fatigue that circumstances had prevented Honey from coming on this trip; I might be quite unfit for it, but I was certainly a great deal fitter than he was. Russell and Hennessey set about making a fire and boiling up a kettle for tea; by the time that was well under way I was feeling better, and able to assist them a bit by gathering the wood.

Tea refreshed us all, though none of us could eat anything. While Hennessey put the things together and began to arrange a camp Russell and I walked over to the wreck. It lay about two hundred yards away, under the stony cliff that had appeared in the photographs. New vegetation had grown up and was covering it over; by next year it would have merged into the forest.

We came first to the bow, to the smashed cockpit where Bill Ward had died, to the broken control columns, the scattered instruments, the flattened and corroded boxes of the radio and radar gear. Then came the broken wing and the engines, and the cabin with smashed seats and burnt upholstery, and the galley stove and lavatory behind it, practically undamaged amongst all the wreckage. I reflected that Honey had been quite right about that; was it to prove that he was right about fatigue as well?

Then we came to the tail.

The starboard side was more or less intact; the port tailplane and elevator were missing completely, as in the photographs and the description of the accident report. I went straight to the broken stumps of the spars still attached to the rear fuselage, that in the tiny detail of the photographs had suggested a fatigue fracture.

They were not as they had been in the photograph. A clean, recent saw-cut had been made to cut both spars through close up to the fuselage. The evidence had been removed.

Russell was dumbfounded, and shouted to Hennessey, who came running. We showed him what had happened. 'Oh, aye,' he said, 'the Russians did that. They cut them bits off with a hacksaw 'n took them away. They took some other bits as well.'

He eyed us with mounting anxiety. 'We thought it was all so much junk,' he said. 'Not important, were they?'

10

MR HONEY TRAVELLED back across the Atlantic in a Lincoln of the Empire Air Navigation School that had been wandering about the north of Canada doing something or other with the lines of flux at the Magnetic Pole. Now it was on its way back to Shawbury and the RAF navigators were glad to oblige by giving Mr Honey a lift back to England. Originally they had been bound straight for their base in Shropshire, but being navigators they rather enjoyed going out of their way in bad visibility on tortuous courses that would test their skill. They landed Mr Honey at Farnborough outside his own office door at half past one in the morning, put him out upon the runway, kissed their hands to him, and took off again for Shawbury in the darkness. Mr Honey was left holding his suitcase in the middle of Farnborough aerodrome in the middle of the night.

Characteristically, he went into the office. He walked in, blinking, to the bright lights of the old balloon shed where the night shift test upon the Reindeer tail was clattering and booming away, and there was young Simmons entering the routine hourly strain readings upon the routine graphs of the distortion of the structure, all of which went along as a perfectly straight horizontal line as the strain graphs of a safe structure should. He blinked at the great clattering thing, sniffed, savoured the familiar atmosphere; everything was all right, and he was home again.

He stayed about half an hour, examining the records; he had only been away for four days, but so much had happened in that time he felt that it was several months, that something must have changed, some catastrophe must have happened to his trial during his absence. But finally he satisfied himself that it was going on all right, and asked if Simmons had been posting the letters to Elspeth properly.

The boy hesitated. 'Well, yes I have, sir,' he said, 'but I don't know that they've been getting to her. You know she fell downstairs the night you went away, and she's been staying with Dr Scott ever since, I think.'

He told Honey what he knew, which was not very much, and satisfied him that Elspeth was not very ill. Honey said warmly, 'It was very kind of Dr Scott to do that. Is he at home now?'

'I think he flew to Canada this evening, sir. He was going to, after his lecture on the "Performance of Aircraft Flying at High Mach Numbers". We all went up to that. It was awfully good.'

It seemed to Honey that there was not much else he could do but to go home and go to bed; he could hardly burst in on Shirley in the middle of the night and demand to see Elspeth, who was apparently being well looked after. As regards getting home, there was a little difficulty. There were no buses at that hour and no RAE transport. Simmons had a motor-bicycle, but Honey could not ride it and Simmons could not leave the Reindeer trial. In the end Honey left the suitcase in his office, and set out to walk the four miles to his home through the deserted lanes and streets.

He got there at about half past three, walked up the path through the front garden, and let himself into the house with his latchkey. He went into the front sitting-room and snapped on the light. The familiar room was somewhat changed in the short time that he had been away; there was a smell of soap that he could not at first identify, and there was a vase of roses on the table. He wondered who could have done a thing like that, and then he remembered that something had happened to Elspeth and other people must have been in the house.

A door opened upstairs, and he heard someone moving on the landing. He went out into the hall and looked up the one flight, blinking, and at the head of the stairs there was a young woman standing looking down, a very pleasant-looking young woman in pyjamas and a kimono. He did not recognise her at first; I don't know what he thought about it. Something that his Fairy Godmother had done for him, perhaps.

She said, 'Mr Honey! We didn't expect you back so soon.'

He said, 'Who is it?'

'It's me,' she said. 'Marjorie Corder.' She laughed a little awkwardly. 'I'd have stayed up if I'd known that you were coming home tonight, but we didn't think you could be here before tomorrow.'

She came downstairs to him. 'You must think it terribly funny for me to be here,' she said. 'But Elspeth was so anxious to get back here, and Mrs Scott couldn't have her for tonight. So I said I'd sleep here with her.' She broke off. 'Did you know she had an accident?'

'They told me something at the office. What *did* happen?' he asked. 'Simmons – he's my assistant there – he said Mrs Scott had taken her into their flat.'

She told him briefly what had been going on. 'Dr Scott wouldn't let anybody cable you about it,' she said, 'because you couldn't have got home any sooner and he thought it would only worry you. She's quite all right now – she's upstairs asleep. She's going to get up a bit tomorrow.'

He said, 'I'll just go up and see her.'

She smiled. 'Don't wake her up, will you? She's sleeping so nicely.'

'I won't wake her up,' he said.

She stopped him as he turned to the stairs. 'Have you had any supper?'

He thought back vaguely over the last few hours. 'We had some sandwiches and things in the aircraft,' he said.

'But when did you have your last proper meal?'

He thought for a minute. 'Gander, I suppose.'

She nodded. 'I'll get you something – you must be hungry. Scrambled eggs all right? Cocoa? Or Bovril?'

'Cocoa, please,' he said. 'But please don't bother —'

'But of course,' she said. 'You must have something.'

He went upstairs and peeped in on Elspeth, who was sleeping, with the washing-up mop in bed with her. On the table by her bedside, pulled forward where she could see it, was another little vase of roses and the photograph of her mother, his Mary, that somebody had taken from the mantelpiece and arranged specially for his daughter, in case she should be lonely amongst so many strangers. Mr Honey closed the door quietly with more moisture even than was usual in his weak eyes, washed his hands, and went down again to the kitchen.

He found Miss Corder at the gas-stove cooking for him; there was a cleaner, fresher air about the kitchen which seemed strange to him and which he did not understand. 'Please let me do that,' he said. 'There's no need for you to stay up now. I'll be all right.'

She turned half round from the stove. 'I feel an awful pig going to bed at all,' she said. 'If we'd thought that there was any chance of you getting back tonight I'd have had a decent meal ready for you.'

He said weakly. 'It's terribly nice of you,' and began to lay the table. 'When did you get here?'

'Yesterday,' she said. 'I brought your letter down to Dr Scott and then I heard that Elspeth was in bed, so I came round to see what I could do. And then she was anxious to get back here, and Mrs Scott wanted to be up in London tonight to see her husband off to Canada, so I said I'd sleep here with Elspeth until you came back. I do hope you don't mind. It did seem the best thing to do.'

'Of course I don't mind,' he said warmly. 'It's so very, very kind of you to take the trouble.'

She brought the scrambled eggs on toast to the table for him on a warm plate, and poured out cocoa for them both. As she supped she told him what they had been doing. 'Dr and Mrs Scott have been so kind,' she said, 'but really, Elspeth's much happier round here. She likes being in her own room and her own bed. I was doing the stairs this afternoon and we could talk, and then after that I made some toffee with her on the gas-ring in her room, and we played Sevens.'

Mr Honey realised dimly that nobody had played with Elspeth like that for many years; perhaps that was what was wrong with her. He said, 'You did the stairs? Do you mean, brushed them down?'

'I washed them,' the girl said. 'They did need it. I hope you don't mind. I did this room, too.'

Mr Honey glanced around the kitchen; so that was what had happened to it. 'It's awfully nice,' he said ingenuously. 'What did you do to the walls to make them like that?'

'I washed those, too,' she said. 'It didn't take long. An awful lot of dirt came off.'

He looked at her in slight distress. 'I didn't know it had got so bad.'

'Of course not,' she said gently. 'One wouldn't, living in the house the whole time. It's only when you come in fresh that it hits you in the eye.'

'I did tell Mrs Higgs to do some scrubbing, only last week,' he said. 'Or sometime. I suppose she didn't do it.'

'I don't think she can have,' the girl said positively. 'I should give her the sack if I were you. She doesn't seem to be very reliable.'

'The one I had before used to steal things,' Mr Honey said. 'Mrs Higgs is very honest, and she's given me a lot of help with Elspeth's clothes.'

The girl compressed her lips and took a drink of cocoa. 'Do you think I might look through Elspeth's clothes tomorrow?' she said. 'I don't want to barge in. But she tells me that she hasn't got any light cotton frocks for summer. Not one.'

'Ought she to have?' asked Mr Honey. 'I wear the same myself all the year round. You mean, like her party frock? I told her she could wear that when it's hot.'

Miss Corder moistened her lips and started off from the beginning to inform Mr Honey what a child should wear. As they talked the cocoa cooled; the first streak of light appeared at the black window. Presently she gathered the cups together. 'Let me have a look at her clothes while you're at work tomorrow,' she said. 'Then I'll make you out a list of what she ought to have.'

He said, 'I would be so grateful. It's so hard to find out, and one doesn't think, I suppose.' He hesitated. 'Could you stay with her till I get back tomorrow evening, possibly? I can fix up something else by then.'

'I could stay till Sunday night if you like,' she said. 'They won't want me at the Airways before Monday.'

His face lit up. 'I know Elspeth would like that,' he said. 'It would be horribly dull for her to be in bed alone here, even if I could get back for lunch.' And then he looked troubled. 'I don't know if that would do, though, would it?'

She said, 'You mean, for me to sleep here?'

'That's right.'

She considered for a minute. 'Not if the neighbours are going to start talking,' she said. 'I suppose they wouldn't like it at the RAE either.'

He stared at her. 'I wasn't thinking of that. It wouldn't matter what anyone at the RAE thought, and I don't even know the neighbours. Elspeth knows the people in No. 23, I think, but I don't know any of them.'

She laughed. 'Well that's all right then. Were you thinking about me?'

He nodded. 'You don't want to get a bad reputation,' he said awkwardly.

She smiled. 'Would it be all right if I put on my nurse's uniform?'

He stared at her. 'Well, I suppose it would. That's rather funny, when you come to think of it.'

'I'll do that if you like,' she said. 'It means I'll have to go back home and get it.' She paused. 'If you like, I'll sleep at home and come over each day.'

He smiled slowly. 'It's an awfully long way.'

She met his eyes. 'I think so, too. I don't mind if you don't.'

'I don't mind,' he said. 'I was just thinking about you.'

'Think about yourself,' she said gently. 'Think about what *you* want for a change; what *you* want out of life.' She put the plates together on the draining-board. 'You go to bed now, or you won't be fit to go into the office in the morning. And I know you're dying to do that.'

He smiled. 'I did look in for just a minute after we landed, this evening.'

'I might have known it. Go on up to bed. It's all made up and ready for you.'

In the door he paused. 'Good night, Marjorie,' he said.

'Be off with you,' she laughed. 'Good night, Theodore.'

He was very tired, but he lay awake in bed for some time thrilled and excited by the thought that Marjorie had come to stay with him, to take some of the aching responsibility for Elspeth off his shoulders, if only for three days. He was deeply grateful to her; from the first moment in the Reindeer when she had talked to him about the weather they would have upon the crossing, he had known that she was naturally kind. He had been right in that; at the first hint of trouble she had come to his house to help him in his absence; she had cared for his little daughter and played with her; she had washed his floors and made him supper in the middle of the night when he had turned up hungry. Now she was going to go through Elspeth's clothes and tell him what to buy.

Only one woman in his life had treated him like that before. Some girls radiated kindness; this one was fit to set beside the memory of Mary.

He drifted into sleep.

She would not let him help in getting breakfast; instead

she sent him up to sit with Elspeth, who was wide awake and sitting up in bed. She told him what had happened to her. 'There was a burglar,' she said, 'so I put on your warm dressing-gown and then I fell downstairs. And then when I woke up I was in Mrs Scott's bed and I was sick seven times and once the basin wasn't there and Dr Scott wiped it up and said it didn't matter.'

Honey said, 'Oh dear. I *am* sorry that happened.'

She reassured him. 'He didn't mind a bit, Daddy, honestly he didn't. He said he could remember being sick in a motor-car when he was a little boy and he wasn't ill at all. He was just sick. I do like Dr Scott. He's nice, isn't he?'

He nodded. 'You like Mrs Scott too, don't you?'

'I like them both, and Monica and Marjorie. Can Marjorie stay till Sunday, Daddy? She said she could if you said yes. Then she's got to go to Canada in the aeroplane but she's coming back on Thursday and she said she'd come down and see me again. Would that be all right?'

He said, 'Who's Monica?'

'Monica Teasdale. She was nice, too, but she's old. She reads out loud awfully well and she kept calling me honey. Why did she do that, Daddy?'

'I don't know. Is she still here?'

The child shook her head. 'She went away the day before yesterday. She said I was to come and spend a holiday with her and go on a dude ranch. What's a dude ranch, Daddy?'

'I don't know,' he said vaguely. 'Something they do in America, I suppose.'

Marjorie called him for his breakfast, a better one than he had tasted in that kitchen for years. She took up a tray and got Elspeth started; then she came down and smoked a cigarette while he finished his. And presently she pushed him off to the office just as Mary used to do, and he with difficulty restrained a crazy impulse to turn and kiss her in the doorway, as he had used to kiss Mary. He walked down to the bus with his old felt hat crammed untidily on his head and his brief-case in his hand, very thoughtful.

He went to the Director's office as soon as he got to the RAE, and stood for a few minutes nervously explaining what had happened at Gander. 'I didn't know what else to do,' he said unhappily. 'Dr Scott had said that it was so important that the aircraft shouldn't fly if there was any risk. And I couldn't make them understand why it shouldn't go on. But I do realise that it has made a very awkward situation, sir. I sent my resignation in to Dr Scott.'

The Director said, 'I know – he came and saw me about it. He tore your letter up.'

'My letter of resignation, sir?'

'Yes. It's not going to help anybody if you resign and afterwards it turns out you were right, Honey. It only makes the matter worse. Leave that for the present and go on with the trial on the Reindeer tail. I won't pretend that I was pleased when I heard what you did at Gander – it's made a lot of trouble. But if it turns out you were justified – well, there's an end of it, of course. And that we ought to know quite soon. I'm expecting a cable from Scott tomorrow or the next day, when he's been up to the wreckage.'

There followed two halcyon days for Mr Honey. At the office he dived straight back into his routine; while he had been absent a report had come in of some work carried out in Oslo on the strain energy absorption of copper alloys with particular reference to high tension electrical conductors, and this report blew a small sidewind on the fatigue investigations. He plunged deep into consideration of what this might mean, and dismissed the Reindeer altogether from his mind; it was for other people, me particularly, to deal with trivial matters like the fate of CATO's North Atlantic Air Service, while he got on with the real work, the stuff that really mattered. That did not prevent him, however, from leaving the office punctually at half past five. He found that Shirley had been round to tea with Marjorie and Elspeth and that they had all been playing Monopoly on Elspeth's bed, a game new to Mr Honey. Elspeth insisted that he should play too, and ruined him without the slightest difficulty, and by the time they all woke up to the time it was half past seven.

He supped simply on a fish pudding and stewed fruit with a milk pudding, all cooked by Miss Corder, and it was with a sense of internal well-being and ease unusual for him after a meal that he sat down with her when they had done the washing-up to study Elspeth's clothes. 'She's all right for winter things,' Marjorie said, 'but really, she's got practically nothing for the summer. Those flannel pyjamas that she wears must be lovely in the winter, but she's awfully hot in them now. And she's got no frocks at all. . . .'

He went through the list with her and she priced the various garments for him. 'She doesn't need all of these at once, of course,' she said. 'In fact, two frocks would do to start with if you could get the washing done at home.' She turned to him. 'I was thinking we might get her up on Sunday for a bit. If we could get her some of these things tomorrow afternoon for her to get up into, it'ld give her a tremendous lift.'

Mr Honey said, 'We'd better get them all at once, hadn't we? I'll have to go to the bank, but I think there's plenty of money. Plenty for this, anyway.'

'I think we'd better get just what she needs for the moment,' the girl said. 'Later on, when she can get about, it would be fun to take her up to London to the big shops; I saw some lovely children's frocks in Barker's the other day, awfully cheap. And she'd get a great thrill out of buying her own frocks in a big shop.'

The week-end passed in quiet, happy intimacy. On Saturday afternoon the Transatlantic stewardess and the research scientist on whose work depended all the lives of people travelling in Reindeer aircraft went out with a string bag to go shopping together down the High Street of the little Hampshire town, and came back loaded with brown paper parcels like any other suburban couple living in more regular circumstances, to have tea in the kitchen and turn over their purchases on Elspeth's bed, and watch the child's delight. Then Honey went down quietly to the front room to consider his more recent calculations on the Pyramid, and presently became immersed in them till Marjorie put her head into the door to tell him supper was ready. And after that, he told her all about it.

On Sunday morning they got Elspeth up after breakfast in her new print frock and sat her in a chair in the garden while Mr Honey mowed the lawn and Marjorie weeded and cooked alternately. They made Elspeth lie down on her bed after dinner while they dozed in the garden in deck-chairs, and then they all had tea together on the lawn. Then it was time for Marjorie to go; in order to be at Heath Row by eight-thirty in the morning she would have to sleep at home in Ealing.

Elspeth said, 'Please, will you come down on Thursday,

like you said?'

She glanced at Honey. 'If your father says I may.'

He said, 'Oh please do. I do wish you could stay on now. It makes such a difference. . . .'

She shook her head. 'I wish I could. But I'm almost sure they'll have a trip for me tomorrow. That means Montreal on Tuesday morning and back again on Wednesday afternoon. I ought to be able to get down here again by tea-time on Thursday,' she said to Elspeth. 'But don't worry if I'm late, because I might not get down till Friday morning. But I will come. I promise you.'

They left Elspeth sitting in the garden with a rug round her and went together to the front door. 'Let her have a little of the semolina pudding for her supper, with some of the jam,' she said. 'I wouldn't give her any more. And she ought to be in bed by seven – it's her first day up, you know. I'd give her her supper in bed.'

He said, 'I do wish you were staying. It's such a help, and it's been so lovely having someone. . . .' He hesitated awkwardly. 'Someone to talk to.'

She met his eyes. 'If by any chance they don't want me at the airport,' she said, 'may I come back?'

He said earnestly, 'Please do.'

She nodded. 'I'll do that if they don't want me, Theodore. But I'm afraid they'll have a trip for me, and in that case it'll probably be Thursday evening.'

He said simply, 'We shall be looking forward to that, both of us.'

She left him, and walked down the road to catch the Green Line bus for London. She hated the thought of going back to work. For her the run to Montreal held little charm; she was tired of serving coffee and biscuits with a smile, like any waitress in a café. The glamour of an airline stewardess was dead for her; she could not rate it equal in importance with the job of making something out of Elspeth Honey, of broadening her warped, one-sided life. For Honey himself she had a deep respect, verging upon love. He seemed to her to be the most unassuming, the bravest, and the cleverest man she had ever met, and she knew that her own qualities could help him tremendously. She was shrewd enough to know that she would never equal him in mental power, but with her cooking and her care behind that power he could do great things.

On Monday morning Mr Honey went into the office thinking mainly of the strain energy absorption factor of copper-tungsten alloys, with a side thought or two to Marjorie Corder; I think he had forgotten all about CATO and my mission in Labrador. It was quite a surprise when he received a message in the middle of the morning that the Director would like to see him; he blinked and wondered what it could be all about, and then remembered that there was some trouble going on about the Reindeer, trouble that was really nothing to do with him at all. He went to the office unwillingly, reluctant to be dragged into the Reindeer controversy again.

The Director said, 'Oh Honey, I want you to keep *au fait* with what Dr Scott is doing about this Reindeer accident. Quite a lot has happened over the week-end. To begin with, this radiogram came in on Saturday night.'

He passed the slip across the table. Mr Honey took it, blinking. It was headed IVANHOE PQ.

'What does this word Ivanhoe mean, sir?' he asked, puzzled. 'Isn't that a book or something?' It seemed to him to be some kind of code, and he was intrigued.

'It's a small town on the Gulf of St Lawrence,' the Director said patiently. 'It *is* a book as well, but it's the name of the place Scott sent that cable from.'

'Oh.'

The message read:

Have visited crashed Reindeer but broken stubs of tailplane spars have been removed with hacksaw stop local evidence states that these and other portions of the wreckage were removed by Russian personnel visiting the scene to recover body of M. Oskonikoff for reburial at Moscow stop suggest demand these parts from Russians as difficult country will make finding of port tailplane uncertain if not impossible stop cable further instructions to me at Ivanhoe – Scott.

Mr Honey handed this back to the Director. 'It's very unfortunate if these parts have been lost,' he said.

'Very,' said the Director dryly. 'I spoke to DRD about it yesterday morning as a matter of urgency and, to cut a long story short, a cable about the matter went off yesterday to our Embassy in Moscow. But I'm sorry to say that

234

the Russians don't seem to be very co-operative in the matter.'

I doubt if he knew more than that himself; it was weeks later that I got something of the story of what had happened in Moscow. The story as I heard it was that Sir Malcolm Howe had rung up M. Serevieff immediately he got the cable and asked for the parts to be sent to England for a further examination. M. Serevieff had countered by saying that he was glad that Sir Malcolm had raised this matter, which was one of some moment. It was certainly the case that the Russian burial party had included certain members of their Accidents Bureau; he could not say whether any parts had been removed and anyway, that was a matter of no importance. What *was* important was that the British Government had tried to trick the Russians, to conceal the evidence of their crime. The body handed to the Russian mission in Labrador was not that of M. Oskonikoff; the dentures did not correspond, and expert examination of the body in Moscow had proved it to be that of a considerably younger man. Would the Ambassador kindly explain this action of the British Government? His manner left no room for doubting that the Russians thought that the accident had been contrived to secure the murder of their Ambassador in a remote place where detection would be difficult, and that the substitution of another body was all part of the plot. Indeed, M. Serevieff said so, in so many words.

I need hardly say that this charge raised considerable stir in diplomatic circles, to the extent that it was impossible even to try any further to make the Russians disgorge the bits that they had taken from the crash. I don't know how it all ended; I doubt if anyone outside the Foreign Office and the Cabinet knows that. I only know that, on that Monday morning, the Director with Mr Honey blinking at his elbow concocted the following cable, which reached me a couple of hours later at Ivanhoe, in the telegraph office of the Royal Canadian Mounted Police:

Foreign Office consider it inadvisable to press for recovery of Reindeer parts from Russians as wider issues are involved stop it is therefore imperative to locate and examine missing port tailplane however long this takes rely on you to do your utmost. RAE.

They sent that one off to me, and Mr Honey went blithely back to his office and the copper-tungsten alloy papers, relieved that he had not been called upon to do something in a matter that held little interest for him.

I got that cable about breakfast time, when by reason of the difference in local time Mr Honey was just going home to lunch to get Elspeth out of bed for the afternoon. The Mounties called me into their office as we were walking from the store where we had slept again in our hammocks, walking down the sunlit main street of that small Canadian lumber town to the café with the French-speaking waitress. I took the message slip from them and read it in dismay, and showed it to Hennessey and Russell and Stubbs in the middle of the street.

Russell went up in a sheet of flame, rather naturally. 'My Christ!' he said. 'The British Foreign Office must be nuts. They just don't know the way we're fixed out here! If that tailplane came off in the air the way you think it did, it might be twenty miles away from the rest of the machine. How do you think we're going to find that in this type of country? Do they suppose a street cleaner'll find it and bring it in?'

I stared at him in despair. 'I don't know what they think.'

We went and sat down at the stainless bar and ordered flakes and eggs and bacon from the French girl. I studied the message again, and compared it with the copy I had kept of my previous one to the Director. I pointed out to them, 'See, I said "finding of port tailplane uncertain if not impossible".'

'You're darn right,' said Hennessey.

'Well, now they come back with this,' I said. I turned to them. 'It just means we've got to do our best to find the thing. After all, it's quite a big unit – over twenty feet long. It might be visible from the air.'

Hennessey said doubtfully, 'It's a chance. It's a pretty thickly wooded section of the country, though, and spruce and alder, they grow pretty fast this time of year. And all the leaves on, too.'

We talked about it for an hour, and then worked out the following programme. We would go up to the lake again in the Norseman, and trek up again to the scene of the crash, prepared to camp there for four days. We would mark out an area half a mile each way from the crash, one square mile in all, with the crashed Reindeer in the centre, and we would search that area minutely whatever the difficulties. If we did not discover the port tailplane there would be a strong presumption that the unit had come off in the air; it was too big a thing for the Russians to have removed *in toto*. That in itself would lend some substance to the theory of failure in fatigue.

After that area had been searched, we would then return to the lake and begin an air search of the district, flying the Norseman low above the tree-tops endeavouring to see the fallen tailplane, flying on closely parallel strips as in an air survey. None of us had much confidence in this procedure, but it was the only thing that we could do.

'One thing,' said Russell. 'We'd better set to work and draft a cable to your chief telling him not to expect too much.' We set to work to do so.

Back in England, Mr Honey hurried home to lunch with Elspeth. He did not normally go home to lunch because the journey from the office to his house took half an hour, or three-quarters if he was unlucky with his bus, and this meant over an hour spent in travelling alone, whereas his nominal lunch-time was an hour only. So he hurried to get Elspeth out of bed and give her a cold lunch and get her settled in a chair with a book to read before he had to hurry off again back to the office. She told him, 'Mrs Scott came and sat with me a little this morning, Daddy. She said she'd come in and give me tea, and you weren't to worry because she'd be able to stay here till you got back.'

He said. 'That's very kind of her.'

Elspeth nodded. 'She said she'd bring some rock cakes round with her, too.'

'Don't let her do this washing up,' he said. 'And don't you do it, either. I'll just leave the things stacked here, and then I'll do it with the supper things this evening.'

He hurried back to the office, and got in three-quarters of an hour late. In the normal course this would not have mattered and no one would have known, because he worked in a watertight compartment and he was apt to stay late in the evenings so that I, for one, would never have bothered him about small irregularities in timekeeping. As luck would have it, the Director had sent for him at five minutes past two to meet E. P. Prendergast, who had turned up at the RAE shortly before lunch to investigate these allegations about the Reindeer tail. The Director had had to hold Prendergast in play with smooth words till Honey had showed up at ten minutes to three, and neither the Director nor Mr Prendergast were very pleased about it.

Mr Honey said breathlessly, 'I'm sorry I'm late, sir. I had some personal matters that kept me.'

The Director said, 'This is Mr Prendergast of the Rutland Aircraft Company, Honey. He has come down to look into this matter of the Reindeer tail.' Mr Honey gazed at the great bulk of the designer apprehensively; Mr Prendergast did not seem to be in a very good temper. 'I have told him the outlines of what we have been doing here. I think, perhaps, if he went with you to your office and you went through the work in detail with him, and bring him back here after that, it would be best.'

Prendergast said, 'Certainly. I shall be most interested to hear what Mr Honey has to say about the Reindeer tail.'

That was about the last thing he said for the next hour, according to Honey. Whatever the little man showed him or explained, the designer did nothing but grunt. This was one of his more offensive techniques; he would stand in silence listening to a halting explanation and then grunt, a grunt expressing an ill-tempered scepticism or plain disbelief. They stood under the great clattering bulk of the Reindeer tail while Honey nervously expounded the harmonics that were being imposed on it; they stood in the office while Honey, nearly in tears by that time, endeavoured to explain his hypothesis of nuclear strain to a designer who knew nothing of the atom and cared less, grunting in disbelief of this newfangled nonsense. He only spoke once, so far as Honey remembers; that was to say, 'I understand, then, that there is no experimental evidence at all yet that confirms the truth of all this theory?'

Honey said unhappily, 'It's too early. You can't rush basic research like everybody here is trying to do.'

The designer grunted.

When finally Mr Honey took Prendergast back to the Director's office he was in a state of acute nervous tension, noticed by the Director, who released him as soon as was polite. As the door closed behind him the designer relaxed, and smiled for the first time that afternoon. 'Queer customer,' he said.

The Director said politely, 'I hope he gave you all the information you need?'

Prendergast grunted. 'He gave me plenty of information. Whether any of it's any good is another matter.' However, when he came to go away he was quite cordial to the Director, almost benign.

The Director did not have time to speculate on that, because as the door closed behind Prendergast, his secretary brought in my cable in reply from Ivanhoe. This read:

Propose search for tailplane an area one square mile around crash intensively estimate this will take four days stop thereafter propose search from air by strip flying an area approximately 100 square miles this may take a fortnight stop am pessimistic of flight search yielding results owing to density of forest growth and recommend all possible pressure on the Russians to surrender parts removed. Scott.

The Director sent for Honey again, who appeared white and nervous and trembling a little in frustrated rage after his hour with Prendergast. The Director showed him this cable; Honey read it without properly taking it in.

'It's no good putting pressure on me, sir,' he said, nearly weeping, handing it back. 'I can't make this test go any faster.'

The Director said, 'I'm not putting pressure on you, Honey. But you're in charge of the Reindeer tail investigation in Dr Scott's absence. I want you to realise the very difficult position that Dr Scott is in, that's all.'

Honey flushed angrily. 'He's not in a difficult position. I'm the one who's in a difficult position, with everybody trying to extract *ad hoc* data from an incomplete piece of basic research. I can't do my work if you keep on badgering me like this – I'll have to give up and go somewhere else. First of all it was Sir Phillip Dolbear and now Prendergast. I've got nothing to show to anybody yet, and every time I'm made to look a fool. And Dr Scott's as bad as any of them.' He was very much upset.

The Director said, 'Mr Honey, I don't think you quite

realise how much you owe to Dr Scott. At last Thursday's meeting with DRD he expressed complete confidence in your estimate of this fatigue failure, in the face of the most damaging attacks, I may say, from both CATO and the company. He staked his own reputation on your work. He told the meeting that he thought you were right, and when he left this country he was confident that if he brought back the parts in question they would prove beyond all doubt that you were right in your diagnosis of the cause of this accident; and that he was right in standing up and putting his whole reputation on your side. Well, now he finds he can't produce that evidence unless he finds this tailplane, and in that country that seems to be like looking for a needle in a bundle of hay.'

Honey stared at the cable through his thick glasses. 'Oh,' he said, 'is that what this means? It wasn't very clear.'

'That's exactly what that means,' the Director said shortly. 'If you were as good a friend of Dr Scott as he has been to you, you'd talk about him rather differently.'

Mr Honey flushed crimson. 'I'm sorry,' he said weakly. And then he waved the cable in his hand. 'May I take this tonight and think about it?' he inquired. 'I'll let you have it back in the morning, sir.'

The Director shrugged his shoulders; he was tired of Mr Honey. 'If you like.'

Mr Honey went back to his office distressed and confused. He was a sensitive little man and absurdly grateful to Shirley and to me for the little trivial things that we had done to help him; the Director had hurt him very deeply by what he had said. He stood for ten minutes in humiliated unhappiness in his office, re-reading my cable and re-orientating his ideas; then he went out and caught his bus back home, lost in deep thought.

His ruminations were rudely interrupted at his own front gate, and he was jerked into another world. Elspeth had been watching for him, and she came rushing down the path to meet him, flushed and excited in her new frock. 'Daddy,' she cried, 'the water heater's come! The men came with it just after you went, and they worked all the time and made a new pipe and fixed it on the wall over the sink, and it's making hot water! They're coming in to paint the pipe tomorrow!'

She dragged him by the arm to show him this wonder in the kitchen. In the front door Marjorie Corder came forward to meet him, with Shirley behind her. 'I came back,' she said simply. 'They didn't want me for another week at the airport, so I came back.'

She did not tell him that she had put in for a week's leave, and got it, after some argument.

Mr Honey said, 'Oh, I *am* glad,' and Shirley standing close behind the girl saw the radiance on his frog-like features, and understood why Marjorie had bothered to come back. And then they all went into the kitchen and admired the hot-water-heater, and gave it its first job to do by doing the lunch wash-up.

He pressed Shirley to stay to supper, and as she was alone in our flat she was glad to do so, so they set to and made a shepherd's pie and put it in the oven to cook. And while that was doing they all had a game of Monopoly with Elspeth, which Mr Honey played unusually badly even for him, so that he was ruined in ten minutes. His mind was so obviously remote from the game that when they were dishing up the supper, Marjorie asked him quietly in a corner by the gas-stove, 'Is anything wrong, Theo?'

'Nothing much,' he said heavily. 'It's been rather a bad day. I had the designer of the Reindeer on my hands most of the afternoon, a Mr Prendergast. He was very difficult.'

Shirley overheard this. 'Everyone says he's difficult. I thought he was such a nice man at the lecture. I hope you told him where he got off.'

Honey smiled weakly. 'He's not a very easy man to tell that to. And there were other things, too. . . .' He hesitated, and then decided to unburden himself to them. 'We've had a lot of cables from Dr Scott over the week-end,' he said. 'He can't find the fractured pieces of the tail.'

Shirley said sharply, 'But they *must* be there!' and Marjorie said, 'Oh, Theo!' Both girls were very well acquainted with the issues that were involved, but none of them had even considered before what it would mean if I failed to find a fatigue fracture in the first Reindeer crash. They pressed Honey for more details of what had happened, and he told them a stumbling and confused narrative, and showed them the crumpled copy of my last cable that he had brought from the Director's office. A sense of disaster descended on them and spoilt their party; they talked through supper in depressed tones with long pauses between each remark. Elspeth, who did not understand what it was all about, asked, 'What's the matter with Dr Scott in Labrador, Daddy?'

Marjorie, to relieve him, said, 'He's lost something, and he can't find it. Something very important.'

'What can't he find, Daddy?'

Honey said, 'A piece of an aeroplane.'

'Is it a very important piece?'

'Very important,' Honey said. 'He's in dreadful trouble.' Shirley, watching him, was interested to see that he had suddenly lost his air of impotent worry. He looked, she said, like a dog just coming on the scent. A funny sort of simile, but that's how she described him.

Elspeth said, 'Oh, poor Dr Scott.'

'Poor Dr Scott,' Honey repeated with deep, emphatic sympathy. 'He's in terrible trouble. And he's been so kind to us, hasn't he? Would you like to try and find it for him with the little trolley?' The two girls stared uncomprehending at them across the cooling food upon the table.

Elspeth nodded vigorously. 'Mm.'

Honey got up from the table, his entire attention fixed upon his little white-faced daugher. 'All right, let's go into the other room and get the little trolley.'

He got up from the table and took Elspeth by the hand, entirely oblivious of the two girls. They moved to the door; Marjorie half rose from her seat. 'Where are you going?' she asked.

Honey turned in the doorway. 'Please,' he said sternly, and there was a confidence of command about him that was new to both of them. 'You may come with us if you sit very quiet at the back of the room, but you mustn't speak at all or interrupt in any way. If you feel you can't control yourselves, you must stay here.'

He went out into the front room; the girls glanced at each other in mystification, and then followed him. They found him pinning a fresh sheet of paper down upon the drawing-board and laying it horizontal on the table at a comfortable height for Elspeth sitting in a chair before it. Then he pulled the heavy curtains to shut out the daylight and switched on a powerful desk reading-lamp upon the table. Next he went to the cupboard and got out two instruments. The first was a small affair of rotating black and white segments, worked by a small air turbine from a rubber bulb held in the palm of his hand; by pressing the bulb he could make the black and white segments alternate at varying speeds. The second instrument was a planchette, a little flat triangular trolley of three-ply wood about nine inches wide, supported on two tiny castoring wheels and a pencil at the third corner. He put this down upon the drawing-board and Elspeth laid the tips of her fingers upon it; Marjorie noted with a shock that she was evidently well accustomed to this routine.

Then he arranged the powerful light to focus only on the rotating black and white segments immediately in front of his little daughter; the rest of the room was in darkness.

'Is that light too strong?' he asked quietly.

'No, Daddy, it's all right,' she said. It was the first time they had spoken.

'All right,' he said. 'Just look at the whizzer.' The segments started to turn white and black in turn before her eyes in the bright light.

He said softly, 'Poor Dr Scott, he's in such terrible trouble. He wiped up the mess you made when you were sick, didn't he?' The black and white segments were changing places more quickly now.

Her eyes fixed upon them, Elspeth whispered, 'Yes.'

'He's been so kind,' he said quietly. 'He showed us how to get the hot-water-heater so that we'll have hot water all the time now.'

She repeated, 'He's so kind.' Her eyes were fixed upon the changing segments in the brilliant light.

'He showed us how to use the washing-up mop, so that we don't have to use the rag,' Honey said in an even tone.

The little girl said drowsily, 'We don't have to use the rag now.'

In the darkness at the back of the room the two young women sat motionless, tense. In Marjorie there was a great tumult of feelings. She was deeply shocked at what was going on; every fibre in her being revolted at the use that Honey was making of his child. At the same time, she could not interrupt; there was a power and a competence about him in this matter that she dared not cross. She must stay quiet now and see it out, but never, never, never should this happen again.

Honey said quietly, 'Poor Dr Scott, he's been so kind to us, and now he's in such terrible trouble, because he can't find what he's looking for. He's so unhappy. It's lost in the forest, all among the trees, in the wild land where no people have ever been.' The black and white segments were changing places quickly now; the white-faced little girl was sitting with glazed eyes, motionless. 'Try and help poor Dr Scott find what he's looking for. Try and help him. He's been so kind to us. It's in the forest, lying somewhere in the trees, where nobody has ever been. It's a big metal piece, nearly as big as this house.'

The faint whirring of the segments was the only sound in the room. The blackness was oppressive, intense, around the girls. Shirley found later that her palms were bleeding from the unconscious pressure of her finger-nails, so great was the tension.

'Poor Dr Scott,' Honey repeated monotonously, 'he's so unhappy, in the forest, looking for it, and he can't find it. Try and help him find it. Try and help him. Try now. Try.'

Beneath the child's fingers the planchette began to stir, and crept across the paper in uneven, jerky spasms.

11

MR HONEY WENT to the Director's office in the morning with the greatest reluctance. He did not like contact with any of his superior officers, ever, on any subject. He regarded technical executives as mean creatures who had abandoned scientific work for the fleshpots, for the luxuries of life that could be bought with a high salary. He had no opinion of any of us, judged as men; for this reason he preferred his own company or the company of earnest young men fresh from college who were not yet tainted with commercialism. He went cynically on this occasion, already embittered by the anticipation of disbelief. It had always been so when he had put forward new ideas; he had not got the happy knack of making people credit him from the start.

He had to wait some time in the outer office, because the Director was engaged. When finally Mr Honey got in to see him he was rather short of time and rather overwhelmed by the pressure of other work; later that morning he would have to entertain and show round a commission of French scientists on a visit to our aeronuautical research establishments. He said, 'Well, Honey, what is it?'

Mr Honey said, 'Is it possible to get in touch with Dr Scott, sir?'

'We can send cables to him. There is a routine in force by which Ottawa can get in contact with the radio in his aeroplane once a day.' The procedure was that a cable from the RAE was telephoned to Ferguson at the Ministry of Supply. It was then radioed to the Department of Civil Aviation in Ottawa, who relayed it to the Royal Canadian Air Force post at Rimouski on the lower St Lawrence. We could reach Rimouski on the two-way radio in the Norseman, and make contact with them each day at six in the evening to receive or transmit any message of urgency.

Mr Honey hesitated. 'I should like to send him a cable, sir. I've got a message here that might be helpful to him.'

'What sort of message, Honey?'

'It's about this tail unit that he's trying to find, sir. I think I've got something that might help.'

The Director stared at him. 'What sort of thing?'

'Automatic writing,' Mr Honey said reluctantly. 'I've had a great deal of experience with that – not in office time, of course. It gives really remarkable results in certain cases.'

The Director wrinkled his brows. 'Automatic writing? You mean produced by someone in a mental trance?'

Mr Honey said eagerly, 'That's right, sir. I got it through my daughter, Elspeth, last night. She's only twelve, but she's really got a remarkable gift. Of course, children do produce the most amazing results sometimes. They don't often retain their powers in later life, though.'

The Director was too busy to allow Mr Honey much latitude to discourse on his researches in that field. 'What is it that you've got?'

Mr Honey produced a small roll of drawing paper, cut from the large sheet he had pinned down on the drawing-board the night before. 'Well, this is what was actually produced,' he said. He unrolled it on the desk.

It was covered all over with pencil jabs, squiggles, and irregular traces. Some of these appeared to form themselves into letters, and some into half words, thus in one part of the paper the letters ING were fairly clear, and in another there was a very definite capital R. Mr Honey turned the paper round. 'This is what I mean, sir.'

Across one corner the squiggles ran consecutively in a fairly straight line. They were certainly writing, jerky and uneven though the letters were; it was not too difficult to decipher the message. It read, UNDER THE FOOT OF THE BEAR.

'I'm sure that means something,' Mr Honey said. 'I think we ought to cable it to Dr Scott.'

The Director grunted, not unlike the grunts that Mr Prendergast had dispensed the day before, and Honey winced. 'We should have to cable some explanation of how the message was produced,' he said.

'Oh, yes, sir. We must let Dr Scott have all the facts, of course.'

The Director suffered an instinctive feeling of revulsion, and I don't blame him. He was in charge of a large Government research establishment of the most serious character. Honey was suggesting that he should send out, in the name of that establishment, a message which could only imply his own confidence in a spiritualistic message produced by a little girl of twelve, the daughter of an official who was believed by many to be mentally unbalanced. This message had to be sent through the Ministry of Supply, who were his parent body, and through Canadian Government organisations. Inevitably its subject-matter would attract attention; it would become the subject of a tea-time joke up in the Ministry. People would start saying he was mentally unbalanced too if he sent out a thing like that.

He said slowly, 'I don't think we should bother Dr Scott with this, Honey. It's too unscientific for us to put forward as evidence.'

That touched Honey on the raw; he was the scientist and the Director a renegade who had deserted the pure field of science for the fleshpots of administration. 'It's not unscientific at all,' he said hotly. 'It's the product of a carefully controlled piece of research extending over a good number of years. The fact that aeronautical people don't know much about research in that field doesn't prove that it's unscientific. They don't know much about cancer research, either.'

The Director was very busy that morning, but he had a

few moments to try and placate the angry little man before him. 'I didn't mean that in any derogatory sense, Honey,' he said. 'But it's not the sort of science that usually emanates from this Establishment, and not the sort that anybody here could possibly endorse.'

'That doesn't mean it isn't true,' Honey retorted.

The Director turned the paper over in his hands. 'Before you can say if it's true or not, you've got to decide what it means,' he observed. 'UNDER THE FOOT OF THE BEAR. The Bear means Russia, I suppose. I told you yesterday that the Russians had refused to release these parts that they have taken from the wreck of the Reindeer in Labrador. Would it not be correct to say that these parts are, in fact, under the foot of the Bear?'

Mr Honey stared at him. 'I don't know,' he said weakly. 'I never thought of that.'

The Director said, 'I merely put that out as a suggestion, Honey, that if this message does, in fact, mean anything, it may merely refer to something we already know about.'

Honey said, 'That might possibly be so. But Elspeth knew nothing about the Russians, sir. I didn't discuss that with her.'

'You knew about it, though,' the Director said. 'Might not thought transference come in? I merely put that forward as a suggestion.'

Honey was silent. He could not think of any answer to that one.

The Director handed him back the paper. 'I don't think we could send that out through official channels in the name of the RAE, Honey,' he said. 'If you feel strongly about it you could write a private letter to Scott, care of the Department of Civil Aviation in Ottawa.'

'Would he get that up in this place where he is, sir?'

'I should rather doubt it. I shouldn't think he'd get it till he returns to Ottawa.'

Honey said irritably, 'What's the use of that? It wouldn't be any help to him to let him have this after the job is over.'

The Director did not think that it would be any help to me anyway, but all he said was, 'I'm sorry, Honey, but that's the only thing I can suggest. Now, if you don't mind, I have a great many things to do this morning.'

Mr Honey said hotly, 'And I bet they're none of them

more important than this,' and flounced out of the room. The Director stared after him a little sadly. Was Prendergast right, after all? He had had doubts of Honey's mental stability himself from time to time, but my faith in the little man had reassured him and had made him stalwart in his defence at the DRD meeting. Now I, the buffer, was away in Canada and he had had a taste of Honey direct from the cup, pure and undiluted. He sighed as he turned to other work. Was another problem looming up before him, another scientist upon his staff who would start pilfering from small shops or behaving rudely in the park?

Mr Honey went back to his office in frustrated rage, not for the first time. He was convinced from his experience in psychic matters that the words they had received were an indication that would be helpful in the future and were not a mere record of current knowledge; he had received too many in connection with the excavation of the Roman aqueduct not to know the style. The flat denial of official methods of communication was sheer frustration to him, because a little reflection showed him that there was, in fact, no possible means of getting into touch with me except through the official channels. He could give no attention to his work, could think of nothing but the grievance that he suffered from, the disregard with which his seniors treated him. He raged inwardly all through lunch, thinking of other jobs that he was going to apply for so that he could shake the dust of the RAE from off his feet. In the middle of the afternoon he came suddenly to his senses. He had done nothing and now he was exhausted by his rage, with a nervous headache. He would do no work that day, and in his present mood he would not stay upon the scene of his frustration for mere office discipline. If the RAE didn't like his way of doing things, well, they could get along without him; he would be leaving before long in any case. At half past three he put on his hat and went home.

He got back to Copse Road in time for tea. Marjorie was in the kitchen laying out a tray with tea for two. She said, 'Oh, Theo, you're back early. You're just in time for tea.' She explained. 'I thought Elspeth had better stay in bed today, so we're having it upstairs. I'll cut some more bread and butter.'

He was naïvely surprised. 'Isn't Elspeth well?'

The girl hesitated. 'She's all right,' she said. 'She was just tired, and I thought she'd better stay in bed.' She did not want to hurt him or to remind him that they had had some difficulty in getting Elspeth out of her trance the night before; Marjorie had carried her upstairs and put her to bed still in a dazed state, and had sat with her holding her hand till she was sleeping naturally. She had certain things to say to Mr Honey about that, but they could wait a favourable chance. She said, 'You must have got off early.'

'I know,' he said. 'Everything went wrong at the office today and it didn't seem to matter, so I thought I'd come home.'

He sounded tired and depressed, and she could guess the reason. She had talked it all over with Shirley that morning, who knew more than she about the workings of the RAE. 'They won't pay any attention to him,' Shirley had said. 'Dennis might, if he was home, although I'm not too sure about that. But everybody else regards him as a joke, you know.'

Marjorie had flushed. 'If that's the way they think about him, the sooner they accept his resignation the better,' she said angrily.

'Dennis believes in him,' said Shirley gently. 'And Dennis is his boss. But planchette at the RAE. . . . It's going to take a bit of stomaching, you know.'

'I suppose it is,' said Marjorie slowly. 'They ought to listen to him, if they're proper scientists.'

'We'll see,' Shirley had said. 'I don't think they're as scientific as all that.'

And so Marjorie said hesitantly to Mr Honey, 'Couldn't you get them to do anything, Theo?'

He shook his head. 'They're so stupid. It's maddening having to work under fools like that. . . .'

'Oh, Theo, I am sorry!' And then, to ease his burden and divert his mind, she said, 'This tray's all ready to go up. If you'll take it, I'll bring up the teapot and the hot water.'

They went up together to the bedroom and had tea with Elspeth. Elspeth was reading *Swallows and Amazons*, bought for her that morning by Marjorie, the first child's book that she had had for over a year with the exception of those she got at school. She told her father all about it. 'It's ever so exciting, Daddy,' she said. 'They did all sorts of things in boats, without any grown-ups with them at all! Can we go somewhere in the holidays and sail a boat, Daddy? Marjorie says there's a sort of series of books all about the same children. May I have another for my birthday?'

He sat looking at Arthur Ransome's pictures with her, his troubles assuaged and sunk into the background of his mind. Presently Marjorie took the tray down to the kitchen to begin washing up, and after a few minutes Mr Honey went down to dry for her. And there he asked, 'Aren't you going to let her get up at all today?'

She was filled suddenly with a great pity for the two of them; he was so completely innocent of any will to hurt. There were things she had to say to him. By the draining-board, piled with the soiled dishes, she reached impulsively for his hand; it was the first time that they had done that.

'Theo,' she said, 'I don't want to be beastly to you. Please don't take offence at this. But honestly, you oughtn't to have done that last night with Elspeth. It's terribly bad for her.'

He blinked through his thick glasses. 'Oh, do you think so? She's done it quite a lot of times before.'

'I know she has,' the girl said. 'But, Theo, she must never do it again. It's a terrible thing to make any child do. And Elspeth's only just getting over concussion. ...' He was silent and distressed. 'I know it was important,' she said gently. 'But Elspeth is important, too. You could warp her whole life by making her do this sort of thing, at her age. You could make her grow up morbid and neurasthenic. She might get fits of depression; she might even become suicidal. Things like that do happen, Theo, I know. I've been a nurse. One always thinks they happen to other people, that they can't happen to you. But they can. And, Theo, children's brains aren't balanced like ours are. They – well, they're just *young*. They can't throw off unhealthy influences like we can. You could do terrible harm to her. Honestly, Theo, she must never do that again.'

She stood holding his hand, looking at him in appeal. She knew that this was a crux in their relations. She knew that she could help him, and she wanted to help him more than anything in the world, but she could only help him if he would accept her ruling in the matters that were properly her sphere. If he took her interference as a slight or turned the matter off with a laugh, she might as well go home.

He stared at her with blurred eyes behind his thick spectacles. 'I never thought of it like that,' he said unhappily.

She squeezed his hand in sympathy with his distress. 'Of course you didn't. But you do want to watch out, Theo – honestly you do. She doesn't seem to know any other children and she talks quite like an old woman sometimes. It's not natural, you know. It's not as she should be.'

He said miserably, 'I know. I know she's not like other children, but I don't see what one can do about it.' He glanced at the girl beside him. 'I know one thing. It makes a very great deal of difference to her having you here.'

'That's only natural,' she replied. 'She's got somebody to talk to, instead of being alone all day.' Gently she freed her hand. 'But do remember, Theo – try and treat her as a child, not quite so much as a grown-up. It's better for her – really it is.'

'I suppose it must be,' he said. 'But living alone as we do, it's so difficult to know where to begin.'

'I know it is,' she said. She stood in thought for a moment. She could not tell him to start playing with his child; he was as he was, and her words could not change his character. If Elspeth got played with it would be through other people, through herself. She turned to the draining-board. 'Let's just wash these few things.'

He dried for her as she washed; as they worked together they talked about the water-heater, about children's books, and about Elspeth's clothes, and presently she said, 'Tell me some more about the RAE, Theo; wouldn't they pay any attention to the message?'

He shook his head, his face clouded. 'I saw the Director. I don't think he believed in it at all. He wouldn't let me send a cable through official channels, and there *is* no other way to get a cable to Dr Scott except through the official channels. They're just afraid of being laughed at, by sending out a cable dealing with matters they don't understand.' He laid down the plate that he was drying and stared out of the window, the cloth drooping unheeded from his hand. 'I'm sure this does mean something,' he said quietly. 'It always did before, when we were finding out about the aqueduct. It's a very well-established means of getting information, this – only those fools haven't bothered to learn about it.'

She was impressed again by his sincerity of purpose. 'Is

there no possible way of letting Dr Scott know, so that he could form his own judgement?' she asked.

He snorted in disgust. 'They said I could write him a private letter. And when I asked when that would get to him they said when he got back to Ottawa! That's after the job is all over!'

'Oh, Theo!'

She took the drying-up cloth from his hand as he stood in abstraction, and dried the last two plates, unnoticed by Mr Honey. Presently she asked, 'Where, exactly, is Dr Scott, Theo?'

He said vaguely, 'In Canada, I think – or else in Labrador. Sometimes they say one and sometimes the other.'

'It's on the north side of the St Lawrence River, isn't it?'

He said, 'I really couldn't tell you. I could find out, perhaps.'

She said thoughtfully, 'Mrs Scott would probably know.'

She sent him up to play a game of dominoes with Elspeth after tea, and told him she was going out to the post. Instead, she walked round to see Shirley in our flat. She said, 'Mrs Scott, can you tell me just where Dr Scott is now? You were quite right about the people at the RAE. They've not been very helpful.'

'Won't they send his message?'

Marjorie shook her head. 'He's awfully disappointed.'

Shirley said, 'I had a night letter from Dennis, from a place called Ivanhoe. He said they were about a hundred miles due north of it, and ten miles to the west of Small Pine Water, and I could look it up on the map. Well, I looked in the atlas, but the map's all just plain white paper north of Ivanhoe.' She pulled out the atlas and they studied it together. 'There's Ivanhoe.'

'That doesn't help much.'

'No.'

Marjorie frowned, staring at the map. 'However did it come to get up there? I've been on the Montreal route for three months, but we don't go north of the St Lawrence at all. We go just south of the Gaspe peninsula, *here*. We don't come to the St Lawrence till we're nearly into Montreal.'

'Dennis said that this machine went to Goose because there was fog at Gander. Goose is up here somewhere, isn't

252

it? It doesn't seem to be marked either – I do think this is a rotten atlas. But I know he told me once the crash was on the line between Goose and Montreal.'

'I see. . . .' Marjorie hesitated for a minute, and then said, 'I wonder, might I use your telephone?'

'Of course.'

She called up Directory Inquiries, and then rang a Wimbledon number. She asked, 'Is that Captain Samuelson's house? Is he there?'

A woman's voice said, 'Well, he's out now.'

Marjorie said, 'Would he be at home if I came round – oh, say in an hour and a half? I'm speaking from Farnham. I'm one of his stewardesses, Miss Corder. I do want to see him this evening, if possible. It's rather important.'

'Well, I don't know if he'll be home before dark. He's down at the Bowls Club and there's been a tournament to-day. He's the vice-captain of the club, you know, and so he couldn't leave before the end, could he? You could go down there and see him on the greens, of course.'

Marjorie said, 'Oh, that would do. The club isn't very far away from your house?'

'It's only just around the corner. That's why we had to have this house, so that he could get his bowls. I'd rather we lived nearer to the shops.'

'Oh, thank you so much,' Marjorie said. 'I'll be along at about seven o'clock.'

She rang off and turned to Shirley. 'Thank you ever so much,' she said. 'I'm going to Wimbledon to see Captain Samuelson. I believe CATO could get a message to them. . . .' She was silent for a minute, standing in thought. 'I wonder if I might ask something?'

Shirley glanced at her.

'I wonder – could you go in and sit with Elspeth, Mrs Scott? Captain Samuelson knows Mr Honey, and I would like Mr Honey to come with me to see him.'

Shirley said, 'I was only going to the pictures. You're going up this evening?'

'I think so. There's a train every half-hour from Aldershot, isn't there?'

They walked back together to the house in Copse Road. Marjorie said, 'Theo, I'm going up to Wimbledon to have a talk with Captain Samuelson. He lives there; I've just rung his wife up. I'd like to have a talk about this thing, getting in touch with Dr Scott. CATO have got their own communications service, you know. There might be some way of getting a message or a letter to Dr Scott through them without it going through official channels at all. Captain Samuelson would know, and I believe he'd help us. Anyway, it's worth trying. Will you come with me?'

He blinked at her. 'That never entered my head. Do you think CATO would help?'

She did not tell him what was really in her mind; it was too long a shot. 'I don't know,' she said. 'They send wireless messages about the aircraft all over the place, of course – to machines in flight and everything. I don't see why they shouldn't be able to get in touch with Dr Scott, if they wanted to. But Captain Samuelson will know.'

Mr Honey nodded. 'I'd like to come,' he said. 'I thought Samuelson was very reasonable. Not like that other pilot, the young one.'

She laughed. 'Peter Dobson!'

An hour and a half later they were at the door of the house in Wimbledon, with the sun dropping down towards the horizon. It was a commonplace, medium-sized house in a suburban road; from somewhere within came the noise of children going to bed, with resonance from the bathroom. The door was opened to them by his wife. 'Oh, Miss Corder,' she said, 'he's still down at the club. There's been a tournament today, and when there's a tournament there's just no knowing when he'll be home. If I were you I should go down and catch him there.' She gave them the directions.

At the Bowls Club they found a few spectators drifting away; out upon the greens there were three or four groups of middle-aged and elderly men in shirt-sleeves, very intent upon their game. They walked round the green till they saw the rather stout, sandy-haired figure of the Transatlantic pilot. Marjorie called, 'Captain Samuelson!'

He raised his head, stared in surprise, and crossed the lawn to them. 'Miss Corder – what are you doing here?' He glanced at her companion. 'I know you. Wait – yes. Mr Honey, isn't it? You got back all right from Gander, then?'

Honey said, 'The Royal Air Force brought me back.'

'Fine.'

Marjorie said, 'Captain Samuelson, I've got something I

want to ask you about. I wonder if we could go somewhere and talk for a few minutes?'

He glanced back at his game. 'Well – we can talk here, if it's not very long.

'I'll be as quick as I can.' She told him what had happened, about the deadlock in Labrador over the location of the missing tailplane, about Mr Honey's trials with planchette. She told her story quickly and well, far better than Mr Honey could have done. 'Nobody can say, of course, whether this information will actually help Dr Scott or not. But it does seem to be all wrong that it shouldn't get to him at all.'

The pilot nodded. 'I see that. But what am I supposed to do about it?'

She hesitated. 'I know you'll think this a terrible suggestion,' she said diffidently. 'But I was wondering if you could fly over Dr Scott's camp on your way tomorrow, and drop a letter to them.'

'Oh, you were, were you?' His manner was not encouraging. 'Where is this place? North of the St Lawrence, isn't it?'

She said, 'There's a lake called Small Pine Water, about a hundred miles north of a place called Ivanhoe, on the St Lawrence.'

He nodded. 'I know Ivanhoe.'

'Well, there's this lake a hundred miles north of it and the crash was eleven miles west of the south end of that lake. That's where they are.'

Behind them came the clink of woods upon the green. The pilot said, 'Well, I can't go rushing off there, Miss Corder. That's a hundred and seventy miles or so off our course.'

'It wouldn't mean that much extra distance, would it?' she pleaded. 'Honestly, it does seem a thing that ought to be done. And after all, it *was* an Organisation aircraft that crashed.'

He said testily, 'Well, yes, I know it was. But if I go off wandering about the world instead of sticking to the route, I'll get myself the sack, Miss Corder, and quite right, too. You can't run airlines in that way.'

There was a long, slow pause. A bee droned past them; from the lawn somebody called, 'Samuelson!' The pilot raised his head and glanced in that direction. 'In about three minutes,' he called. 'Roll for me, Doc.' He stood looking down, kicking the turf at the edge of the path irritably. 'The Russians took away the spar stumps, did they? And you reckon that you've found the other part by planchette?'

'I don't quite go so far as that,' Mr Honey said cautiously. 'All I've got is a sentence – "UNDER THE FOOT OF THE BEAR". But that was produced under well-controlled conditions, conditions that were identical with those of another research, in which we got some quite remarkable results.'

'I see.' The pilot stood deep in thought, his mind back on what had happened at DRD's meeting. Many people, Prendergast amongst them, took the view that this small man with the weak eyes was off his head; others, Dr Scott, and the Director, were emphatic that he wasn't. He had oscillated from one view to the other, himself, several times; on the balance he was now inclined to believe in Mr Honey. But God, what types that Farnborough place did produce!

He asked, 'Do you still think Bill Ward had this fatigue trouble?'

Mr Honey blinked. 'Bill Ward?'

'The machine that crashed in Labrador. Do you still think that that one had fatigue trouble?'

'Oh, I see. Well, yes, I think that's very probable,' Mr Honey said. 'I think that's very likely indeed. In fact, I should be rather surprised, if they ever find these parts, if they don't show a very marked fatigue fracture.'

The pilot stared at the gabled line of the suburban roofs behind the almond trees. 'That bloody old fool – that Group-Captain of the Accidents Department, I've forgotten his name – he said it was pilot's error of judgment. I've never heard such cock in all my life.'

'I shouldn't think it was that,' said Mr Honey. 'It would be a very remarkable coincidence if the pilot had made an error of judgment just at the time when we could reasonably anticipate a failure in fatigue.'

Samuelson said keenly, 'At the same time, I suppose you can't prove that it was failure by fatigue unless Scott comes back with that tail?'

'Well, no. I think you'd have to have some evidence from the crashed parts if you're going to upset the accident investigation.'

Marjorie Corder said, 'Surely the Organisation would be interested in finding out what actually happened? Enough to

256

let you go off your course a bit to drop a letter?'

'I don't know about the Organisation. . . .' The pilot stood in silence, staring out across the level greens. Bill Ward was dead, and vilified after his death when he could not defend himself. Small, stupid people said that he had come down from altitude to check up his position, and had hit a hill, like any pupil on his first cross-country. He had been furious when first he heard of that report; he was furious still. He had spoken his mind at DRD's meeting; he would speak his mind again, at any time, to anybody who would listen. That was not how Bill Ward had met his death.

Professional pride was very strong in him, and the memory of Bill Ward in many a pilot's room, in many countries.

'All right,' he said. 'Let's have your letter and I'll see what I can do.'

*   *   *

We searched that square mile of Labrador forest for three days, and it was a terrible job.

Before I went there I thought that Labrador was a country of rocks and sparse, scattered trees. I mentioned that to Russell once, who told me that it was, all except this particular bit. That bit was dense jungle – there is no better word. On the first day we did no more than cut a trail round our square mile, blazing the trees and cutting a track through the undergrowth as we went, sinking deep in the swampy muskeg in the bottoms and clambering over hills strewn with rotten, fallen trees. The flies were sheer torment all the time; we had fly-nets to protect our faces and streamed with sweat in them; our hands and wrists grew puffed and swollen with the bites.

The others were more used to these conditions than I was and they were certainly in better training, but I found that I could keep pace with them in the work. The very novelty of these conditions was a stimulus to me; moreover, I knew that as a scientist from Farnborough I was expected to be a passenger, useless in the woods, and I was determined to show them that a scientist can also be tough. I found that I could do as much as they did or a bit more, but there is no doubt that at the end of the three days I was far more exhausted than they were. I couldn't have kept up much longer.

On the second and third days we split up into two pairs

and set to work to traverse the area in twenty-yard strips; in places the vegetation was so dense that even that left quite a possibility that we could pass each side of the tailplane and never see it. We found the starboard aileron and the No. 6 engine. We did *not* find the port landing wheel assembly, the No. 3 propeller, or the port tailplane and elevator. The position on the evening of the third day was therefore still inconclusive; we had not found the parts that we were looking for, but that was not to say they were not in the immediate vicinity. The port landing wheel and the No. 3 propeller were almost certainly lying somewhere very near us, and we had not found them.

That evening we were tired to death; I was so tired myself that I could eat nothing, though I drank some tea. Only a small piece of our self-imposed task remained to be done. We planned to finish that in the forenoon, and get down to the Norseman on the lake shore after dinner, and fly down to Ivanhoe and rest for a couple of days before commencing the air search. I remember I was deeply depressed that night and hardly slept at all.

We were all anxious to get finished with the wretched job. The fourth morning we were up at dawn and started off after a cup of tea and a few biscuits. It was better early in the day; it was cool and the flies did not get going in full strength until the day was well advanced. We worked for a couple of hours and knocked off for breakfast a little after eight, with only a trifle left to do. We were still sitting smoking when the Reindeer flew over at about a quarter to ten.

She came from the south-east, flying very low, only about five hundred feet above the tree-tops. She passed to the east and north of us and came round in a great circle to the west; then they evidently saw our camp, because they turned directly for us and flew over. From the port window of the cockpit someone waved to us and we ran out into the clearing in among the crosses of the graves and waved back to them; she flew over us so low that we could see the faces of the passengers at the windows.

I cannot describe what a beautiful sight she was, that summer morning, above the fronds of the spruce trees, shining in silvery silhouette against the bright blue sky. She was flying well throttled back, a great shining lovely thing that slipped through the air without effort, with only a murmur

258

of noise. I stood and watched her, fascinated by her beauty. Down in the forest we were tired and hot and grimy and bitten to death by bugs of every sort, but up there they were clean and well fed and comfortable and safe, up in the clear air in that lovely, lovely thing. I remember looking at her perfect lines and at the great clean grace of her, and thinking it was worth while, after all, to bear with Prendergast, who could turn out so wonderful a design as that.

They went well over to the east and turned again, and now they came so low that they were not a hundred feet above the trees. We stood out in the little glade amongst the graves and as she came to us I saw someone's head half out of the starboard window of the cockpit, and I recognised Samuelson, whom I had met in London a few days before at DRD's meeting. I doubt if he would have recognised me. His arm was out of the window and he was holding something with coloured streams flying from his hand, and as they approached he let this go, and it came parabolically down to us, its bright tails flashing in the sun. It landed on the edge of the clearing and Stubbs ran to get it; the Reindeer opened up her engines and climbed away from us towards the west.

Stubbs came back with the message bag and gave it to Russell, who opened it. It contained one letter, addressed to me in the uncouth scrawl that I had come to know as Mr Honey's writing. I slit it open; there were two sheets of notepaper. As I read it, I sighed with disappointment. It was just sheer stupidity; it seemed that he had been playing with planchette, and he sent me an incomprehensible message that he thought must be important. Honey again. . . .

I raised my eyes, and the other three were standing there looking at me eagerly, waiting to hear what it was all about. I smiled wryly. 'I don't think it's very important,' I said. I hesitated, embarrassed. 'One of my staff has been messing about with spiritualistic stuff – planchette. He got a message that he thought might be useful to us.'

Russell laughed. 'Oh!'

'I know,' I said ruefully. 'You know what people are.'

'What's the message?'

' "Under the foot of the bear," ' I said.

'That's all? Just "Under the foot of the bear"?'

'That's all,' I said. He turned away; I think he was as disappointed as I was. When we had seen the message bag flash down we had expected something that would help us.

'Which foot?' asked Hennessey, with ox-like stupidity. He was a good bush pilot, but he was pretty slow sometimes.

'I don't know,' I said irritably.

'The one he stands on, I suppose,' he said. 'That's what it must mean.'

Russell knew him better than I did. He turned back suddenly. 'Say, is there a place round here that's called Bear anything?'

'Dancing Bear Water,' Hennessey replied. 'That's the only Bear I know of round these parts. But it's the heck of a long way from here.'

I stared at him. 'Which way is it?'

He looked towards the sun. 'Over that way,' he said, pointing. 'East – east with a bit of north in it, maybe. Thirty – forty miles.'

Russell said quickly, 'Back along the course to Goose, from here?'

'I dare say it would be,' he replied. 'It's right next to Piddling Dog.' He turned to me. 'I guess these names sound kind of funny to you,' he explained. 'This section of the country was mapped out first by an air survey, back in 1929. Nobody hadn't ever been here, only a few Indians, maybe. When they got the survey all laid out in Ottawa they found they'd got the heck of a lot of lakes they didn't know about, so they set down to give 'em all names from what they looked like on the map. I got a map down in the Norseman that shows Dancing Bear. Just like a bear it is, with a little island for the eye, 'n everything.'

And there, that afternoon, we found the port tailplane of the crashed Reindeer. We saw it first from about a thousand feet as we flew over; it was standing nearly vertical between the spruce trees, about a quarter of a mile due south of the sole of the foot of the Dancing Bear. It was about thirty-seven miles from the crash. We might have found it ultimately in our air survey if we had gone so far, but I think we might have stopped short of that.

We landed on the lake and taxied in to the shore, and beached the Norseman on a little bit of shingle. The going was fairly easy upon land and we reached the tailplane in about a quarter of an hour. And when we got to it, it was a clear case if ever I saw one; a fatigue fracture of the top front spar flange, the metal short and brittle and crystalline at the break. The rear spar had been twisted off after failure, and the metal there was good.

Bill Ward must have kept her in the air for five or six minutes after losing half his tail, before they hit the trees and they all died. One thing puzzled us a lot at first; how was it that they had not managed to get out a wireless signal in that time? Then we found the insulators of a wireless aerial on the tip of the tailplane, and that too was explained.

12

I GOT BACK TO England three days later, and I was very tired indeed. I had slept very little, because the itching of the bites that I had got in the woods was with me still when I got home; indeed, they took a fortnight to subside completely. Moreover, the strain and tension of the travelling and the research were having their effect, preventing sleep. I should have asked some doctor to prescribe for me, but I could not wait for that. I felt it urgent to get back to Farnborough without delay.

We landed at Heath Row from Montreal about midday. A car was there to meet me; I had a packing-case for luggage and we got it into the back seat with difficulty, and drove to Farnborough. I went straight to the main office block, to the Director's office.

I got in to see him at once. 'Good morning, sir,' I said. 'You got my cable?'

He got up from his chair. 'Yes, thanks.' He looked at me, and then said, 'Rather a hard trip?'

'It was anxious for a time,' I said. 'I thought at one time that we weren't going to find it.'

'You brought some samples back with you?' he asked.

'Oh yes. They're in a crate outside. I couldn't transport the whole thing, of course, so I cut off all the bits that seemed to matter. I've told the Transport to take them to the Metallurgical. It's absolutely clear, sir. It's a straightforward fatigue fracture of the front spar, the top spar flange.' And I told him what it looked like.

'Really. ...' He stood in silence for a moment. 'Well, that's very satisfactory from our point of view,' he said. 'We come well out of it. That's not what matters, though. It's shocking bad for CATO and bad for the country. This means that all those machines will have to come back for modification, and that means the end of the British Transatlantic service for the time being, I'm afraid. But there's nothing for it, now.'

I made a small grimace. 'It's just one of those things. It's a frightful shame. The Reindeer's a delightful thing to travel in.'

'You crossed in one, did you?'

'Both ways. It's a lovely job.'

'I know it is,' he said. 'Still, I don't know that I'd have fancied it myself, in the circumstances.'

I laughed. 'You have to shut your mind to that,' I said. 'Be like an ordinary passenger. Forget about the structure and take an interest in the stewardess.'

He glanced at me quizzically. 'I understand that Mr Honey has been doing some of that.' It's extraordinary how the Director gets to know what's going on.

'A very good thing, too,' I said.

'Oh, very.' He turned the conversation back to business. 'I'll wait until those parts are ready for me to see and we've all seen them,' he said. 'Then I'll ring up DRD and I expect he'll want to call another meeting.'

'Had we better let Prendergast know, unofficially?' I suggested. 'He had a bit of a drip last time because we kept him in the dark.'

He nodded. 'Yes, we'd better do that. Will you get in touch with him, Scott?'

We stood talking over details for a few minutes. Then I said, 'There's just one more thing, sir. I got a note in Ottawa from Captain Samuelson, the pilot of the Reindeer, asking me not to broadcast the fact that he'd dropped that note from Honey to us. It seems that he went a long way out of his course without telling the Organisation anything about it, and he'd rather like to keep it dark.' I grinned. 'If Sir David Moon had seen him assing about down among the tree-tops in the middle of Labrador, he'd have had twins.'

'I see. . . .'

'I spoke to Russell and Group-Captain Porter,' I said.

'They won't let it out from Ottawa.'

The Director said slowly, 'I think it might be rather a good thing to gloss over all the automatic writing side of this business.' I smiled. 'After all, you went out to find and to examine this wreckage, and you found it and you examined it. That's all that matters to anybody. I'm quite sure the Foreign Office would very much object to any publicity about the Russian element.'

'And we should very much object to any publicity about planchette,' I said.

'Exactly,' he replied. 'Until that type of research becomes one of the regular activities of this Establishment, which I hope won't be in my time, the less said about it the better.'

I nodded. 'I should think so, sir.' I turned towards the door. 'Everything has been all right in my party while I've been away, I hope?'

He said, 'So far as I know.' He glanced down at his desk. 'There's a new job coming on. They're having trouble with the Assegai.'

'They were bound to do that,' I said. The Assegai was one of the jet interceptor fighters coming into squadron use. For rapid climb it had the new Boreas engine; in level flight at over thirty thousand feet it was probably capable of exceeding the speed of sound. Because the forces on the structure were still very much a matter of guesswork in the trans-sonic range, its speed in level flight was supposed to be limited to Mach .90. People who knew the fighter pilots said from the start that those young men would never pay attention to that sort of restriction, and they hadn't.

'They lost one of them about a month ago,' the Director said, 'and then they lost another one last week. Both with structural failure of the wing. Then the day before yesterday they lost a third, but this time the pilot got out safely with his parachute. Apparently he was looking out along the wing and saw the whole thing happen. He says he saw a line of light along the leading edge before it broke.'

I stared at him. 'A line of light?'

'That's what he says he saw. It seems he's very positive about it.'

I was dumbfounded. 'But what could cause that?'

He smiled. 'I don't know, Scott. That's what we've got to find out.'

I said ruefully, 'Well, that's a new one.'

'I said that it had better wait till you came back,' the Director said. 'They'll send the pilot here to see you and tell you the whole story in his own words, as soon as you like. Who would you put on it?'

'Morrison,' I said. 'It's right up his street.'

He nodded. 'I think so. The only thing is, Morrison is having trouble – oh, that's since you went away. His wife has got TB; she's got to go into a sanatorium. I think that you may have some difficulty in getting any useful work out of him for a month or so.'

'I'm very sorry to hear about Mrs Morrison,' I said. 'I'll have a talk with him. He's certainly the man who ought to handle anything like this.'

I went back to my office. My desk was piled high with dockets and papers that had come in during my absence, waiting for my attention. I told Miss Learoyd to put them all on the side table, and I rang down for Mr Honey and asked him if he would come up and see me. When he came I told him all about it, the success of his fatigue estimate and the success of his automatic writing. He did not seem very greatly interested in either, except technically; success did not thrill him in the least. He regarded a success merely as a convenient platform from which to plan a further advance.

He was, however, viciously pleased at the effect the news would have on Prendergast. 'These ignorant fools in the design offices,' he said angrily, 'they don't know what they're doing, half the time. They come down here and strut about and treat you like so much dirt. If only they'd pay some attention to the people who know something about the job, they wouldn't have these accidents.'

He displayed a characteristic reaction to the news that the entire British Transatlantic service would be suspended for an indefinite time by the grounding of the Reindeer fleet. He asked if we could get hold of the tailplanes of two of the grounded aircraft for further experiments. It seemed a golden opportunity to him. 'If they can't fly they won't want their tailplanes,' he pointed out. 'It really would be a great assistance if we could carry through a complete research on tailplanes of one type.'

He was deeply grateful to Shirley and to me for the little we had done for Elspeth. 'I don't know what to say to thank you,' he muttered. 'If Mrs Scott hadn't come round that morning and found her, I – I don't know what would have happened.'

'Forget about it,' I said gently. 'You'd have done the same for us. But, Honey, if you don't mind my saying so, you ought to make some arrangements that Elspeth isn't left alone quite so much. It's taking a bit of a risk.'

'I know it is,' he replied. 'As a matter of fact . . .' and then he stopped. He began again. 'I've got somebody staying with me now, for a little while. I do agree with you, it's very bad for Elspeth so much alone.'

'It's none of my business,' I said. 'But it's a bit hard on the kid.'

He said ingenuously, 'I'm very hopeful that I'll be able to do something before long.'

I thought of Marjorie Corder, and kept my face as straight as a judge. 'That's fine.'

They rang through from the Metallurgical Section a few minutes after that and said that my crate was there, and they were opening it. I rang the Director, and we all went down together to inspect the bits that I had brought back with me from Labrador. There was a little surface corrosion, as one might expect from parts that had been lying for some months in thawing snow, but there was general agreement that the evidence was absolutely clear. I went back to my office and rang up Prendergast.

'Good afternoon, Mr Prendergast,' I said. 'This is Scott speaking. Yes, this morning. Oh yes, thank you – not quite a holiday, you know, but very interesting, all the same. Look, Mr Prendergast – I'm sorry to say that we found a very definite fatigue fracture. I brought the parts back with me – yes, I cut the spars beyond the fractures and brought the fractures back. They're here now if you'd like to come down and see them.' And I told him where the fractures were.

He said, 'Really? How very, very interesting. I should very much like to see those pieces.' He spoke very pleasantly; I was amazed. He went on to discuss the repetitive stresses on the tail for a little; he was cordial, benign, and considerate. 'I had a most interesting visit to your department while you were away,' he said. 'Mr Honey showed me the research that you have going on. I was very much impressed.'

So had Mr Honey been, but I would not tell him that. I

said, 'I'm very sorry about the Reindeer, Mr Prendergast. I'm afraid this is bound to mean that all those aircraft will be grounded now at seven hundred and twenty hours.'

He said genially, 'Oh well, worse things happen at sea. I expect we shall get over it, one way or another.'

Well, that was one way of looking at it. I wondered if Sir David Moon would take it quite so philosophically when he was told that all his Reindeers were going to be grounded for an indefinite period, but that was none of my business. I talked to Prendergast for a few minutes more, and the extraordinary man was as smooth as silk when I had expected him to be as a raging demon. I put the telephone down, wondering if I should ever understand designers.

It was five o'clock, and I was very tired. I had to start something going on the Assegai before I could relax, and I rang through to Mr Morrison. After some delay the girl answered the call. She said that Mr Morrison wasn't in the office; he had not been in that day. His wife was very ill; he had taken her to the sanatorium at Bognor Regis. No, she didn't know if he was coming in tomorrow.

The Assegai, it seemed, was going to be my baby.

I had a wife; I had not seen her for ten days and about nine thousand miles. I rang up Shirley at our flat and said, 'Darling, I'm back.'

She said, 'Oh, Dennis, *dear*. Where are you now? In the office?'

'That's right. Will you come and fetch me with the car? I've done all that I'm going to do.'

She came, and we drove home together to the flat, and mixed a drink. Everything was strangely as I knew it; it was curious to think of all that I had seen and done since I had been home last. We had a vast amount to talk about; I had to tell her what had gone on in Canada and she had to tell me what had gone on in Mr Honey's little house in Copse Road. 'I crossed over in the same machine as Monica Teasdale,' I said. 'We had a long talk in the middle of the night.'

'That poor woman,' she said softly. 'I did like her. Was she very much cut up, Dennis?'

'I think she was,' I said. 'It's hard to tell with an American, especially an actress like that. You can't tell if she's putting on an act.'

She was silent for a minute. 'I can't help thinking about

her,' she said at last. 'She was awfully fond of him, you know. I think it was heroic of her, to go away like that. Do you think we'll ever see her again, Dennis?'

'No,' I said, 'I don't think so. Only on the screen.' I rubbed my wrists and hands; they were itching again like fire.

Shirley said, 'Dennis, come and let me put something on those bites. I've got some cream that will soothe them.' We went into the bedroom and she put it on for me, and then she said, 'What about our holiday, Dennis? You really must take one this year; you're looking awfully tired. The Reindeer must be just about cleaned up, isn't it? Couldn't we go away now, before anything else crops up?'

I grinned at her. 'Too late,' I said. 'It's cropped.' And I told her about the Assegai.

'Oh, Dennis! Someone else must deal with that. You can't go on for ever without a holiday.'

'I'll have to hold the fort till Morrison gets back,' I said. 'I don't suppose that'll be so long. I'm seeing the pilot in a day or two.' I stared out of the window of our little bedroom. 'I can't make out why there should be a light,' I said. 'It doesn't make sense.'

She laid her hand upon my arm. 'Forget about it now,' she said gently.

I roused myself to talk of matters that were more up Shirley's street. 'How's Marjorie Corder getting on with Honey?'

'Oh, she's a dear. You know, I wouldn't be surprised if they got married.'

'So they ruddy well ought to,' I replied. 'From what you tell me they've been living in sin for the last week.'

She turned on me. 'Oh, Dennis, they haven't! Mr Honey wouldn't know how.'

'Don't you be too sure about that,' I said. 'Are they engaged?'

'I don't think so,' she said. 'Not yet. But her leave's up at the end of the week. Perhaps they will be then.'

As a matter of fact, they got engaged that night. Mr Honey went back to his little house that evening anxious to justify himself in Marjorie's eyes. What she had said about his treatment of Elspeth had made a deep impression on him. He regarded her as a woman of the world and more knowledgeable than he: somebody who travelled repeatedly to

Canada and the United States and liked it. He had a deep respect for her. Curiously, she seemed to have a deep respect for him, and in this she was unusual; most people treated him with very little respect. He did not want to lose her regard.

He went into the kitchen and beamed at her through his thick glasses. 'Dr Scott's come back,' he said. 'The message we sent got to him all right. Captain Samuelson flew over and dropped it.'

Her face lit up. 'Oh Theo, I *am* glad. Was it any good?'

'Yes, it was. There's a lake there called Dancing Bear and they found the tailplane just south of its foot.'

'Theo! So it was under the foot of the bear, after all?'

He nodded. 'I knew it must be something like that. It was just the same with the aqueduct. You couldn't understand the message till you'd thought about it for a bit. But in this case, of course, we hadn't got the data. We didn't know there was a lake called that.'

'It's wonderful!' she exclaimed. There was a light of admiration in her eyes that he could not mistake.

He coloured a little. 'Well,' he said diffidently, 'it just comes of proceeding in the proper scientific manner. So many people start off right, but then when they come up against something they don't understand, they turn round and say the whole research was started on wrong lines. But I *am* glad this turned out to be useful, because of Elspeth.' He looked at her appealingly. 'You don't really think it did her any harm, do you?'

She laid her hand impulsively upon his arm. 'Of course not, Theo – don't worry about that. We must find her and tell her – she'll be thrilled!'

He said, 'Do you think that's wise?'

She stared at him. 'But don't you want to tell her?'

He blinked at her through his glasses. 'Well, what do you think, Marjorie? Won't it impress it on her mind? I thought you wanted to forget all about that sort of thing.'

'Wouldn't you tell her at all?' she said thoughtfully. 'Just forget about it?'

'Well, yes – I think I would. After all, it's not important any longer. Tell her in some years' time, when she's a bit older. She hasn't talked about it again, has she?'

The girl shook her head. 'That's very sweet of you, Theo,' she said soberly. 'You really are the kindest man I've ever met.'

He coloured; it was a long time since anyone had said that sort of thing to him. 'There's another thing,' he said unsteadily. 'It *was* a fatigue fracture.'

'Oh, Theo! So you were right in that, too?'

He blinked. 'I thought it must have been. It's really very satisfactory, because it adds another trial without wasting our time, if you understand. This trial that I'm doing at the RAE becomes a confirmatory experiment – it means that we're about six months further ahead than we thought we were. If this one confirms the results of the first, the Labrador accident, we really will be on a firm foundation, so that we can go ahead with confidence.'

She did not understand what all that meant, but it was evidently something very near his heart, and so she said, 'How splendid!'

He beamed at her. 'It's really very satisfactory,' he repeated. 'I think we're on the way to getting something useful now.'

She thought for a minute, and then asked, 'Theo, what's going to happen to the Reindeer if it gets fatigue like this? Can they go on using it?'

'The Reindeer? Oh, you mean the machines they're using now. They've got to stop, I think. Dr Scott said something about grounding them all. I think he said they could go on to 720 hours – that's half the estimated time to failure.'

'Oh. ...' With her knowledge of the Organisation she tried to visualise how the Montreal and New York services could be run without any Reindeers, and failed. 'I suppose they aren't safe any longer.'

'I should think they'd be all right up to 720 hours,' he said. 'But after that they ought to stop. I think Dr Scott's quite right in that.'

She said slowly. 'Then the one at Gander must have been very dangerous, Theo.'

He laughed, almost boyishly; his success and her approval had lifted years of care and grief and worry off his shoulders. 'You know, I think it was. I'm rather surprised we got across all right, really I am. It did 1,430 hours, that one, without breaking. The only thing is, Dr Scott says the Canadians are quite certain that fatigue fractures are governed by the temperature, that they come sooner when it's cold. That's one of the parameters I haven't dealt with yet, that and the question of electrical conductivity. It might possibly explain why that one didn't break, because it had been operating in the tropics, you see. There's a whole field to explore' he said enthusiastically. 'All sorts of things.' He was like a little boy let loose in a toy shop, uncertain which of the attractive treasures to pick up first.

Marjorie said, 'If you hadn't pulled up its undercarriage, Theo, I should have gone on flying in it. And I should have been killed, like Betty Sherwood and Jean Davenport.'

He stared at her dumbly, blinking in distress at the idea.

She said thoughtfully, 'I wonder how many lives you've saved, Theo? How many people are now living who would be dead by now, or just about to die, but for your courage and your genius?'

He blinked at her in silence. Much more important to him at that moment was the curve of her throat as it slid into her dress and a small curl of hair beside her ear.

'You're a great man, Theo,' she said quietly. 'This was all your doing. But for your work and your devotion other Reindeers would have crashed and other people would have been killed – hundreds, perhaps. Captain Samuelson would have been killed, as Captain Ward was killed. I should have died, as Betty and Jean died. I happen to know about it, so does Captain Samuelson. The passengers who would have died but for your courage and your work, they'll never know. But I can speak for them. Thank you, Theo, for all that you've done for them, and for their wives, and for their children.'

Mr Honey was never a very articulate man. He just put his arm round her shoulders and kissed her. As Marjorie put it to Shirley, that kind of broke the ice. By the time Elspeth, who was reading Arthur Ransome lying on her bed upstairs, awoke to the fact that she was hungry and came down to see what was happening about tea, her father was engaged to Marjorie Corder. Elspeth, who had been expecting that to happen for some time, thought it was a very good idea.

Marjorie went round and saw Shirley alone at tea-time on the following afternoon. 'I know it's no good trying to kid you and Dr Scott,' she said candidly. 'You think I've worked for this, that it's been all my doing. Well, up to a point, it has.'

Shirley smiled. 'I don't think anyone that Mr Honey

married could expect to be exactly passive in the matter,' she observed. 'Any girl would have had to have done most of the work.'

Marjorie nodded. 'I think that's true. But that doesn't mean that we aren't going to be terribly happy together.'

'My dear, I know you will,' said Shirley. 'I can tell you one thing – he's an awfully kind man.'

'I know,' the stewardess said softly. 'You wouldn't think it, but he's brave too – and just terribly clever.' She turned to Shirley. 'I'm not a very clever person,' she said, 'and I don't really understand very much about his work. But I do know this – it's just about as important as a man's work can be. I've only known him a short time, but in that time I've seen him save hundreds of lives – literally hundreds. When you think of what might have happened to the Reindeers if he hadn't found out this about fatigue —'

'I know,' said Shirley. It was in her mind to say that I had had a bit to do with it as well, and so had Marjorie herself and Captain Samuelson, but she did not want to be ungracious or to spoil her pleasure.

'All my life,' the girl said, 'ever since Donald got killed, I wanted to be in aviation. That's why I manoeuvred to get this job with the Organisation, to be a stewardess. I love being on aerodromes and seeing aeroplanes. It's a sort of bug that gets in you, you know.'

Shirley nodded. 'I've got it, too.'

The stewardess said, 'Serving teas and drinks and asking passengers to fasten their safety belts and helping them to do it – that's one way to work in aviation. It's all right if you can't do anything more important. But then when I met Theo, when he pulled the undercart up out at Gander, I started wondering if that was really the best thing I could do. He's such a – such a *big* little man,' she said. 'His work is so vastly more important than mine, and he does need someone's help so very, very much.'

'My dear,' said Shirley softly.

Marjorie said, 'I never went to college and I won't be able to do much to help him in his work. I don't think he'd want that, anyway. But I can help him for all that, in all the things he can't do properly himself. And I can make him young again, I think, and make him enjoy things. If I can do that, he's bound to do better work even than he does now.

And I think that's a better way to work in aviation than just serving teas and drinks and telling the passengers when to do up their safety belts. . . .'

*   *   *

DRD called his second meeting on the Reindeer tail two days later, at 11.30 in the same room in the Ministry of Supply. I killed two birds with one stone, that day, by arranging for the pilot of the Assegai to meet me an hour previously in Ferguson's room.

His name was Flying-Officer Harper. He was a dark-haired, fresh-faced boy of twenty-one or twenty-two, who adopted the pose that everything was a joke and nothing really mattered, whether being crossed in love or being killed in an Assegai. He came into the room warily, as if walking into a trap.

'Flying-Officer Harper?' I said. 'Good morning. My name is Scott and I'm from Farnborough. We've got to start a special investigation into these accidents that you've been having with the Assegai, and I asked if you could meet me here to tell me just what happened.' I motioned him to a chair and gave him a cigarette. 'Tell me, what happened first of all?'

'Well,' he said, 'the wing came off.'

'I know. Any idea why it came off?'

'I suppose it just isn't strong enough.'

'Tell me just what happened,' I said. 'It's my job to try and make it stronger. First of all, what height were you at?'

'About thirty-five thousand, I should think. Anyway, between thirty and forty thousand.'

'Were you alone or were there other machines about?'

'There were other machines up at the time, but nobody near me. Nobody else saw what happened.'

'What were you doing? Were you flying level or diving?'

'I was in a shallow dive, sir.'

'What speed were you going at?'

'I don't know,' he said evasively. 'The air-speed indicator goes all haywire – it was flipping about all over the scale.'

'What was the Machmeter showing?'

'I never look at that,' he said. 'It's no bloody good, that thing. Half the time it's U/S.'

One has to be patient. I said, 'Would you say that you

were near the speed of sound?'

He said reluctantly, 'I might have been. It's rather difficult to tell.'

I smiled. 'What about the restriction on the speed of the Assegai? The one about not doing more than .90 Mach?'

He laughed cynically. 'That's just a bit of bloody nonsense. Nobody pays any attention to that.'

'You mean, in combat practice you go faster than that in Assegais?'

'Of course. Everybody does. It's just a lot of nonsense put out by the boffins, that.'

I grinned. 'What's the fastest you have ever been in an Assegai?'

He said proudly, 'I got it up to 1·2 on that Machmeter thing. That was in about a thirty-degree dive. I believe you'd get her faster than that if you started at about fifty thousand.'

1·20 Mach it getting on for a thousand miles an hour. 'Did you have any trouble getting through the speed of sound?' I asked.

'It's just like being inside a kettledrum,' he said. 'Everything's sort of hammering at you, very quick, and it gets bloody hot. Then as you go through it all gets smooth again. Then it's the same as you slow down and come back through.'

I stared at him. It had never been contemplated that ordinary squadron pilots would do that. 'Have you done that often?' I asked.

He shrugged his shoulders. 'Half a dozen times,' he said. 'It's rather fun.'

'Does everybody do this?' I asked.

'Of course they do,' he said. 'Wingco hands out a raspberry if he hears anyone talking about it. But everybody does it.'

RAF discipline was no concern of mine; my job was simply to do what I could to see that aircraft were built strong enough to be safe in the way that they were used. I said 'Let's say that you got out of control when flying at ·90 Mach and inadvertently approached the speed of sound. I suppose it was around that region that this accident happened?'

He grinned. 'That's right. I got out of control.'

'Well now, what happened?'

'She stuck in it,' he said. In the kettledrum, I mean. I suppose I wasn't going fast enough to go through. I think you've got to make it quick or not at all. I tried to get out of it by slowing down, but the stick was jammed or something, and everything you touched was vibrating like one of those electric shocking coils, you know. Everything was getting bloody hot to touch, and I thought, "Oh Momma!!"' He laughed. 'Well, then I looked at the port wing, and there was a sort of line of light right from the root to the tip, right along the leading edge, and then there was a bloody great bang and the whole wing was gone — just like that. Well, then I pulled the blind down over my face and the seat ejected all right, and there I was sitting in the air with bits of metal all around me. So I pulled the chute and came down normally.' He paused. 'I can't think of anything else.'

He had had a most miraculous escape. I thought about it for a minute, and then said, 'This line of light along the leading edge. What did it look like?'

'It looked sort of incandescent,' he replied. 'Like the crack of light you see at a furnace door.'

I could not make head or tail of that. 'Do you remember how it ran?' I asked. 'I've got an Assegai wing down at Farnborough. If you came down there, could you mark that wing with a pencil to show exactly where you saw the crack of light? Or don't you remember well enough for that?'

He said, 'Oh yes, I could do that. I know just how it went.'

Well that was something to start from; at any rate we had a description of the symptoms, if the cause of the disease was quite obscure. I talked to Harper for some time, but he could add little more. He treated it as rather a joke, regardless of the fact that his Assegai had cost the taxpayer about twenty thousand pounds. He was taking his girl friend to see *Lovely Lady* at the Hippodrome that evening, so I fixed for him to come to Farnborough next day and draw his line upon my Assegai wing.

I went on down to DRD's meeting, in the same conference room as the previous one. I had had the bits of spar that I had brought from Labrador sent up from Farnborough and placed at the end of the table, in case there should be any argument about it from the diehards. As each member came in for the meeting he made for these bits of structure and examined them. E. P. Prendergast pulled out a pocket

274

magnifying glass and examined the fractures for a long time, grunting sourly when anybody spoke to him; he was in no genial mood that day. Carnegie and Sir David Moon examined the parts gloomily, talking in low tones. Group-Captain Fisher came in just before the meeting opened, red-faced and irritable; he did not examine the parts because he had seen them the afternoon before.

DRD opened the meeting by saying that the representative of the RAE had brought back certain parts from the Reindeer accident in Labrador, some of which were on the table. Technical opinion was unanimous that they indicated a fatigue fracture of the front spar flanges of the port tailplane. He would ask Dr Scott to outline his investigation to the meeting.

'There's not much to say,' I remarked. 'When we reached the scene of the accident we discovered that the spar fractures at the fuselage had been removed for examination by the Russian burial party who had come to exhume the body of their ambassador.' There were incredulous smiles and raised eyebrows round the table. DRD nodded shortly. 'It therefore became necessary to locate the tailplane itself. We found this thirty-seven miles east-north-east of the scene of the accident – that is, back along the course to Goose. These fractures on the table, there, were cut from the tailplane as it lay. There was, of course, no means of bringing the whole unit down to the coast for shipment. I think that's all about it. I'm sorry not to have both parts of the fracture to show you, but I understand that political difficulties have prevented that.'

DRD said, 'I'm afraid that is so.' Then he turned to the Inspector of Accidents. 'I don't know if you have had an opportunity to consider the matter, Group-Captain?'

The old man raised his head. 'Not yet,' he said definitely. 'I have not received any report of this investigation from Ottawa, and until I do so the matter must remain *sub judice* so far as I am concerned.' He was so ill advised as to go on, clutching at a straw, 'I understand that the wreckage from which these parts were cut was found thirty-seven miles from the main crash. That seems to me to be a very long way away. It is at least possible that these parts do not belong to the Reindeer at all, but to some other accident. I think that point wants some investigation.'

With that, I think, the bowler hat descended firmly on his head. Prendergast stuck out his great jowl and said, 'What on earth do you mean?'

DRD interposed hastily. 'The identification of these pieces is clearly part of the procedure, Mr Prendergast.'

The designer grunted offensively. 'I should have thought that was hardly necessary, since I am present at this meeting. I am not accustomed to wasting my time investigating casual bits of aircraft junk. These are all portions of the front and rear spar structures of the Reindeer tailplane.'

DRD said, 'Well, that settles that. It seems that this first machine had flown 1,393 hours up to the time of the accident, and these samples clearly show that the cause of the disaster was fatigue failure of the nature postulated by the investigation undertaken by the RAE. We now have to consider what action we must take.' He turned to me. 'Dr Scott?'

'I have not changed my views,' I said. 'Action must be taken by some other body. But I think that some modification to the present design of the tail structure is clearly necessary, and until that has been carried out no Reindeer should fly more than 720 hours. That's my opinion.'

Carnegie said, 'Based on Mr Honey's work and on this evidence?'

'That's right,' I replied. 'Some rather unfortunate things were said about Mr Honey at our last meeting. I should like to point out that he's the only one among the lot of us who has been consistently right all through. If he hadn't damaged that second Reindeer at Gander, you'd have had another accident, beyond all doubt.'

There was a glum silence. It was broken by Carnegie, who said, 'That aircraft might as well stay at Gander, if we can't use it. In fact, I suppose it will have to. I suppose I may take it that that one, which has flown something over 1,440 hours, is grounded from now on.'

DRD said, 'That is an executive decision, to be taken as a result of this meeting. But I think it's very likely.'

Sir David Moon said, 'Mr Chairman, the news that we have heard this morning is bad news for us, as you can suppose. It entails laying up a fleet of Reindeer aircraft for a major modification, probably for a matter of months, if our past experience is any guide. That means, this country must cease to operate a Transatlantic service, unless we care to do so by reverting to the obsolete and uneconomic types that we lately discarded. And, in fact, there are too few of those now available to enable us to maintain our services. That is a very heavy blow to us, and to this country.' He was speaking quietly and seriously. 'We do not question its necessity, but we ask for a hand in framing what restrictions on the Reindeer are deemed necessary, with a view to making the optimum use of the aircraft.'

I was not paying much attention; I was thinking of the Assegai. The Reindeer was over, so far as I was personally concerned; what happened now was for others to decide. The Assegai was vital and urgent. It had never been intended that the Assegai should be flown in the trans-sonic region, but the young men were doing it and doing it every day. It had already killed two of them. It might well be impossible to prevent the fighter pilots from getting the most out of their machine; they were not of the temperament to submit to restrictions based on safety. Either the Assegai must be taken away from them or it must be strengthened, and strengthened quickly, to withstand the forces that they put on it. What those forces were was very little known. It was a complete mystery to me, at that time, why one thin line along the leading edge should have become incandescent. And till we found the answer to that one, the Assegai would go on killing the young men.

I came back to the meeting with a start. DRD was saying: 'The first thing is to find out what modifications are necessary.' He glanced down the table at the designer. 'Perhaps Mr Prendergast can give us some indication of what will be involved?'

Prendergast reached for his attaché case, pulled out a whiteprint, and opened it upon the table. 'I have given this matter a good deal of attention, personally,' he said ponderously. 'Clearly, there is no alternative to increasing the mass of the spar flanges at the root and for several feet out from the root, and it is desirable that the elastic modulus of the spar flange should be increased as well. I propose to insert a steel channel section, nesting into the existing duralumin flange.' And he went on to talk about families of nesting sections, one of his structural fetishes, and fitted bolts in reamed holes prepared on the spar drilling jig. He showed us his drawing.

Carnegie asked gloomily, 'What's the delivery of these special steel sections?'

'Enough for two machines will be available on Thursday next,' the designer said. 'The remainder will flow on after that as required.'

We stared at him incredulously. Carnegie asked, 'Do you mean to say that we can get these special steel sections without any delay at all?'

'I am not accustomed to having my word doubted, Mr Carnegie,' said the designer haughtily. 'I have been thirty-seven years in this industry, and I hope I know what I am talking about. I have chosen this particular solution, one of several, because it seemed to offer certain production advantages, though at a small cost in extra weight. We already have the necessary dies, prepared as part of our policy of laying by the dies required for all our nesting sections.' He glared down the table at the Treasury official. 'And I may say, in passing, that we experience continual and increasing difficulty in obtaining payment for dies which are not immediately required for our contracts. If it were not for our foresight and prudence in preparing these dies in the face of all the obstructions thrown in our path by the officials of this Ministry, I should not be able to assist you in this way.' The Treasury official made a note upon his pad. E. P. Prendergast swelled himself out like a fog. 'The great company which I have the honour to represent,' he said, 'has placed the full facilities of its Sheffield steel plant behind this matter, with overriding priority, in anticipation of our requirements. I see no reason to suppose that we shall be held up for materials.'

DRD remarked, 'Well, I'm sure we all feel that that is very satisfactory, Mr Prendergast. Have you been able to prepare any estimate of the time that the modification is likely to take?'

'I have.' The designer pulled a paper from his case. 'In the first place, I have assumed that you will give me verbal authority to commence work now – this morning – upon the preparation of the necessary parts, which are, in fact, already in hand.' The man from the Treasury frowned, and then laughed. 'I also assume that you sanction night-shift work upon this contract, and overtime excepting Sundays. Am I correct?'

DRD was somewhat at a loss. 'I think so.'

The designer grunted offensively. 'Well, you must make up your minds if you want this work done or not.'

Ferguson leaned over and whispered to DRD, who said, 'Yes. We can give verbal instructions to proceed, Mr Prendergast.'

Sir David Moon said, 'Mr Chairman, in view of the extreme urgency of this matter to us, may I ask if Sunday work can be authorised?'

E. P. Prendergast stuck out his great jowl and said, 'On no account would I agree with that. If you want work done on Sundays, you must go elsewhere. It is uneconomic upon any account, and it strikes at the root of family life, which is the basis of the greatness of this country.' We stared at him, blinking. 'God comes before the Reindeer, gentlemen,' he said.

DRD said smoothly, 'Of course. On the assumptions you have made, Mr Prendergast, how long do you suppose this job will take?'

The designer consulted his paper. 'We can accept the first machine for modification on Monday the 18th, and the work will be completed by the evening of the 21st. Thereafter we can modify one machine in each four complete working days.'

We stared down the table at him. Sir David Moon said, 'Am I to understand that each aircraft will only be out of service for four days?'

'That does not include the time of the delivery flights to and from our Stamford works,' said Prendergast.

Carnegie said impulsively, 'But that's fantastic.'

Prendergast glared at him. 'I am not accustomed to that language in relation to my statements,' he said harshly. 'If you are unable to accept our estimates, you must take your work elsewhere.'

All good designers are difficult men or they could not be good designers; I think everybody at the table was more or less aware of that. We set ourselves to mollify the great man, and I say that with sincerity. A great man he was, a great designer, and a superlative engineer. But not an easy man to deal with. No.

In the end Sir David Moon said, 'This represents a different picture altogether, Mr Chairman. If the company can

279

do the necessary modifications in so short a time, there will be no need to interrupt our present schedule of services at all.' Prendergast nodded. 'We can allocate the machines off service one by one for this work to be done. The general public need not know anything at all about it.'

DRD said, 'I think that's very desirable. It never does any good to have a garbled version of these troubles in the newspapers.'

The Director leaned across to me. 'They'd only print half the story, anyway,' he remarked. 'They wouldn't believe the other half.'

The meeting broke up. I said to him, 'I had a chat with that Assegai pilot, sir. It was at the speed of sound, of course; it stuck for several seconds in the region of high drag. He said he'd been through to the supersonic zone several times. He was quite positive about that incandescent line along the leading edge. He's coming down tomorrow to sketch it on the wing.'

He nodded. 'Morrison back yet?'

'Not yet,' I said. 'I think he's coming in tomorrow. I hope he sees more daylight in this matter than I do.'

He smiled gently. 'It'll come,' he said.

Honey got married to Marjorie Corder about a month later, and on the third day of his honeymoon the test tail broke, at 1,296 hours only, which gave him something to think about. Flight-Lieutenant Wintringham said it was a wedding present for him. He came hurrying back from Bournemouth, where they were staying, to view the body, and I sent him back to his honeymoon with a flea in his ear. But I don't know what kind of a honeymoon they had after that, because he came back to the office with a considerable extension to his nuclear theory of fatigue, expressed in twenty-six pages of pure mathematics.

That autumn I was restless after office hours. I had nothing much to work at in the evenings and I was very worried about the Assegai. I tried reading Shirley's novels, but I can't take any interest in those things; real life always seems to me to be so much more stimulating. I tried listening to the wireless and got fed up with that. And it was much too soon to write another paper for the Society.

One evening Shirley laid her sewing down. 'Dennis, I wish you or somebody would write up some of these things that happen, like the Reindeer tail. I mean, write literally all about it, not just the scientific part. All about Monica Teasdale, and Elspeth, and planchette, and the Director going to Kew Gardens – all the bits that made it fun. We shall forget what really happened in a few years' time and we'll have lost something worth having. I'd like to try and save some of the fun we're having now, to look at when we're old.'

I stared at her thoughtfully. 'That's not a bad idea,' I said. 'It'ld be better than sitting worrying about the Assegai.'